IT FELT GOOD TO BE ONE OF THE CHOSEN.

"Welcome, gentleman," the Wing Commander began. "You are here as prospective members of what is hoped will be only the first of a series of fully integrated NATO specialist fighter squadrons. If we are successful here, others will follow. Here at November One, come what may, and with an extremely limited time frame, we intend to weld you into a single, tight, supremely efficient fighting unit. At November One, you will be taught to fly lower, faster, higher and tighter than you ever thought possible. Gentlemen, you may not be low-level ground attack pilots, but at November One, you will be expected to carry the fight to *any* level. Nowhere is to be safe for the enemy, whoever he may be."

TROPHY

Julian Jay Savarin

HarperPaperbacks
A Division of HarperCollinsPublishers

This is a work of fiction. The characters, incidents, and dialogues are products of the author's imagination and are not to be construed as real. Any resemblance to actual events or persons, living or dead, is entirely coincidental.

HarperPaperbacks *A Division of* HarperCollins*Publishers*
10 East 53rd Street, New York, N.Y. 10022

A hardcover edition of this book was published in 1989 in Great Britain by Century Hutchinson Ltd.

Cover art by Attila Hejja

First HarperPaperbacks printing: December 1990

Printed in the United States of America

HarperPaperbacks and colophon are trademarks of HarperCollins*Publishers*

10 9 8 7 6 5 4 3 2 1

For Tornado drivers and back-seaters, who know the edge.

Beginnings

Chapter

Early summer, high noon, the Grampian coast of Scotland.

Two sleek aircraft were lined up on the brand-new runway, their twin engines winding up to full military power as they began their take-off roll. Then four sunbursts of blue-white flame with orange tails seared backwards, as the afterburner nozzles flared open. The multiple explosion of sound came as one, and the aircraft hurtled down the wide concrete, accelerating with astonishing rapidity. Soon they were off the deck, wheels tucking away while they were barely clear of the ground. Then with breath-taking suddenness, they reefed into the vertical and roared skywards.

They rolled 180 degrees while still in the climb, pulled onto their backs, rolled another 180 upright, and streaked out to sea. The afterburners were cut with a barely audible *plop*, bringing an abrupt reduction in noise that was almost silence. It had been a quite spectacular take-off.

Flight Lieutenant Mark Selby, RAF, was driving his metallic blue Ford Sierra XR4x4, sunroof open, along the coastal road from Cullen, making for the newly-established airbase. The A98 skirted the high dark cliffs and he was enjoying the view of the vast waters of the Moray Firth over to his left, when the sound erupted. Recognising it instantly, he pulled into the lay-by a short distance ahead and got out to watch.

The May noontide was bright and clear, with visibility limited only to the distance the eye could see. Blessed with the sight required of a top fighter pilot, he quickly picked out the fast-climbing aircraft and watched them with envy.

He had time in hand. Even though he had stopped off in Aberdeen to look in on his younger sister Morven, who was at university there, he still had a couple of hours or so before his new commanding officer at November One would be expecting him. He liked to keep an eye on Morven: not that she needed it, but both their parents were dead—their father eight years ago, of a classic businessman's coronary, their mother the previous winter, run down one icy morning by a skidding lorry not half a mile from her home—and he and his sister had no other close family, so he felt responsible.

This morning he was dressed in a civilian outfit, jeans, trainers, and a white polo shirt. Only just under six feet, his compactness made him seem shorter. His closely-trimmed hair was dark, his face squarish, with a prominently defined jawline, his nose underscored by a neat moustache. He had the eyes of a sea captain, blue, piercing, and distant. His hands were broad and strong, coarse almost, yet those who knew said that when flying, his touch was supremely gentle.

He leaned now against the car and stared at the receding dots until they had vanished into the unending blue of the sky. Soon he himself would be piloting one, flinging one of those beautiful machines into the air, to dance with it within its domain, leaving those less fortunate far behind, earthbound.

Mark Selby got back into the car, sighed contentedly. It felt good to be one of the chosen.

Slowly the Royal Air Force Wing Commander got to his feet. Physically he was unremarkable, of medium build, clean-shaven, with regular features, dark eyes, and slightly receding sandy hair, yet instantly he dominated the crowded briefing room. There was an intensity to his gaze, a power generated by his presence, that drew all eyes. A hush fell upon his audience of uniformed airmen. On the dais with him were two fellow senior officers, from West Germany and from Italy. They remained seated at the long briefing table. Outside, the early evening sun shone brightly upon the expanse of concrete.

"Welcome, gentlemen," the Wing Commander began. "Welcome to Scotland, and to November One. You are here as prospective members of what is hoped will be only the first of a series of fully-integrated NATO specialist fighter squadrons. The more observant among you will have noticed the fin identification N-01 on all parked aircraft. This stands for NATO Zero One, the first such squadron. If we are successful here, others will follow. The initial requirement is for ten squadrons. We hope that will only be a beginning.

"We consider ourselves extremely fortunate. Not only have we been entrusted with a brand-new and enormously expensive aircraft, but we have also been given a brand-new station, built upon the site of an old one, from World War Two. But of course nothing comes free. In return for all this a great deal is expected of us. Some of you have come to us from Tornado squadrons. Others from the Trinational Tornado Training Establishment at Cottesmore. Some are from the flying services of other NATO countries and still others are straight from advanced flying training, with no operational experience. Here at November One, come what may, and within an extremely limited time-frame, we intend to weld you into a single, tight, supremely efficient fighting unit.

"Given recent media comments on the subject of low flying, many people can be forgiven for thinking that young men such as yourselves go out to your aircraft, look keenly up at the sky, pat your ship, then climb into it and immediately search for a convenient mountainside to pile noisily and expensively into."

There were brief snuffles of subdued laughter. The Wing Commander cut them off, his gaze unsmiling.

"You and I know better. We know the dangers, and we also understand the narrow edge of public acceptance that we tread, even when operating over lightly-populated areas such as this. Nevertheless, at November One you will be taught to fly lower, faster, higher and tighter than you ever thought possible."

His eyes scanned his audience, as if seeking out each man in turn.

"Why fly low? you may ask. We're fighter pilots, not mud-movers. Well, gentlemen, you may not be low-level ground attack pilots, but at November One you will be expected to carry the fight to *any* level. Nowhere is to be safe for the enemy, whoever he may be. The new Tornado excels at sustained low-level transit. Nothing can match it. That ability may well save your lives one day. During service with your previous units some of you have participated in bombing and air-to-air combat competitions for trophies. Here, however, while your conversion to the new aircraft may well include such competitions, the real trophy is already in your possession. You do not have to fight to win it—you must fight to *keep* it. That trophy, gentlemen, is life itself. Dead pilots and navigators are no good to me.

"I want no circus fliers. But I do want the sort of men who should we—God forbid—find ourselves at war, will go out there and give the other guy a thoroughly bad day, *and* live to give his friends more of the same. There may be some among you who, as time passes, will come to feel we are not for you. I expect such people to have the courage to say so. No one will think the less of you for it. The fact that you are already here speaks volumes for your capabilities. Your careers will not be affected by an unsuccessful time with us and you will be doing none of us any favors if you brazen it out. Not only could you kill yourselves. Worse, you would almost certainly take others with you. A word of advice: I have a great deal of respect for the man who knows when it's time to quit, and none at all for the man who does not."

The Wing Commander now introduced each of his companions on the platform.

"These gentlemen are . . . Fregatten Kapitän Dieter Helm, and . . . Tenente Colonello Mario da Vinci. And no artistic jokes, please—the Colonello's bite is infinitely worse than his bark."

There was a dutiful rumble of subdued chuckles. The Colonello gave a thin smile, and dusted an invisible speck from his sleeve. He was a small, neat man. A dark-haired Mediterranean, in complete contrast to the angular West German by his side.

"Their equivalent rank is Wing Commander,"

the speaker continued. "The same as mine. They are your senior flying instructors and you will listen to them and to their staff, as if they were messengers from the Almighty." He folded his arms. "A very brief word about the variable-sweep wing of your new aircraft. Those of you from other Tornado units, and the F-111, will need no introduction. All versions of the Tornado have variable sweep, with four main configurations. Full spread at 25 degrees is the normal landing configuration and is also used for low-speed hard maneuvering. Forty-five degrees is the mid-position for cruising, and can be used up to about Mach.88. Fifty-eight degrees and the sixty-seven degrees full sweep are for high-speed flight. Thus in one aircraft, you have both a hard-maneuvering and high-speed fighter. Our particular version, like the F2A and F3 ADVs, has fully automatic wing-sweep and this means that in combat, the aircraft will select the optimum configuration for a given situation. The IDS, of course, is manual sweep only.

"Your aircraft are advanced versions of the standard F3 Tornado. They have a thirty percent increase in power, giving a thrust-to-weight ratio that's better than an F-15 Eagle's or an F-16 Falcon's. Any Americans among you will appreciate what that means."

Someone cried out, "Oh, we do . . . we do!"

The Wing Commander smiled briefly. "I'm pleased to hear it. Other modifications have been made to this special ship in order to give extra maneuvering capabilities, including control beyond the stall limits of the conventional F3. Our new ship does not as yet have an official designation. Here at November One, we call her the Super Tornado. You may also hear her referred to as the Air Superiority Variant, or ASV. Handle her properly, and she'll get you through anything. She'll even suffer fools gladly—up to a point. Take liberties, however, and she'll bite. Hard.

"It now only remains for me to introduce myself. My name is Christopher Jason, and my call-sign is November. I've a head start on you all in flying the ASV, so when one of you can take me I'll know he's getting there. And to show you just how informal I can be, you may call me 'sir'."

Wing Commander Jason smiled again, this time more warmly, and put on his cap. The meeting was over. As he left the platform he looked back at the eager, experienced young aircrew in the briefing room. If they were successful, he'd told them, other elite squadrons would follow. He wished he felt as confident as he'd sounded: the truth was, even November One was living on borrowed time. Nothing was certain. Not even beyond the end of the month. Still . . .

Powerful forces in government were against it; against both the basic concept, and the expenditure it represented of tax-payers' money. In these days of *perestroika* the cash could be spent more usefully on . . . on what? Nobody ever cared to specify. In the meantime, the underlying strategic theory of deterrence without resort to nuclear weapons was conveniently forgotten.

Wing Commander Jason sighed. They'd bloody well better be successful. One mistake, and it might be just the excuse the pinchers and the scrapers needed to close him down. And they were wrong—of that he was convinced. But the trouble was, it would take a war to *prove* them wrong, and nobody in his right mind wanted that. He paused at the rear door to the briefing room and touched Da Vinci's arm, politely gesturing for him and Dieter Helm to go out first.

As the three men disappeared the assembled aircrew began to drift out through the main doors into the warm May evening. Uncharacteristically, there was no wind off the waters of the Moray Firth to cool the baking runways. Some of them gathered in groups, talking animatedly. Others were more thoughtful, aware of the challenge ahead and remembering the events, mostly unplanned, that had brought them here to November One.

Chapter

"Did you say something?"

"Just that I knew I should have brought my water skis today."

"Don't worry. You won't get wet."

"That's what you always say, Herr Baron."

Axel von Hohendorf smiled against the pressure of his oxygen mask. With variations, the short exchange was usually the same at moments like this. Despite grumbles from the back seat he knew he was in fact lucky enough to have the best Weapons Systems Operator on the *Marineflieger* squadron. Johann Ecker might not be biologically nerveless, but in the rear cockpit of a Tornado he gave a good impression of it.

Hohendorf checked the radar altitude at the top right hand corner of his Head-up Display. The green numerals (for their height) said 20. He smiled again. 450 knots—825 kilometers an hour—at 20 feet above the surface of the Baltic, and at night. No room for nerves when your life was so completely in the hands of another. Johann deserved his little grumbles.

Hohendorf held the stick and throttles firmly, but with the light sure touch of one in complete affinity with his machine. A flashing glance past the HUD at the twin engine rpm indicators on the lower right of the main instrument panel, told him both engines were spooling smoothly at 80 percent. He eased the throttles forward minutely. Instantly, the percentage numerals in the small windows at the bottom of the dials went up to 82, while the needles on the dials inched their way round until, its wings at full sweep, the aircraft was being hurled forward at 500 knots.

Hohendorf loved the Tornado and considered himself a very lucky man to be flying it. They made a good team. He barely needed to use the 4-way "coolie hat" trim button on top of the stick to adjust to the new wing configuration. The controls remained light and crisp, just as he liked them.

In fact, of course, the feel was artificial. There were no physical connections between the controls and the systems they operated. All was done by electrical signalling, the control inputs having been interpreted and acted upon by the on-board computers. For all his skill, Hohendorf knew that flying this low at such speeds in the Baltic night required the precise sensitivity of the computers to keep the aircraft stable and in one piece. It was the time when you trusted your instruments and systems implicitly.

There was no actual horizon in sight, no exterior reference points for the brain to refer to. If the instruments said you were upside down and about to hit something but your brain insisted there had to be thousands of feet between you and the big splash, you believed your instruments. You were well-advised to. There were lots of areas of land and seabed around that bore grim testimony to what could happen if you didn't.

"Right, right, zero four five," came Ecker's voice. This time, as navigator, he spoke in English, standard practice for all operational communication.

"Zero four five." Hohendorf confirmed the new course.

He eased the Tornado up to 100 feet, banked steeply to the right, and pulled the stick firmly. The aircraft went into a 4g turn, giving its occupants four times their own weight to cope with. G-suits inflated, embracing their lower bodies tightly, keeping the blood from flowing into their legs.

Hohendorf levelled out on the precise heading. The G-suits relaxed.

"Zero four five," he said, and took the aircraft back down to 20 feet.

It had been necessary to climb. Twenty feet above the rushing sea was not the height to go into a 4g turn, especially at night. Even with the wings at full sweep, the Tornado still had a span of just over 28 feet; which would mean a mere six feet between its lower wing tip and oblivion . . . if you got everything right.

"I'm glad you did that," Ecker said, relapsing into German.

"Did what?"

"Climbed first." Ecker was a veteran of Hohendorf's bat turns at low level.

Hohendorf had been known to spread the wings to their full span of just over $45\frac{1}{2}$ feet, roll the aircraft over into a 90-degree bank and pull sharply on the stick, engines on full afterburner. Once, they were so low, Ecker swore the wingtip drew a circle in the water. That was the stuff of legend. Theoretically the aircraft would have cartwheeled, but Ecker still swore by it.

Hohendorf said: "Tonight I'm doing things the easy way, Johann."

Ecker's reply was a grunt of disbelief: then, back in English, he said: "Left, left, zero one zero."

"Zero one zero." And Hohendorf repeated his earlier maneuver, this time rolling left onto the new heading.

Five miles out to their left and 200 feet up, another Marineflieger Tornado was carrying out identical manoeuvres. Though they were a combat pair, neither aircraft communicated with the other. The night's exercise required total radio silence: but the planning had been so meticulous that at exactly the correct times, each aircraft went into its routine, choreographed by the mission brief. Later, on return to base, infrared recordings combined with the head-up-display videos, would be analyzed to determine the success of the exercise and the performance of the crews.

"I have three targets," Ecker said calmly, "at fifty miles."

Hohendorf glanced at the small window in the top left of the horizontal situation indicator. The red glowing digits were counting off the closing range, and the needle on the HSI was now pointing 20 degrees to the left. It continued to creep left.

"Three," Hohendorf said. "All nicely grouped?"

"Yes. They're playing tonight."

The targets were surface ships.

When the HSI needle had now moved 30 degrees, Ecker said: "Left, left, three four zero."

"Three four zero."

Hohendorf turned onto the new heading. The HSI needle had swung to point straight ahead.

"Range 25 miles," Ecker went on. "If we keep on this track, we should pickle them nicely."

The targets were three NATO vessels, representing hostile ships. They knew of the impending simulated attack but not when, nor from what quarter it would come. They were in a temporarily shipping-free zone and to make visual acquisition difficult for the attackers, the ships were blacked out;

not even their navigation lights were showing. But they were still sitting ducks in infrared.

If either of the attacking aircraft was detected, a pulsing tone would sound in the headphones of the crew, warning them that they were being tracked. A low-pitched continuous tone would indicate a radar lock-on; and a high-pitched continuous tone would denote a simulated surface-to-air missile launch. It was up to the crew of the aircraft to break lock before matters reached that stage.

"They'll be picking up Beuren and Flacht in the other plane soon," Ecker commented at 15 miles to target.

"That will keep them occupied while we enter the back door," Hohendorf said with quiet satisfaction. The second aircraft, he knew, would not be flying so low.

Then Ecker was saying sharply: "I have a fourth target!"

"What? We were told to expect three."

"This one's bearing one two zero and coming up fast. Too fast for a trawler. Range thirty miles. Probably our friends from the east coming out for a snoop. Range to original target now fifteen miles."

Hohendorf concentrated on flying the plane. Ecker would monitor the new ship's movements. As yet, no warning tones had sounded.

"Original targets breaking formation," Ecker announced. "They must have detected Beuren and Flacht."

"All the better for us. How's our new friend doing?"

"Still on the same course, but range is now thirty-five miles and increasing. We're going away from him, of course."

"Why didn't we see him before? Submarine?"

"Possibly. Range ten miles to targets. Two of them right across our track. We can take the other one out later."

"Good. At two miles, I'll begin the pull-up to pass over their sterns. I'll trigger the cameras at pull-up. We should have some nice pictures."

"They must be asleep. Good thing for them we're not firing Kormorans and they're not hostile. You've done it again, Axel."

"Wait till we get there. They might still get a lock-on." Hohendorf wasn't counting his chickens. Nothing was certain until the pictures were in the cameras.

At two miles, he began the pull-up, triggering the cameras as he did so.

A dark shape swept with a sudden roar out of the black night, hurtled low across the NATO ships, and was gone before anyone realized what had happened.

"Jesus!" a young American lieutenant on the bridge of one of the ships exclaimed. "What the hell was that?"

His vessel, a Spruance class anti-submarine destroyer, was heeling over now in a tight turn to starboard, but much too late.

A seaman standing next to him, amused by the officer's attempts to remain steady, said: "A bat out of hell, sir."

"Don't get smart with me, sailor!" the lieutenant snapped.

The sailor, whose name was Lebreaux, came from the Louisiana bayou country, and claimed Choctaw Indian blood in his ancestry. His now impassive face in the subdued electronic glow on the blacked-out bridge made one believe it.

"Sir!" he said.

The captain had eavesdropped on the exchange from his high chair. "Lieutenant Street?"

"Sir?" Street crabbed his way towards the captain. The ship was still leaning into its turn.

"We were just creamed, Lieutenant. What are you aiming to do about it?"

"Do, sir? Well, I guess it's a bit late now to—"

"How long have you been with us, Lieutenant?"

"A week, sir."

"A week. And before that?"

"Shore duty at Pearl, sir."

The captain sighed. "So this is your first exercise of this type."

"Yes, sir."

The captain sighed once more. "From the

warmth of the Hawaiian Islands to the cold Baltic."
He paused, as if deep in thought.

"Lieutenant Street," the captain at last began
patiently, "the attack is not yet over. There's another plane out there, maybe more. I don't want us
caught with our pants down again. As of now you're
the radar officer on this bridge. It's not going to happen again, is it?"

Street was stunned. "Radar officer, sir?" He
glanced at the stocky figure next to Lebreaux. "I
thought Lieutenant Commander Gruder was . . ."

"The lieutenant commander is standing down
for the next pass. Is that right, Lieutenant Commander?"

Gruder did not turn. "That's right, sir. I'll just
go check on that sub-on-surface contact." He
sounded as if he might be smiling.

"There you go, Lieutenant," the captain said.
"All yours."

Street swallowed. "Yes, sir."

The captain lowered his voice. "And
Lieutenant . . ."

"Sir?"

"I don't want to hear you yelling at my sailors
on my bridge again. Do you read me?"

"Sir!"

"Now back to your post, Lieutenant."

"Sir!"

The barest of smiles creased the Choctaw profile of seaman Lebreaux as the destroyer heaved itself into another sharp turn in the icy Baltic waters.

The Tornado was again approaching the ships, again at 20 feet. This time the attack would be more difficult, because the opposition was fully awake now.

Ecker was saying: "One of those captains really knows his business. He's still not detected us but he's evading like mad. I think a simulated Kormoran will take him."

"Go ahead, Johann. A Kormoran it is."

Hohendorf and Ecker were a total team, almost a single unit. On such occasions, Ecker was virtually in command of the aircraft. To work successfully together, a pilot had to sit on his ego. Hohendorf's ego did not give him trouble. When all was said and done, he was still the pilot. The front cockpit was still the best place to be, despite the high respect he had for Ecker both as a fellow professional, and as a man.

The fact that none of the ships had yet picked them up on radar was a tribute to Ecker's tracking skill. Radar illumination of the targets was kept down to five-second intervals, which meant the Tornado was broadcasting its presence only in brief spasms. The constantly updating navigation systems kept it zeroed on target, even during the periods when it was flying blind.

"Left, left, two seven zero," Ecker said.

"Two seven zero," Hohendorf confirmed, reefing the Tornado round onto the new heading.

A virtually invisible shape, and still unde-
tected, it hurtled towards the wheeling destroyer.

"I have lock," Ecker announced. Pause. "I'm
launching."

Hohendorf threw the Tornado into a wrenching
turn away from target and lit the burners. Twin
gouts of flame seared the darkness as the aircraft
climbed into the night. No need now for stealth: the
instruments told him their attack had been successful.

On the bridge of the destroyer, the loud tone that sig-
nified a direct hit filled Lieutenant Street with chagrin. They all saw the twin glows of the Tornado's
afterburners as it rocketed away.

"He's giving us two fingers," the captain said.
"Mister Street?"

"Sir?"

"You never picked him up, did you?"

"Er . . . no, sir."

"Jesus," the captain said in disgust.

"Message from the Dutch frigate, sir," Lebreaux said to the captain. "They nailed the other
Tornado, sir."

"Goddammit!"

"Sorry, sir," Lebreaux said.

"Not your fault, son."

"No, sir."

"Goddammit!" the captain said again, heaving
himself off his chair. "Stand down from general

quarters. Let's go see what that mystery sub's playing at. Goddammit!" One leg was stiff from sitting
and he slapped at it in frustration.

The destroyer's lights came back on, and
trailed by her accompanying ships now also with
their lights on, headed towards the submarine.

A short while later, Lebreaux had another message.

"Sonar reports the sub's dived, sir."

The captain said nothing. Warsaw Pact, certainly—it was always the way. Altogether, he was
having a thoroughly bad night of it.

The Tornado was at a thousand feet and heading
back towards its Schleswig-Holstein Marineflieger
base, West German Naval Air Arm. The second Tornado, its nav lights also winking, was now flying in
loose formation with it. There was still no communication between the two aircraft. Radio silence would
be maintained all the way to touchdown at base.

"I think Beuren and Flacht were taken," Ecker
announced with some satisfaction. He'd gone back
to German. "I've picked up some coded stuff between
the ships."

"We won't know for certain until debrief. I'll
back Flacht myself."

"If I'm wrong, I'll buy you dinner in the Alt-
stadt." There was a restaurant in the preserved old
part of Schleswig that was a favourite. "If I'm right,
you buy."

"I'll take a meal off you any day."

"We'll see." Ecker sounded sure of himself. The entire exercise had been recorded by the aircraft, right down to their inter-cockpit communication. "You're going to lose."

For some moments silence descended between them, broken by the sounds of their breathing of oxygen through their masks, and the muted hum of the twin RB-199 engines spooling behind them. From within, the Tornado was a remarkably quiet aircraft.

Then Hohendorf said: "I'm going to let her take us in now."

"All right," Ecker agreed. "I've got the flight plan ready."

Hohendorf relinquished control of the Tornado to its computers. The inertial navigation system would take them with accurate precision right back to base. Then Hohendorf would assume control again for the actual landing.

Ecker set up the return flight plan, giving the system its waypoints, areas to avoid, beacons to take note of, then left it to its devices. In the second Tornado, the same procedure was taking place. Then in the winter darkness, the two aircraft, computer controlled and spaced three minutes in tandem, headed for home.

Instead of the customary manually-performed fighter break over the runway, the approach was long and straight so as not to unduly disturb the sleeping citizens below. Despite the known reliability of the system, Hohendorf always felt uneasy with this particular operation. He didn't really mind the automated transit and attack mode—there was always airspace should anything go wrong—but approach was something else entirely. He knew such feelings didn't make sense, especially since he trusted the machine to carry out auto terrain avoidance at well over 500 knots, but there it was. His one comfort was that he could always over-ride the system and revert to manual control.

Ecker, who was quite aware of how Hohendorf felt, said: "Look at it from my point of view, Axel. Whether I like it or not I've got to put up with you pilots most of the time. Now if only we had fully automated take-off and landing, we back-seaters could do the job all by ourselves."

"Everyone knows a back-seater is only a frustrated pilot."

"You pilots love to believe that. It polishes your egos."

"Jealous, jealous."

The banter continued until Ecker said: "All right, genius. Time for you to play with your stick again. Come on, driver. Get me down."

Hohendorf grinned in his mask. "Yes, sir. It's nice to know you're needed."

He carried out another of his perfectly smooth landings.

Ecker said: "One of these days, I'll catch you out doing a rough touchdown."

"You'll have a very long wait."

"Pilots are so vain," Ecker went on as they began taxiing back to the hardened aircraft shelter. The navigation system remembered its original starting point and would know when it was back home.

"And beautiful," Hohendorf reminded him. "Don't forget that."

"You've been watching the movies again."

The second Tornado touched down just as they reached the HAS. Another pair of Tornados took off soon after, to continue the night's exercise.

At the debrief, Beuren and Flacht were looking sheepish.

Beuren, the pilot, said: "The Dutch nailed us on the first pass. We got a hit in. But that's not much good if you're shot down as well."

Ecker was surprised. Willi Beuren was an excellent pilot. "How did that happen?" He turned to Flacht. Electronic countermeasures were the backseater's responsibility.

Flacht said: "They've got a good crew on that ship. They were really on the ball. I was jamming like mad; but I'd waited as long as possible before starting, to cut down our radar signature. Too long, in fact—they were on to us like that." He snapped his fingers. "As Willi just said, we got the hit, but we wouldn't have made it home in the real game."

Hohendorf, who'd been unzipping his G-suit, straightened and said: "You were too high. You should have gone lower." He placed the suit on a perspex-covered map table. "Even at night, 200 feet is too high these days. Once we had reached the attack phase, you should have copied and taken her down."

Hohendorf was exactly six feet tall, with the palest of blue eyes, and a crop of fine blond hair. Without the cumbersome flight gear, his body was slim and tough-looking. His unlined face was deceptive. At twenty-eight, he looked like a teenager, until you saw the life experience in his eyes.

"You should have gone down to the sea," he insisted.

Beuren was indignant. "And hit it?"

"Trust the auto. Besides, in the real thing, you would have died anyway. You just said so."

"But it's not the real thing, is it, Axel? Remember that."

"And you remember, Willi . . . if the real thing should ever happen, I don't intend to die; and if that means going down to *five* feet, that's where I'll be."

Beuren looked at Ecker. "What do you say to that, Johann? It will be your neck too."

Ecker decided to remain neutral. "War is war, and an exercise is an exercise."

"That's not an answer."

"Axel is a very good pilot . . ."

"So am I."

"Everybody knows that, Willi. You were just

unlucky tonight. Don't worry about it. Come on, Herr Baron. Let's get this gear off."

As they left the debriefing room and went down a corridor to the small room where they would hand in their helmets, G-suits and lifejackets, Ecker continued: "You were a bit hard on him."

Hohendorf said: "I know Willi is a good pilot, Johann, but he must use more aggression. He'll be one of the first people we lose, and Wolfgang with him, should we ever have to do it for real, and I don't want that to happen. If he can't hack it, I think he should transfer to something else."

"You know how he feels about Tornadoes. He'd never fly anything else."

They had reached the gear store. A civilian in his fifties was waiting behind a small counter.

"Good evening, Herr Stöcken," Hohendorf greeted as he put his gear on the counter. "We're keeping you up late tonight."

Herr Stöcken, a former serviceman, was used to night exercises. "No more than usual," he said. "How did you do, sir?"

It was Ecker who answered as he placed his own gear next to Hohendorf's. "How can you ask? I have a pilot who needs water skis. Two passes, two scores. You should see the video."

"I don't know why you do it," Herr Stöcken said to Hohendorf, putting the first batch of flying equipment neatly away. The G-suits went on shelves, the helmets and lifejackets being hung next to their owners'. "You wouldn't catch me up in one of those things." He had never flown, but liked being near aircrew. Even in these times they were the nearest thing to heroes.

Hohendorf smiled at him.

" 'wiedersehen, Herr Stöcken," he said. "Danke."

"Gute nacht." Ecker yawned.

" 'wiedersehen, meine Herren," Herr Stöcken said, sorting dockets as he settled down to wait for the next crew.

Hohendorf and Ecker went farther down the corridor, turned into another which led to a row of small changing rooms. Each went into one where he undressed and, wrapped in a towel, went to the shower room. After showering they changed into civilian clothes and made for the small squadron Mess.

The pine-lined room was partitioned with shelves and well-tended pot plants into a dining area and a lounge bar with comfortable armchairs. A television set stood in one corner, a coffee machine in another. The walls were decorated with squadron photographs: aircraft, people, events. There were also badges and insignia from other units that had paid visits down the years. Off to one side, a swinging door led to the kitchen. There was a light on in the bar, but no one seemed to be around.

As they entered, Ecker said: "A coffee? Or would you prefer a beer from the kitchen fridge?"

"A coffee, thanks, Johann."

Hohendorf went over to a window and looked out. The lights of the airfield glowed like so many stars in the night. On the ground snow lay thickly, the black gashes of the cleared roads like deep wounds across it. In the distance, plows moved to and fro, their lights swinging in bright swathes. The weather people had said no further snow was expected.

"It wouldn't be like this," Hohendorf said, his forehead against the cold glass, "in a real war. So neat and tidy."

"Would anything still be here?" Ecker queried drily. "Come, Axel. Your coffee's ready. Come and sit down."

Hohendorf came away from the window and took a seat next to Ecker at a small, low table.

"I know Willi likes to fly Tornadoes," he said. "And I know he's good. But if he thinks he will kill himself by going lower, one day he might decide to . . . and then he *will* kill himself. And Wolfie too, of course."

"What are you trying to say?"

Hohendorf took a swallow of coffee. Glared at it.

"What's wrong?" Ecker asked innocently.

"You forgot the sugar."

"Oh, I'm sorry."

"You're not," Hohendorf told him. "Ever since you gave up sugar, you've been trying your crusade on me."

"Do you good."

"God save me from the converted. I remember when you gave up cigarettes. But I was lucky then, never having been a smoker. The sugar, Johann. Please."

Ecker gave in and got the sugar.

"Thank you," Hohendorf said drily. "What am I trying to say about Willi?" He put two teaspoonsful into his mug, stirred, then laid the spoon down. "Wilhelm has a wife and two children. Wolfgang has a wife and a baby. I don't want to see either of them go. Someone has to get Willi to come to terms with flying low. If not, then—"

"Not everyone's like you, Axel. Willi handles two hundred feet well enough. He's a very safe pilot."

"I know that."

"So what are you going to do? Tell the boss what you think?"

Hohendorf stared at his back-seater. "Are you crazy? I can't do that to Willi."

"Then what?"

"I'll talk to him."

"And how are you going to do that without upsetting him?"

"I'll find a way."

"I wish you luck."

"I'll take him up in the trainer. We can work it out up there."

"Oh yes." Ecker was skeptical. "*You're* going to

give Willi Beuren a check-ride? A man who was on Tornadoes two years before you were? Oh I can just see it."

"I'll ask him to give *me* a check-ride."

"He's not going to fall for that. After tonight's performance, how are you going to persuade him you need a checkout? How are you going to persuade the boss, for that matter?" Ecker shook his head. "Give it up, Axel. Willi is all right . . ."

"Look, Johann. Wolfgang felt they should have gone lower tonight. He didn't say so in there, but I know how he felt. I've flown with him. He's not as good as you, but he's very, very able. In a little while, he'll be snapping at your heels. And already he can handle the ski level. He knew that's what they should have done tonight." Hohendorf sighed. "All right, Johann. I'm going to leave it for now. But I tell you there's an ugly feeling in my gut about this, and it worries me."

They finished their coffees and stood up to leave. Ecker took the mugs into the kitchen to rinse them out. Hohendorf went to the main entrance to wait for him.

On a wall near the double doors was a large frame containing passport-type photographs of squadron aircrew, past and present. Each carried a small caption beneath denoting name, rank, and period of service with the unit. Beneath a few something else was appended: a small inked-in, black cross. There were four beneath the newer photographs; people who had died, two into the sea off Bornholm.

Hohendorf read his own entry silently. KAPI-TÄN LEUTNANT AXEL Baron Von WIETZE-HOHENDORF. Next to his, was Ecker's. KAPITÄN LEUTNANT JOHANN ECKER.

Footsteps made him turn. Ecker approached, and looked at him questioningly.

"The board interests you suddenly?"

Hohendorf said nothing. He turned back to the board, searching for two other names. KAPITÄN LEUTNANT WILHELM BEUREN, and OBER-LEUTNANT ZUR SEE WOLFGANG FLACHT. He imagined one day seeing small black crosses beneath those names.

Ecker's own eyes followed the direction of Hohendorf's gaze. "Come on, Axel," he said. "It's time to put your worries away. We've had a long day of it and I'm ready for home and bed."

Just as they were going out, Beuren and Flacht went past, their debriefing over, on their way to change out of their flying suits.

Flacht waved cheerily. Hohendorf and Ecker responded, then went wearily out into the cold, still night.

The car park was a short distance from the squadron buildings. Hohendorf glanced up at the sky. A faint sound of jet engines came to him.

"The boss on his way back?" he remarked to Ecker.

Ecker glanced at his watch. The dial glowed faintly at him. "It should be. It's just past midnight. His ETA's in five minutes."

Hohendorf was sure Ecker was correct. The squadron commander always made his estimated time of arrival.

"Are you going to wait for him?" Ecker queried.

Hohendorf shook his head. "No. I told you I'd leave it for the time being." He walked to his car, a dark red Porsche 944 Turbo. A rich man's toy.

Ecker accompanied him, and stood to one side as he unlocked the car and climbed in. He started the engine. Ecker was still standing there. He lowered his window.

"What's up, Johann?"

Ecker came forward, leaned on the car, and lowered his head. "Why don't you come over and spend the night with us?"

"I've got a perfectly good bed waiting for me."

"You've been in that house by yourself for a month now. My Erika's worried about you. You know she is. Ever since Anne-Marie went back to Munich . . . Erika thinks you're going to sell the house and move into the Fliegerhorst Mess. You can't do that. There's never anyone there except a few green Fähnrich officer candidates waiting for assignment. You'll be bored out of your mind."

"You tell my little cousin I'm all right." Hohendorf smiled. "Who would have thought it? I take my back-seater home for a weekend and the next thing that happens, my cousin's married him. Nothing can be worse for a pilot than to have a navigator in the family."

"She feels I have to look after you."

"She would. As for my wandering wife . . . tell Erika things will sort themselves out. She's not to worry. Anne-Marie and I understand each other."

"But—"

Hohendorf grinned. "Goodnight, Johann."

He put the car into gear. Ecker stood back, and he accelerated out of the car park. As he turned into the road that would eventually take him to the main gate, a pair of Tornadoes curved in to land, their presence betrayed by the noise of their engines, and the winking of their nav lights.

Ecker stood in the cold car park, watching the tail lights of the Porsche until they eventually disappeared.

Then slowly, he made his way towards his own car.

Chapter

"So what does it feel like to be a paid killer?"

"Better than being an unpaid one."

"Touché!" she said, almost approvingly. "Either you've had practice dealing with awkward questions, or someone's been teaching you how."

"I hate to disappoint you, but no one's been teaching me. I haven't had to answer silly questions like that before, either." Selby glanced at the revelers. He and the girl were almost shouting to make themselves heard above the racket. "But I expect tonight may well make up for it."

"You don't really like us, do you?"

"To tell you the truth, I have no strong feelings either way."

"Contempt, then. I see."

He said nothing. He didn't know the young woman looking mockingly up at him, and he didn't want to.

About the time that Hohendorf was leaving his base in Schleswig, it was 23.15 in London. A winter's ball was in full swing and the guests, having had their fill of a substantial banquet, were settling down to an evening of serious dancing and drinking.

The ballroom and main restaurant of one of the bigger London hotels had been engaged for the night, and one of the three hired bands was onstage. People in dinner suits and ball gowns were moving gracelessly to the disco beat of the music. A few of the younger men had removed their jackets, while their partners had abandoned their shoes and hitched up their long skirts, to dance more freely. There was a lot of leg showing.

Selby and his companion were standing on a balcony overlooking the dance floor. His eyes were searching the crowd below.

"If you're looking for that pretty girl who was at your table, she's over there, I'm afraid, being monopolised by the dreaded Reggie."

He looked, and in a far corner recognised the long sweep of dark hair, a man's hand resting possessively on the shoulder beneath it.

"Not jealous, are you?" his pushy companion teased.

He turned to look at her. Small, neat body. Short black hair, thickish eyebrows and wide-apart dark eyes full of mischief. A small, sharp nose, but a generous mouth. She wore a black gown with gold highlights, and an intricate gold necklace gleamed at her throat. Black earrings hung from small lobes and a small, black-dialed watch on a gold band encased her left wrist. On her feet were golden sandals. Unusual, but interesting, he thought. And very expensive.

"Will I pass?" she queried, tilting her head to one side as his eyes surveyed her.

"You'll pass."

"Well! I did expect a little more enthusiasm."

"You mean like those drones who've been hovering about you all evening?"

"Ah ha. So you did notice me."

"It was difficult not to."

"Oh dear. I detect a note of censure and . . . Oh do look! It would seem that Reggie's having a go at kissing your girl . . . but she does not appear to want him to. You must have quite a hold on her. Reggie's usually quite devastating."

"He looks fat and conceited from here."

Her eyes narrowed. "If you find us so hard to stomach, why did you come?"

"Morven got the invitation. She needed an escort. I agreed to provide one."

"Morven," she said, dragging out the name thoughtfully. "And she needed an escort. So she's not your . . . girlfriend."

"My sister."

"Your sister." Below them the band stopped playing. As the reverberations faded she lowered her voice. "What's this? Big brother foresakes the skies to chaperon sweet little sister and keep the big bad wolves at bay?"

"Who told you about me?" he countered.

"You're not the only one who's observant, you know. In passing, I heard someone ask a friend what you did for a living. You know how it is at these functions . . ."

"No. I don't."

She smiled. "What a lovely chat we're having. I think it's time we introduced ourselves. One never knows how the evening could end." Her glance was daring him. "I'm Kim Mannon. That's right," she continued as he started, "Mannon, of Mannon Robinson, merchant bankers. I'm the host's daughter." She offered her hand in an almost businesslike way.

He shook it. "Mark Selby. I—"

"No need to apologize."

"I wasn't going to. You called me a paid killer."

"Oh dear. We're arguing just like an old married couple. This is going to be an interesting evening, after all. I was getting quite bored with these people."

"And now you've found a convenient distraction."

"Don't be so hostile, Mark. I saw you up here all alone. You looked bored too, so I thought I'd come up and say hello."

"You have a unique way of saying it."

She tilted her head again. "I'm going to make you like me, you know."

"You've got that on good authority?"

She didn't reply. Instead, she asked: "Are you really a jet fighter pilot?"

"Yes."

"What are you?"

"What do you mean?"

"What rank?"

"Is that important?"

"I'm just curious."

"Snobbish, you mean. I'm a Flight Lieutenant."

"And what's that in *real* rank?"

Selby shut his eyes in weary resignation.

"Well, you can't expect ordinary people to know these things," she said defensively. "I understand about majors, captains, and colonels and so on . . ."

"If you need a translation, it's equivalent to a captain."

"Army captain? Or navy captain?"

"Army captain."

"It's not much. But it'll have to do, I suppose."

"Thanks."

"Well, I've got to know what I'm going to marry."

"You're *what*? First I'm going to like you . . . now I'm going to marry you?" He laughed, amused in spite of himself. "All in the space of an evening?"

"Well, not this evening . . ."

"You're crazy."

"Daddy won't be pleased, of course. He wants

me to marry Reggie. Something in the City, you see, and all that crap."

"You *are* crazy."

"But nice. Underneath all the rudery." She looked away. "And speaking of the devil, here he comes, towing your clearly undevastated sister."

Selby peered over. The plump, sleek-looking man with the winter tan was bounding up the rich carpet of the curving stairs towards them. Behind him came Morven, hands holding her skirt clear as she climbed.

The confident Reggie arrived, thrust out a hand to Selby. "Reggie Barham-Deane. Your sister's been telling me all about you. So you're one of those jolly chaps who tear madly about the sky and crash into mountains and so on."

He laughed uproariously, then recoiled as Selby's eyes hardened. Morven, coming up behind, stared apprehensively at her brother. She knew the pictures flashing through his mind: a laughing Sammy Newton, his friend and hers, a smoking crater in a hillside, a grieving widow, a fatherless baby boy. . . .

Barham-Deane said quickly, "Just a joke, Selby. You don't honestly think I meant that, do you?"

Selby's voice was dangerously quiet when he finally replied. "Barham-Deane, you're a prat. Worse, you're a drunken prat. Those 'jolly chaps' you've just joked about are dedicated men, with more skill and bloody talent than you could ever dream of. For your information . . ." He glanced at Kim Mannon. ". . . and for yours too, out of every six thousand applicants who come to us wanting to be pilots, three hundred at the most make it through preliminary selection. Of that lot, half may become pilots and about fifty of those may actually make it to fast jets. And even that number will be further whittled down before they arrive on an operational squadron. We work bloody hard to do what we do. And for what? So that if we inadvertently frighten a field of cows or disturb a sleeping village, questions can be asked about us in Parliament. And if one of us should cop it, prats like you can joke about it."

He turned away, disgusted, and stared blindly out over the empty dance floor. The band had changed now and new, fashionably bizarre musicians were tuning their instruments. Suddenly, he swung back to Barham-Deane.

"And do you know what I find really sickening? That we stick our necks out every day in order that pampered sods like you can make your killings in the market place, and sleep easy in your beds. Christ . . . if our friends from the East ever come marching down Whitehall you'll be first out there in the queue to sell them something."

Briefly, he passed a hand over his eyes. He shook his head. Then he pulled himself together.

"Goodnight, Miss Mannon. Thank your father for inviting us and tell him we've had a wonderful evening. Come on, Morven—let's get out of this place. I've had enough of it."

He walked quickly away. Morven followed him, after a sheepish smile at Kim Mannon.

Barham-Deane, watching them make their way down the stairs, said: "I certainly pressed the wrong button there. Bit gung-ho, wasn't he? Those types can never take a joke."

Kim Mannon said: "God, Reggie. You can be such a dick sometimes."

"Language, darling. That's what comes from fraternising with the troops. What would your father say?"

"Oh shut up!" she snapped, and strode angrily away in the direction of the upstairs bar.

He stared after her. "I do believe our Kim is smitten with the sky warrior," he murmured. "Well, well. What do you know."

They'd hailed a taxi and were on their way to Elgin Avenue, to a flat belonging to absent family friends.

"I'm sorry, Morven," Mark said. "I shouldn't have blown up like that. But people like him really do get on my nerves."

She touched his arm lightly. "I think you lasted quite well, all things considered."

"I've spoilt your evening."

"No you haven't. I had a good time. I was dying to get away from Reggie, anyway." She smiled. "As a matter of fact, I'd already told him you had to get back because you were on duty in Leicestershire to-morrow morning."

"Not to mention the hundred miles I'd have to drive to reach Cottesmore."

They both laughed.

"As long as you're sure you didn't mind leaving," he said after a while.

"I didn't. Honestly."

"All right."

"I think Kim Mannon fancies you," Morven said, checking his face in the gloom of the taxi to gauge his reaction.

"I doubt it. Women like that are always taken by a new diversion on the horizon. She's bored with her Reggie for the time being. Perhaps she wants a pilot for her list. She can count this one out."

"I think you're wrong about her."

"Oh yes?"

"You didn't see her face when Reggie made his stupid remark. If looks could kill, he'd be bourguignon."

"As long as I didn't have to eat him."

They laughed again.

The big, first-floor flat in Elgin Avenue had three bedrooms, and was very comfortably furnished. Morven and Mark had taken a guest bedroom each, leaving the owners' master bedroom untouched.

Morven said as they entered: "I'm doing some shopping with Tricia in the morning, so I'll catch the

15:40 plane back to Aberdeen. You don't have to get up. Have a lie-in, and I'll see you by midday at the very latest."

"Do you need to go back? It's . . ." he glanced at his watch. ". . . Friday now. Why not spend the weekend? Penny and Anthony won't be back for another week. We've got the place to ourselves."

"I'd love to, Mark," she said regretfully, "but I shouldn't even have come. I've got a paper I'm supposed to be working on. If you want your little sister to become a famous marine biologist, she's got to keep at her work." She gave him a hug. "But I wanted to see you. What with me being at university up in Scotland, and you always on some training program or other, we never get to see each other."

Which was certainly true. Within the past six months, they had met just once. Now she began to feel guilty.

"Will you be all right on your own here?" She looked worriedly at him.

"I'll be fine. I'll spend a quiet weekend here, then go off to the squadron on Monday. I'm not flying till the afternoon."

"You're sure?"

"Of course I'm sure. Now who's the baby of the family around here?"

"You could always get in touch with Kim Mannon." Morven looked at him sideways. "I bet she'd set the weekend alight."

"I'd need my head examined."

"Oh come on, Mark. She's not that bad."

"She's worse."

"I'm obviously not going to change your mind. Coffee before bed? I can make some."

"No thanks. I think I'll turn straight in. By the way . . ."

"Yes?"

"I meant what I said about blowing my top back there; but when Barham-Deane made that asinine comment about crashing, I couldn't help thinking about Sammy. I was the one who had to tell Charlotte. I still see her face in the night sometimes."

She patted him gently on the arm. "I know, Mark," she told him softly. "I know."

She was a strongly built young woman, with the clear complexion of someone who spends much of her time in the open air. Her dark hair, thick and lustrous, fell well past her shoulders. Her eyes were a luminous green, her face heart-shaped with a firm chin, her forehead high and curving. The nose was strong but the mouth, in complete contrast, looked soft and vulnerable. When she smiled, her eyes seemed to twinkle. In the blue, high-necked ball gown, she was ravishing.

"Mo," he now said, "I think you were the belle of the ball tonight. And given the number of Reggie lookalikes who were buzzing around you, a lot of other people thought so too."

"I'm your sister. You've got to say that." But

she was pleased. "Kim Mannon wasn't exactly a frump, you know."

"Unimportant. And how are things with Adrian?"

"It's only a student thing. I don't really want to get involved with anyone at the moment. He serves as a good buffer."

"Does he know this?"

"Oh yes. We're good friends."

"I must meet him."

"Oh no. You always scare my boyfriends away."

"Any man who really deserved you wouldn't let himself be scared off."

"Mark, you can be very terrifying to someone who doesn't know you." She smiled, leaning forward to say, "Goodnight. See you in the morning, or whenever you get up. Coffee will be made."

" 'night."

Affectionately he watched her go. After the death of their father when she was nine, Selby had virtually been a second father to her. Now twenty-two, she had grown into a stunning young woman and, like any father, he felt protective towards her.

At the ball, Kim Mannon was talking to a youngish man whose bow tie was undone, and who looked seriously the worse for wear. He could barely stand.

"Have you seen Angela Ward?" she demanded.

"An . . . Angela?" He looked vaguely around.

"She . . . she was being groped by Reggie the Smooth some . . . somewhere over there a while ago. Probably has her under a table by now. Oops. Oh dear, Kim. Shouldn't have said that. Reggie and you are . . ."

"No we're not," she snapped. "Pull yourself together, Jeremy. Be more specific."

"Speci . . . spec . . . specific? Who wants to be specific? This is a ball, not a board meeting, for God's sake. Relax. Take off your iron knickers. Get under a table yourself." He giggled fatuously. "Oh dear. Done it again. Shouldn't talk to the boss's daughter like that."

She looked at him pityingly. "Captains of industry." She turned away to continue her search.

"I'd be better for you than . . . than Reggie the Smooth, you know?" he called after her. "I mean that. Any time, any place. Jeremy's the name. . . ."

She ignored him. She was looking for Angela. And if she could embarrass Reggie at the same time, so much the better.

Loud knocking brought Mark Selby out of a deep sleep. Despite the suddenness of his awakening, he felt refreshed. There had been no nightmares to disturb his dreams. He yawned through the continuing knocks, picked up his watch. Ten thirty. Morven must have forgotten to take her key when she'd left.

"Coming, Mo!" he called. "Hang on!" He picked up the previous night's dress pants from a chair, pulled them on and hurried out on bare feet. "Coming!" he called again.

He reached the door, and opened it.

"Good God," he said.

"That's one way to greet me," Kim Mannon murmured as she slid in past him. "I will come in, thanks."

He turned dazedly, to stare after her.

"Do close the door, Mark," she said, smiling at his utter confusion. "You're letting in a positively Siberian gale."

He pushed it shut. "What are you doing here? How the hell did you find this place?"

"That's not a nice welcome, considering the trouble I went to." Mockingly her eyes surveyed his bare upper body. "Mmm. Nothing like being prepared."

Completely taken off guard, he said weakly, "My sister will be here soon."

"Hiding behind sister's skirts? A big warrior like you? Morven won't be here till midday, perhaps a little later. We've got nearly two hours."

"How do you know . . . ?" His voice faded.

"You should congratulate me as a tracker. All I had to do was check the seating arrangements, find out whose guests you two were and the rest was easy. Angela Ward, who's with the company's legal department, had a quota of six guests. She invited Tricia Balcombe, who included your sister and escort on the list. Lucky for me, the escort turned out to be you. This morning, I called Tricia who very nicely told me where you two were staying, and that she was meeting Morven for a late breakfast and some shopping."

Selby ran a hand through his stiff dark hair, unsure of how to handle the situation. "Would you like some coffee?" He needed time to think.

"Can I sit down first?"

"Oh. Yes, yes. Please do." He gestured towards the sitting room. "Er . . . I'll take your coat."

She removed the full-length sable with a flourish, and handed it to him. He swallowed hard. She was wearing the shortest of skirts, and a plain T-shirt. Her legs were bare. Clearly there was no further clothing beneath the T-shirt.

He swallowed again. Her obviousness was almost laughable.

"I see I didn't give you time to dress properly," she said, eyeing his crotch.

And now, his own body was betraying him. Marvelous.

He hurried away to hang up her coat and to get the coffee, aware of her challenging smile, following him. While the water was heating he fetched himself a shirt.

When he returned to the sitting room with two mugs, she was gone. Then he saw the low-heeled shoes she had worn, on the floor by the settee.

"This is a lovely room."

He turned at her voice. She was coming out of

the master bedroom. Her barefoot walk caught at his breath.

She came right up and kissed him. There was not much he could do with a mug of steaming coffee in each hand.

"Coffee," he said.

She did not take one. Instead, she stayed close in front of him, her breasts lightly brushing his chest. He stepped back.

"I've completely wrecked your poise," she told him. "I thought you fighter pilots were fireproof."

"Are you going to have this coffee, or aren't you?"

"Don't change the subject." She leaned forward, kissed him again; hard.

"Christ," he said against her searching lips, "You'll scald us both!"

"Put the bloody things down then."

With difficulty, since she would not stop, he placed the mugs upon a small glass-topped table. No sooner had he done so than she tripped him neatly, they stumbled onto the settee, then rolled onto the floor.

By now she was holding him off. "Don't be in such a hurry," she said.

"What?" he gasped. "You must be joking. Wasn't it you who—?"

"My prerogative." She was very still. Suddenly the game was over. "Now you've got to deserve me."

They were still sprawled the way they had

fallen. She was beneath him, her mouth challenging his. Her legs moved slightly, sending waves of excitement through him. A shiver traveled up his entire body: there was an intensity in her dark eyes that pulled at him in a manner that was almost physical. His hands began to work at her clothes. The T-shirt and skirt came off without effort, and she was naked beneath them.

Without speaking, breathing shallowly, she started on his trousers, her hands pushing at them as if rolling down a stocking. As she pushed, her body made shifting movements over him. He gave a low groan, lifted his hips to make her task easier, and tore at the buttons on his shirt. His trousers dealt with, now her naked body was trembling against him. Every part of her seemed to be moving. Now she was beneath him, now on top, then beneath him again.

"Oh please," she begged, lips and tongue caressing his mouth. *"Come in."*

When at last he entered her she gave a sharp intake of breath and made a high-pitched, mewling sound. She screamed softly, and from deep within her throat came faint gasping sounds.

Selby felt as if his entire body had plunged into her. They rode together with increasing urgency. Beneath him she arched suddenly and screamed a second time, as if in pain. Her body tightened, pressed itself hard against him. Then she gave a long, drawn-out moan and her moist body slowly relaxed, legs spreading languorously.

"Oh God," she said in a voice thick with satisfaction, "that was wonderful. *You* were wonderful." She passed a gentle caressing hand across his face and kissed him with soft full lips.

Suddenly she bit him. "But don't think this means you can control me."

He frowned. "Why should I want to control you?"

"And that doesn't mean I'll let you ignore me, either."

He propped himself on an elbow, chin resting in the palm of his hand. "You like things both ways, don't you?"

"And why shouldn't I?" She was unrepentant. "I'm worth it."

By about midday, Kim was sitting, alone and reflective in a booth in a small restaurant she favored, in a quiet backwater off Sloane Street. An unannounced presence made itself felt. She looked up.

"What are you doing here, Reggie?" she asked unenthusiastically. "Shouldn't you be at some watering hole in the City?"

He sat down. "Mind if I sit?"

"Yes. I want to eat alone."

"Now, now, darling. I'm curious. Did you find the noble defender of our skies?"

She stared at him silently.

"You shouldn't be surprised, darling. Angela told all, in between aspirins. Holding a ball on a Thursday is not a good idea. There are plenty of aching heads about the office, and not a lot of work being done."

"You, I take it, are working?"

"But of course. I've merely come down here to keep up to date. Rang the house in Marlow, found you weren't there. Rang the Chelsea house, ditto. Where, I wondered, could our young Kim be? Tried this place as a last resort. Well? Did you find him?"

Barham-Deane looked at her closely. "Ah," he said softly. "A blush, and a suffused glow of the face in general. Yes. Clearly, you found him and, I would think, a good time was had by all."

"Don't play the injured suitor with me, Reggie," she said coldly. "In the first place, you're not my suitor, whatever ideas my father may have, and in the second, when Angela refused to play she tells me Arabella Grant was more than happy to accommodate you. So please, cast no stones in this direction."

Barham-Deane took this calmly. "I wonder what your father would say about this Selby."

His expression at that moment reminded her of a weasel's. "Going to tell him, are you?"

"Knowing your liking for family conflict, I imagine I can count upon you to do that for yourself. But what about this Selby? Have you told him of your little hobby? The anti-nuclear one? He may not like that at all, and neither will his masters, even if you are the daughter of the great Sir Julius. I'd be very careful, darling. You may not always be able to control the little games you play."

"Reggie . . . *go*."

Barham-Deane stood up slowly. "All the nice girls love a uniform." He made it sound like an insult.

"Are you still here?"

"I'm going. See you in Marlow at the weekend."

"I'll be in town this weekend."

He paused. "I see. This is serious." For the first time, he appeared to find no humor in the situation. "We have our little adventures, darling, but do remember who you are, and what your future is."

"And *you* remember. . . . I'm not a platform for your ambitions."

His face hardened. "A man becomes a fighter pilot first and foremost, because he's in love with the damned thing. Fighter pilots have careers and when push comes to shove, the machine wins over a woman anytime. That's why he can be what he is."

"As usual, you're talking about a subject of which you have little knowledge."

"Do you think I haven't talked to pilots? Some of them are even gents, you know. I've met them at the Club."

"And that makes you an authority."

He nodded slowly, not agreeing with her, but coming to a particular conclusion about something.

"An about-turn within twenty-four hours," he said. "You used to say such people were just big boys with expensive toys. How are the mighty fallen." He leaned forward, knuckles on the table. "Just remember, darling . . . he has a career, and careers . . . can be damaged."

He chose those words upon which to make his exit.

"Bastard," she said quietly, her dark eyes drilling into his back.

In Elgin Avenue, Morven Selby, anxious not to miss the Aberdeen plane, rushed into the flat and paused, sniffing. The lounge betrayed no signs of previous occupation, and was as tidy as when she had gone out.

"Mark?" she called.

"In here!" The voice came from the direction of his room.

She did not go in search of him but remained where she was, looking slowly about her. "Has someone been here?"

He did not reply and took his time before joining her. He was fully dressed, in a pair of gray trousers, open-necked shirt and a lightweight sweater. He carried a black double-breasted blazer which he laid carefully on the back of one of the two settees in the room.

She looked closely at him. "Someone has been here. A woman, judging from the scent, and that smug expression on your face."

"Maybe it's this new aftershave I'm using."

She gave him a sideways look of disbelief. "This is your sister you're talking to. My nose works, and if I didn't have a plane to catch, I'd spend the weekend itemising all the little clues that betray you. I'll settle for a straight confession. Who was she, as if I didn't know?"

"If you know, why ask?"

She ignored him, and began walking round the room, peering about her.

"Do you want me to drive you to the airport? Or are you staying to play detective?"

She ignored that too. "I sniff with my little nose, something very expensive. Something beginning with K. How am I doing?"

"I don't know what you're talking about."

"Ha!" The derision was undisguised. She extended her prowl to the master bedroom.

He watched the open door with amusement, until a cry of triumph came from within.

"Guess what I've found," she crowed. She reappeared, holding something aloft.

"Oh my God." Melodramatically he covered his eyes with one arm.

Morven was displaying a pair of minute red knickers. They were a bright red.

Morven said: "I have been told I've got sexy underwear, but I don't think this belongs to me. Any ideas, brother?"

He cleared his throat. "The cleaning lady?"

"Give up, Mark," she said. "Miss Kim Mannon was just letting you know the territory's been staked. And don't look stunned. Men stake their claims. Why shouldn't we? Better get used to it." She gave a knowing chuckle. "So she came after you in the end. Good on her. I did wonder why Tricia kept delaying me when I wanted to get back. Kim must have spoken to her earlier. So, you're going to have that sort of weekend, after all."

"What sort of weekend?"

"Oh ho-ho. Listen to him." She tossed the red flimsy at him. Instinctively he caught it and self-consciously rolled it into a tight ball which he shoved into a trouser pocket. "I wouldn't put it there. Just imagine what will happen when you pull out your keys."

"Go and get your things if you want to get that plane."

"Seeing her later, are you?"

"Morven . . ." he began warningly.

"I'm going. I'm going."

While she went to collect the small travel bag she'd brought with her, he returned to his room to find a hiding place for Kim Mannon's underwear. He tried six places before deciding on his own travel bag.

"You're excited by her, aren't you?" Morven yelled at him from her room.

"That's right . . . tell the whole street."

"Well? Aren't you?"
"No," he said.
"Liar!"
Which was true enough.

Chapter

*Just over 1600 kilometers to the south of Ham-*burg and a little eastwards, a pair of F-104S Starfighters belonging to the *Aeronautica Militare Italiana,* the Italian Air Force, were high over the Adriatic and curving round to head back to Rimini for a landing. They had been engaging in a high altitude interception exercise with a pair of USAF F-15 Eagles that had come from the air combat maneuvering range at Decimomannu on Sardinia, for the occasion. The Eagles were well on their way back to base, somewhat miffed.

The humble Starfighters had laid a well set-up ambush and had nailed one of the mighty American birds. The Eagle pilots, confident they were at the controls of the world's most capable and potent fighter, had allowed their confidence to leave them vulnerable. An adversary who already knows he's the underdog, will make up in cunning what he lacks in capability. The result had been a nice video shot to be crowed over later, of an Eagle framed squarely by the gunsight of an aircraft which owed its genesis to the late fifties, and its first flight to the early sixties.

The pilot responsible for the unfortunate Eagle's embarrassment was the newly-promoted Capitano Niccolo Bagni. The rank was a mere two days old, and his flying suit still bore the *tenente* insignia. His colleagues called him Nick the Greek because his family originally came from Syracuse in Sicily, and his unofficial call sign was "El Greco." Bagni was himself a native of Florence.

By all the rules, Bagni should not have been a fast jet pilot, and particularly not of an aircraft as unforgiving as the needle-sharp Starfighter. Virtually a missile with stub wings, the F-104 had claimed many an unwary pilot.

Bagni was at once frightened of, and in love with it. He was also frightened of and in love with flying. The fear, no one, not even his instructors during training, suspected. The love was patently obvious to all. Bagni's worst moments were take-off and landing, with landing being the greatest of nightmares. Yet once off the ground, he became transformed. The air was his element and in his hands the capricious Starfighter became an artist's brush, tracing elegant patterns in the sky. His fellow pilots always insisted his nickname had less to do with his Sicilian ancestry than with the artistry of his flying.

That artistry had enabled him to win today's aerial contest.

The Starfighters, built for speed rather than turning capability, had looked like easy meat for the agile Eagles. But Bagni and his partner had used their assets, high speed and small size, to turn the tables. The two F-104s had flashed past the Eagles splitting into different directions. Taking the bait, the Eagles had turned after them. Bagni had gone high while his number two, Vittorio Baldassare, had streaked earthwards. They had also listened on their adversary pilots' channels. The eavesdropping had proved interesting.

"I've got lock-on!" one American voice had crowed. "He's moving, but I've still got him!" Baldassare had been the intended target.

"Shit!" came the other Eagle. "Goddammit, mine's gone!"

"I'm hanging in! I'm hanging in!" exclaimed Baldassare's pursuer. "He's not getting away!"

Bagni meanwhile had gone almost vertical and had cut after-burner. As speed bled off, he kicked left rudder, pivoting on his wingtip and was heading down again as his own pursuing Eagle had begun to turn. It was a mistake by the F-15 pilot. Using height as energy, Bagni slammed into burner and began to catch up. The F-15 obeyed the laws of physics. Pulling hard Gs, even if you're a powerful fighter, will still cost you in speed. High speed does not a tight circle make.

Bagni knew he could not hope to turn with the Eagle. His one chance lay with cutting into the better aircraft's circle and if he misjudged it, the Eagle would not give him a second opportunity and he'd be nailed. The initial surprise would be gone and the Eagle pilot would be waiting. Fast and furious was the way to do it.

Coming down diagonally enabled him to curve behind the F-15 whose pilot was still looking for him. Despite the tightness of its circle, the American aircraft was still moving very fast indeed. Bagni didn't want to lose it, and he kept his nerve as the range closed. At the moment when the Eagle's path began to fly it towards the F-104's gunsight, Bagni knew he had won.

"Good afternoon," he had said in English. "Have a nice day."

"Oh *shit!*" had come a furious, embarrassed voice, and the Eagle had violently reversed its turn. But the kill had already been made. "Goddammit, Rattler. You should have been covering me!"

The second Eagle had been getting seriously annoyed with Baldassare's tiny, darting Starfighter.

"Hold still!" the pilot was saying as the designator box kept prancing all over the sky and the attention-getter kept beeping away. His colleague's sudden call ruined the shot. "Dammit!" he swore quietly.

The Starfighter had got away.

"Knock it off, knock it off," the nailed Eagle had

then called disgustedly, using the prescribed signal for termination of an engagement.

As the two Italians now headed towards Rimini, Baldassare said: "How does it feel, Capitano 'El Greco,' to have zapped the mighty Eagle?"

Bagni knew his wingman was gleeful. A small legend was in the making. Bagni decided to enter into the spirit of things.

"Just a normal day's work for an artist."

"Oh to be a great sky magician," Baldassare began wistfully. "What are we poor ordinary pilots to . . ."

"Check my tail!" Bagni interrupted suddenly, voice sharp.

Though taken by surprise, Baldassare immediately positioned himself behind the other aircraft in order to do a visual inspection.

"There's nothing wrong with your tail."

"The fire warning light is giving me the slow blink. Have a good look."

Seconds passed tensely while Baldassare carefully manoeuvred his aircraft as he gave Bagni's tail a more detailed scrutiny.

"Still nothing. No extra smoke." The J79 turbojet often tended to leave a slight trail. "Perhaps you've got a malfunction with the light."

"I hope so. Keep with it and warn me the moment you see anything."

Baldassare acknowledged.

Fire is every pilot's horror and in a fast jet, with

all that high-octane fuel about, it is even more so. Given his own secret battle with landing, it was Bagni's worst nightmare come true. He crossed himself, praying devoutly that someone had not checked the light properly. Already, despite his terror, his mind was clinically assessing the choices of action if there was indeed an incipient fire.

"Still nothing," came Baldassare's voice.

Bagni made a wry grimace in his mask. He was being repaid for being so unashamedly pleased by the Eagle pilot's discomfiture. Still, it felt good to take an Ego Driver down a peg now and then. The chance did not come very often.

"How is it looking?" he now asked his wingman.

"Still clean. And the light?"

"I've still got it. Engine temperature's normal, so far." Perhaps he would make it down all right, after all. He didn't fancy ejecting, but that would be better than trying to land with a burning engine that might die at any moment.

He checked his instruments. All had normal readings. If they were to be believed, the engine appeared to be in perfect health. He told himself to remain calm. He could not ignore the winking light, but he would not let it panic him.

As if on cue, Baldassare's voice said in his ear: "You're still looking good."

Bagni decided to warn Rimini of a possible

emergency. "Striker One to Goddess," he began, using the day's call sign. "Striker One to Goddess."

"We have you, Striker One."

"I have a fire warning. Repeat. A fire warning."

He could almost see the sudden stiffening in those who'd heard that message and knew its implications. When the voice came on again, it was measured, as if trying hard not to spook him.

"Roger, Striker One. Understand fire warning. We're getting ready for you."

His smile was bitter, only a grim twist of the lips. Getting ready. By now, the fire engines would be racing to take up station, followed by the ambulances . . .

No. Put that out of your mind.

"Advise on your current state," Goddess was saying.

"All readings normal except fire warning. No engine surge." He checked that his straps were secure, just in case.

"Vittorio?" he said to Baldassare.

"Looking good," came the reply. "You're clean, Nico."

They continued their descent, having been given priority over all other traffic heading for the base. For Bagni, it would be a straight run in. Baldassare would wait until he was safely down, then come in for a normal landing.

The Starfighter was handling perfectly. If only

that light would behave itself! He felt as if he were sitting on a bomb, waiting for it to go off.

Baldassare was saying: "Don't wait in there if it looks like trouble, Nico. She's not a glider. Punch out if it looks bad."

"We're not there yet. She's handling perfectly. I'm watching her. Don't worry."

"Don't worry, he says."

The descent continued without drama, then it was time to set up for the landing. The tower left him to it, wisely choosing not to distract him with useless queries. If he had a problem, they'd soon know about it.

Speed was now down to 250 knots, just over 460 kilometers per hour. Time to lower the flaps and gear. The wheels came down and he trimmed the aircraft in the new configuration. No control problem. No fire. But not the time to be complacent. The engine could blow at any moment. Flaps fully extended to landing configuration. Engine to 93 percent, boundary layer blowing coming on, helping the flaps to give more lift. 180 knots now, creeping down to 175.

Runway threshold coming up. Speed over it at well over 300 kilometers an hour. Nearly 325. Air brakes out. Throttle back. 75 percent power now. 152 knots. Here's the runway. Wham. Braking chute out, streaming behind the tail. Powerful retardation. Slowing down. Safe. *Safe!* Fire warning light still blinking. Lousy malfunction. Must be. But still no chances to be taken. Drop chute. Fire engines following, just in case. Ambulances too. Sorry, boys. No trade for you today.

Sweat was on Bagni's brow, and his entire head felt sticky within the helmet. He taxied off the runway and stopped well away from other aircraft. He shut down the engine. The warning light was still on. He shut down all systems swiftly. Snap harness release. Canopy open. Someone had put the ladder against the aircraft: one of the fire crew, in full gear.

Bagni started to climb out, keeping his helmet on. He glanced at the instrument panel. The fire warning light was out. Even so. A hot engine can still explode. He got out of the Starfighter quickly and hurried well away from it. What had taken seconds, had seemed a lifetime. Seconds only, from landing to a full stop.

He removed his helmet, and turned to look as Baldassare swept over to break for entry into the circuit. He glanced at his own aircraft now surrounded by the fire crews, waiting for something to happen. Nothing did. The aircraft was perfectly all right. The ambulance gave him a lift back to the squadron.

Baldassare landed smoothly, giving the ambulance a thumbs-up as he taxied by.

After the debrief, Baldassare was hushed. A quick check of the aircraft by the ground crew had discovered two things: the fire warning light had indeed malfunctioned: chillingly, however, a hairline crack had been found in one of the fuel feed pipes that ran atop the main tanks, beneath the Starfighter's spine. Had Bagni continued hard maneuvering and used the engine robustly, the crack might have widened to spew fuel all over the hot engine, resulting in a catastrophic fire.

"So all along," Baldassare was saying in wonder, "you did have an emergency, Nico." He shook his head, marvelling, and held a forefinger and thumb together. "That close to a fire. A guardian angel made that warning light blink. I think I'll ask the Colonnello to keep me flying with you. You're lucky. A pilot needs to be lucky sometimes."

Bagni smiled. "You don't need me, Vitto. You're a good pilot."

"Perhaps, but not an artist like 'El Greco.' You must teach me how."

Bagni put a hand on the younger pilot's shoulder. "I don't think there's much I can teach you—but if the Colonnello agrees, you can be my wingman for as long as you like."

Baldassare grinned. "That's what I wanted to hear. Now to some real business. I hope you're not going far this weekend because the guys and I have planned a little something tonight to celebrate your advancement to capitano. After your close shave with the fire, we intend to make it something you'll remember. You'll need the weekend to recover! The squadron bar this evening."

"I'll be there, but it can't be an all-nighter. I'm off up to Milan in the morning."

"Bianca?"

"Yes. I promised her last weekend, and couldn't make it because of standby duty. I cannot let her down again."

"Why don't you two just get married and solve the problem?"

"She's not ready yet. She has her business up there. Very successful. And I'm not ready either. We like it the way it is. What about you? Why don't you marry that little girl of yours?"

Baldassare was horrified. "Me? I'm only twenty-two!"

"And I'm twenty-five. Plenty of time for us both."

"Are you going up in that roller skate of yours?"

"Careful. You're talking about the car I love."

The "roller skate" was a beautiful, wedge-shaped Fiat X 1/9 in gleaming black. Bagni treated it like gold.

"Get yourself a real car," Baldassare teased good-naturedly.

"We can't all have millionaire fathers." Baldassare's family were industrialists and his father had given him a red Ferrari Dino for his twenty-first birthday.

"Oh he's not a millionaire," Baldassare said

with the ease of someone who was close enough to millions not to care. "Not in cash, anyway."

"You mean he still needs a hundred lira, or so?"

A *sergente maggiore* came up to them. "Sir," he began to Bagni, "Tenente Colonnello Croce wishes to see you."

"Thank you, Sergente. I'll be right there."

"Sir. And sir, it was good that you got that Eagle. We all heard it. Well done, sir."

Bagni smiled. "Thank you, Sergente Magliano. It's for the squadron."

Magliano went away delighted. A little stencil of an Eagle would appear on the squadron notice board, to join others of different aircraft types nailed by the squadron pilots during air combat exercises. Among the Phantoms, F-16s—two lucky shots—Jaguars, and Tornado ground attack aircraft, would be Bagni's Eagle; a true prize.

Baldassare said: "You're his hero for life. No one else is going to get another Eagle. I'll bet the old man wants to congratulate you."

"More like extra duty for something I should or should not have done."

It was lightly said. Their commanding officer was fierce, but he was also fair.

"You'd better go and find out," Baldassare advised. "You don't want him to send Magliano a second time."

"You're right. See you later."

"See you, Nico."

Croce, a big man with a drooping moustache who had difficulty squeezing himself into the Starfighter, was smiling when Bagni entered his office. The moustache made him look like every schoolboy's idea of a seventeenth-century pirate.

"Ah. The great 'El Greco' himself," Croce greeted warmly. "Come in, Bagni. Come in!"

Bagni moved farther into the room.

"I hate losing good pilots," Croce went on abruptly.

Bagni stared at him. "We lost someone?"

"No, no. I don't mean in a flying accident. I'm talking about you. You were excellent today. Not only did you get us our first and quite probably last Eagle, you handled that emergency with the sort of skill and calm under stress that I need on the squadron."

Bagni was still staring at his boss. "Then who are we going to lose, sir?"

The moustache twitched sardonically. "I have no choice. I've been ordered to make you available for transfer to a new squadron. It's a very new and elite unit, made up of NATO crews. I'm afraid you're going to have to learn to fly with a back-seater."

"Tornadoes?"

"Yes, but up-graded—not the ones you've seen. These will be very fast and very special aircraft. Someone's read your confidential file and decided you're just the man they need. As I said, I've no choice in the matter. I'm proud they want you, but reluctant to let you go."

"Will there be anyone else from the squadron?"

Croce shook his head. "You're the only one going from here. I hear there's a little party in your honor later on in the squadron bar. Am I invited?"

"Of course, sir."

"Good. I'll see you later."

"Yes, sir. May I ask where this new unit is to be based?"

"Scotland."

"*Scotland?* My God—at this time of year?"

"It's not exactly the Arctic, Bagni."

"No, sir. But it might as well be. My blood belongs to the Mediterranean."

"Your blood belongs wherever the AMI sends you. Besides, the actual posting won't come through for several months yet. They're still building the base, apparently."

"Yes, sir."

"And Bagni . . ."

"Sir?"

"Not a word to anyone. As far as you're concerned, the subject is classified."

"Tenente Baldassare was with me when Magliano brought the message."

"If he wants to know why I sent for you, I'm sure you can give him a suitable answer."

"Yes, sir."

"All right, Nico. That's all. See you in the bar.

And by the way—" Croce leaned forward across his desk. "That was truly magnificent flying today. Your personal score on the board is now two Phantoms, two Jaguars and now, the Eagle. Impressive trophies."

Bagni smiled briefly, nodded, and went out.

A full hour after he had left Tenente Colonello Croce, Bagni still sat in his room at the Mess, facing the wall. The day had been mild, but in winter darkness came early. He had not turned on the lights.

He stared at the unseen wall, hands gripping the sides of the chair as his terror during the landing was at last allowed to surface. There had been other rooms, and other chairs.

After a while he sighed deeply, left the chair, and turned on the lights. Then he began to prepare himself for the night's revelry in the squadron bar. He stared at the face in the mirror, and paused in the act of brushing back the dark curls of his hair.

It was a Roman face with a high forehead, strong planes and a proud nose. His dark brown eyes were lustrous in the reflected light. He was not a big man. At five inches under six feet, his body was compact and seemed just right for the small Starfighter cockpit. Yet there was an elegance about him that belonged to a much taller man. Seen together with Baldassare, it would be easy to mistake them for brothers, for they had the same unhurried manner.

Bagni frowned at his image in the mirror. He

had forgotten to ask the Colonello about making Baldassare his permanent wingman. Given the news about the posting to the special squadron, it probably didn't matter now.

He rubbed his face with his hands. A new aircraft to get used to and someone else to think about as well, in a back seat. It was bad enough to have an unquenchable terror of smearing himself all over the runway, without being responsible for another man's life as well.

He stared at the reflection. "Tell the Colonello," he said to the face before him. "Tell him you won't do it. Tell him why."

He could just imagine Croce's reaction to that admission. He sighed. As with all past occasions when the matter came to haunt him, he knew he had an even greater terror: that of being grounded.

A shiver went through him, like the shedding of a skin. The persona of "El Greco," dogfighting artist, was back. He shut the door to the room on his terror, and went to meet his waiting colleagues.

In Schleswig Holstein, it was 1300 hours. Half an hour before, Axel von Hohendorf, leader of a pair of Tornadoes, had swept along the main runway to go into a classic fighter break before landing. The second aircraft was again crewed by Beuren and Flacht. Their day's mission had been a series of attacks on simulated dense concentrations of coastal surface-to-air missile batteries, with Beuren's aircraft impersonating an electronic combat and reconnaisance Tornado. Hohendorf had been detailed to attack the SAM sites after Beuren's ECR Tornado had first cleared the fire control radars.

The attacks had been successful, with Hohendorf taking his aircraft ultra-low along the designated stretch of coast. Unfortunately, despite Beuren having acquired targets and successfully achieved launch parameters, his aircraft would again not have survived the mission.

Hohendorf, now in civilian clothes, knocked on the door to the squadron commander's office, the damning evidence of the mission videos weighing heavily upon his mind.

"Komm!" ordered the voice from within.

Hohendorf pushed the door open and entered. "You wanted to see me, Chief?"

Korvetten Kapitän Hans Wusterhausen was a lean man, his close-cropped dark hair with a silver-gray streak at each temple. His gray eyes had a directness about them that gave the impression they were being permanently zeroed onto a target. His was a sometimes unnerving stare, a clear warning that he did not suffer fools gladly. A pilot making a dodgy landing, for instance, would be far better advised to admit it, than offer a lame excuse. His unofficial designation was "Sea Eagle." No callsign could have been better chosen.

Wusterhausen was highly experienced, and had flown a wide variety of fast jets, including carrier-borne US Navy F-14 Tomcats while on secondment duties.

He looked up from his desk as Hohendorf entered and shut the door.

"Ah, Axel." He noted Hohendorf's jeans and sweater. "Ready to set off?"

"I'm hoping to get to the Hamburg tunnel by 1500 at the latest, otherwise I'll catch all the commuter traffic and be there for hours. You know what it can be like."

"You'll make it easily in that Porsche of yours. Besides, I won't keep you long. That was good work this morning, by the way. You and Johann Ecker have got the highest score of all Blue Force crews, including mine." He smiled, a little sheepishly. "Well done. You two are a great team."

"Thank you, sir. But the fact remains, we lost my number two again. Very expensive if we were doing it for real."

"Willi's a good pilot, and Wolfgang is second only to Johann as a weapons systems man. What happened?"

Hohendorf found he could not put his anxieties into words. He couldn't make a firm accusation against Beuren, using his hunch as the only basis. He couldn't endanger a man's whole career. On the other hand . . .

He said: "The units playing Orange Force were a little wise to us, I think. After all, in the past, some of them have played the role of the Blue Forces themselves."

Wusterhausen nodded, moved on. "Even so, you still managed to inflict heavy casualties. A destroyer and a frigate, plus ten SAM batteries taken out. As I've just said, the highest individual score. Not a bad performance. In any case, we'll not get the full picture until all the reports from the participating units have been analyzed, now that the exercise is over. My guess is that it will take at least two weeks before we get to see the results." Wusterhausen gave another smile. "But that's not why I called you in here. The information I'm about to give you is not to be repeated to anyone . . . not even to Johann Ecker . . . until I say so. Is that clear?"

"Yes, sir," Hohendorf acknowledged formally.

"A special squadron is being formed," Wusterhausen went on. "It is to be a fully-integrated NATO squadron, made up of crews from the Alliance countries. This will please you, Axel. The aircraft will be brand new, Super Tornadoes; fighter variants with a major increase in engine thrust. You're always going on about wanting more power. Well, you'll have plenty to play with."

"I'm going to be part of this unit?"

"A confidential directive has gone out to a series of units, requiring commanders to recommend personnel. I was asked to supply one crew. I've recommended you. I believe that what they're planning will suit you perfectly, and they'll be pleased with you too. Well? Do you want it?"

Conflicting emotions went through Hohendorf. Despite the fact that he already flew an outstanding airplane, the thought of being given a truly powerful Tornado excited him. On the other hand, he did not want to leave the squadron. He didn't want to leave his friends. Further, Wusterhausen was a good CO. He didn't want to leave him either, for some unknown person he'd have to learn to understand and work with all over again. The new Tornado was powerful bait, but . . .

"I can almost hear the argument in your mind." Wusterhausen's shrewd, target-wise eyes were amused. "You don't have a choice. My recommendation can be read as an order. If a fancy new squadron is being created, I want this squadron to be represented. You're going to be our ambassador."

Hohendorf stiffened. "When you put it like that, Chief, it's very difficult to refuse."

"Believe it."

"So Johann and I will be leaving—"

"Ah," Wusterhausen interrupted. "This is the part you're not going to like. Johann will not be accompanying you."

Hohendorf looked at his commanding officer in disbelief. "But we're a tight crew. We've been together for—"

Again Wusterhausen interrupted. ". . . a very long time. I know, Axel. You work well together;

which is why you're my top crew. Under normal circumstances, I would not split such a team . . . but these are very special circumstances. I'm sending my best pilot away. I cannot send my best back-seater as well. I need Johann here to bring the newer boys up to scratch."

There was a knock on the door.

"Excuse me," Wusterhausen said to him, then: *"Hierein."*

A Bootsmann entered with a sheet of paper. "This just came in, sir," the communications petty officer began. "Leutnant Müller thought you should see it immediately."

Wusterhausen took the decoded message. "Thank you, Aurich."

He began to read as the Bootsmann went out. Hohendorf watched him, waiting.

"You'll find this of interest, Axel," Wusterhausen eventually said, looking up from the paper. "Two United States Air Force F-15 Eagles were buzzed this morning at high altitude by a pair of Fulcrums who had come up for a look at our exercise. They had a mock combat with the Americans, before heading for home."

Hohendorf raised his eyebrows. "Fulcrum" was the NATO name for the MiG-29, a formidably agile and powerful Soviet single-seater.

"Then a little later, two Royal Air Force Tornadoes . . ." Wusterhausen checked the message once more. ". . . F.3s on a practice long-distance patrol were met by a pair of Su-27 Flankers, this time off the coast of Norway. They too played a game with the RAF, before heading home."

"How did the Tornadoes do?" The Su-27 was larger, even more formidable than the MiG-29.

"It doesn't say. Nothing about the Eagles, either."

"Ever since the MiGs showed-off at Farnborough, they've been getting a little bolder."

Wusterhausen said drily: "You must admit they were very impressive."

"They've got their weaknesses. A good pilot could exploit them in a proper stand-up fight."

Wusterhausen's smile was speculative. "Think you could take them?"

"With more power in my engines . . . yes."

"So I was right to recommend you. I cannot give you details, but I can tell you that the new aircraft will be all you could wish for."

"About Johann . . ." Hohendorf began, trying again.

Wusterhausen shook his head slowly. "It's no use, Axel. The matter is not for discussion. Flacht will be going with you . . ."

"Wolfgang?"

"Yes. What's wrong with him?"

"Nothing. He's a very good back-seater."

"Then why this surprise?"

Hohendorf was unsure of what to say next.

"Well . . . but what about Willi Beuren? He'll need a replacement."

"He'll have to break in one of the newer boys."

"But who will be his real back-seater, Chief?" Hohendorf dreaded the answer he knew would be coming.

"Johann Ecker. Who else? Johann knows how Willi flies, and will be a great help with the new man. Some of the time, though, Johann will fly with me. Axel? Are you all right? You look upset. Is something wrong?"

What could he say? How could he tell the CO about Beuren, when he had absolutely nothing with which to back up his fears? And yet, Johann with Beuren—it didn't bear thinking about. But Beuren was a good pilot; a very good one.

"Axel?" Wusterhausen was saying. "Is something wrong?" he repeated.

Hohendorf pulled himself together. "I'm fine, Chief. I was thinking of something else—having to see Anne-Marie this weekend—"

"Ah yes. I'm very sorry about that, Paul." The flimsy excuse seemed to have got past Wusterhausen. "But you'll have to sort your marriage out before you leave for the new unit."

Hohendorf nodded, relieved to have managed to deflect the Sea Eagle for once. "We'll be having a serious talk. One way or the other, it will be resolved before I go."

"Good. I don't mind telling you that in some

quarters the opinion is that you'll not be waiting too long for your Korvetten K."

The news drove all other thoughts from Hohendorf's mind. "Whose opinion?"

"Mine, for a start. Now off you go, or you'll be blaming me for getting you caught in the tunnel. Try to have a good weekend."

"Thanks. See you on Monday."

Wusterhausen nodded and watched the other man leave. "You may have trouble with your wife, Axel . . . but that's not your real worry. Don't think I fell for that explanation for one minute."

As he walked away from Wusterhausen's office, Hohendorf heard Ecker's voice behind him.

"Ah, Axel," Ecker called. "What did the Sea Eagle want?"

Hohendorf turned, keeping his expression neutral. "He wanted to give us a pat on the back for a job well done, and also to talk about Anne-Marie."

Ecker was pleased about the pat on the back, sympathetic about Anne-Marie.

"How are you going to handle it?" he asked. From the little anybody had been able to gather, Anne-Marie was not the easiest of people to deal with. The squadron members were on principle solidly behind Hohendorf, even though publicly they kept well out of the family quarrel.

Hohendorf smiled. "I'll think of something."

"I expect you'll have to. Don't forget, we're here if you need us."

"Thanks, Johann. I won't forget."

"Fine. See you on Monday."

"Tchuss."

"Tchuss, Axel."

Ecker waited until Hohendorf had turned a corner before he thoughtfully began to retrace his steps. He was passing the squadron commander's office when Wusterhausen called to him through the half-open door.

"Ecker. In here."

Wondering what was up, Ecker did as he was told.

Wusterhausen was at his desk.. He gestured absently. "Sit down, Johann."

Ecker, feeling like a schoolboy who'd been summoned for some unspecified misdemeanour, took a chair facing the desk.

Wusterhausen went straight to the point. "What's bothering Axel Hohendorf?"

"I don't quite understand the question, Chief. Everyone knows his marriage has come apart, and of course that bothers him. But it certainly does not affect his flying."

Wusterhausen gave a brief smile that could have meant anything. "How quickly you leap to his defense. Don't worry, I'm not about to ground him. . . . So you feel his marriage is all that's causing him concern?"

"Of course, Chief. What else could there be?"

"What indeed." Wusterhausen slowly placed the palms of his hands upon the desk and raised himself off his chair. He paced the small room slowly, now and then pausing before a framed photograph of an aircraft he had flown, or a group of colleagues past and present. The walls were hung with mementoes of his flying career. Now he stopped before a recent one. It was a picture of him in full gear, standing next to a Tomcat on the massive flight deck of an American aircraft carrier. Ecker observed him warily.

He turned from the photograph to face Ecker. "Either my officers have suddenly become simpleminded, or they believe *I* am," he began, his tone of voice clearly warning anyone against such a dangerous course. "Axel Hohendorf is almost certain to command his own squadron one day, yet when I practically handed him his double K, he was as indifferent as it was possible to be without being rude. Oh he made all the right noises, of course. But for a man as passionately committed to fast jet flying as he is, it was a strange performance. His mind was somewhere else and don't . . . don't repeat it is to do with his wife."

"With respect, Chief, it must. She wants him to leave the Service and fly with her father's airline. And as if that's not bad enough, she carries on with . . ."

Wusterhausen raised a restraining hand.

"That's between the two of them. No. It's something else. Something is digging at him. There are good pilots, competent pilots, mediocre pilots, and bad pilots. None of the last are on my squadron, I'm pleased to say. We have many good ones, but one genius. Axel Hohendorf. He has the instincts of the old, pioneer flyers, combined with a total empathy with today's high-tech machines. It's a rare gift and because of that, I trust his instincts. If something's on his mind, I expect him to tell me, no matter how trivial it may seem to him. And yet he refuses to admit it. Have you any idea why that could possibly be? As his back-seater *and* a family member you're closer than most of us."

Ecker was in a quandary. Should he mention Axel's comments about Willi Beuren? Clearly Axel himself had not mentioned it to the boss, and would not forgive him for going behind his back with this. It was up to Axel to do the telling, especially as he himself was not at all sure that Willi was at risk.

"I'm sorry, Chief," Ecker said, "but I really don't know. It could be any number of things. I could be shooting in the dark and say the completely wrong thing. For example, I know he's thinking of selling his house and moving into the Fliegerhorst. He's been living in that house by himself ever since his wife moved back to München. Something like that is bound to prey on his mind. But I wouldn't swear it's the most serious matter he's giving thinking time to."

"I happen to agree with you," Wusterhausen said. "I am sure it is not the proposed sale of the house. Besides, given his workload on the squadron the house must be a positive haven of quietness."

"He misses her, even if he doesn't say so."

Wusterhausen shrugged. "You know the man better than anyone on this unit. All right, Johann. I'm letting you off the hook for now . . . but don't let it get really serious before you tell me. Are you receiving me?"

"Loud and clear, sir." Ecker stood up. "I can tell you one thing. Whatever's on his mind, it's not affecting his flying."

"If I thought that," Wusterhausen said, "I'd have grounded him weeks ago."

Hohendorf was lucky. He made it to the Hamburg tunnel ahead of the main rush and was delayed only by five minutes. As he headed out on Autobahn 1 towards Bremen, the cassette of one of his favorite singers, Dinah Washington, was interrupted in the middle of "September Song" by the *Verkehrsfunk,* the traffic advisory service.

As the tape was paused by the radio station giving the information, a female voice told him that an accident was causing a seven-kilometer jam between the Soltau-Sud and Dorfmark exits. Dinah Washington came back on as the message ended. He had no cause for worry. His ultimate destination for the day was in Westphalia, the family home near Tecklenburg, where he'd be spending the night with his mother, and the traffic snarl-up was away to the east on another autobahn, between Hamburg and Hannover.

As he listened to the song and the Porsche hurtled fast along the relatively traffic-free motorway, he suddenly remembered that Anne-Marie had never liked this tape, and this song in particular. He sighed as the song ended, but hit the replay button. He was saddened by the breakdown of the relationship, but not as devastated as most people thought. Their families had expected the marriage ever since they were teenagers, and so had their friends. Unfortunately, neither the expectations of family and friends nor a profitable business partnership—a thriving domestic airline combined with a pharmaceutical company with outlets in practically every town and city in the country—guaranteed a lifetime of marital bliss.

In truth, neither should have married the other. They would have been good friends, he now thought; he had never loved her, and now the wrongness of the marriage had turned Anne-Marie into a person he could not even like. Its collapse had let her become the perfect stereotype of a spoiled little rich girl.

He was not looking forward to seeing her in München. Dinah Washington continued to tell him about September in the rain as the Porsche took him towards Tecklenburg.

*   *   *

Schloss Hohendorf lay in secluded grounds outside Tecklenburg, at the edge of the Teutoburg forest in Westphalia. A long tarmac drive threaded its narrow way through a thick colony of tall beach trees that seemed to form a guard of honor on either side. Stripped of their foliage by the winter, their trunks rose skeletally into the night.

The lights of the Porsche blazed at them as Hohendorf accelerated along the final stretch. As a boy, this section had always made him feel as if he were coming to the end of a tunnel. That feeling was still with him and his acceleration had been an unconscious response, an eagerness to be home at last.

He came to the small bridge that spanned the streamfed moat surrounding the castle. The building itself dated back to the 15th century, but many updates and repairs had given it a thoroughly post-Bismark look. Designed as a shallow U-shape, it had a steepled turret attached to its right wing. A wide patio about two meters above ground level was at its center, flanked by two broad flights of steps that descended to the wide gravelled circle into which the drive led. The center of the circle was occupied by a bare patch of ground which in spring and summer became a brightly colored flower bed. A cobbled strip crossed the bridge, to pass between two square pillars, each topped by a graceful stone urn.

Positioned centrally in its own small tower on the steep roof of the castle was the white face of a clock. Lights from the gravelled circle played upon it, making it a beacon when seen from the darkness of the tree-lined drive.

Hohendorf slowly guided the Porsche between the pillars and drove round, tires crunching loudly on the gravel, to park nose-on between the steps. As he turned off the engine the patio lights came on and tall double-doors, paneled with thick squares of glass, swung open. By the time he had got out of the car and bounded up the steps with his small travel bag, his mother was waiting for him.

She was a tall, slim woman with a regal air. But the warm smile of welcome transformed her features into an expression of almost girlish pleasure. Her blonde hair was as rich as when she was younger.

"Axel!" she whispered, hugging him.

He kissed her quickly. "Inside, Mother. I don't want you freezing out here." He put a protective arm about her, taking her back inside.

"I'm not an invalid, Axel."

"You're not well, either," he countered, shutting the door. The entire building, during its most recent period of alterations, had been efficiently modernized and was pleasantly warm. "After all, you're not as strong as you used to be."

"Nonsense. I am as strong a Bavarian as I ever was. It's just my usual winter chill. I've borne two strong children, and I'm still only fifty. So don't try and write me off as yet, young man."

Hohendorf smiled, kissed her on the forehead. "I wouldn't dare."

His words pleased her, as her own smile showed. "Your father's away in Japan on business, so it will just be the two of us for supper."

"Thank God. We won't need to be formal." He sounded relieved.

"Now, Axel," she admonished, though not too seriously. "You must try and come to terms with your father. You've had enough time."

"I'll never have enough. He must learn to face the fact that I make my own decisions about my life. He's had plenty of time too." He turned her to him. "Do you know, you're a very beautiful woman?"

"You're flattering me, child. What do you want?"

"Nothing, dear Mother. I merely spoke the truth. You're beautiful, you're clever, and you're loyal. What more could Father ask for? Why does he try to hang on to Anne-Marie too?"

She nodded slowly, understanding. "What are you going to say to her when you go down to München tomorrow?"

"I don't know."

"Your father's very upset by all this."

"I'm not the only one who's at fault. He expected her to be someone like you. But she isn't, and I am not he. He's more worried about the severing of business ties between the two families. God knows we don't need the tie-up financially. The land and property we own in Westphalia alone gives us sufficient revenue. He holds positions of importance in the community, and policemen salute his car when they see it. What more does he want?"

"You're not being fair, Axel. He only wants what is right for you."

"He's not being fair to me—he must realize by now that being married to Anne-Marie is definitely not right for me. It's not right for her either." He gave his mother a squeeze. "Now look at us, you and me. I came down to spend a quiet night with you, not to argue about what Father wants and whether I should stay married to Anne-Marie. I'm going up for a quick wash and I'll join you in the small dining room."

"I wish I could help, my dear."

"Just be the mother you've always been. That's all I ask."

She gave another of the smiles that served to take the years off her. "It's too late for me to change."

"Which is exactly what I want." He kissed her forehead, then went quickly out of the galleried entrance hall.

In the staircase hall, a rich Persian carpet partly covered the polished wooden floor and wide stairs of dark polished wood wound their way upwards in three flights, to the first floor.

As he reached the top landing a thin man in

his late fifties, dressed in a dark suit, came out of a nearby room.

"Good evening, Herr Baron," he greeted respectfully. "It is good to see you at home."

"Good evening, Hans. It's always good to be here. Has my mother been well?"

"You know how it is with the chill, sir. But she is strong."

Hohendorf smiled. "So she's just been telling me."

"You will be having supper in the small dining room, sir?"

"Yes, Hans."

"I shall see to it."

"Thank you."

Back erect, Hans gave a little nod. "Herr Baron," he acknowledged, and went down the stairs.

Hohendorf watched him for some moments. Repeated attempts over the years to get the manservant to address him less formally had failed. It had been "Herr Baron" and it always would be.

As he made his way to his room, he glanced at the ancestral portraits that graced the walls of the corridor. Most of the male members were in some form of military attire, from the early days up to the present. There was even a portrait of Axel himself, the ultimate modern warrior in full flying kit, helmet beneath his arm, but that one took pride of place down in the drawing room. His mother's wish. It was hung next to his own favorite: the portrait of a naval commander in best blues, cap at a rakish angle. His maternal grandfather.

His mother always maintained he took after that particular grandfather, a man who had died long before he was born and whose sole child had only been four at the time.

The Count, Axel's businessman father did not think the dead commander a good role model, and frequently said so.

Supper was quiet and enjoyable and at the end of it as they had coffee, the Countess said: "I almost forgot, your commanding officer called with a message."

Hohendorf was surprised. "Wusterhausen? What did he want?"

"Nothing. He's given you some extra time off. He says you can take two days, but be back by Wednesday. Is it about Anne-Marie?"

Hohendorf nodded.

"This is not hurting your career?"

"No, Mother. Wusterhausen is a good CO."

"Oh, Axel. I wish I could do something for you both." She stroked his arm, as if to comfort him.

He smiled at her. "I'll work it out."

"With all this on your mind, it must be difficult when you're flying. All those crashes one reads about . . ."

"It does not affect my flying. Believe me. Wusterhausen is very sharp. If he thought I was slipping, he'd ground me very quickly. In his place, I'd do the same. So don't worry."

"I won't," she said; but the smile she gave him was less certain.

Hohendorf finished his coffee, and leaned over to kiss her cheek. "And now, I'd better get myself off to bed. It's an early start for me."

"Goodnight, my son."

"Goodnight, Mother. Coming up?"

"No. I think I'll stay down for a while."

"All right. But not too late, or Hans will be ordering you off."

She gave him a hug. "Away you go. You've got that long drive to München."

After he'd gone, she went into the drawing room to stand before the portrait of her father.

"Look after him, *Vati,*" she said. "I don't want to lose him too." She turned to her son's portrait. "And you, Axel," she said to it softly, "take care in that machine of yours. Take care."

Chapter

Saturday morning, the Welsh mountains.

Flying Officer Richard Palmer was twenty-two and was aware that if he couldn't hack this low-flying, he wouldn't live to be twenty-three. He'd just caught himself keeping his eyes glued to the elusive Hawk twisting through the valleys ahead of him, almost to the exclusion of the rest of his environment. Yet he knew that situation awareness was paramount to continuing survival: target-fixation easily led to a premature acquaintance with the ground.

The instructor flying the target Hawk advanced trainer in front of him with such fiendish skill was totally determined to make life as difficult as possible for his pursuer. Palmer knew his every move was being analyzed by another instructor in another Hawk, lurking somewhere. Between them, the two instructors had him in a psychological sandwich, putting on the pressure. If he couldn't cope, he'd be no use as a front-line fighter pilot.

And Palmer very much needed to cope. It was of vital importance to him.

The mountains were terrifyingly close. He listened to his ragged breathing within the confines of his helmet and mask. He was determined to fight this fear. Too much was at stake.

His urgent desire to fly had begun at the age of twelve when his father had taken him to the Royal Air Force Museum at Hendon. He had spent most of that visit staring at the imposing bulk of the Lightning operational prototype, the P.1B. Neck craning at the towering white shape, the "over-under" configuration of its powerful engines and its strange, coned nose intake, he'd felt it *wanted* to fly, even as it quietly stood there.

"I want to be a pilot," he told his father.

And his father, a World War Two baby who had not known Service life, said: "To be able to do that, you must do your homework and learn well at school. Only an officer will fly something like that, and they won't let you be an officer if you don't do well at school."

"I'll do well," he vowed.

He'd done better, and a proud father had seen him go on to university and come away with a first class degree. He had got his first taste of flying with the university's air squadron before going on to the RAF College for officer training, academic work, more flying, months of praying he'd make it, and watching others fail. Making it and going on to more advanced training, now a real officer, father and mother very proud. He'd done it all: the propeller-driven little Bulldogs; the Jet Provost, for his first experience of jet flying; then the red and white Hawks for the beginnings of true fast jet experience and now, the sharp end was getting nearer. Now, he was at the advanced stage, piloting a Hawk in air superiority light grey colours, chasing a wily instructor in a sister aircraft, its low-level grey/green camouflage pattern making it difficult to acquire visually, even against the snow-mottled background of the mountains. General visibility, thank God, was perfect.

Three pressure-filled years of sweat and here he was. Not bad for the son of a man who owned an electrical appliance shop in Reading. Fear or no fear, he would hang on to that dancing Hawk.

Then it was gone.

Oh shit, he thought. *Shit shit!*

Don't panic. He's still there. He must be. He hasn't gone over the top or he'd have been silhouetted. There, that valley. Into it.

Palmer stood the Hawk on its wingtip, hauled the stick towards him, eased off, reversed the turn. The agile little aircraft threaded its way through. The ground rushed by above the canopy, speckled walls rising towards the sky. 400 knots on the HUD.

Where's that bloody instructor?

"Are you with me, three-six?" The voice in the helmet daring him to say otherwise.

"I'm with you."

But I'm not. Christ, oh Christ. Where is he?

The area had been cleared of other aircraft for the duration of the sortie, but that did not allow complacency. Anything could happen. People had met each other coming over the tops of mountains and certainly in the real game no enemy was going to conveniently tell you where he was going to be.

Keep the eyeballs working. Be conscious of the HUD. *Don't* stare at it. Don't get mesmerised by the ground rushing past. Monitor, monitor, monitor. Be aware! Watch for his pull-up. He'll try to do it when he thinks you're not looking. Then he'll be away between the mountains and you'll have lost him. He'll be waiting for you when you land. What were you doing, Palmer? Daydreaming? The taxpayer didn't fork out nearly three-and-a-half million quid on you, to allow you the luxury of a daydream in one of Her Majesty's aircraft.

Oh dear God, where is he? Christ. The ground's close! Don't panic. You're two hundred feet up. There. On the HUD. You're OK. Engine's spooling smoothly. Nicely on the throttle. That's it.

The light gray Hawk flashed between the rising walls of the mountain slopes in pursuit of its prey. Palmer held the controls firmly, but without undue pressure. The terrain rolled this way and that as he sped by, tearing the air with his passage.

And then, he saw it. A speck seeming to leap up the side of the mountain. He was on to it, keeping it firmly in sight. He trailed it all the way back to base.

When they had landed, the instructor said: "Did you lose me at all, Palmer?" Gray eyes seemed to stare into his very soul.

"There was a time when I thought I had," Palmer said, warily covering his options.

"I never would have thought it. Well done, lad. You can buy me a beer later."

"Yes, sir!" Palmer flushed with relief.

The instructor smiled. "A little bird tells me, Rick, that a choice posting's coming up soon. Tornadoes. I think you'll like it."

Palmer stammered incoherently, at a loss for words, so great was his pleasure.

The qualified flying instructor, a hardened Squadron Leader, clapped him on the shoulder. "Don't thank me, lad. You did it all by yourself." He smiled again. "With a little help from your friendly QFI, of course."

The QFI began to walk away, then paused. "And Palmer, I don't want to hear you've bent any of those nice Tornadoes . . . or I'll come looking for you. Got that?"

Palmer grinned. "Yes, sir."

When the QFI had gone, he found himself remembering just how much the mountains had scared him.

* * *

Munich was cold at midday, but the sky was clear of cloud. Low banks of hard-packed snow bordered the dry streets. The red Porsche cruised along a wide, spotlessly clean road towards an exclusive residential area in a northern part of the city.

Hohendorf slowed for an approaching corner. To his right, a cobbled pedestrian path with a paved cycle track running alongside, probed into a snow-covered park. He turned left into the side street. A hundred meters later, he turned right. Another right turn took him into the short drive of a large, two-storeyed house. There was enough room for four cars. Only one stood there: a big, gunmetal gray BMW coupé, gleaming in the cold light of the winter's day. It was washed daily by one of the family chaffeurs.

Hohendorf parked next to it. He was glad she was in. Better to have it out now, than to sit waiting for her return. He turned off the engine, picked up his bag, climbed out of the car, and shut it quietly. He walked up the short flight of steps. As he got to the porticoed entrance, the tall door opened.

"Hello, Axel," she said. She never called him dear or darling. Too common.

By any standards, Anne-Marie was a beauty. Her long hair was a burnished gold, her eyes almost white in their paleness, and the fine bones of her face bespoke of noble breeding. She was elegantly tall, and curvaceously slim. Her voice was deep and capable of sensuousness. One of the von Ettlingens before her marriage, she was a countess in her own right, with a family schloss deep in the Bavarian hinterland. She was dressed as if she was on her way out.

She came forward to kiss him full on the mouth. "Come in. I'll make you something to eat." It was not what he would have expected of her. Summons to a servant would have seemed more her style. "You look tired," she went on as he followed her inside. "A bad drive?"

"No. It was quite enjoyable. But I've been flying long hours this week. Perhaps it's caught up with me at last."

She appeared about to say something, but changed her mind.

"I see you're ready to go out," he began. "I don't want to interrupt your business."

"Just a lunch date," she said. "I'll cancel. It's not a problem. Go and freshen up. We'll eat in the breakfast room."

"Where are Manfred and Ute?"

"Ute's looking after the schloss for the weekend, and Manfred is driving Father to Stuttgart. You might even have passed them on the way. Father will be going on to the schloss, so Manfred won't be back either. We'll be all alone."

"Is that what you want? I can find a hotel if you've got . . . people coming."

Her eyes did not turn away from his. "If by 'peo-

ple' you mean Gerhard . . . no, he's not coming here.
I would not do that."

"You go to his apartment instead."

"Yes." She was not coy about it.

"Is he the lunch date?"

"Yes. He's not flying today."

"Then don't cancel your lunch. I can make my
own . . ."

"I said it is no problem. I'll simply tell him I
can't come."

She did not say Gerhard would just have to put
up with it, but that was implicit in her tone. Hohendorf almost felt sorry for the man. A senior pilot with
the Ettlingen family airline, it could not be easy trying to keep on the right side of the boss's already
married daughter. One false move and bang would
go a flying career. It would be very difficult to get a
job with another airline based in the country. A
vengeful Anne-Marie could be fearsome.

"I'll do that freshening-up," he said. "See you
in the breakfast room."

She nodded. "Axel . . ."

"Later. We'll talk later."

She nodded again, and left him to it.

The Munich town house was expensively decorated, expensively furnished, its valuable paintings
and objets d'art protected by an unobtrusive but
comprehensive electronic security system. Anne-
Marie, Hohendorf reflected, was certainly a luxury
the handsome Gerhard Linden would find difficult

to afford, despite his generous salary with Ettling Luft. Presumably she would not want to change the high-priced style into which she had been born—on the other hand, perhaps she was attracted to Linden's way of life, which must seem to her bohemian by comparison. It was all relative. Many people would consider Linden's lifestyle very enviable indeed. But guessing which way Anne-Marie would jump next had always been a hazardous occupation.

They ate off plates of crested silver and with crested knives and forks. The meal was washed down with a nicely chilled Rhine wine.

When they'd finished, he said: "That was very good, Anne-Marie. Thank you. You always were good at this."

When she lived with him in Schleswig-Holstein, her dinner parties had been much sought after by his squadron colleagues.

"No better than your cousin Erika," she said. "We were taught at the same school." But she was pleased by the compliment.

"You're better," he said, "and you know it."

She gave a tiny smile. "How have you been eating?"

"Most times at the house . . . but Erika and Johann often invite me to eat with them. I also use the restaurants and of course, during a lot of flying, I eat at the squadron. I am quite well catered for, as you can see."

She was looking intensely at him. "Let's go to bed."

"What?"

"What's so strange about a wife wanting to go to bed with her own husband?"

"Now?"

"Now." She'd stood up and was walking away, undoing her long golden tresses as she went.

Hohendorf stared after her, at the used plates and dishes before him, then back again at his departing wife. Her behind swung with undeliberate provocation, her long legs . . .

He stood up. To hell with Gerhard. Anne-Marie was still his wife. He followed her up to what used to be their bedroom. She had run ahead of him and was lying on the bed, already naked. Her expensive dress had been flung to the floor, her underwear a trail leading from it. Her golden hair was spread out in a fan about her head. Her eyes watched him.

He paused. Despite everything, she had aroused him. The eyes told him she knew he wanted to take her.

"Anne-Marie . . ." he began.

"Don't talk, Axel. Just take those clothes off."

No, he thought, I won't.

Part of him wanted to take her, then walk away from her with indifference; pay her in some way for the humiliation of her past behavior toward him. But he decided against it. Why play her game?

She saw the changing mood in his eyes and responded by being even more outrageous. She moved suggestively on the bed.

"Come, Axel. You know you cannot resist . . . You know . . ."

But he was walking out of the room. Her eyes narrowed, blazing their anger at him. But she said nothing and after a while, she joined him in the breakfast room, dressed again, her face still and pale. She considered the remains of their lunch, then looked across at him.

"Is it another woman? No," she went on, without waiting for his reply. "It wouldn't be. It's that wretched airplane of yours. You're in love with it."

"Anne-Marie . . ."

But she was not listening. Already feeling ill-humoured because of his rejection, she was not in the mood for explanations.

"Or perhaps you are paying me back for Gerhard?"

He decided not to answer her. When Anne-Marie wanted to savage something or someone, no amount of reasoning could stop her until her need had run its course.

But she was changing tack. "Oh Axel," she said, "why did you make me leave you?"

The unexpectedness of her move made him take his time before replying. "If I remember rightly, you left of your own free will. I came home after a night mission to find your car gone and your wardrobe empty. There was not even a note to tell me why."

"I had discovered I could not be a service wife."

"I was already with the Marineflieger when you married me. You knew right from the beginning when you and Erika and I were all teenagers together, I wanted to be a Marineflieger pilot. It was no secret."

"Yes, but I did not expect you to be one forever. When we got married, my father expected you to leave to join the company. You could be on the board, a vice-president."

"And what would your brother have to say about that?"

"Rolf?" She was dismissive. "Give him a yacht in the south of France and plenty of silly girls to play with and he's happy, as long as the money keeps going to him."

"He's older than you or I, and the one who should succeed your father."

"Don't be ridiculous, Axel. Rolf is useless. He would destroy the company with his follies. Don't you see? We need you. My father . . . your father-in-law . . . would pay any salary you'd like and if you're so desperate to keep flying, I wouldn't mind. We'd have the Citation to fly anytime we wanted . . ." She paused.

Hohendorf had sat up and was shaking his head slowly. "It's no use, Anne-Marie . . ."

"What does the Marineflieger pay you?" Her

manner had again changed, and she was looking at him, eyes no longer wishing to reason. "What kind of pittance do you get?"

"It's not the money. I'm certainly not doing it for the money. You've got to understand . . ."

"Understand what? That I must be happy for you to climb into your litle airplane, while I sit like a good little wife waiting, hoping someone is not going to come and tell me they've found pieces of you spread all over the place?" Her voice had risen and her eyes were blazing. *"And for what?* And don't tell me it's for democracy and freedom because I'll throw something at you!"

"I wasn't going to. It's much more complicated than that."

"Whatever it is, I don't want to hear."

"That's what I was afraid of."

"Oh, Axel," she said, voice pleading again. "You know I love you."

"I know you don't."

"How can you say that? Have you forgotten how we were? We have always been good together."

"You're attracted to me sexually . . . I don't deny it. But love me?" He shrugged. "I think not. You married me almost out of habit."

"And you? Didn't you ever love me?"

He looked at her and was about to reply but, afraid of his answer, she interrupted him.

"Is there another woman?"

He wanted to laugh. "Of course there isn't," he

replied. "Where would I find the time for another woman?"

"I suppose I can understand that," she said with some irony. "You barely have time for the one you've already got."

It was not going to be an easy weekend. But then he'd never thought it would be.

First Lieutenant Elmer Lee McCann swung the new stone-gray Corvette off the main trunk route, and onto the side road that led to the gates of the Cotswolds USAF unit where he was stationed in England.

McCann was a native of Kansas City. He would make a point of informing anyone who would listen that meant Kansas City, Missouri, and not Kansas City, Kansas, which he considered to be hicksville. He was a city dude, not a farm boy. Easy-going for a streets man, there was one thing that really got up his nose: being called a cowboy. His father, a well-off banker, had made him a present of a brand-new Corvette for his twenty-first birthday, and a new model had followed every year since. McCann, an only child, was now twenty-four.

Shortish, with a round chubby face and a crop of corn-colored hair that became unruly beyond the length of one inch, there was a cockiness about him that sometimes rubbed people the wrong way. His bright blue eyes and a button of a nose gave him the look of a slightly malicious imp.

McCann had joined the service desperately wanting to become a fighter pilot; he saw himself flinging fast jets about the sky with omnipotent abandon. His eagerness had in the end been his undoing. After several over-confident and bad landings, and one crash that had injured his instructor but had left him unscathed, he had been washed out of flying school.

With the expectation that he'd refuse, get out of the air force and everyone's hair, he had unenthusiastically been offered a chance at navigation school. To the chagrin and surprise of his superiors, he had accepted. To their even greater surprise, he had turned into a first-class navigator and weapons man. In navigation and bombing competitions, his aircraft frequently came first. But there were still flaws in his character, apparently irredeemable.

McCann pulled up at the gate. The military policeman, American, recognised him and came up to the car.

McCann showed his pass.

The policeman saluted. " 'Mornin', Lieutenant. How was London?"

"Don't ask, Browski." Dead pan. "Don't ask."

"That bad, Lieutenant? I don't believe it. You never have a bad time."

Suddenly McCann grinned. "It was that *good*, man. I'm telling you."

Browski smiled back. "I figured it would be something like that."

"Browski."

"Yes, Lieutenant?"

"Do I get to enter the base?"

"Oh. Sure, Lieutenant."

Browski went off to raise the barrier, saluted again as the Corvette rumbled past. He ambled across the road to talk to the other gate sentry.

"That Lieutenant McCann. Always having a good time."

"He's a dickhead," the second policeman said uncharitably.

"What's with you, Canelli? Lieutenant McCann's one of the main men on this goddam base. Never uptight. Never pulls rank."

"So that makes him a good officer? Goddam rich kid. If I'd had his chances . . ."

Browski frowned. "I get it. You want to make Airman First Class to Colonel in one day."

"Fuck you, Browski."

"Have a nice day," Browski said, unmoved, and walked slowly back to his post.

In the Officers' Club, McCann heard someone say: "Elmer Lee?"

"Yo." He looked up from his cup of coffee to see a fellow navigator, in captain's uniform.

"The man wants to see you," the captain said.

"Colonel Crane himself?"

"Who else? And I'd get out of those civilian

clothes, if I were you. What have you been up to this time, Elmer Lee?"

McCann shrugged. "Beats me. I haven't run over anybody. And last time I looked, old ladies still had their purses."

"A word of advice."

"I'll listen, but I don't promise to take it."

"Try not to come on flippant with the colonel."

McCann gave one of his impish grins. " 'Flippant.' Now there's an English word. But then you Boston boys are almost English. Or perhaps you've been over here too long."

"You've got twenty minutes, McCann."

"Yes, sir," McCann acknowledged, none too seriously.

But he was in Crane's office on time, smartly in uniform.

Crane, a greying man who looked as if he'd seen too many things he hadn't liked, was studying a thick file. Outside, a fully loaded F-111 low-level bomber trundled down the runway, and staggered into the air on widespread wings. Much bigger than the Tornado, it looked ungainly and strangely unsuited to its environment.

"Lieutenant McCann," Crane began without looking up, as the sound of the jet's engines faded, "I have here records which by any standards make fine reading . . . that is, until I look at the rest of them." He paused, and looked up, jabbing at the file briefly with a forefinger. "Lieutenant, part of what's

in this file tells me you should have been a captain
by now. Any ideas why not?"

"No, sir."

The wide blue eyes didn't fool Crane. He
grunted, went back to the file, began to read aloud:
"First at Navigation School. First in a bombing competition at Nellis, during Red Flag. First, first, first."
He shut the file with a snap. "Dammit, McCann! If
competence in the air alone gave rank, you'd probably be one of the youngest majors around." He
opened the file again, studied an item in it. "Calling
your pilot a dipshit is no way to make friends and
influence people, especially when *he's* a major, and
you're a rookie second lieutenant . . . even if you were
top of your class."

McCann cleared his throat. "I apologised afterwards, Colonel. I'd got over-excited."

"Over-excited. Is that what you call it? To
Major . . . now where's his name . . . to Major Ives,
it was crass insubordination. He recommended at
the time that you be kicked out. Did you know that?"

McCann was genuinely surprised. "No, sir."

Crane looked at him. "A pity. You might have
learned something if you had. You've got a good flying record, McCann. Before you came to us, you were
on Rhinos." Rhino was slang for the Phantom, the
aging but powerfully brutish twin-engined fighter
bomber.

"Yes, sir. I was on F-4Es."

"Again, your flying record during that period

is excellent. But you apparently got into an argument with another major, on tactics, *during* a hard turning fight. Do you always pick arguments with majors, Lieutenant?"

"Not if I can help it, Colonel, sir. The incident you mentioned took place during Red Flag at Nellis. We were coming out of Coyote North when we were bounced by a couple of Gomer F-5s." McCann meant the Tiger II used as MiG simulators against which participating aircraft had to fight. "I called a break and he ignored it. I could see the Gomer, and he couldn't. He had zeroed in on the Gomer's buddy and had become fixated. He wouldn't let go. I called the break again, but got no reaction. He was determined to nail that little F-5. But his buddy nailed us first. I got angry. We could have taken them both if he'd listened. I told him what the hell use was it having a back-seater if he wasn't going to listen."

Crane remained silent for a few moments, again reading the file.

"Someone ought to paint two gold oak leaves on your cockpit rim," he said. "You've certainly nailed two majors."

McCann did not smile. The Colonel was not smiling.

"Some people say," Crane went on, "you're a spoilt rich kid. I don't happen to agree . . . but you do have a slight problem with superior officers, especially those you think know less than you." Crane's eyes, seeming to hold the wisdom of the ages, fastened upon McCann. "A special memo has been passed to me. There's a requirement for top crews to form an elite group of squadrons. I've recommended you."

McCann would not have been McCann if he had not snidely suggested: "Getting rid of me, sir?"

"No, Lieutenant. I may be doing you a favour. I may be the only person in the entire United States Air Force who believes it, but I think you have it in you to make the grade to high rank. You might even carry a general's star one day, if you're not busted out first. If these new squadrons hold their promise, you'll be among some of the most envied aircrew in the Western Alliance."

McCann thought about that for a while, then asked: "Why me, Colonel?"

"In the first place," Crane said, "I consider you good enough."

"And in the second?"

"And in the second place, I want you to give someone else a headache for a change."

He closed McCann's file, shunted it to one side, and picked up another. He opened the new file and started to read. The interview was clearly over.

That night, in London, Mark Selby woke up sweating, in the grip of his nightmare. Once again he'd had to watch Sammy Newton's screaming face melting in flames. It hadn't happened that way, of course—Sammy's death must have been instantaneous, the flames had come later, and Mark had been miles away, back at the station—but in his dream the face was always screaming, and always melting. And as it melted it was replaced by Charlotte Newton's, her expression one of bitter accusation.

Selby sat bolt upright in the darkened room, trembling. Someone put her arms around him. Kim.

She said nothing, merely held him tight.

"Oh Christ," he muttered.

They stayed thus for a long while in silence. It was two in the morning and outside in the tree-bordered Chelsea square all was quiet.

"Did I make much noise?" he asked her. "I was shouting for someone to help. Loud enough to wake the whole city."

"No," she told him. "Perhaps in the dream you were, but I only heard a whimper. You woke me when you sat up. Was it your friend again?"

"Yes . . . Oh God, why can't I let it rest? There was nothing I could have done. You see, we'd been paired for a low-level but on the threshold, just before take-off, I had a leak in my LOX system. That's liquid oxygen—there's a converter on board that makes the stuff we breathe up there, and it's bad news without it. I had to abort. Another crew was due to join with us a few minutes later. They were ready to roll, so they took my slot. It was on the flight with them that Sammy and his nav went into the mountain. Not that I could have done anything, even if I'd been there. Even so, Charlotte's face always seems to be accusing me."

"And did she? Did she ever accuse you?"

"Of course not. Charlotte understands what it's all about."

"You're the one who's doing the accusing, Mark. You're blaming yourself for something you know you're not responsible for. Whatever happened that day would have occurred whether you were there or not. Everyone who flies knows the risks they take. Your own words. Remember? You said that to me only days after we met. There was something on the news about a fighter crashing in Germany."

He nodded slowly. "We'd better get back to sleep."

"Would you like a hot drink first? I can make you one."

"No," he said. "I'll be all right."

He settled back down and she wrapped herself about him, holding on to him tightly.

She had changed subtly since the winter, and though she was still wilful and unpredictable, she had begun to understand a little of what was required of someone in his line of work.

Her father had been alarmed by her staying power, expecting her to have ditched Mark Selby as swiftly as she had other passing fancies. But if anything, *she* was the one afraid of being ditched. As for Reggie Barham-Deane, he was becoming increasingly obnoxious as the relationship continued.

She didn't care. There was not a hope in hell that she would marry Reggie, whatever her father's wishes. She did not exist in order to provide a commercial dynasty for him; even if in the end things turned sour between Mark and herself, she still would not be marrying Reggie.

"Not a chance," she murmured.

"Did you say something?"

"No, darling," she replied softly. "Go to sleep. You're off to the squadron tomorrow, and I want you refreshed. I don't want you going into any mountain." She kissed him gently on the cheek.

About them, the otherwise empty house made its own soothing noises.

In the morning, she watched him closely as they sat in the large kitchen, eating at the breakfast bar. She was wearing something she called a dressing gown. Selby thought it was almost invisible.

"You'll shock your neighbors," he said, enjoying the sight.

"They can't see in. Besides, no one peers around here."

"There's always someone," he countered, "everywhere."

She smiled. "I bought it specially, to wear for you."

"Your father would just love it if he walked in now."

"He's not likely to. He's in New York for a week."

"And Reggie the Smooth?"

"I can handle Reggie."

"Isn't this place like a second home to him?"

"My father allowed it. Not me. Reggie won't come here while Daddy's away, if I don't invite him."

"Are you sure?"

"Quite sure. If I complained to Daddy about him, he'd be out of a job. He knows it, so we've got an armed truce. He's absolutely furious that I'm still seeing you, but daren't do anything about it."

"Nothing open, you mean."

"What can he possibly do? He'd have tried something long before now, if he'd been able to."

"I hope you're right." Selby did not sound convinced. "He'll have powerful contacts at that club of his."

"Don't worry about Reggie. He's old news." She looked at the kitchen clock, mischief in her eyes. "We still have some time before I drive you to the station."

"I thought you said last night you wanted me refreshed."

"This will refresh you."

They barely made it to the station on time. He had decided to leave his car back at the unit up in Leicestershire, letting the train take the strain to London, as the ads had proclaimed. Unfortunately, he'd had to share the trip down with a regiment of football supporters. Today's journey back was mercifully free of them.

Selby paused by the barrier. "I nearly forgot," he said to Kim, pulling a postcard from his jacket pocket. He handed it to her.

It was from Morven, and addressed to him at his squadron. The picture was of Union Street, Aberdeen. Her message on the back read: "Who would have thought it? The great hunter tackled and brought down by Diana herself. Congrats to all."

Kim studied the card: "I think I'll keep this, to remind you it won't be easy to get away from me. I like the way your sister gets to the heart of the matter. Diana was the goddess who hunted, wasn't she?" She reached up to kiss him on the lips. "Better go to your train or it will leave without you. Do they send military policemen after missing pilots?"

He smiled at her. "They might."

"See you soon?"

He nodded, and they kissed quickly. She remained where she was, watching him hurry along the platform. She waited for his parting wave as he climbed aboard, before turning and hurrying back to where she'd left her car. The train began to move almost immediately.

As he took his seat, Selby thought about the other message he'd received, and which he had not told her about: the official notification of his posting to a new unit in the far north of Scotland at the end of May.

Chapter

Flight Lieutenant Neil Ferris sat relaxed in the back seat as the Tornado IDS scooted low up a Welsh slope and dipped into the valley beyond. Maintaining a height of 200 feet above ground level, it roared between two high ramparts of bare terrain. Though it was noon, the April day was dark and angry, and the cloud base seemed to be just above the cockpit.

The aircraft was flying itself, responding to the navigation program that Ferris had given it, while he himself sat back and enjoyed the ride. A tuneless humming from the front seat came to him on the headphones. He smiled. Jock Urquhart, his pilot, was again pretending nonchalance. Ferris had yet to meet a pilot who was totally at ease with the system.

He marveled at his own equanimity. It had not always been so. A Flight Lieutenant in the Royal Australian Air Force, he had been seconded to the

RAF, and had found himself posted to the training unit in Leicestershire, where Tornado ground attack crews received their initial schooling in flying the aircraft.

Climbing into the back seat of the Tornado to do the navigator's job had been a new experience for him, coming as he had from the right hand seat of the RAAF F-111C Aardvarks. He had been given the ride of his life on that first, familiarisation flight, but it had convinced him he would never learn to operate such an aircraft himself.

Slowly he had grown to like it and its systems; liked the way it handled itself, as if it knew exactly what it wanted. Twenty-three sorties, covering twenty-nine hours of intense flying training, had now turned him into a fully-fledged Tornado back-seater. The syllabus reeled off in his mind as the aircraft tilted itself over on a wing, and hurtled round a mountain. It then reversed the turn to pop over a ridge and into another valley.

Transition, navigation. The Tornado tilted again, wing seeming to brush a cliff face; an unnerving illusion. Formation flying, weapons aiming. Its systems had found another slope, steeper this time, and were lunging for it like a dog taking the scent. Auto terrain-following, night flying. The Tornado screamed up the slope and flung itself down the other side. Attack profiles.

He'd done it all.

The aircraft was changing course for the umpteenth time. A Red Spot fly-around. Red Spots were locations within the flight plan that had to be avoided: schools, population centers, hospitals, farms, wildlife sanctuaries, and many more . . . The entire UK was a mass of Red Spots. Measles, he called them; and it sometimes seemed there was more rash than healthy open country.

Ferris, eyes in and out of the cockpit in a continuing sweep, allowed part of his mind to dwell agreeably upon the news he had received just before suiting up for the flight. The Chief Instructor had told him of an impending posting to Scotland, at the end of the coming month. When told he'd been selected because of his outstanding skills, he'd grinned in some embarrassment; unusual for him. Ferris, a tall, well-muscled man, was no shrinking violet.

He grinned now, remembering. "Someone up there must like me."

"Did you say something, Bondi?" came Urquhart's voice as the Tornado banked to avoid a low hill.

"Go back to sleep, Jock," Ferris retorted. "The navigator's in control. I'll wake you when it's time for you to try and persuade me you know how to fly this plane."

"Hah!"

Bondi . . . Ferris shook his head slowly. At least, he'd been spared Bruce, Cobber, and Digger. Still, since coming to the old country, he'd found that most people had preconceived ideas about Australia: kangaroos, dingoes, aborigines and Bondi Beach prominent among them . . . with the odd lager-drinking crocodile in there somewhere.

Coming as he did from the best state in the nation as far as he was concerned, Western Australia, Ferris had never been anywhere near Bondi. What about the seclusion of Two People Bay, or the sight of ferocious breakers off Cape Leeuwin, or the petrified stillness of the Pinnacles at sunset? You could have Bondi and its bronzed beef-cake gods for free.

The Tornado had been on a straight course and a gentle climb for some minutes now. The ground had disappeared, and all about it was the dark rain cloud. It knew it was approaching home.

Ferris looked at the weather unenthusiastically. "Some spring," he said.

"You've been spoilt out there in the Antipodes," Urquhart said. "This is normal, as you should know by now. You've been here long enough. Can I now have my airplane back, please?"

"What's the matter? Withdrawal symptoms?"

"You navs will never understand."

"Sounds like a stick fetish to me. Penis envy."

"You're a vulgar Australian."

"Coming from a Scot who speaks like an Englishman, I take it as a compliment."

"Give me my plane and shut up."

They were good friends.

The Tornado came down out of the murk for a feather-light touchdown on the streaming runway.

Then a tyre burst. It swerved sharply to the left, heading for the turf at speed. Urquhart corrected swiftly with the rudder, coaxing it back to the center line. The nosewheel was still off the deck, so the thrust-reversers had not yet gone into their routine.

For what seemed an age, the nose held off while he kept the thumping machine as straight as possible on the wet runway. Then the nose was down and the buckets at the tail deployed as the thrust-reverse sequence came on, slowing the aircraft. The headlong rush was abruptly cut, but it still seemed to be moving fast. Urquhart was reluctant to use the toe brakes just yet, in case only one was working. That would cause the Tornado to swing violently, with all sorts of unpredictable consequences.

There was still plenty of runway left so he decided not to force it. At last, he felt speed had been sufficiently reduced to enable him to try the brakes. He canceled the buckets, and eased the toe brakes. Braking was even. The aircraft came safely to a halt in the pouring rain. He taxied off the runway and came to a halt for the second time. Through the canopy, they could see fire engines and ancillary vehicles hurrying towards them.

"Next time you feel like killing us," Ferris said, "give me some warning, will you?"

"I'll try."

A silence fell between them. Then Ferris said: "That was a bloody good landing, mate."

"If I say so myself, it wasn't bad. Not bad at all."

The vehicles had arrived.

"Let's shut down and get out of this thing," Ferris said.

"We'll get wet."

Ferris and Urquhart laughed, a little hysterically perhaps, in their relief.

Wing Commander Christopher Jason stood at the Grampian end of the wide main runway and felt pleased. A camouflage-pattern anorak over his RAF No. 2A dress, he looked along the newness of its surface, towards the Moray Firth.

He could not see the Firth from his position, for the runway appeared to dip slightly, so that its still unfinished end was out of sight. A light breeze was coming off the water, bringing with it the mechanical sounds of the continuing work. The reconstruction was being carried out seven days a week and this Saturday was thus no exception. Despite the time of year, this part of the Scottish coast sometimes had unusually mild weather while the rest of the country froze; and despite the known ferocity of its winter gales, he felt the site was well chosen for their bold experiment.

Jason had good reason to feel pleased with himself. Thirty-six years old, there were many who considered him a fast rising star, and the rejuvenation of the old wartime airfield was seen as ample proof of it. He looked about him, appraising the new hardened aircraft shelters, the tall traffic control tower bristling with up to the minute electronic aids, the radar towers and beacons, the comprehensive landing system, the new personnel accommodation, the large hangars, and the ten-foot-high electronically-alarmed perimeter fence. Distantly construction vehicles churned the ground with their fat wheels and tracks, and the whole area was loud with the activity that went into the building of an operational flying station.

It was the culmination of nearly four years of hard work, and it seemed, furthermore, that the project would be completed on time. The genesis of the idea had come to Jason years before, during his time as an operational evaluation pilot on the first of the Tornado air defense variants, the F.2. He had immediately felt that more power was needed, and when, with the F.3, a new version of the engines gave 10 percent extra power, he still had not been satisfied. Admittedly, fully automatic sweep of the wings with manual over-ride would make the pilot's life less hectic in combat, but Jason still wanted more.

In his reports and evaluations he gave his idea full rein, asking for 30 percent more power, even on the F.3, added aerodynamic surfaces for better agility, and strategically substituted composite materials to reduce weight and improve thrust-to-weight ratio. He also requested a more powerful main computer, even more advanced avionics with an integral

helmet sighting system that could work autono-
mously, as well as with the radar and infrared scanning and tracking sensors, through the fire control
computer. As if that had not been sufficient, he had
come up with the broader notion of a new fully-
integrated operational force, made up of crews from
the NATO Alliance which would be autonomous,
and the leading edge of the organization's conventional defences. It would be the first into battle, buy-
ing time during a sudden emergency for the member
countries to sort out their priorities regarding the
commitment of their national forces.

Jason personally felt that one of NATO's
chronic weaknesses had always been an apparent
lack of any concerted response to a possible threat.
His proposed NATO force would be the shield behind
which the Alliance nations would have breathing
space in which to co-ordinate their actions. He envis-
aged at least ten such squadrons made up of eighteen
aircraft each, as a nucleus that would be stationed
strategically throughout Europe. He saw a requirement for more to follow, and believed that other alli-
ances, such as SEATO, would benefit from the
system. But that was for the future. His prime concern for the moment was Europe.

Such aircraft, he had proposed, would need
funding from all the Alliance states, and would be
manufactured concurrently with other versions of
Tornado. He put the idea to his superiors, expecting
them to wince. They did, but they listened too, and

spent months deliberating. Then he was asked to submit his plans in detail. More months passed and he despaired. Then, slowly, he began to receive support; but even with support, the fight was a long and bruising one. He never weakened and in the end, after much hesitation and protestations on the grounds of cost, it was grudgingly decided to go ahead with the project. It helped that a spirit of closer unity in Europe was showing the beginnings of a tidal flow. But he was not complacent. Support was not universal. The merest whisper of change in the political climate, and that which had been given could very easily be taken away. And the really testing times were still to come.

Jason, the holder of the Air Force Cross and a Master's Degree in the Arts, squared his shoulders and lifted his head to sniff the springlike air. Then he turned towards an approaching sound. A staff car was coming towards him. As it drew nearer, he saw the two-star vehicle plate and pennant of an Air Vice-Marshal. He drew himself to attention.

The car stopped and a tall slim man, with the single broad and single thin ring of rank on his greatcoat shoulders, climbed out. Air Vice-Marshal Robert Thurson.

Jason saluted.

Thurson smiled and returned the salute. "Walk with me, Chris," he said.

They went a short distance from the staff car before Thurson continued: "Master of all you survey? You must be feeling quite pleased with yourself." He shook his head slowly. "I still can't believe you actually managed it."

"With plenty of help from you, sir."

"Oh, I know a good idea when I hear one. That was all yours. Getting it implemented was quite another matter, especially when one had to deal with national vested interests. Your refusal to back down shook many people, especially when you offered to resign." Thurson smiled again. "Shook me too. Did you really mean it?"

"Absolutely."

Thurson paused to look at his younger companion. "Yes. I believe you." They continued walking. "You'll be pleased to know the first batch of aircraft will be arriving at the end of the month and your first crews in the latter half of May. You could, of course, accept command of the Station. It's yours, should you want it. All of this is, after all, your personal trophy."

Jason shook his head. "Thank you, sir, but I would prefer to fly with the squadrons and be involved with the work-up. There'll be three here eventually, plus the Operational Conversion Unit, and the Evaluation Unit. I'd like to keep close to it."

"I suspected as much, so you'll be happy to know who'll be coming in to take command as Group Captain; someone who'll back you to the hilt. Jacko Inglis." Thurson waited for the reaction.

Jason beamed. "Could not be better. We were at the F.2 OEU together."

"I thought it might please you," Thurson said drily.

"Thank you, sir."

"Our necks are on the block, Christopher. We both know it wouldn't take much. Try not to lose any men, or any aircraft."

"I'll do my best, sir."

"Let's hope for all our sakes that that will be sufficient."

They walked in thoughtful silence for some moments, then Jason said: "May I speak informally, sir . . . and frankly?"

"Please do, and I shall brace myself." Thurson smiled thinly. "I know by now just how frank you're capable of being."

Their leisurely steps continued as Jason went on: "You know what I think of politics and politicians."

The Air Vice-Marshal made no comment.

Jason glanced at him, and continued: "The recent military jet crashes have brought all kinds of Luddites out of the closet. Ban this, ban that, stop low flying . . . It's a bloody funny thing, you know—airliner fall out of the sky, smash into each other on taxiways, plow into mountains, or burn themselves out on runways taking scores, sometimes hundreds of people with them, yet nobody calls for an end to civilian flying. Trains run off the rails, disasters occur with ferries, and tubes catch fire underground . . . yet nobody, *nobody* tries to ban train services, or ferries. Nobody says close down the underground system.

"We fly at the edge, where we must if we are to do our job properly. If these people would stop long enough to *think,* and to compare our casualty rate with those of the organizations responsible for civilian transport, they would soon see sense. Any crash, civilian or military, is a tragedy. People die, families suffer. But if we are not allowed to carry out our training without hindrance, then they may as well disband the air force . . . because no commanding officer will be responsible for sending untrained crews into battle should that occasion ever arise. The entire expensive air fleet that everyone's so exercised about would be wiped out within the first half-hour of combat—together, of course, with their expensive crews.

"I do wish that just for once these people would think of the national interest, rather than of how good their bleatings will look to their constituents, or whatever special interest group they're pandering to at any given moment. More than anything else, sir, we need continuity. To build a successful team here, we've got to be able to believe in tomorrow, next week, next month. Even the month after that. All I ask is that somehow, sir, you keep these people off our backs. Then I can teach the crews who come here to *think* their aircraft into combat, the way someone once taught me."

"That was quite a speech." Thurson stopped, turned to look back at his staff car. Its distance made it look strangely small. He raised an arm and signaled. The car began to move. "Give you a lift?" The snow still had not made up its mind about falling.

"No, thank you, sir. I want to walk a little longer."

"Very well, Christopher. I'll do what I can for you." He removed his cap and carefully brushed his sleeve across its top, removing dark drops of moisture. "But do remember, our necks are still very much on the block."

"Are those the words of the former QFI who taught me how to think my aircraft into combat? Or are they of the Air Vice-Marshal who has to mind his p's and q's?"

The car had glided to a stop and its driver, a smart young woman in civilian clothes, got out and opened one of the rear doors.

"Both," the Air Vice-Marshal said. Turning quickly as Jason saluted, he entered the car. His warning had been delivered. Further questions or answers would be pointless.

Chapter

The British Embassy, Washington, an evening in early May.

"I may have a defector for you." The words, in impeccable English, were softly spoken, yet Buntline clearly heard them above the general chatter.

The party was being hosted by a junior Western diplomat and Charles Buntline had a glazed look that those who didn't know him would mistake for the onset of drunkenness. Those who did, would recognize the signs. Buntline wanted to leave. Of this, the speaker was well aware. He had known Buntline for some time.

Buntline turned, the glazed look fading. "Surely not, Sergei," he said with mild skepticism. "What with *glasnost, perestroika,* and even elections? I'd have thought the defection business was going out of fashion. Nobody's wanting to leave anymore. Why should they? Sad thing is, it'll put people like you and me out of business, old son."

Sergei Grigorevich Stolybin, KGB Lieutenant-Colonel ostensibly a journalist on Moscow's leading monthly, laughed softly. "If I believed that, I'd give up malt whiskey. *Glasnost* is ripping us apart. The old guard are not pleased and everyone's waiting for the counterattack."

They were standing next to a buffet table. Buntline stared at its gaudy delicacies unenthusiastically. "There's nothing there that I'd like to eat." He glanced about him. "God. I hate these occasions. I don't know why we bother to come. Attachés of every hue pretending to be enjoying themselves, but really just desperate for something less than totally boring to fall their way."

"Such as the kind of information I've just given you . . ."

"Which I'm expected to believe."

"Why don't we move a little further from the common herd? Enough to be out of immediate earshot, but still within sight . . . so that no one gets the wrong idea. Especially not my sour-faced but ambitious young KGB major over there who's trying to make it with that young American lady while keeping an eye on me."

As they moved from the table Buntline staggered slightly, giving the impression of having reached his limit.

"I do hope this is not one of your misinformation games, Sergei. Are you working for us on this? Or for your people?"

"Questions, Charles. Which do you want answered?"

"The one that really matters. Is it true?"

"Very true. Not an ordinary defection, either."

They had secured a quiet corner in the vast apartment. They smiled insincerely, as they talked in keeping with the people around them. Buntline was supposed to be an export-import businessman.

Stolybin looked at him speculatively. "You don't believe me."

"Should I?"

"You don't have a choice."

"That's original."

Stolybin hesitated for a split second, then made up his mind. "A pilot is going to bring out an operational prototype of a single-seat, single-engined fighter. The West suspects that it exists, but knows absolutely nothing about it. Like the MiG-29, early variants have been in squadron service for years. It took you long enough to find out about the 29. You're getting a chance to find out early on this one. It's an F-16C beater. At least, that's the thinking behind the design and it will complete the triad with the Su-27, and the MiG-29."

"What's this wonder machine called?"

Stolybin said drily: "You don't sound convinced. Stories have been floating around in the West about it . . ."

"Not one of your special brand of leaks, I suppose? Rumors about something that isn't really there?"

"You mean the way the American Stealth fighter hasn't really been 'there,' Pentagon leaks notwithstanding. Until, of course, persistent rumors forced *them* to publish a single, crudely-doctored photograph which is causing even more confusion. No, Charles, what I'm offering you is the chance to get your hands on something tangible. Quite a coup for you, Charles."

"You still haven't told me what this technological marvel is called."

"You in the West, tend to go in for educated guesswork. I've seen it referred to in some quarters as the MiG-35. We have not yet given it a name."

Buntline still looked skeptical. "It must have a Design Bureau Identification number."

Stolybin appeared to dodge that. "It does have a nickname . . . a little joke by the pilots. They call it *Krivak . . .*"

"Krivak? But that's a naval ship . . . a class of destroyer."

"As I said, a pilot's joke. They think their new aircraft is so good, it will destroy all before it."

"They can live in hope, I suppose."

"Don't dismiss them, Charles. I believe it to be an excellent airplane. The MiG-29 took you all by surprise and even now, you've still not had the chance to assess the Su-27 properly despite the Paris air show. I'm offering you something quite special."

"Do the Americans know one of your pilots is planning to deliver this precious toy to the West?"

"Of course not. This is for you as I've said, Charles, and I want it kept strictly in-house. This is not another Belenko."

Here Stolybin was referring to the MiG-25 pilot who had taken his aircraft in a blaze of publicity to Hokkaido in Japan, in September 1976, supposedly under inducement from the West. The Krivak pilot was apparently defecting unasked.

"Just supposing I do believe this wild story, what do you want of me?"

Stolybin's eyes were very still. *"Supposing . . . I understand your skepticism, Charles, but you already know you have no real choice. If I'm lying, you'll get nothing. But what if I'm not . . . ?"* He deliberately left his words hanging. "What I want from you is an escort of your fighters waiting for him, and a tanker to give him fuel for the remainder of the flight. For obvious reasons, he cannot leave with long-range tanks. He's a test pilot and his program requires him to test the aircraft within rigidly-controlled fuel parameters. Most times he flies on half fuel only. But on occasion, he must go with full tanks, and on one of these he will make the flight West."

"Why the escort?"

"To stop your side shooting him down." Stolybin gave a wide, suddenly genuine grin. "Or ours, of course."

Buntline said nothing for some moments as he digested what he'd been told. He glanced with apparent uninterest about the room. The KGB major was clearly still trying to impress the young American woman with his suave Russian wit, but every now and then his eyes would stray towards Buntline and his companion.

Buntline cleared his throat. "When is all this to take place?"

"I'll be in touch. Soon, I think. The pilot has been planning it for years—now it's simply a question of his test program. . . . By the way, I must insist you bring as few people into this as possible. An absolute maximum of three, in fact. I must insist."

"Three . . . ?"

"That is so. Any more, and the whole operation may be compromised. You know the terrible reputation your people have. Soviet bugs in every room. Israeli spies camping in the chandeliers. . . ." His eyes hardened. "I won't risk the pilot's neck, and I won't risk mine either. You understand that, Charles? I protect myself. At any cost, I protect myself."

Buntline nodded. Stolybin first, the pilot very much second. "Who is this pilot?"

"I know him personally."

"Good." So the man's name was being kept for later. "Do you also know why he intends to do this?"

"Revenge."

*   *   *

"Revenge, Mr. Buntline?"

"That's what he said, Minister."

"Do you believe him?"

"Not revenge against Mother Russia, sir. Not even against the Soviet system. It's the hard-liners in the military he can't forgive—they gave his father a rough time, I gather—and it's them he'll be able to hurt if he comes over. First-hand information about how perestroika is being betrayed by some of their own generals."

"Generals are like that, Buntline. It never does any harm to shake them up." The minister considered. "We'd have to give 'em their plane back, of course."

"Paperwork, Minister. Bound to take long enough for our technical people to . . . look it over."

"There is that."

"According to Stolybin the thing's pretty innovative."

"He'd have to say that."

It was a week later, and Charles Buntline was back in London. He had gone to the one man he felt he could trust, his former boss in the foreign service, who was now a cabinet minister.

"Sergei's been very clever. If we take him up on it and it's all a big con, we lose very little. But if it's genuine, and we turn him down, then—"

The minister nodded. "So the fact is, whether

we believe him or not, we might as well act as if we do."

"Exactly. If the Krivak is what he says it is, then it's the only fully operational aircraft in squadron service anywhere in the world with fly-by-light controls." Buntline noted the minister's incomprehension and elaborated. "They're a system of optical fibers that, unlike more conventional fly-by-wire systems, are immune to the effects of the sort of electromagnetic pulses that accompany a nuclear blast. Fly-by-wire systems are of course far more efficient than earlier, purely mechanical linkages, but they employ computer-interpreted electrical impulses to move the controls, which make them very vulnerable to local electromagnetic disturbances. . . ."

The minister glanced ostentatiously at his watch, but Buntline in full technical flow was unstoppable. "Many top combat aircraft of the West are now fly-by-wire, and for a long time we believed that the MiG-29 owed its astonishing agility to a fly-by-wire system. When we discovered that this is not so it was thought in some quarters to be due to a lack of technical ability. I happen to believe that the retention of manual controls was a deliberate policy. Like fly-by-light, they are of course EMP proof, and therefore able to operate in the vicinity of nuclear explosions. And now, possibly, the Soviets have made the jump directly to fly-by-light. We're working on FBL, but we're nowhere near operational status. If the Krivak has it, then they've made an astonishing breakthrough."

As Buntline stopped speaking the minister gathered his wandering attention. "Very well, Charles. What concrete measures do you have in mind?"

"That we should provide the escort, but not from aircraft from an RAF squadron. We should approach the special new NATO unit being created up in Scotland."

"Ah. The November Project."

"Exactly, sir."

"You do know, of course, that an awful lot of people would like to see that particular venture stillborn. An indulgence, they insist . . . waste of taxpayers' money, so forth. Do you think we should attach ourselves to it? Would that be wise?"

Buntline looked sly. "If they make a mess of it, they will have blotted their copybook, perhaps terminally. If on the other hand they perform well, the credit will be yours. You will have pulled off quite a coup." He thought of what Stolybin had said to him in Washington. "And so will I."

The minister looked thoughtful, but in fact he had already come to a decision. "We need a liaison man. Someone who can handle that firebrand who's responsible for the November Project. What's his name?"

"Jason. Wing Commander Jason."

"Ah yes. Jason. He's giving a lot of people sleepless nights; and I'm not talking about the local crofters. He's a spender, and he doesn't take no for an answer. Personally I wouldn't trust him an inch. I expect you've got someone in mind for the job?"

"I'm thinking of someone who would be perfect." Buntline was looking pleased with himself. "Air Vice-Marshal Robert Thurson. He'll be able to crack the whip when necessary."

"Thurson. Yes, of course. Jason's a sort of protegé of his. Good choice, Charles. I like the idea of Thurson."

"Thank you, Minister. Does that mean we go for it?"

The minister nodded slowly, eyes fixed upon Buntline. "It does indeed. Are you quite sure you can trust Stolybin?"

"One can never be sure of anything in a case like this. That could have fatal consequences. But I've worked him for some time now. He's given us some good info. . . ."

"When it pleased him."

"He could be telling the truth on this one. If, as he claims, he does know the pilot, his reasons could be quite personal. This glasnost thing has got everyone on the hop over there. Normal analysis no longer applies."

"Got us on the hop too. As long as we don't let our guard down."

"Which is exactly how Jason thinks," Buntline

said. "So you see, Minister, his November unit is just right for the job."

The minister's eyes were speculative. "It would be a damned spectacular prize. A secret combat aircraft from the other side, dropped into our laps. Yes, Charles. Go for it."

Whitehall, London, that same week.

Air Vice-Marshal Thurson was ushered into the large, richly-furnished office by a middle-aged woman in a severe suit. She closed the door quietly behind him.

"Glad you could make it, Air Vice-Marshal," the minister said, rising to his feet and coming round his polished desk to show Thurson to a deep leather armchair. He took a seat opposite. On a small table between them, tea for two was laid out. "Will you join me in a spot of tea?"

There was another man in the room, in a dark city suit. He was not introduced. Thurson was himself in civilian clothes. The city suit was Buntline.

"Yes, thank you, Minister," Thurson said as the minister began to pour.

"We have a proposition," the minister said. "Sugar?"

"No, thank you. I'll only have the milk."

"Very well." The minister handed the fine bone china cup over. "This gentleman will explain the proposition to you." He settled back as Buntline came over.

Buntline did not sit down. "At some time in the near future," he began, "a Soviet pilot will defect with a new, pre-production fighter aircraft which is far in advance of anything currently in service with their squadrons. The defection route, via the North Cape, is already set. We shall be needing a defensive escort for him. The aircraft is a single-seater, and is believed to have fly-by-light technology. We also believe, though this is not fully confirmed, that it possesses some Stealthy properties."

Buntline paused for effect. "The escort will not be made up of aircraft from a standard Royal Air Force squadron. It will be made up of aircraft and crews from the November unit that both you and Wing Commander Jason have fought so hard for."

The minister chose that moment to join in. "Good opportunity to test its feasibility, don't you think, Air Vice-Marshal?"

Thurson stared at each of them in turn. "With respect, Minister, I . . ."

"I do hope you're not going to turn me down," the minister interrupted. The veiled threat was laid neatly behind the words.

"I was about to say, Minister," Thurson began firmly, "that we're a long way from having crews capable of undertaking such a risky venture."

"Risk is part of a figher crew's life."

"Again, I must correct you, Minister. Wing Commander Jason does not train risk-taking crews.

That would make them far more dangerous to each other than to the enemy."

"If you keep to schedule," Buntline put in smoothly, "you should be fully operational by the time we're ready. We expect the best crews to be put forward for this mission. We cannot afford any mistakes. If things should go wrong, they must be able to take care of themselves. Naturally, we expect nothing to go wrong."

Thurson said: "You're telling me these crews may actually have to shoot their way out? I want to make quite certain that's what you're really saying."

"What's the value of a fighter crew that can't shoot?"

Thurson's eyes hardened as he looked at Buntline, then he turned to the minister. "I must consult with Wing Commander Jason, sir. He—"

"Have things changed so much within the RAF?" the minister wondered. "I was not aware that Wing Commanders could give orders to Air Vice-Marshals."

Buntline shot his cuffs. "Well, Air Vice-Marshal?"

Thurson could be seen controlling himself. He turned back to Buntline, but the minister stepped in quickly.

"Gentlemen, gentlemen," he said pacifyingly. "We are all on the same side. You are to say nothing to the Wing Commander," he went on to Thurson, "until you receive specific authority to do so. Let him continue as normal."

"In short, Minister, keep him in the dark as long as possible."

"I see you understand the situation perfectly."

"And the crews eventually selected for the mission? Are they to be kept in the dark too?"

"They'll already have quite enough to worry about. I'm told a modern fighter crew has an immense workload. Let's not burden them any more than we have to, shall we?" The minister smiled. "After all," he went on, "there is much in this for your Wing Commander. There are some very powerful forces ranged against him, who would like to see him fail, and the project halted. I would think he would grab this opportunity to show the merit of his plans. He would be proving a very valuable point.

"After all, I believe he is of the opinion that we should not succumb too readily to the current blandishments from the East. In some quarters, he is seen as a warmonger."

Thurson said stiffly: "Wing Commander Jason is no warmonger. That is a scurrilous . . ."

"I did not say it, Robert," the minister interrupted mildly, becoming unexpectedly informal. "I happen to agree with your man."

"He is still no warmonger," Thurson repeated.

"Precisely. I'm on his side." He clapped his hands together and rubbed them warmly. "I want the November Project to succeed."

*   *   *

Jason lifted the Super Tornado off the main runway within 300 meters of ground roll and at 130 knots, raising the gear as he did so. With the wheels nicely tucked in and afterburners roaring, he reefed the aircraft into a vertical climb. In the seat behind him his navigator, Squadron Leader Armiger, blew out his cheeks to clear his popping ears.

The Tornado hurled itself skywards, spread wings automatically moving to full sweep as the speed built. On the HUD, the digital airspeed display blurred in a swirl of numbers. At 30,000 feet, barely thirty seconds had passed. The numbers had begun to slow down as he eased the throttles back to full military power, canceling afterburners. Behind them the tiny fishing village a few miles down the road from the base was a thumbnail-sized blur of gray slate roofs. The Tornado still flung itself towards the roof of the sky, the thinner air allowing it to maintain its phenomenal rate of climb, even with the burners out.

At 60,000 feet, Jason eased out of the climb and brought the aircraft level. The wings began to spread. He throttled further back and speed decayed to 400 knots and at that velocity, the Super Tornado headed out towards the coast of Norway.

Behind Jason's aircraft, was another Tornado F.3S from November One, crewed by Flight Lieutenants Tingey and Morgan, pilot and navigator respectively, which was keeping station with him at ten miles separation and 5,000 feet below. Exactly one minute and thirty seconds had passed since take-off.

As he settled down and checked his systems within the remarkable quiet of the cockpit, Jason again felt the elation that had come to him the very first time he had flown the new aircraft. It had come to the airfield in late April, the first of the complement that would eventually make up the Operational Conversion Unit, and had exceeded all his hopes and expectations. Now in May, with test pilots Tingey and Morgan on temporary secondment, the aircraft for the first operational squadron were already arriving. So far, everything was working out as planned, and for the moment the Air Vice-Marshal appeared to be doing a good job keeping potential wreckers at bay.

The Operational Evaluation Unit was up to strength and the station that was itself November One had received nearly all its requirement of ground personnel. Jacko Inglis was already in place as Station Commander, or Base Commander, as he would be officially called, November One being in real terms a NATO base rather than a straight RAF station. This was a slight departure from normal practice where all stations, irrespective of the nationality of the forces housed within it, remained an RAF unit. However, the Base Commander would always be RAF. When other such bases became operational in Alliance countries, their commanders would be a national of that country.

Jason knew everything depended upon his being able to make the project viable, and quickly. So far, luck appeared to be remaining with him, and the vagaries of politics seemed to be leaving him to get on with it.

The day's mission called for a high and low-level intercept off the Norwegian coast. Playing the Aggressor role would be an unspecified number of USAF F-15 Eagles, and Norwegian air force F-16 Falcons. Their attack plan was unknown. It would be up to Jason and his wingman to detect and "destroy" the hostile aircraft without aid from a ground controller. It was to be an autonomous intercept.

From the cockpit, which seemed even roomier than the already roomy office of the standard Tornado, Jason looked out of his aircraft. Certain familiar aspects of the other Tornado variants had been altered. The main body was slightly longer and sleeker than the standard F.3, and where previously the engine intake lips could be seen slightly to the rear on either side of the cockpit, they were now hidden beneath leading edge root extensions. The LERXes reached forwards, curving gently and narrowing until they eventually diminished to nothing as they ended just behind the nose radome. The position of the LERXes served to clear the housing panel for the retractable fuelling probe on the left side of the cockpit.

The intakes, Jason knew, had been slightly redesigned to enhance the airflow into the powerful new engines, and to fit into position with the root extensions. The main computer, already increased in memory capacity from 64K to 128K for the standard F.3, was now a computer with 256K. Jason wanted 520K, but for the moment he was more than happy with the current power.

The cockpit also revealed many changes. Most of the analogue instruments had given way to three large, multi-function displays which could furnish him with a wealth of information, depending on what was called up by the selector buttons that surrounded them. For all that, he was pleased that some standard instrumentation had been retained, a sort of "get you home" kit if a systems malfunction or potential battle damage took out the displays. Like many pilots, he did not believe in 100 percent infallible systems.

In the back seat Miles Armiger, Squadron Leader and one of the navigation instructors at November One, was also pleased with his up-graded equipment. His radar, which could track and scan simultaneously, had a max range of 150 nautical miles. With the Super Tornado's advanced weaponry and dogfighting ability, all this added up to a uniquely lethal long-range and close-range killer. Furthermore, Armiger knew he was being flown by the best pilot he'd ever ridden with. He was ready for those F-15s, wherever they were.

Jason, head encased in an advanced helmet that could project the HUD display on its visor as well as possessing a point-lock-and-shoot capability, listened to his own breathing, keeping it slow and calm as his eyes searched the sky about him. His hands, on the throttles and stick, were ready to react instantly in response to whatever threat showed itself. Throughout the coming encounter, there would be no need for him to remove them: various switches and buttons on each control would enable him to conduct the fight while retaining full authority to maneuver the aircraft.

Jason continued his non-stop scanning: of the world outside, of his displays and instruments. At this height, visibility was limited only by the range of his vision. A good 30,000 feet below, wisps of cloud were made invisible by a thicker blanket several thousand feet beneath them.

The Eagles, Jason knew, would be coming up once the fight was on; but the F-16s would choose the medium and lower levels. The best course would be to take out the F-15s at long range, then deal with the F-16s. It all depended on how many Aggressors were playing today.

"Any trade for me?" he asked Armiger.

"Patience," came the reply, "is a virtue."

"Bloody navigators," Jason muttered.

Armiger gave a tight grin in his mask, and studied his display for signs of incoming targets. He knew Jason was tense. Jason wanted a complete kill. After all his struggles to bring November One into being, it was now up to him to prove the effort had been worthwhile. It was necessary to prove that the November One squadrons could do the job and take out potential adversaries as far away as the region of Norway's North Cape, over a thousand miles from base.

Though the aircraft of a fully operational November One squadron would carry a warload on combat air patrol, for this training mission Jason's Super Tornado and that of his wingman carried only inert missiles, a full complement of ten. Four were carried under-body, the high-speed advanced medium-range air-to-air missiles, a newer generation specially designed for fitment to the Super Tornado. Known as HAMRAAMs, they were named Skyray. The six short-range missiles carried beneath the slightly larger and longer wings were the HAS-RAMMs, and these were named Krait, after the deadly and venomous little snakes of the Indian subcontinent. Both missiles were lighter, smaller, and faster than their predecessors. The Skyray had a kill range of over 100 miles and while this was slightly less than the formidable American Phoenix carried by Tomcats, three Skyrays could be had for the purchase price of one Phoenix.

The Krait, replacing the AIM-9 Sidewinders normally carried by other Tornado variants, was for close-in missile engagements and could achieve a speed of Mach 3.5 in three seconds. Its range was up to twenty miles. For closer engagements still, the

Super Tornado had a six-barrel, variable-speed 20mm rotary cannon.

Both Skyray and Krait had nasty tricks up their sleeves. Their twin seekers allowed them to lock onto decoys while still being able to use the free seeker to continue target lock. They could also identify the intended target, predict its flight path, and even switch off and commit suicide if the target turned out not to have been hostile.

For the day's mission, all the missile and gun firings would be simulated by the computers and the kill tone would sound in the target pilot's helmet, should he allow himself to be caught out. Jason and his wingman would hear the same "death knell" should they be the ones who were caught.

"Still nothing?" he now asked of Armiger.

"What is it with you pilots?" Armiger countered. "I'm the one sitting back here, and I'll tell you when."

"Yes, boss," Jason said drily and continued to search the sky.

Sometime later, they made a rendezvous with a Victor air tanker for a top-up of fuel and then resumed patrol while the tanker headed back.

They had passed Iceland long since, and were approaching northern Norway when Jason began to feel itchy. The hostiles were out there.

It should be soon, he felt. It would not do if the "invading" force had somehow escaped detection.

The two Super Tornadoes, in their air-superiority grey colour scheme with the low-visibility NATO four-pointed star in its blue circle on their fins and forward fuselages, continued to hunt for their adversaries. Their call signs were Hunter Two-One and Hunter Two-Four respectively.

At November One, in the fighter control room, Flight Lieutenant Caroline Hamilton-Jones—recently arrived for secondment to the USAF at Brize Norton and still settling in at the November mess—stared at the huge wall screen that would map every stage of the coming battle. Computer-generated images of the pair of defending Super Tornadoes were on it. Plan or side view could be selected, and all information about the mission could be called up on various windows. As this was to be a fully autonomous flight, no instructions would come from control. Those in the room would simply watch and record.

The room was tense with expectation. Everyone's attention seemed glued to the vast screen, and in every heart was the wish that the boss, Wing Commander Jason, would succeed.

Suddenly a collective sigh filled the control room. Creeping in from the lower right of the screen were the first images of the Aggressor force.

Caroline watched them avidly, her mind flying out to where the Tornadoes patroled. She had a dream she told no one: she wanted to be a fighter pilot. Within the RAF, of course, there was little chance of that happening, so instead she selflessly devoted herself to the complex electronic world of the control room, and whenever possible imagined herself up there in one of the pilots' seats, planning how she would conduct herself in the coming fight. She was a romantic at heart, and flying was her first love.

"Well, well, well," Armiger murmured. "The boys have come out to play at last."

"What have we got?" Jason asked.

Armiger, who to minimise broadcast of their presence had been using the radar intermittently, had still managed to get his targets on screen. The radar, remembering, continued to show not only the target positions when last detected, but also their predicted positions according to the obtained track. It would update and modify this information at the next sweep.

"We've got six bogeys," Armiger replied. "Four F-16s. Two at 1000 feet, and two at 5000. Then we've got two F-15s at 15,000."

The radar had annotated the targets A to F, holding each in track. From its memory, it had compared radar signatures and had correctly identified the aircraft, a readout coming on-screen briefly for each designated letter. It had also decided that targets A and B, the two F-15s, were priority.

Armiger studied his screen. Top left corner was the super Tornado's speed of 475 knots. Top center

was the current heading at 045 degrees, and at top
right, was their current height at 55,000 feet. Beneath the heading was target A's bearing at 010 degrees which was constantly changing as track
information showed it was moving from left to right.

"There'll be more," Jason was saying, searching the sky above.

Armiger did not contradict. Instead, he
switched radar on for a quick upward sweep.

"Shit!" he said. "Two more bogeys. F-15s at
70,000. Bastards. That's sneaky. I'm altering priority." The two new targets, G and H, were earmarked
for early attention.

"I knew there'd be more," Jason said drily.
With eight targets to deal with, at four different altitudes, it was going to be a hot fight. Surprise would
improve the odds. "Let me have some of your picture
on the HUD and pass the situation to Hunter Two-
Four."

Flight Lieutenants Roger Tingey and Phil Morgan—pilot and navigator respectively—were in the
second ASV. Secure datalink communication between the aircraft ensured a swift transfer of information, free from eavesdropping. A burst of code,
and within seconds, one of the screens in the rear
cockpit of Hunter Two-Four displayed the same tactical situation as Armiger's.

On Jason's HUD, all the relevant details necessary for the intercept were now displayed.

"We'll take the high boys in each group," Jason added.

Armiger passed this on to Two-Four. No other instruction was necessary. Tingey would go after the medium-level Eagles, and the low-level Falcons.

As yet, there had been no warning tone in their helmets to indicate that the Eagles had scanned them.

In Fighter Control, Caroline Hamilton-Jones watched the encounter develop. The Tornado images, though clear on the huge screen, were not real-time replicants. Because of the use of composite materials in the ASV, its radar signature was substantially degraded. The computer had used a basic source to enhance the image, creating an accurate line drawing of the aircraft. Little trails came from each wingtip: a continuous one for the left tip, a dashed one for the right. As each aircraft manoeuvred, the trails would mark its passage, sometimes crossing as it rolled. It was a graphic display of how each pilot used his mount.

She heard a sudden flurry of movement and looked up to a low balcony at the far end of the room. Someone had come in and was standing next to the senior controller. She recognised the Air Vice-Marshal, Thurson, in flying overalls.

The controller had clearly been caught on the hop. She was herself taken unawares. No one had warned of Thurson's impending visit.

After a brief chat with the controller, a Squadron Leader, Thurson made his way down from the balcony. She drew respectfully to attention as he approached.

He gestured quietly with one hand. "No need for that, Caroline." He studied the screen. "I hear November's up."

"Yes, sir."

"Think he'll make it?"

She looked at the screen, seeing Hunter Two-One, Jason's aircraft, do a ninety-degree turn and begin to climb.

"He's gone into a zero-Doppler turn to blind the F-15s," she said, "in case they're trying to light him with their radar. He'll make it."

"You're talking like a pilot," Thurson remarked, mildly amused.

"I'm around pilots all the time, sir," she said, with the ease of one who knew what she was talking about. "You pick things up."

Thurson stared at the screen. "It's an interesting move. Let's see how it develops."

Armiger said: "They're still together. They can't have scanned us."

"So much the better," Jason said. "Let's wake them up." Then moments later: "I have a Skyray lock on target."

"Skyray lock on target G," Armiger confirmed. "Better let him have it, then take H out. We've got

4.3 minutes to visual range and counting. If we let them get to visual, we've blown it."

Jason squeezed the missile release. "Skyray launched. I have lock on the second target."

"Target H locked," Armiger confirmed again.

"Launching. Launched. Are we recording?"

"Every breath. No one's going to be able to deny they've been taken."

"He's launched at them!" In the control room, Caroline Hamilton-Jones was tense with suppressed excitement. She watched avidly as the computer, having checked that the launch parameters had been achieved, sent electronic pulses racing towards the F-15 images.

Their pilots had evidently received the threat tones in their helmets, for they immediately went into a tight, turning break, hoping to ruin the shot. But they had left it too late. The pulses continued their inexorable journey, following the twisting images until each merged with its selected target. The F-15 images turned into glowing coffins.

Someone had selected the Eagles' comm. channel and put it on the speakers.

"Goddammit!" came an irate voice. "I've been nailed."

"And me, brother," came the other. "We're out of the fight. Let's go home."

"Goddammit!" came the first voice, sounding

furious. "Goddammit!" he added a third time for good measure.

Caroline turned to look at the Air Vice-Marshal.

Thurson had a satisfied smile upon his face.

"Good shots," Armiger said. "Now for the F-16s."

"What's the news on Two-Four?" Jason took the ASV into a turning dive. The fight was far from over.

Armiger watched as one of the Eagle targets flared off the screen. "They've got one, but missed the second. Ah. Two-Four's got a third launch going." A pause. "Oh dear. Another miss."

"What the hell are they up to?" Jason demanded sharply. "They should get their fingers out!"

"That Eagle driver's a wily bird. He's moving about pretty niftily and jamming like mad."

The Eagle and the Tornado were performing their frantic skydance beyond visual range of each other, the battle being conducted on their radar screens. Having only one pair of eyes in his cockpit, the Eagle pilot was at a disadvantage; but he was using his formidable machine's capabilities to the full. Tingey, frustrated by his two misses, was keeping his distance.

Armiger said: "Two-Four's not letting him get close. But they'll have to end it soon—the F-16s are coming up to have a look. We're still out of their range, but they're well within ours. Do we help Two-Four first?"

"No. Let them sort their mess out. Good thing this is not a hot fight. Let's go after the 16s."

In Fighter Control, all eyes were glued to the screen, watching the epic battle between Two-Four and the lone, belligerent Eagle. The Eagle kept trying to get close, hoping to use its legendary turning capabilities with which to nail the Tornado. Tingey was using the Super Tornado's phenomenal acceleration to run out of the fight, giving himself room before turning back for a head-to-head, but the Eagle was having none of it.

Each time Tingey came hurtling back, the Eagle would go vertical, forcing Tingey to break or risk being pounced on from on high. While the watchers in Control were enthralled by the patterns being traced on the screen, they all knew this particular fight was taking too long. In a real fight, the outcome would have been decided long since. He who sees first should win. It was beginning to look as if a draw would be the official outcome.

Thurson was still standing next to Caroline.

"The Eagle will have to leave soon," he said quietly. "He must be close to bingo after all that hectic maneuvering."

"Bingo" was the very last moment when a pilot would have sufficient fuel for a safe return to whichever airfield he'd taken off from, with enough of a

margin for a further diversion should an emergency
arise. Staying in the fight beyond bingo was stretch-
ing the limits of the safety margin.

"November's going after the F-16s," she said.

"I have Skyray lock on target C," Jason said. They
were now down to 20,000 feet.

"Confirmed," came from the back seat.

"Launching." Jason squeezed the missile release. "Lock on D. Launching." He squeezed again.
"Two off the rails. Lock-on's good."

"He's taken two F-16s," Caroline reported excitedly.

Thurson said: "He's certainly proving his point.
The ASV's a winner." He looked at the portion of the
screen where the second Tornado and the Eagle were
still dancing round each other. "As for Two-Four, at
least the Eagle has not been able to get him so far.
If this were for real, the hostile aircraft would have
been tied up, wasting fuel, until its pilot would probably have to eject in the end. He certainly wouldn't
have been able to get back. Who are the crew?"

"Flight Lieutenants Tingey and Morgan, sir."

"Chris Jason shouldn't be too hard on them.
They got that Eagle's partner, and they've effectively neutralised him. Ah! The Eagle's leaving the
field of battle. I knew it—he's reached bingo. I'd call
that an honorable draw. That was good flying on
Tingey's part. Now let's see how he copes with the
F-16."

*　　*　　*

"Eagle's going home," Armiger said. "He's thirsty, I'll bet."

"Two-Four should have had him," Jason said.

"Oh, I don't know. They didn't do so badly. Brand-new aircraft they're not yet at ease with . . . first time against something like the Eagle . . . not to be sniffed at. They got one, and tied his buddy up in knots. In the real thing, they'd be coming back home."

Jason made a sound that could have been a grunt.

"Does that mean you agree?" Armiger queried.

"Don't push it."

Armiger grinned in his mask. "Just the two Falcons now, and it's home for us. How do you want to handle it?"

"A fast pass using the Krait, and the helmet."

"Target A's our meat. I'm giving B to Two-Four."

"They'd better get him."

"Go easy on them, Chris. They're a good crew."

"I know," Jason conceded.

He switched HUD symbology to the helmet, looking past it as he searched the sky about him. The Krait seekers had found nothing as yet to excite them. He rolled the Tornado onto its back and pulled the stick firmly towards him. The G readout whirled to 7. He made a straining noise to combat its onset as his G-suit squeezed at him, preventing the blood from draining to his feet. G pressure relaxed as the change of direction was completed.

The aircraft flung itself earthwards. Jason slammed the throttles against the stops. The afterburners came on instantly, twin tongues of pulsed flame searing out of the trail. Wings at full sweep now, the ASV was like an arrowhead, the power of its engines canceling out its own weight and making it seem to flash across the sky.

In Two-Four, Tingey and Morgan had performed an almost identical maneuver. Like twin gray sharks, the Tornadoes fell upon the unfortunate F-16s.

Jason was looking to ten o'clock when the designator arrow appeared on the helmet symbology, pointing to the right. He turned his head. The arrow shortened as his line of vision acquired the designator box.

"I've got him," he said.

They were still beyond kill range, but the Krait was making its weird modulated hissing sound, indicating that it knew the target was coming into range. The hisses pulsed ever more quickly, as if betraying eagerness for the kill.

In the back, Armiger had the outline of an F-16 on one of his screens. Superimposed upon it were temperature patterns, graded from violent red at the core of the engine, flaring out into orange to yellow to various levels of green and finally to blue around the "coolest" areas. The blue areas extended well beyond the target, showing that even its passage through the air generated sufficient infrared signatures for the Krait to lock-on to. He tuned the seeker so that blue areas would act like a beacon to target.

"I have lock-on," Jason said as the Krait's hiss changed to a continuous drone. "Launching. One off the rail."

Seconds later, the infrared image of the F-16 on Armiger's screen winked out.

"I don't think he knew what hit him," Armiger commented drily. "Home, James, and don't spare the horses. Ah! You'll be pleased to know that Two-Four's just scored."

"I should bloody well hope so too," Jason retorted.

In Fighter Control, Air Vice-Marshal Thurson gazed upon the computer-generated carnage with satisfaction.

If the squadron as a whole performed as well as this when they arrived, there'd be no problem with the minister's defector. Last news was, he'd had to delay his break. He was a test pilot, apparently, and modifications were setting back his program. "Seven kills, one draw, no hits taken, plenty of missiles still on the rails, and more than enough fuel with which to get home. And all this, out on the edges of the UKAIR region. I think we can indeed say Jason's made his point." Thurson turned delightedly to Caroline. "It would be a good idea, I believe, to invite a few doubting Thomases here to see the action for themselves one of these days. Is that a look of uncertainty I see, Flight Lieutenant Hamilton-Jones?"

"I was merely thinking, sir, that the Wing Commander might not . . ."

Thurson smiled at her. "I'm quite certain I shall be able to persuade him. Don't you?"

Despite the smile, Caroline knew the matter, when it arose, would not be open to discussion.

Wings swept, the Super Tornadoes came screaming low over the main runway to break hard, wings spreading as speed decayed. Each did a complete roll before setting up for the landing. They touched down in formation. It was a neat display.

Later, in one of the smaller debriefing rooms, the two crews watched the reply of the entire mission, on video. The Fighter Control's computer recording was included. Tingey's epic tussle with the F-15 was described in series on intricate trace patterns. Every turn, every run-out, every zoom and roll was there. Any part of the fight could be halted and studied, so that Tingey would see where he'd made mistakes.

At the end of the viewing session, Tingey said to Jason: "I'm really sorry about those two misses, boss."

"Not to worry, Roger. There's some good stuff in that recording. You were clearly dealing with a hot shot. You anticipated, he anticipated. You both knew what you were on about. Next time, you must simply out-think the bastards you meet." Jason gave a brief smile. "Who knows? I might not have taken him either."

Tingey's expression was one of relief. "Thanks, boss."

Jason went to his office to find Thurson waiting. They settled themselves on either side of his desk.

"Did you see it all, sir?"

"Yes," Thurson said. "I did. Good work. I know Tingey missed one, but I'd say he was lucky not to get tapped. That Eagle was ferocious. Tingey's no slouch."

"In a real fight, he might have been killed."

"I say he would have lived to fight another day."

Jason gave Thurson a sideways look. "Are you having an argument with me, sir?"

"No. But I have an idea."

Jason eyed his superior warily.

"You look as if you think I'm going to ask you for a loan," Thurson commented drily. "The fact is, I was impressed with what I saw today. I'm glad I decided to make this unannounced visit. It occurs to me that it would help our case, strengthen our arm quite considerably, if we could arrange a visit by some of our detractors."

Thurson paused to let his words sink in.

Jason was not fooled. *We* meant the AVM

would arrange the visit and Wing Commander would agree to it.

Jason said: "MPs and the like?"

Thurson nodded. "And the odd local councillor who may have received low-flying complaints."

"MPs . . ." Jason drummed his fingers on the desk. "It was an MP, a minister, who some time ago, mistakenly decreed that the advent of missiles made fighters obsolete. Decades later, we're still paying for that piece of brilliance. If his line of thinking still carried any weight, we would not have had Tornado at all, never mind those ASVs out there."

"Tornado nearly didn't make it," Thurson reminded him. "Don't forget that. And the 'anti'-lobby's still very active. I feel it would greatly help if we did invite a few up here."

"This is a sensitive unit, sir."

"It also belongs to the taxpayer. You can't keep him out, Christopher . . . at least, not out of everything. I think they should see the combat screen. The screen itself is no secret, only what makes it work."

Jason knew he had lost. His playing of the sensitivity card had been a last desperate try. It was simply that he knew from experience that the anti-lobby did not wish to be convinced—it would remain stubborn no matter how good his case, and he had no wish to waste his time trying to sweeten them. There were more important things to do.

"When would you like this visit, sir?"

"When would *you?*"

"Not before the first squadron's operational. Two months. At least."

Thurson nodded. "That's quite acceptable."

With this visit to hurry Jason along, he thought, they'd be well on schedule for the minister's little project.

Jason was in the control tower. At one end of the main runway, a standard Tornado F.3 had received clearance for take-off. Thurson was in the front cockpit.

No one, Jason thought, could accuse his old instructor of being a desk warrior.

The Tornado dipped its nose slightly as Thurson opened the throttles on the brakes. Then the brakes were released and the aircraft roared forward. Thurson hit the burners halfway through his ground roll. Soon, the sleek nose was coming up.

Thurson lifted it off the deck steeply, burners echoing to the Grampians, wheels tucking in. He continued the climb until the aircraft disappeared from view, its roar fading reluctantly until a relative silence fell upon the airfield.

"Showing us he can still do it," someone said.

Jason made no comment. He was thinking that perhaps Thurson would forget all about the proposed visit in time. But he knew it was a forlorn hope.

He looked down the main runway once more. Two of his Super Tornadoes had lined up on the threshold, waiting to fling themselves into the air.

The sight made him feel good.

Chapter

Pyotr Ivanovich Kukarev rolled the Krivak onto its back, gave the stick a little backward pressure and felt his G-suit squeeze at him as the aircraft pulled itself into a seemingly impossible, tight split-S. He had started the maneuver at 10,000 meters, but had reversed his direction with the loss of less height than he would have in the MiG-29. And all on full afterburner.

Once he was again in level flight, he canceled the burner. Fuel had to be saved. Despite having taken off with only half capacity, he would be expected to return with 25 percent of that in the tanks.

It was a beautiful aircraft. He had thought so the very first time he had climbed into its uncharacteristically roomy cockpit. Even the '29, though one of the top three frontline fighters, was still relatively cramped. Out-of-cockpit visibility of the Krivak was also superb, particularly to the rear . . . the vulnerable, all-important six o'clock position immediately astern.

Kukarev was a major at twenty-eight, of average height, a little stocky, with blond hair and a clean-shaven boyish face with dimples. The face was a good mask that was at once disarming and which hid his thoughts effectively. A veteran of Afghanistan, he had earned his spurs flying the ground attack Su-25 between the arid mountains. He had gained a reputation for being absolutely fearless and had somehow been less worried than most by the Mujahideen Stinger surface-to-air missiles. He always hit his targets with all his ordnance, wheeling back to rip at the same target with the 23mm six-barrelled rotary cannon. Somehow, he repeatedly managed to return unscathed. He always flew closer to the mountains than anyone else, tilting the aircraft onto a wing tip to get through the narrowest of passes. His flying skills had become legendary.

But it had all been part of a secret, wider design, conceived in bitterness years before.

Highly decorated, he had been posted home and selected for conversion to MiG-29s. Soon he was again coming to the notice of his superiors. A posting to one of the top-secret Krivak squadrons had followed. These earlier versions of the plane that he now flew had not in his opinion been more agile than the -29, but the model he was now testing far outstripped in every possible way the previous aircraft.

This, he thought, was a real combat ship for the next century, single-engined or not.

A transfer to operational test flying had followed his promotion to major. It was a prestigious posting and confirmed to him the success of his years of planning. He had deliberately thrown himself into the thick of the fighting in Afghanistan. If he had been shot down, then that would have been the end of it. But he had survived, and had emerged with his loyalty to the Motherland finally proved beyond all possible doubt. In spite of his father, no one could now question his own political soundness. He was a hero.

His father, fighting against the Germans, had once been a hero also. But his father had not remained a hero. The *Zampolits* had seen to that. Afraid of his influence towards detente in the post-Stalinist years, the hardliners had fabricated evidence of his political unreliability, and General Kukarev had ended his days in internal exile. All rank, privileges and property were unjustly stripped from him and he died, still young, a broken man, leaving his son a cadet with one over-riding obsession: to avenge a cruel wrong.

Kukarev pushed the bitter memories out of his mind and concentrated on his preparation for the landing. He roared low over the long runway, broke cleanly, bringing the wheels down even as he reversed the turn to position himself right over the threshold. The Krivak responded as a thoroughbred

should. This variant was one of only three operational prototypes, and it would not do for him to bend
it. Nevertheless, his approach had a dash and a flair
that none of the other pilots seemed capable of emu-
lating. He throttled back, brought the nose up.
Gently, the aircraft sank to the runway. Another
flight complete. Another stage in his plan.

That weekend, in England, Mark Selby drove to
Buckinghamshire. Kim had invited him to the family home and it was with some reluctance that he
had accepted. Her father was going to be there, and
he hoped Barham-Deane had not also been invited,
by Sir Julius himself.

A couple of miles before Marlow, he took a side
turning onto a B-class road, as she had instructed.
It was a glorious spring day, and the countryside
looked quite beautiful. He felt his spirits lifting.

Presently, he turned off the road and onto a
long meandering drive that traversed open country
and went up a gentle slope into well-kept woods. On
two of the bends, a fast-flowing stream bordered it.
The drive finally straightened as it left the woods,
and it was only then that Selby saw the house.

The drive speared its way through a vast land-
scaped garden to end in a large parking area before
an immaculate Queen Anne mansion. Kim's white
Mercedes was already there. Another white car, a
Rolls-Royce Corniche, was parked next to it.

Selby parked on the other side of the Mercedes,

and climbed out. No one seemed to be about. He looked about him, his gaze caught by a stunning, uninterrupted view of the Buckinghamshire countryside. The sound of a horse's hooves made him turn. Kim Mannon on a magnificent gray.

She brought the animal to a halt close to him, and studied him from her perch, a smile playing about her lips.

"So you made it. I was afraid the thought of Daddy might have scared you off."

"I almost had second thoughts," he admitted.

"What made up your mind?"

"You."

Her smile widened. "Mmmm."

The horse moved forward. Unused to horses, Selby took a cautionary step backwards.

"Don't be afraid," she said, voice hinting at laughter. "Nero won't bite. He's just making friends. He knows you're OK."

"I'm glad he does. Nero. I might have known." Selby looked at the house. "Nice hut." And at the countryside. "Nice view."

"It will do. Welcome, sir, to Grantly Hall, home of the Mannons of Bucks." She grinned down at him. "The daughter of the house is graced with untold charms and has a great desire to go to bed with you at this very moment."

"What of the master?"

"Probably watching us from his study, so it will have to wait."

The horse moved its hooves with leisurely patience, stretched its neck to nuzzle at Selby.

"See?" she said. "He likes you. Didn't I say he would? He's never like that with Reggie. He even bit him, once."

Selby took another step backwards. "I thought you said he didn't bite."

"Only people he doesn't like. Don't be a baby. I thought all fighter pilots were brave."

"We are. We are. It's just that horses with bone-crusher jaws are scarce up there, especially ones called Nero."

The horse pricked up its ears and came closer. Selby stood his ground, but watched the animal warily.

"Speaking of Reggie," he went on, "will there be another guest this weekend?"

"There'll be other guests . . . none of whom will be Reggie. That's what you wanted to hear?"

He smiled up at her. "I feel better already."

"Good. Jarvis will show you to your room while I put Nero away. I'll give you a proper welcome later." Her eyes promised all. "By the way, do you ride?"

"Not really."

"Never mind. I'll give you a lesson. Once we get away from here who knows what we might get up to?"

"Who indeed."

"Now I suppose you'd better go and meet

Daddy. And not before time—you've been avoiding him for months."

"I haven't been avoiding him."

"I suppose I've been keeping you away from him," she amended.

"That's more like it. But I don't expect he'll be all that pleased to see me. I *am* messing up his plans for you."

A flash of hardness danced briefly in her eyes. "I make my own plans for myself." She wheeled the horse abruptly and set off at a trot.

Selby watched her disappear behind a wing of the building. Footsteps made him turn again towards the house. A man in butler's uniform was approaching. Clearly Jarvis.

Jarvis was a new breed of butler, young and fit, not at all the conventional image of a family retainer.

"Good morning, sir. If you'll let me have your luggage, I'll show you to your room. Miss Mannon instructed that you should be given the Blue Room. You'll like it, sir. Splendid view of the county."

Selby opened the 4x4's hatch and took out his gear. He shut the car as Jarvis picked up his things.

"Here. Let me take this . . ."

"No need, sir," Jarvis said firmly. "I can manage."

I'm sure you can, Selby thought, and followed Jarvis inside.

The Blue Room, furnished in Regency style,

was as splendid as the promised view. After he had been installed for a few minutes, Selby heard a knock on the door.

"Come in."

The door opened, and Kim Mannon, still in her riding gear, entered, shut the door and launched herself at him. The huge four-poster bed was close enough for them to fall onto, instead of the floor where the force of her lunge would otherwise have landed them.

After a while, she paused for breath.

"Don't you think," he put in quickly, "that I ought to at least meet your father, before you ravish me in his house?"

She was lying on her back now, arms and legs spread, breasts heaving. He leaned over to kiss her. Immediately, her arms entwined themselves about him and she manoeuvred her body beneath his, legs clasping at him. The heat of her thighs seemed to burn through his clothes and, despite himself, he felt desire growing.

Abruptly, she released him. "Oh shit!" she said in exasperation. "But I suppose you're right. Let's make ourselves presentable." She inspected herself in a mirror. "I'm coming in here tonight," she promised, "when everyone's asleep."

Sir Julius Mannon was younger-looking than Selby had expected. He was, given his strong-minded daughter's height, also taller than expected. A full head of silver hair was neatly trimmed, with tiny wings curling above and behind his ears. Dressed in the tweedy hounds-tooth of a country gentleman, he had received Selby in his study where, Selby noted, an unrestricted view of the drive could indeed be had.

Kim had brought him in, and then had left the two men to it.

Mannon had his daughter's dark eyes and they now studied Selby keenly.

"So you're the young warrior Kim's been keeping from me."

"Hardly, Sir Julius . . ."

"Bullshit," Mannon interrupted bluntly. "She's been biding her time. And for good reason." He laughed unjovially. "Drink?"

"Er . . . no. It's a bit early for me."

"I shall have one. Keep a stock in here. Not flying within the next seventy-two hours, are you?"

"No, sir."

"Oh well. Suit yourself." Mannon poured himself a generous scotch. He showed Selby to a deep leather armchair. "Take a seat." And when he had also sat down, continued: "You're quite different from the usual butterflies my daughter invites from time to time. Frankly Selby, that is a cause for worry."

"I fail to understand, Sir Julius."

"Call me Julius. Leave the 'Sir' to the toadies. You don't look like a toady to me."

Selby shifted uncomfortably on the polished leather.

"Usually, when Kim invites young men she has met," Mannon went on, "she introduces them within a day or two, dragging them up here like puppy dogs for my inspection. It's her way of letting me know she cares so little about them that if I disapprove, out they go.

"You, however, are very, very different. You are the first one she's kept from me. That tells me my disapproval in this case will count for little. She has also given you the Blue Room. If I had any doubts before about how serious she was, this has wiped them away. It was my son's room." Mannon paused, as if in remembrance. "She idolised him," he continued briskly, "and putting you in there speaks more loudly than she could have done herself. She is sending me a message that is both a confirmation of her intent, and a warning to me not to interfere."

Mannon paused, swirling his scotch round the glass.

"What happened to your son?" Selby asked.

"Died with his mother in a helicopter crash in Portugal. We had a villa there, in one of its most beautiful provinces, the Beira-Alta. The villa was close to the Sierra Estrella. The helicopter pilot had not been one of our regular people. He died too, of course. Went into the mountains. I sold the place soon after."

"I'm sorry. I can understand your feelings. I lost a very good friend not so long ago."

The dark eyes studied Selby. "One of your colleagues?"

Selby nodded. "His aircraft burned on impact. He never got out."

"Then we both know what it's like," Mannon said after a long silence. "That is why I hope you will appreciate what I am about to say. People like you are a special breed of young men. You have high intelligence, and exceptional skills. You perform a duty that few of us ordinary mortals are capable of and when the Reggie Barham-Deanes of this world are placed next to you they come in a very poor second.

"However, even the Barham-Deanes have their place in the scheme of things. Reggie is a prize shit . . . oh don't look surprised to hear me say it . . . I am well aware of what he is. And Reggie is also the most efficient financial barracuda of his generation that I've come across. He's on my team, and I've watched him put together a multi-million pound deal in one week, while our competitors had been struggling over it for months. They simply hadn't done their homework. Reggie did his and pounced while they were still arguing among themselves.

"I was about to say he has the same hunting instinct that you fighter boys employ so well in the air, but I can see that would scandalise you. I'll put it another way. People like Reggie make the money that pays for your wonderful high-tech machines. Basically they make the money that buys your aircraft, so that you can keep the skies free of intruders, so they continue making the money to buy the aircraft to enable you . . . and so on. It's the way of the world. Clearly, to judge by your expression, you don't agree."

"I'd like to think my friend died for rather more than that."

Mannon looked at Selby with the barest hint of pity. "I have no doubt my daughter believes she is in love with you. I shall not interfere in her relationship with you, any more than I interfere in her anti-nuclear work. I allow her that, because to actively oppose her would only increase her stubbornness. But I ask you to consider this. You have yourself just indicated what a high-risk profession you follow. If you marry she will always be wondering when she may become a widow. Barham-Deane, on the other hand, will always be there. He'll be good for her, and good for the company."

"With respect, sir, we have not spoken of marriage. I happen to agree with you about the risks involved in my work. I am personally of the opinion that fast jet pilots should not marry. I don't say it's the right opinion . . . but I was the first to see Sammy's wife after it happened. I'll never forget the look on her face. Others think I'm wrong. Many commands, as a matter of fact, prefer married men.

More stable, less prone to taking chances, so the thinking goes."

Mannon said: "I'd have thought that by now you'd know that when Kim puts her mind to it, she gets what she wants. Your views on pilots marrying won't stand a chance once she's made up her mind."

"Are you asking me to discourage her, so that Barham-Deane can fulfil your game plan?"

"Oh no. If you behaved out of character, she'd smell a rat in an instant. She's my daughter and she's inherited certain attributes that I recognise only too well. I'll handle Reggie. He'll have to be patient, just as I'm going to be."

"You would marry your own daughter to a man you yourself have called a shit?" Selby was appalled.

"In terms of humanity, he *is* a shit. In terms of marriage, however, he will be biddable. And in business terms, he is the brightest star on my horizon." Mannon waved a hand. "Take a look at all this. It has produced the young woman who now enthralls you. She is a product of her environment."

"And you would waste her . . ."

"Not waste, young man. Not waste. I'm proud of her, despite her apparent eccentricities. She's tough, and quite clever. She'd be more than a match for Barham-Deane, within a marriage. This house, and those like it, were built by the Barham-Deanes of this world, but held together by women like my daughter. It's an unfair equation, but true. A harsh reality."

Selby took his time before speaking. "She won't let you, you know. I may not be the one she eventually marries . . . but it won't be Barham-Deane. She's like you. She won't back down."

Mannon was quite unperturbed. "We shall see. You know, it's a pity. You're right. She is like me, and she knows how to choose. You've got spine. None of the gadflies she's tagged to herself from time to time would have stood toe to toe with me. Even Reggie watches his step. But you . . ."

"Your money may buy the aircraft. It does not buy me."

"Doesn't it? Who pays your salary if not we, the taxpayers and moneymakers?"

Before Selby could reply that to receive a salary was not the same as being bought, Kim entered. "You two have had enough time to get acquainted," she said cheerfully. "Mark, I've saddled a horse for you, and there's some riding gear that I'm sure will fit; so if you're up to it, a quick gallop's in order."

"I'm not so sure about a gallop. A leisurely walk will do."

"Baby," she accused, then went up to her father to kiss him on the cheek. "Well? What do you think?"

Both men had stood up and now Mannon's eyes held Selby's briefly before he turned to smile at his daughter. "A man not easily frightened."

"Mm hm." She turned to Selby. "In case you're

wondering, that's a major compliment. Right. Come on. Let's get you on that horse."

The two men's eyes met for another brief lock, before Selby turned to leave with Kim.

"Did you bring evening wear?" Mannon called to Selby as they went out.

Selby glanced back. "Yes. Kim warned me."

"Good. Then I shall see you at dinner."

Mannon flexed his knees, as if secretly amused by something.

"The gear's in your room," Kim said as they walked away. "I'll meet you at the stables."

"And where's that?"

"Jarvis will show you. You seem thoughtful. What did Daddy actually say to you? You appear to have got on quite well."

"He gave me a lesson in reality. I hope he's wrong."

"Care to tell me?"

"No."

The dark eyes looked at him anxiously. "We're not going to have a bad weekend, are we?"

He smiled at her. "Whatever gave you that idea?"

While Mark Selby was being introduced to the delights of Buckinghamshire, Nico Bagni was having a difficult time in Florence. He stared past his companion, unenthusiastically out of the restaurant window, at the Piazza della Signoria.

It was a bright, warm day, and the sun's rays fell starkly upon the square, fortress-like shape of the Palazzo Vecchio, its castellated clock tower a proud sentry standing guard. Bagni's displeasure was not for the tall arches of the Loggia, nor for the great statues, the silent onlookers of the square. He was as proud a Florentine as any, of his city's history. It was the droves of tourists filling the cobbled square that had briefly distracted him from the girl at his side: the coaches parked like airliners, the horse-drawn open carriages awaiting camera-laden passengers.

He told himself wryly, he was being unfair. People came to Florence because his home city was beautiful, and ancient. History spoke to you here.

His eyes wandered, pausing to study the open-air café beyond the Loggia. Every table was occupied. At last, he returned his attention to his companion. She was staring at him, face pale, eyes with a hint of moistness.

"So," she began softly, "that's your last word on it?"

"I don't have a choice, Bianca."

"Of course you have a choice. Everyone has a choice."

"You know I cannot leave the Service."

"Why not?"

"And what will I do? Come to Milano with you and join the fashion world?"

"That was unkind, Nico."

After a pause, he said: "I didn't mean it to sound that way. But you must understand. I am a fighter pilot. That's what I want to be until they tell me I am too old, or no longer fit. You're following the career you want. Why shouldn't I?"

"Mine is not dangerous. It will not kill me."

"You could walk out of here and be hit by one of those tourist coaches."

She sighed. "You know what I mean."

"What I do is less dangerous than driving a car. The statistics prove it."

"And now, you're going away, and won't tell me where." She decided to ignore casualty statistics. She smiled, ruefully. "Who would have thought we'd be sitting in this place one day, feeling so miserable? We've known each other for ten years, Nico, since we met for the first time here in the piazza. You were staring at the Rape of the Sabine."

He smiled, remembering. "And a sixteen-year-old girl came up to me to ask what I thought of it."

"I wasn't really interested in the statue."

His smile widened. "It took me a while to work that out. I went into a boring explanation."

"You were shy. I liked that."

"Not a macho Italian."

"Enough of those around."

"And now?"

"A lot of my women friends think you're a macho fighter pilot and are crazy about you. But I know you're still the Nico I met all those years ago. You don't have to impress me."

"I'm not trying to impress you. I simply want to remain a pilot. I love flying, just as you love designing clothes. Your name appears in the glossy magazines. People buy your fashions in New York and Paris and London. When you decided you didn't want to get married, I understood and let you follow your career, and I followed mine. You travel to London, Paris, or New York, and I go where the Aeronautica Militare sends me. We each have our responsibilities."

She stared at him. "I'm afraid, Nico."

"Of what?"

"I'm afraid for the future."

"Because I won't tell you where I'm going?"

"You've always told me before. How do I keep in touch? How can I write to you? Can I telephone?"

"I'm sure I'll be able to tell you. I'm not authorized as yet. That's all it is. There's nothing to worry about."

"And your parents? Do they know?"

"Not yet."

"I went to Fiesole to see them last weekend."

He nodded. "They told me."

"Your mother's worried too."

"She's always been worried about my flying, for as long as I can remember. I've never crashed, even in training."

"Never an emergency?"

"There are always possibilities. There are emergencies in everyday life."

"You didn't answer the question."

"Bianca . . . we are not here to talk about emergency situations in flying. I am here today, with the most beautiful, most elegant woman in all of Tuscany, and I intend to enjoy her company in every way I can. Are you going to let me?"

"Since you put it like that . . ." She smiled, but her eyes were guarded.

In Schleswig, Hohendorf was on stand-by duty. His navigator was still Ecker. Ecker now knew of Hohendorf's impending move to the new unit and though each was unhappy with the enforced change, they had come to terms with it.

Hohendorf had recently carried out several missions with Wolfgang Flacht in the back seat and had found the younger navigator as proficient as had been expected. For his part, Ecker had gone on a few sorties with Willie Beuren. He worked well with Beuren, and had told Hohendorf so. Despite this, Hohendorf found himself unable to lose the feeling of uneasiness; but he had still not told Wusterhausen about it.

Now, however, as they sat in the squadron lounge with the two other crews on duty, they were discussing a forthcoming visit to Nellis air force base in the States, for participation in a Red Flag exercise. It was to be a joint visit, with two Marineflieger aircraft in company with two RAF IDS Tornadoes. The crewing would be Hohendorf and Flacht, Beuren and Ecker. Hohendorf was pleased, despite the crewing. It still meant he would be flying on one more tough exercise with Ecker before it was time to leave for Scotland.

Ecker said: "Two weeks, and we'll be in Nevada. I'm looking forward to showing them what a Tornado can really do."

Hohendorf smiled. "I think we'll have a few surprises for them, Johann."

That evening at Grantly Hall, the reason for Sir Julius Mannon's sly amusement became clear. He had invited Reggie Barham-Deane for dinner. Kim was furious and throughout the entire meal said as little as possible, her face pale with anger, her dark eyes cold. The seating had been so arranged that Barham-Deane was next to her, while Selby had been stuck at a far end between a mother and daughter, neighbors of Sir Julius, who were driving him to distraction with silly questions about flying.

From time to time a look of mutual sympathy would pass between Kim and himself, and, on one such occasion Barham-Deane leaned intimately towards her and murmured, "Must be terribly frustrating for you, darling. He's over there between the harpie and her daughter, while you're here with me. Sir Julius has a sharp sense of humor, don't you think?"

Kim brought her head close to his, smiling sweetly. Seeing that, Selby felt gloom descend upon him and wished he had not come. It was going to be a miserable weekend, after all.

Barham-Deane glanced at Selby in triumph as Kim put her lips against his ear.

"Fuck off, Reggie," she told him, still smiling.

His head jerked away, and he went a bright red.

Selby noted it and felt immediately better. Sir Julius had also seen the brief drama at his table. He glanced at each of the three in turn, noting their expressions. His own expression gave nothing away as he returned his attention to the guests closest to him, and smoothly continued his conversation.

At last, the dinner came to an end. Some guests were staying the night and as soon as he decently could, Selby retired to his room. Mannon took Barham-Deane into his study. Clearly, Barham-Deane would also be staying the night.

Selby lay shirtless on his bed, annoyed with himself. For someone who had always been careful not to become seriously involved with a woman, he wasn't doing very well. He could no longer deny that Kim Mannon had become important to him.

"You're an idiot, Selby," he now said aloud. "You understand airplanes, not women. Mach 2 at 40,000 feet is your territory. That's where you live. Any day now you'll be talking marriage, and that's simply not on. Make what you can of the weekend, then get the hell away. Go back to what you know."

He paused for long reflective moments. "God, but she was beautiful tonight," he added softly.

He must have dozed, because a soft knock made him start.

He sat up. "Come in." The bedside light was still on. He glanced at his watch. Two in the morning.

Kim entered, pushing the door shut and locking it behind her. She stood against it, and watched him. She was in her dressing gown, a deep blue affair that gleamed darkly and added luster to her eyes. Her face was still pale, as if from a continuing anger.

He returned her gaze. Even in anger, she was beautiful.

"I'm sorry for tonight, Mark," she said at last. "It was inexcusable of Daddy to invite Reggie without first warning me. He knew how I felt. I think he realizes now that he overdid it tonight. After you came up I told him what I thought of him for springing Reggie on us like that."

"And what about the man himself? What did he say while you were telling your father off?"

"He had the grace to keep out of it and look sheepish."

Selby was skeptical. "Reggie Barham-Deane wouldn't know how to be sheepish if it bit him on the nose. He was probably smirking, just as he did all through dinner."

"Oh Mark. I'm so sorry you had to sit through that. I wanted this to be such a good weekend for us."

"It won't be spoiled," he said.

"Promise?" She seemed to brighten.

"Promise."

"I'm all tense and angry."

"I have a cure for that . . . but not if you stay over there."

She tilted her head to give him a sideways look then slowly, she began to remove her dressing gown. "You'll have to be patient and gentle with me."

"I can be patient, and gentle," he assured her.

Beneath the dressing gown she was completely naked. She walked with slow steps toward the bed and stretched her body down upon him.

"Show me it's going to be a lovely weekend," she said against his lips as she pressed herself to him. "Show me."

"The lights . . ." he began.

"Sod the lights."

As their bodies fused together in eager passion, Selby found uppermost in his mind the thought that when all the flowery phrases were removed, this was what he was employed by the taxpayer to protect. The man trained to blow an invading bomber to smithereens was only protecting his right to make love to Kim Mannon.

In the event, the weekend turned out much better than had been expected. Sir Julius had to leave for an urgent meeting abroad, with Barham-Deane forced to accompany him in what was clearly a deep sulk. Left to their own devices, Selby and Kim Mannon had themselves a high old time, most of which was spent in bed. Jarvis was discretion itself, and had kept well out of the way.

Selby returned to his unit on the following Monday, to find he was one of the selected crews to take part in a forthcoming Red Flag exercise, in company with two West German Tornadoes. His backseater was to be an American, Elmer Lee McCann, who had been posted in to undergo Tornado conversion training.

He had flown with McCann several times at Cottesmore, and had found that he liked the quirky, rebellious American. It was on one such flight that McCann had confided in him of an expected posting to a special unit. Selby had said nothing of his own posting, preferring to wait and see how things eventually turned out. If McCann became his permanent back-seater at the new unit, he wouldn't mind.

The second Red Flag Tornado was being crewed by Urquhart and the Australian, Ferris. Selby liked Ferris, and had also worked with him. The teams had been well-selected, he felt. RAF Tornadoes had scooped trophies in previous competitions in the States, and he hoped his team would do well at Nellis.

He had been designated leader of the RAF teams, and had been told that the West Germans would be led by a Kapitän Leutnant Hohendorf. At Nellis, lead of all four aircraft would alternate by mission, between Selby and Hohendorf. He wondered anxiously what Hohendorf was like. What kind of pilot? What kind of man and most importantly, what would he be like to work with in a team?

They would not actually meet until Nellis. Normally, all crews would work-up together, sometimes for weeks, before going on to the vast "war zone" in the Nevada desert, but on this occasion the mission had been planned so that the two pairs of aircraft would simply rendezvous over the North Atlantic, and then continue on together to Nellis. Selby felt certain the mission had been planned that way as a prelude to the eventual posting to Scotland.

Two weeks later, McCann was putting on his country boy accent in the back seat of Selby's aircraft: "Ah've got two bogeys at zero four five, 800 knots. Angels three zero." McCann meant 30,000 feet, their own current cruising altitude.

"Bogeys? Angels? Where do you think you are, Elmer Lee?"

"Let me have my fun. Wow! Those guys are hitting it."

"They're on time and spot on," Selby said. "They seem to know their stuff."

"They look like hot shots to me. Wonder what they'll be like on the ranges?"

"We're not competing with them, Elmer Lee. They're on the team."

"Even so," McCann said, always eager to pit

himself against any newcomers. "They'll be on us . . ." he continued, ". . . now!"

The RAF Tornadoes were cruising at a steady 450 knots. The two Marineflieger aircraft tore past on either side, wings at full sweep, to pull into a steep climb. They snapped into a quarter-roll and belly to belly, continued the climb. They reversed wing to wing and spreading their wings forward, pulled over the top to double back on their track, upside down. They flashed past, going the other way to pull into a dive, levelled out, having completed the entire maneuver in perfect formation.

Their exhibition over, the Marineflieger Tornadoes were now coming up fast, but slowing down to match speeds as they drew closer. The leading aircraft gave the impression of coming to a halt as it matched exactly Selby's airspeed.

Selby glanced to his left, and gave a brief salute. So this was Hohendorf.

McCann looked out at the newcomers, noting how they had slotted neatly into formation: the lead ships now side by side, the wingman on each outer wing and a little to the rear.

McCann selected the pre-arranged frequency. "We've got some smart-ass fliers here, Mark ol' buddy," he said, knowing the other aircraft would pick him up.

"Very impressive," Selby concurred.

"Glad you think so," came a new voice. "Think

you know the way to Nellis?" The voice spoke English with only the slightest of accents.

"Any time, baby," McCann answered. "Any time."

The helmet was turned their way again. "Then lead on."

Back on the cockpit frequency, McCann said: "Sounds like he's got a sense of humor."

"That's always a help," came Selby's comment.

There was a Tristar tanker up ahead to top them all up, then it would be on to Nellis.

Nellis. Red Flag: a vast airbase packed solid with aircraft of all types, and of various Western air forces. Beyond it, thousands of square miles of Nevada emptiness; baking desert and dragon's teeth mountains. A simulated war zone where the unwary pilot could be "killed" by wily Aggressors pretending to be the enemy, or be truly killed by his own mistakes. The mountains and the desert floor, and the air, were not kind to the unwary.

When they arrived, Selby had immediately been struck by the seemingly limitless visibility. The cloudless sky, the heat and the vastness, could not have been more different from what he was accustomed to in Europe. He had previously been to Maple Flag up in Canada where the terrain and weather were more familiar, even if the available area for combat flying was infinitely more generous. Of the four NATO crews, only McCann was returning to a known stamping ground. He promised to show them the ropes.

Using maps of the range area, he showed them the favored ambush points of the Aggressor pilots who invariably flew the tiny, difficult-to-acquire F-5, but who could be supplemented at any time by other students flying Eagles or Falcons. Some of these students might well have been to Red Flag before and would have some dirty tricks up their sleeves. He warned them of the simulated surface-to-air missiles, hidden out there in the mountains and the desert, which would be eager to make the Tornadoes their meat.

"These SAM birds are operated by nasty little enlisted personnel," he told them, "who like nothing more than nailing some hot shot pilot. Take it from me, guys. They're after our asses."

By the time they went into their first mission pre-brief, they felt they had already acquired a subtle edge over their fellow lambs to the waiting slaughter. Their first flight was to be a familiarisation mission over the ranges, to see what was in store.

Selby had found that he had been accepted easily by the West German crews, with the exception of Hohendorf, in whom he had sensed wariness. They had been like two stags, carefully assessing each other; and when Hohendorf had extended a hand in greeting, despite the accompanying smile Selby had seen a challenge in the eyes. He knew then that Hohendorf would be the one to watch. And he wasn't surprised: after the fancy approach over the Atlantic, he had suspected that the leader of the Marineflieger Tornadoes would be a tough one.

For his part, Hohendorf viewed Selby with his own watchfulness.

"That one," he confided later to Ecker, "is somebody to watch."

"Mark Selby?"

"Oh yes. Mr. Selby thinks he can show me a thing or two."

"And can he?"

Hohendorf smiled. "Johann, Johann. Prepare to get dust in your eyes. Flacht and I are going to take out more targets than our friend Selby. We're going to tear the throats of the SAM crews. Just make sure you get Willi Beuren to follow me in when he's paired with me."

Ecker said nothing, but smiled in acquiescence. He wished he would be flying with Hohendorf, but this was a perfect opportunity to acclimatise Wolfgang Flacht to Hohendorf's at-the-edge flying. It was Flacht who would be going to Scotland with Paul. Ecker felt regret at this, but kept his silence.

The four Tornadoes flew low across the desert, Selby in the lead.

"Good God," he said, looking out at the pitiless landscape. "I wouldn't like to go down here."

"I got news for you," McCann said. "I wouldn't

like to go down anywhere. Just keep right on being a hot shot pilot, will you?"

Selby smiled in his mask. "So what's down there, Elmer Lee?"

"All the wonders of creation . . . bull snakes, side-winders, rattlers . . ."

"That's quite enough, thank you."

"There's lots more . . . tarantulas, a wonderful landscape of sagebrush, scrub . . ."

"McCann—"

"Had enough?"

"More than enough. I promise not to put you down."

"I just hate walking, is all."

"So do I. Rattlesnakes. Ugh!" Selby was grateful they were not earmarked for desert survival training during their stay. Some of the other visitors, he'd learned, had been selected to undergo the ordeal. The majority of them had been from the US forces; though he'd heard a couple of French, Jaguar-flying pilots had been put on it. Given their probable posting to Chad, he was not surprised. "Better them than me."

"Did you say something?" McCann queried.

"Just pilot talk."

High above them, F-15 Eagles were mixing it with the Aggressors. Invisibly in the distance, the high-G contest whirled spectacularly. At any given time, all sorts of aircraft were engaged in furious maneuvering, all across the range area. But today, this would not concern them.

The sortie was completed without incident. No Aggressors tapped them—they were not supposed to—but McCann had warned against complacency. So they kept low all the way. Legend had it that an RAF Buccaneer pilot had once left wingtip trails on the desert floor, so low had he gone.

The next day's sortie was a different thing altogether. They were given, in McCann's words "a real bitch." The mission brief had assigned them two target areas. One was a clutch of SAM sites, an airfield, a convoy of trucks, and a railroad. The other, more SAM sites, a helipad, and a pipeline.

Hohendorf and Selby decided to split forces on the approach, each of them leading a pair. Selby would lead Beuren's and Ecker's Tornado, while Hohendorf would have Urquhart and Ferris. It was to be a low-level transit all the way to the targets and back, using maximum ground cover, and maximum jamming to neutralise the defences.

Take-off was on time. They were lucky. Due to the heavy concentration of aircraft waiting for the off, some left for their designated areas later than planned. Hohendorf and Selby intended to use that to advantage. Some of the late ones were Aggressors. Selby did not think this advantage unfair. In a real war, a potential enemy would be snagged by all sorts of organizational problems. It was inevitable on either side. Maximizing all advantages was the name of the game.

The two pairs of Tornadoes hurled themselves into the air, and headed for their allocated targets.

In the target areas, the ground defense operators were on the alert. Their simulated armament was as close to the real thing as was possible. Their target videos would record all passes and all "kills," precluding any arguments from indignant pilots. Those videos were the stuff of humiliation; true ego deflaters. But at least, the "dead" crews would still be alive to learn from their mistakes. Knowledge that in a real war they wouldn't have made it was supremely chastening.

In both their minds, Selby and Hohendorf, fully aware of the accuracy of the defences, nursed a determination not to get nailed. They kept their aircraft low, twisting and turning against the high ground, using the terrain to mask their approach.

Target area. An operator was getting excited.

"We've got a . . . what's this? It's a Tornado!" he exclaimed. "And he's giving us all kind of jamming, and I mean heavy. He's low down in the dirt and . . . he's gone! Let's get a track on this guy," he added wearily, defeated by the Tornadoes' electronic counter-measures.

Someone else picked up the refrain. "I've got him! There he goes. We're locked on, we're firing on this guy . . . we broke up. Let's see if we can acquire this guy again. And . . . we're tracking . . . we're track . . . there he goes. No. Boy . . . he's ECMing us bad here on something . . . he's way out of range now.''

Hohendorf threaded his Tornado between two ramparts of high ground, safely through the first line of defense.

"Good work, Wolfgang," he said to Flacht. "I think you turned their tracking into a mess. Now for the next line."

The second operator was speaking. "Here's another Tornado! His wingman. We're tracking. We've got ECM here. Giving us some stuff. This guy's ripping through. Good job. Good job. And he's gone. No chance."

Urquhart followed Hohendorf's reefing Tornado, hugging the ground, through the SAM barrier.

Watching the world tilt this way and that, Ferris said: "Don't you dare lose that nimble lad out there."

"I'm on him, Bondi. I'm on him."

A third operator had picked up Hohendorf's aircraft. "Here he comes, here he comes! I've got him! I've got . . . goddamn Tornado . . . Oh shit! I missed him. let's see . . . no, no. I've lost this guy. And here's his buddy. Keeping low. Good masking. Oh some good stuff here. I just can't acquire this guy. Some heavy manoeuvres. We've lost him. We've lost him. He's long gone."

They were through. The first target, the railroad, was coming up.

From the back, Flacht said: "Do you want manual on this? Or shall I set it up?"

"It's all yours, Wolfgang. You deserve it. We'll go for auto-release."

As Flacht set up the run-in, Hohendorf uncaged the weapon release button on the stick and waited for Flacht's word. At the bottom of the HUD, two dashes began sliding towards the middle. When the fall line from the center entered the space between them, they would be on target.

"Left, zero one two," Flacht said.

Fifty feet above the terrain, Hohendorf eased the Tornado onto the new heading. Bare, oven-baked rock faces blurred past. The dashes continued to move right.

"All right," Flacht continued. "Finger on the button."

Hohendorf pressed it. Nothing would respond until optimum release parameters had been achieved. He kept the pressure on as the aircraft hurtled towards the railroad.

"Weapon gone!" Flacht called. "We've got a hit!"

"Now for the next one," Hohendorf said with satisfaction.

Selby was entering his selected hostile area. He took the aircraft at high speed, constantly reversing his turns, never flying straight and level for more than four seconds, never allowing the same length of time between the changes of attitude. A one-second break could be followed by a three-second turn, then a two-second, then a one, and so on.

McCann, continuously scanning the world outside as well as his displays, crowed: "That's it, baby! Let's rock and roll!"

On the ground, Selby's antics were making life miserable for the defending SAM and anti-aircraft teams. One radar operator in particular, a woman, was having a hard time of it.

"Ooh . . . he's giving us a lot of ECM," she was saying in a voice that was close to exasperation. "We're getting nothing on this guy. What are we gonna do? Looks like a Tornado." Suddenly she got excited. "And we're locked on this guy! ECM, but we've got him!" Her words came faster now. "No. We're barely keeping up with this mother. One point two degrees elevation . . . he's diving . . ." The words were almost running into each other. "Do we have a launch on this guy? Yes! Launch complete . . . no. And he broke us up. We're going to have to abort that launch."

*   *   *

Selby was through, sweeping along the desert floor. Behind him, Beuren's Tornado popped over a ridge and plunged towards the SAM gauntlet. But as the seconds ticked away, the operator was still chasing Selby, determined to nail him.

"There he is again," she said. "Let's get something on this mother. He's got some good manoeuvres. Down in the dirt. This guy's in close. Do we have launch? No. He broke us up again." She didn't say fuck, but she was thinking it. "This guy's done some outstanding ECM. C'mon. Where are you?" She was almost seductive about it. "OK. I've got him again. This guy is down low. Tornado. We're getting nothing here. Fuck it all," she added, giving in.

Beuren was close on Selby's tail. The operator had taken their measure and was out for blood now. The slightest mistake by the attacking aircraft was going to give her a kill. She was determined.

Beuren entered the fray.

"Here's another one," the operator said. "I've got lock on this guy. He's got some manoeuvres, but I've still got him. ECMing . . . breaking us . . . but I'm still with him." Her voice was beginning to rise with the excitement of the chase. She counted off range parameters rapidly. "ECM momentarily, but I'm with him. We're launching on this guy. Launch complete. No manoeuvres, no nuthin. Just straight plain flying. We've got this guy." She sounded very pleased.

Selby went on to hit his targets, swung back for the SAMs. Behind him Beuren wheeled, hitting targets but in reality out of the battle.

Knowing they had downed one Tornado in their sector, the operators there were eager for the leader. This time, a male operator was tracking Selby.

"OK," he said. "We've got an inbound Tornado. Jamming good. Terrain masking. We've got a lock. No we don't. There he goes."

"I think we'll call that a miss," someone next to him said.

"I reckon," he said.

They laughed sheepishly.

"And here he comes again!" the operator began excitedly. "Oh boy! He's in close and coming right for us." The roar of the Tornado seemed to fill the desert as it screamed overhead, almost touching. *"Woo!* Crazy too! Can't touch him. Let's see if we can get his wingman."

In his sector, Hohendorf was wiping out his targets. Urquhart and Ferris in their Tornado were being almost as devastating. They turned for the SAMs.

* * *

On the desert floor and among the rocks, the defense teams waited, chagrined by the lack of success so far.

"I've got this Tornado here." The operator who'd had the first fruitless encounter with Hohendorf hunched forward over his screens. "He's in real low and oh man he's giving us some jamming and we'll never get on to him. He's down, down in the dirt, just about ready to get out and walk. Some ECM here. Ain't nothing we're gonna do about it. There he goes." A sense of having lost. "Masking and jamming, and on his way. And there's his wingman. Gone too. We've got nothing on these guys. Tornado. Yeah."

The four aircraft made a low-level rendezvous at Yucca Flats and headed back to Nellis. They'd done a good day's work, marred only by Beuren's taking a hit. Later, the videos showed only too graphically what had happened.

Beuren had not gone low enough.

Afterwards, when they could talk privately, Ecker said to Hohendorf: "It was his first time out, Axel."

"That's not good enough, Johann, and you know it. I had Urquhart and Ferris down there with me. They used the terrain and survived. Selby feels let down . . ."

"He didn't say so . . ."

"Would you in his place? Let's be honest, Johann. The Englishman must be furious. He could have had a perfect mission. We beat the defences and eluded the fighters. If Willi had gone down low, we would have had a clean day. I will fly against Selby anytime, but that doesn't mean I want him handicapped. Next mission, I'm pairing Willi with me . . . and I want him down on the deck for the attack."

But the next time, Beuren still held off. His avoidance manoeuvres were good, and he hit a fair number of targets. His only problem appeared to be the ability to go below 100 feet. He was happier at 200. He was good at eluding the defending fighters. However, during the Red Flag visit he fell victim to the SAMs and anti-aircraft guns no less than four times. None of the others had been acquired long enough for a successful launch, and had escaped unscathed.

When they returned to Schleswig Hohendorf let the report on the deployment speak for itself to Wusterhausen. It contained all the relevant information. Besides, as Ecker pointed out to him, many US aircrews had fallen victim to the ferocious enlisted personnel in the rocks, and none had been grounded because of it.

Hohendorf was in as much a quandary as ever. He had no liking for ruining a man's career, yet an incident that had taken place the day before they had begun their return flight to Europe only added to his worries. An F-111 crew had over-cooked it on a low-level pass, and had ploughed into the mountains. Both the F-111 crew members had died in their aircraft.

As time drew near for his posting to Scotland, Hohendorf felt no better, but chose to say nothing to Wusterhausen. He hoped he would not regret the decision one day.

A forward airbase on the Kola Peninsula, spring into summer.

Kukarev, the high boots of his summer everyday dress gleaming, stood by the control tower and watched as a pair of Sukhoi Su-27 interceptors, twin-tailed and twin-engined, hurtled down the vast 4.6-kilometer main runway. Made up of geometrically precise oblong blocks of concrete, it resembled a great road that came from nowhere on its way to nowhere.

Kukarev kept his eyes upon the Su-27s as they lit their after-burners and leaped smoothly into the air. They were going out on routine patrol, and would not be back for at least an hour. This was not to be an extended mission.

Ever since his detachment as test pilot to the forward base six months before, he had gradually worked up into a specific routine. He made it his business to know the movements of the other aircraft with which he shared the base. This aroused no suspicions, as his test flight program called for various exercises with and against those very aircraft. There were formation routines, air combat practice, ground attack manoeuvres, tanker exercises, recce patrols, and so on. He engaged in mock combat with both the Su-27s, and the MiG-29s, noting the styles of the pilots involved.

For example, he knew of one particular Su-27 pilot who in close combat, always began his attack with a high-speed approach; but instead of putting out his airbrakes to slow down and prevent the overtake thus warning an alert potential victim, would go into a high-G barrel roll, displacing about the target aircraft and keeping out of sight while he took the shot.

Kukarev had a counter to that particular move, but never used it. When he eventually made his break, if it was discovered this might be one of the pilots sent to chase him. Painstakingly, he had made himself familiar with each pilot's idiosyncracies, in preparation for the day of his final take-off.

His detachment was made up of the one aircraft, but there were two other pilots who shared the test program with him; a captain, and the detachment commander, Lieutenant-Colonel Melev. Kukarev felt sorry about Melev, whom he considered a good man. The Lieutenant-Colonel would be severely dealt with for the loss of the aircraft; but he was simply unfortunate enough to be in the wrong place at the wrong time. Kukarev was determined to carry out his plan.

His expression betraying nothing of his thoughts, the young Russian studied a big Ilyushin

I1-76 as it trundled onto the runway in readiness for take-off, its four underslung turbofans whistling as the pilot throttled back and came to a stop. This was a tanker version and Kukarev had carried out several refueling exercises with it. Did its departure mean that the Su-27s were on an extended patrol after all? he wondered. If so, this was a change from normal practice. He would have to watch for these sudden changes in future. It would not do to take-off on his final flight, only to find a tanker set up to attend to his pursuers' fuel needs.

The base was home to a wide variety of aircraft. It was a special unit, not normally on the operational roster of bases in the area. But it was kept in a constant state of readiness as a deployment and exercise unit. The current occupiers were his own detachment, plus a 28-aircraft regiment of Su-27s, 2 I1-76 AWACS and 2 I1-76 tankers, with an assortment of utility and transport aircraft making up the entire complement.

The I1-76 was winding up to take-off thrust; then with a quadruple roar, the high-tailed aircraft urged itself down the runway. Kukarev watched it rumble on its take-off run, sluggish by comparison with the hurtling '27s that had gone earlier. Now the nose was coming up and the large aircraft heaved itself into the air, heading north.

Kukarev knew that Murmashi, to the northwest, was an active interceptor base. So was Malyaur, still northwards but a little to the east. A

2-squadron regiment of MiG-29s had recently been rotated there. Here on his detachment base, the Su-27s were due for rotation southwards to the Central Front, but that did not necessarily mean they would be staying there. Whenever he left, if his destination was guessed there'd be plenty of high-tech machinery to send after him.

He had already decided upon the circumstances, though the exact date of his defection had not yet been selected. It would be at the end of the detachment, towards the beginning of autumn. When the Krivak's test program was over he had already been detailed to fly the aircraft back to one of the manufacturer's airfields. On that day, it would be flying with full tanks . . .

"Comrade Major!"

Kukarev turned at the familiar voice, not showing the irritation he felt.

Captain Anatoly Zitkin was the base's most junior political officer. Kukarev's antipathy for *Zampolits* exceeded even his late father's but unlike his father he knew how to keep his thoughts to himself. General Kukarev had often said loud enough for anyone within earshot to hear that there was nothing about patriotism that any political officer could teach him. He spoke with the assurance of a man who at twenty had hurled his fighter into massed formations of enemy aircraft during the Great Patriotic War with a ferocity that had stunned even his comrades. He had become one of the youngest squadron commanders and in later years, one of the youngest generals to command an air army.

But even that had not made him immune to the schemes of those who had sought his downfall. And even today *glasnost* and *perestroika* would not prevent the old guard from resisting fiercely. In fact, the possibility of reform would ensure it. The Russian spring, if there were to be one, would have a hard time of it. Which was why the general's son was leaving. What had started as a blind desire for revenge had matured into the belief that he could do more for his country from outside it.

Zitkin arrived, slightly out of breath.

"I hope," Kukarev began good-naturedly, "you're not going to scold me for not keeping up with my hours of political instruction."

Zitkin smiled, but it failed to reach his deep-set eyes. "No, Comrade. I have . . . a favour to ask of you."

Wondering at the nature of this favor, Kukarev waited.

"Comrade . . ." Zitkin began and paused, seemingly unsure of himself.

A revelation, Kukarev thought. *Zampolits* were not normally uncertain, even with someone of higher rank.

"I've been meaning to ask you for some time," Zitkin went on. "Some weeks ago, you had a visitor. I have since discovered him to be a senior officer with the KGB." Zitkin paused a second time, looking slightly embarrassed. "Comrade Major, I do not wish you to think me . . . impertinent . . . but you appear to have good relations with the Comrade Colonel. I am eager to serve the Motherland as best I can and I thought that perhaps the next time you saw the Comrade Colonel . . . well, you know my work—if you would put in a word for me, then perhaps. . . ." He tailed off.

Kukarev wanted to laugh. The little bastard was ambitious and wanted a push through the back door, in the time-honored fashion of those his father had spent all his life resisting . . . What, he now wondered, would Zitkin say if he knew that the KGB senior officer, Sergei Stolybin, was not only a good friend but was also, in Zitkin's terms, a traitor? That without Stolybin, the plan to take the operational prototype to the West wouldn't work?

Without Stolybin, there would be no tanker, and no NATO escort. Not, of course, that the KGB man could help him get to the rendezvous alive. Not an easy matter, even with the Krivak prototype. If pursuit were mounted, he would have to deal with it while having nothing with which to defend himself. The Krivak was not yet cleared for live firings. That was another part of the test program, to be carried out in September at a different location. In the meantime, the aircraft carried only inert weapons and simulated firing equipment.

Kukarev looked at Zitkin, stifling his distaste. "I'll do what I can," he said, turning to watch an Antonov An-12 transport trundling toward the take-off point. He kept his eyes firmly upon it, until Zitkin got the message and left.

The An-12, a high-winged four-engined turbo-prop, rumbled on, but Kukarev was not really interested in it. He turned to walk on, and saw someone just passing Zitkin and approaching. Kukarev immediately felt better as he recognized Sergeant Yuri Tikov. They had both been in Afghanistan together where Tikov, a nerveless Ukrainian, had serviced his Su-25 under fire from the hills. Tikov was such a good crew chief, Kukarev had managed to have him posted to almost every unit in which he'd subsequently served as a pilot.

Tikov was his one regret. He would not be able to say goodbye to him. Tikov would not understand. For though the sergeant heartily despised the Zitkins of the world, and had a healthy dose of Ukrainian nationalism within him, it would never stretch to understanding a flight West. Mercifully, the sergeant would be going to the new location some days before the detachment ended.

There would be no awkward goodbyes, Kukarev thought. No inadvertent betrayal of what he planned to do when he climbed into the cockpit on that last flight.

The An-12 took off with a relative whisper of its turboprops as Tikov saluted and reminded him he had a cockpit check to do within the hour.

Chapter

The end of May saw cars of a large variety of makes and sizes turning up at the gates of November One, on Scotland's Grampian coast.

Hohendorf, in civilian clothes, pulled up by the guardroom, his Porsche packed with his gear. He had been able to take most of what he needed for the time being. As he was now virtually single, he'd be living in the Mess.

He climbed out of the car, and looked beyond the guard barrier to where two World War II Mosquito fighter bombers, acting as gate guardians, were parked nose-on, on either side of the access road.

"They're the real thing, sir," the airman at the reception hatch said to him. "Not those plastic replicas some of the other stations are having." He clearly disapproved of economy drives and plastic replicas. "They used to be based here during the war."

"Those very two?"

"Yes, sir. Anti-shipping strikes in Bergen fjord was their game."

How strange life is, Hohendorf thought. *One of them may well have killed my grandfather.* The commodore's destroyer had been sunk in Bergen fjord.

"May I have your name, please, sir?" the airman was saying.

"Oh. Yes, of course. Hohendorf."

The airman consulted a clipboard. "Hohendorf . . . Hohendorf . . ." he murmured as he checked his list. "Yes, sir. Here we are . . . Kapitän Leutnant Wietze-Hohendorf." He said it correctly. "Sign here please, sir, for your pass. And if I could see some identification . . ."

Hohendorf produced his Marineflieger ID, signed and was handed his pass, complete with photograph and other relevant details. The Porsche's license number was also recorded by the airman.

"Right, sir," the airman went on. "Here's your information pack. It gives you all details of the unit as it relates to you. There are directions to the Officers' Mess. If you'll Warn In before doing anything else, sir."

Hohendorf took the sealed, substantial folder. "Thank you," he said.

"Thank *you,* sir. I hope you'll enjoy it here with us."

"I'm sure I will."

As he spoke, Hohendorf heard a fierce roaring

sound, increasing in volume as it approached. He looked up. Two sleek fighter aircraft passed overhead, wings at mid-sweep. Their Tornado parentage was obvious, but they looked meaner and much deadlier.

As he continued to look, the Super Tornadoes swept their wings fully. The burners came on in a quadruple thunder and the aircraft rocketed upwards in a steep climb. Hohendorf stared in awe as they hurtled vertically, their tails flaming. He kept his eye on them until they had disappeared into the blue of the summer sky. The whole thing had taken fleeting moments. He could barely wait to get his hands on one of those ships.

He looked at the airman. "I shall enjoy it very much."

The airman smiled. "Thought you would, sir. That's what all the gentlemen say."

"Have many arrived?"

"Quite a few, sir. And there's more to come. The Mess will be fuller than some I've known."

"Well . . . thank you again."

"Thank you, sir."

Hohendorf got back into the Porsche and drove slowly towards the barrier. He showed his pass, and was allowed through. A sign said: STATION LIMIT 20 MPH.

Hohendorf smiled to himself as he followed directions on the map from the info pack. The real station limit was more like Mach 2.5—at the very least.

The place had the sparkle of its newness. Even the utility vehicles gleamed. He pulled up in the Mess car park and went to Warn In at Reception. After he'd been allocated his quarters, he unloaded his gear and began to settle in.

Then he went in search of Flacht, whom the receptionist had said had arrived a day previously.

The roar of an aircraft taking off penetrated even the thick walls of the Mess. Hohendorf smiled again, deeply excited by the prospect of climbing into the front seat of one of this new breed of Tornado.

Selby had come to November One two hours before, and had taken the earliest opportunity to inspect the new aircraft. Apart from the more obvious changes, he had studied with interest the new tailerons. They were larger in area, and had been moved slightly aft. They also had dogtooth leading edges, rather like the F-15 Eagle's, though the overall Tornado design had been retained.

The station itself, he'd found, while having the familiarity of an RAF establishment, was subtly different. Most apparent, was the flagpole at Station Headquarters. Where normally a solitary RAF ensign would have been flown, two emblems now flew, with the blue of the NATO flag occupying the top position. The uniforms worn by the various people on the unit were those of their respective nationalities, but all wore the NATO shoulder patch in the shape of a shield on the left, with another shield of the national flag, on the right.

The Mess building, he'd noted, had followed the standard RAF design; but again, there were differences. Perhaps it was the newness of the three-storeyed structure.

He walked along a carpeted corridor on the ground floor, heading for the anteroom. His footsteps slowed as he recognised someone coming towards him. He stopped by one of the doors.

Hohendorf came up to him. "So . . . we are to be here together. But you do not look as surprised as I am." Hohendorf held out a hand.

Selby shook it. "I met up with your back-seater an hour ago . . ."

"Ah . . . Wolfgang."

"Yes. He told me you were expected."

"Do you know where he is now?"

"Looking at one of the new aircraft."

Hohendorf smiled. "It should please him. I saw a pair demonstrating a remarkable climb."

"The Wing Commander was in one of them. All the crews will be getting an official welcome from him later today."

"And you . . . you have seen the ships?"

"Oh yes."

"And?"

"Beautiful."

Hohendorf nodded. "I think so too. I am anxious to fly one."

"We'll be getting the chance soon, I shouldn't wonder."

"Any other Red Flag people here?"

"McCann's with us," Selby replied, "and Ferris, but not Urquhart . . . which is a shame. He's a very good pilot. But perhaps they'll send him through later. He works well with Ferris. There's a small Italian contingent. I've met one of them, Nico Bagni, not much to look at, but by all accounts, he's quite fiendish in the air. Nailed an Eagle not so long ago. In a one-oh-four, would you believe."

"A Starfighter." Hohendorf grinned. "We shall have to look to our laurels."

"Possibly."

They were still fencing with each other, still wondering about the other's mettle. Their eyes held each other's for a brief speculative moment, probing.

Selby said: "Care for a coffee? I was just about to have one in the anteroom."

"I should find Wolfgang, but he can wait. Yes, thank you. I will have one."

As they entered, another Super Tornado roared into the Grampian sky.

"Did Bagni himself tell you about the Eagle?" Hohendorf asked.

"Oh no. Strikes me as the slightly shy type. He'd never raise the subject. Usual grapevine stuff. One of their ground crew talked to a couple of RAG bods and it filtered through. They call him 'El Greco.' "

"An artist. We really shall have to watch him."

Selby poured the coffees, then raised his cup. "Cheers. Here's to whatever this is going to be."

Hohendorf raised his own cup. They were challenging, as well as toasting each other.

McCann breezed into the anteroom a few minutes later.

"Well hi, guy!" he greeted Hohendorf, genuinely pleased. He grabbed Hohendorf's hand, shook it briskly.

"Hello yourself," Hohendorf said, amused.

"First some of that coffee." McCann went to pour himself a cup, returned to join them. "So the Red Flag gang's been sent up here. I guess somebody somewhere wanted to see how we'd shape up first. I've seen Wolfie, and old Bondi Ferris. I've recognised a few other Red Flaggers too. One of the French guys, and a bunch from Stateside. France is not strictly in NATO, but what the hell. They're part of the Alliance. And where are your other guys, Axel?"

"Johann and Willi will not be coming."

"Shame. I liked Johann."

"Are there many Americans?"

"A whole crowd. There's a couple of Navy guys rolling around in shades making like they're Hollywood stars, and even a pair of shaven-headed gyrenes, for Christsakes."

Selby said: "Elmer Lee has a phobia about US Marines."

"As long as they keep out of my way, is all."

Hohendorf said soothingly: "We're all on the same side."

McCann snorted. "A Marine's on only one side . . . his own. Wait till we start ACM, eh Mark?" he continued, meaning air combat maneuvering. "We'll nail those guys."

"That we shall," Selby agreed, pacifying his back-seater.

But McCann had pushed the unwelcome Marines to the back of his mind. "Seen the birds?" he asked Hohendorf. "They're something special."

"I saw two of them doing a very impressive climb when I arrived, but not close to."

"Wolfie's out on the flight line having a good look at one. You'll be even more impressed when you get into the front seat. Boy . . . I've been waiting for a ship like this all my life." McCann gave Selby a warning scowl. "Just don't bend it when I'm with you."

Selby gave a tight smile. "I'll try to remember, Elmer Lee."

About an hour after Hohendorf had arrived, Richard Palmer pulled his laden Vauxhall Cavalier estate to the side of the B-class coastal road that led to November One. He had come from the direction of Portsoy, and beyond the road on a bluff to seaward were the remains of an ancient castle. It seemed to be almost directly under the flight path and he made a mental note of it. It was a good reference point. A path near a stream led to it.

He got out of the car, and looked up. A pair of Super Tornadoes had streaked over, going low out to sea. He recognized them by their differences. Now their burners came on together and reefing onto their tails, they tore upwards with a knife-edged sound of thunder. Palmer knew he would come to recognize that distinctive roar anywhere.

As he watched them leap into the blue, he felt a heartbeat of excitement. A mix of emotions were coursing through him. It was like the first day at school, at university, at flying training. The questions were always the same. Would he be able to hack it? What were the others like? And as usual, the greatest of fears was that of failure.

As he watched the aircraft turn into specks then disappear, he felt a burst of pride too. He had been selected to fly one of these things. Many had not. It was something to hold on to. He climbed back into the car and continued on his way, following the winding road that eventually took him to the main gate.

Once past the guard there, Palmer unpacked in his allocated room in the Mess. He put his various items away with studied calm. The room was extremely spacious and comfortable, with a bathroom en suite. While it was undoubtedly of RAF Mess pattern, there was a continental feel to its decoration and furnishings.

When he had finished, he went downstairs to have a look around. He wandered into the billiards room. Two men in flying overalls were having a game. He was astonished to recognize one of them.

They paused in their game to look at him.

"Welcome, Sparrowhawk," the taller of the two said with a smile. "So you made it."

His old instructor from his Hawk days, Squadron Leader Tom Wells.

"Yes, sir."

"Don't look so surprised, lad. I've come to make sure you don't bend one of those shiny new airplanes."

"Yes, sir." Palmer wasn't sure whether the prospect of being put through the training wringer a second time was something to look forward to, but it was nice to see a familiar face.

"Settling in OK?"

"Yes, thank you. The accommodation is rather generous."

"Shows what can be done when we all put our heads together. This is Mick Thirsk. He's a back-seater instructor. I'm about to thrash him."

Palmer nodded at Thirsk, also a Squadron Leader. "Sir."

Thirsk smiled at him. "I've heard good things about you, Richard. I'll see if we can get a decent back-seater to hold your hand. Seen the aircraft yet?"

"Only in the air, sir. They look quite fantastic."

The older men glanced at each other know-
ingly.

Wells said: "They are fantastic, and very, very
fast. Highly responsive too. You'll have to think far
ahead of that airplane. Think of the Hawk as a nippy
Ferrari sports car. The ASV is a full-blown racing
machine with almost limitless power on tap, even
more agile, seemingly ready to come back at you before you've moved. But once you've become one with
it, it's no more frightening than the Hawk. It will
take you to regions of your skills you never thought
possible. I'm here to make sure it does. You won't be
letting me down, will you, lad?"

"No, sir."

"Good. Got all your general bumpf about the
Mess and the unit?"

Palmer nodded.

"Good," Wells said again. "Now off you go and
have a look at your shiny new toy while I complete
the slaughter of this poor unfortunate. And don't forget the Wing Commander's seeing all students in the
main briefing hall."

"I've got it in the info."

"All right, lad." Wells smiled at him. "Glad to
have you with us."

"Thank you, sir."

Palmer left them to their game.

Hohendorf, who had changed into uniform, finally
caught up with Flacht by one of the aircraft shelters.

An ASV had just landed, and was being pushed backwards into the shelter by an aircraft towing tractor, with the crew still aboard, to allow the inertial navigation system to recognize its original starting point.

They shook hands in greeting then stood to watch as the aircraft systems were shut down.

"Oh ja," Hohendorf said. *"Sehr schoen."*

Flacht said: "I'm glad I came. I've sat in the back pocket of one of those on the line. A dream. You'll like your office."

Hohendorf was staring at the aircraft with something akin to love. "I'm sure I will."

The Super Tornado was now silent and the crew were climbing out. About the aircraft, the technicians were already busy with its servicing. The pilot came towards them. A Wing Commander. He glanced at their name tags.

"Welcome, gentlemen," he said. "Can't wait to try one?"

"No, sir," Hohendorf answered.

"That's the spirit." The Wing Commander studied them with probing eyes, then held out his hand. "I'm Jason and for my sins, mainly responsible for most of this; so if any of you cock up, it's my neck."

"We'll take good care of your neck, sir," Hohendorf said.

"I like your thinking. Hohendorf and Flacht. Heard about what you did at Red Flag. Good stuff. Selby's here too."

"I've seen him."

"Good man, Selby. Good pilot. With Bagni, you three are my star pilots. Glad we could get you all." Jason grinned. "Surprised? You shouldn't be. I've studied everyone's files over the past months. Believe me, there are no passengers here." He glanced up at the clear sky. "I'll leave you to continue your tour. Nice day for it."

"I'd like to try an office," Hohendorf said.

"Check with the Chiefy. If the lads are not going into the cockpit, be my guest."

"Thank you, sir."

Jason went on his way while Hohendorf approached the senior non-commissioned officer in charge.

"May I have a look at the cockpit, if you're not working in there as yet?"

"Of course, sir," the Chiefy said. "We won't be going in for a little while yet."

"Thank you."

Hohendorf climbed up the ladder and eased himself into the front cockpit. It was noticeably roomier than the already quite spacious IDS version. He recognised much of the instrumentation and was pleased there had not been change for change's sake. The newer displays he approved of, though for the moment they were switched off. He laid his hand gently upon the controls for feel, acquainting himself with the positions of the various switches and buttons on the throttles and central stick, to judge them for ease of swift operation. They fell nicely to hand. Someone had done his homework well.

His hands reached about him, fingers expertly identifying familiar switches and controls. The rapid take-off panel had been left in its usual place near the base of the control stick. The central warning panel, with its fifty-eight rectangular warning lights, was where he expected to find it, in the lower right hand corner of the main instrument panel. Even the switch for the raising and lowering of his seat was still tucked away on the far right of the right hand side console. In the rear cockpit, if the normal layout pattern had been followed, the navigator's seat control would have been replaced by the command ejection selection lever, with the seat switch repositioned slightly to the rear on the lamps test panel.

Hohendorf continued to familiarise himself with the enhanced cockpit, liking especially the wide-angle holographic HUD.

Flacht had come up the ladder, and was peering in. "Well?" he began. "Do you like it?"

"Wolfgang," Hohendorf told him, "this is the airplane I've wanted for a long time. If it goes as well as it looks, I shall be a very happy man indeed. And to judge by the way I saw this one perform earlier, I think my prayers have been answered. And you? How is your seat?"

Flacht looked very happy. "I was in one down

the line and I stayed in so long, they had to throw me out . . ."

"We're ready now, sir!" someone called from below.

"And," Flacht continued, "it seems it's your turn for the boot now."

Hohendorf nodded, reluctant to leave. "You're right. We'd better get out of their way."

Flacht went back down the ladder while Hohendorf climbed out and followed him. The Chief Technician was waiting for them, a look of benign tolerance on his face.

"Well, gentlemen? Do you like what you've seen?"

"We like it very much, Chiefy," Hohendorf replied. "Very much," he repeated. "Thank you."

"We're here to please, sir. You fly 'em, we keep them healthy."

"I am sure you do." He extended his hand to the Chief.

After a brief hesitation, the Chief shook it, then saluted. "Thank you, sir."

Hohendorf returned the salute and followed by Flacht, left the shelter.

The Chief watched them depart. A corporal had come up to stand by him.

"Keen lot," the corporal remarked.

"Good bloke, that," the Chiefy said. Like all astute senior NCOs, his short comment spoke more volumes than any number of glowing reports in a confidential file.

A Tornado streaked low on full burner.

The corporal glanced at it. "Noisy sod," he said.

By early evening, all the expected crews had arrived and they filed into the main briefing hall, to be officially greeted by Jason. They watched as he stood on the dais, flanked by a seated, senior German and Italian officer.

"Welcome, gentlemen," he began, "to Scotland, and to November One . . ."

When it was all over, Selby took McCann to one side. "That was your voice, wasn't it, Elmer Lee? Someone's little joke with the Wingco about welcoming the increased power of the new ships. Someone said: 'We do, we do.' I thought it sounded rather like your dulcet tones."

"Yeah. That was me."

"A word of advice, old son. Never, never interrupt a British Wing Commander in mid-flow; even one who's a fighter jock. Bad for the health."

"He seems an OK guy."

"So does a tiger. Magnificent beast; but you wouldn't put your head in his mouth."

McCann grinned. "That's one way of looking at it."

Chapter

Three weeks later, Air Vice-Marshal Thurson flew his Tornado F.3 to November One in the late morning, on one of his unannounced visits.

"Well, Chris?" he began, entering Jason's office in flying overalls. "How goes it?"

It was the first knowledge Jason had of his arrival, having spent the better part of the morning in the air combat simulator section. He stood up quickly at Thurson's entry.

"It goes rather well, sir," he replied. "Conversion's progressing smoothly. Both actual flying and simulator work's at full chat."

"I can certainly vouch for the flying. My word. I had to wait for a landing slot. Who would have thought it, eh? A few months ago we were standing on a deserted airfield. Today, it's a regular Heathrow. Well done."

"Thank you, sir. Can I get you some coffee?"

"Actually tea, Chris, if you can wangle it."

"Tea it is. Please have a seat, sir."

"Thank you."

Jason pressed the intercom button on his desk as the Air Vice-Marshal sat down. "Sergeant Graham."

"Sir?" came a female voice.

"Rustle up some tea for the Air Vice-Marshal, will you, please?"

"Yes, sir."

As he cut transmission, he said to Thurson, "She should have warned me."

"I asked her not to. No need. And no need to stand on ceremony. Do sit down. She seemed a nice young girl. Loyal too. She definitely did not approve of my barging in on you like this, and showed it. I fancy my rank does not send her into fits of awe."

"If she was insubordinate—"

"Absolutely not. She has spirit. Leave her be. I'm certain she knows her limits. She probably thinks I'm checking up on you."

Jason let the matter rest. "And how are things in Whitehall?"

"We're still in good shape, but it's early days. Our detractors, if not in retreat, are keeping their heads down and waiting to fight another day. There's no talk at the moment of excessive defense spending. Their case is made rather more difficult by the fact that the treasuries of other nations are also involved. However . . ." The AVM's voice grew serious. ". . . any accidents, should they occur . . . will bring the wolves howling for blood."

"We're minimising the chances by putting in plenty of simulator work, both in the air combat and full-mission roles. The procedural sims are in full swing."

There was a discreet knock on the door.

"Come in, Sergeant," Jason called.

Small and very pretty with short, gleaming black hair, she came in with a full tray which she placed on a low table next to Thurson.

"I've made you some coffee, sir," she said to Jason.

He smiled at her. "Thank you."

"And thank you, Sergeant," Thurson said.

"Sir. Shall I pour?"

"No. That's quite all right. Let it stew for a bit."

She placed Jason's mug, which had a transfer of the NATO emblem on it, on the desk, and went out.

Thurson said: "Have any rising stars begun to show as yet?"

Jason nodded. "At first, there were the three pilots I expected: Hohendorf, Selby, and Bagni. Then the performance of one of the youngest, straight from the Hawk school with no Tornado experience, caught my eye. His name's Palmer. He's good, and will be better with time. For the navs, Ferris, Flacht, and McCann. Now there's a character." Jason chuckled. "If I were a policeman, I'd say he had a record as long as your arm."

Thurson began to pour his tea. "What nationality?"

"American."

"Oh well," Thurson commented, as if that explained everything. "Good, is he?"

"Brilliant, and absolutely aggressive when he's after a target. He's a failed pilot. I believe the Americans are glad to have him out of their hair."

"Hm. Keep an eye on him, just in case."

"I'm already doing so. Bit of a rebel, but gold in the back seat."

"Who's his best pilot?"

"There are two he seems most compatible with. Selby, who is a first-class fighter jock, and oddly enough, Palmer, our novice. They achieve good results. I think he respects Selby, and sees Palmer as a sort of younger brother. We shift them around to get the best possible mix. Hohendorf and Flacht are like cement. Selby works well either with McCann, or Ferris. Ferris is also good with Bagni, and Palmer. I think the primary crewings should be Selby-McCann, Hohendorf-Flacht, Ferris-Palmer. Ferris is more stable. Just right for Palmer."

"What about Bagni?"

"There's a nav from Italian Tornadoes, Tenente Spacio, who's converting very quickly and who'll make a good intercept man; but for some reason, his results with Bagni are less than perfect. I've teamed him with a US marine, and they seem to be getting on famously. Bagni and the second marine, who happens to be a back-seater formerly on Phantoms, are working rather well together. There's a moral there somewhere. The marine's called James Henry Stockman III, and is a captain. Father owns a Ferrari dealership on the West Coast. Perhaps that's it, even though Bagni owns some souped-up Fiat.

"There's an odd thing, however," Jason continued. "Hohendorf and Selby."

Thurson's eyes were alert. "What about them?"

"Nothing to cause worry . . . yet. They were on that Red Flag deployment together . . ."

"I saw the reports. They performed excellently."

Jason nodded. "Yes. Their results were very good indeed."

"Then what's the problem?"

"There's . . . an atmosphere between them. Oh they're civil to each other . . . no breach of conduct or anything so obvious; but there is something, an undercurrent that I cannot quite put my finger on."

"Does it affect the performance of their duties?"

"Absolutely not. Red Flag proved they cannot be faulted professionally."

"Then I believe you have no cause for anxiety. From what you've told me, we're dealing with two exceptionally skilled men serving in the same unit.

A competitive spirit between them is inevitable, perhaps to be welcomed. They're both good material. I've heard that Hohendorf would not have had any great difficulty in getting his own command back home in the near future, had we not deprived the Marineflieger of his services. Let's make good use of his talents." Thurson finished his tea. "And now, for some slightly irritating news which I thought I'd leave till the end."

"Ah," Jason said warily.

The Air Vice-Marshal gave his thinnest smile. "A few letters have reached me, about low-flying. Not a deluge . . . not even a trickle; but I felt you ought to know. It's not a problem. We're still in the honeymoon period, and are likely to remain there . . . provided no one disfigures himself and his aircraft on a mountain."

"We'll keep an eye on stray mountains."

Thurson looked at him speculatively. "Yes. Good. One other item."

Jason waited, knowing this would be more "irritating" news.

"Remember our chat some time ago about a VIP tour of the control room?" Thurson said mildly. "I can see by your expression you hoped I'd have forgotten."

"Not much chance of that, sir."

"None at all, Chris. I want you to send me a convenient date. You did say the summer, if I remember correctly."

There was nothing wrong with the AVM's memory, Jason thought ruefully.

"Yes, sir," he admitted.

"Good. I'll be arriving with a group of all-Party MPs, and local councillors. Let them see what we're up to . . . within reason. Let them feel involved. Get to meet them."

"Do I have to?"

"If you wanted an easy life," Thurson remarked, at his most dry, "this was the worst possible career to choose, and certainly not this project."

"I'm obviously a glutton for punishment."

Thurson stood up. "Well, glutton, take me around your little operation and show me how it's getting on. We'll start with the air combat simulator."

"By the way, sir," Jason said as he too stood up, "we're organising November One's first Summer Ball . . ."

"I'm invited, of course."

"Naturally, sir."

"Good. In addition to my wife, I'd like to bring an extra guest. All on the same card."

"Of course, sir. I'll see the invitation's altered. May I know who—"

"Antonia. My daughter."

"Antonia? Last time I saw her she was only a child."

Thurson laughed. "She may have seemed like that to you, Chris, but she must have been at least sixteen. Anyway, she's a young woman of twenty-one now. Time passes, you know."

"Don't remind me, sir."

"It's all right for you, man. Still in the first flush of youth, feller like you. Don't read too much into this, but you ought to take a look at her—if you can get past the young tigers, of course. She creates havoc wherever she goes, these days. Fact is, her mother and I reckon she could do with a steadying hand." He glanced at his watch. "Well, come along now, Wing-Commander. We mustn't keep your simulator bods waiting."

He strode away. Still rendered speechless, Jason followed him.

Jason paused by the hatch in the entrance corridor to the vast simulator building. The corporal behind the grille looked at him. Thurson waited patiently to one side.

Jason showed his pass. "The Air Vice-Marshal is coming in with me."

The NCO peered round to check, looked at Thurson uncertainly before saying: "Very good, sir." He pressed a hidden button and the double doors blocking the exceptionally clean corridor swung open.

As they went through, Thurson said: "He checked me out first, despite the rank. I like that. Take nothing for granted. I must tell Jacko Inglis I like the way you two seem to be running things."

"Let's hope you continue to, sir."

"That depends, Chris."

"On what, sir?"

Thurson had moved on ahead. "On how happy you keep me."

The Wing Commander gave his superior officer's words some thought. There were things he wasn't being told. He looked up. "Left here, sir, for the air combat section."

Their rubber-soled shoes whispered on the highly polished floor as they walked. Presently, they came upon the large doors that led to the air combat section and entered. Here, the floor was covered with standard-issue hard-wearing synthetic material.

They had entered the computer room with its high banks of machines, and a large curving console stacked with display units and controls. A wide window beyond the console showed three huge domes in a hangar-sized room. Unseen within each dome was a perfectly reproduced cockpit of the particular aircraft being "flown." Modular design enabled several different aircraft to be simulated, by simply altering the internal configuration. Currently, the cockpits were all of Super Tornadoes.

In the computer room were two instructors—one pilot, one navigator—civilian technicians, and a small group of pilots and navigators. All turned to look as Jason and Thurson entered, the military men coming loosely to attention as the Air Vice-Marshal entered. The low hum of powerful machinery formed a constant background noise.

"Please, gentlemen," Thurson said to them. "No ceremony. In here, we're all jocks and navs."

They relaxed. Thurson went across to the pilot instructor whose screen showed the images of two aircraft clearly locked in combat.

"Who's up?" he asked.

The instructor, a Flight Lieutenant, said: "Palmer, sir. He's matched against Selby."

"Is he? And how is he doing?"

The instructor turned down the corners of his mouth. "Having a hard time of it, I'm afraid, sir. But to be fair, he is up against a pretty tough opponent. Selby's very good. Selby's red aircraft, Palmer blue."

On the screen, one of the aircraft had just fired a missile. A hit.

"Oh dear," the instructor said. "Another Fox Two on Palmer." That meant a short-range missile hit. "That's his third. But he'll improve. He's done better than any other green student, all things considered. People like Hohendorf, Selby, and Bagni have taken to the system like ducks to water, but many of the other students need time to adjust. We've even had a few people get air sick on us. Palmer, however, is very keen to mix it. Ah! Good maneuver. He's twisted nicely out of the way of that missile. Good use of infrared jamming and flares. He'll be all right, sir."

"I don't doubt it," Thurson remarked. "Can we hear what's being said?"

"Certainly, sir."

The instructor flipped a switch and immediately the sounds of aircraft in flight, plus inter-ship communications, came up on the computer room speakers.

In the "blue" cockpit, Palmer craned his neck backwards as he looked upwards through the bubble canopy at the computer-generated sky. The blue of the sky and the ground features beneath were so well simulated that he had no difficulty in suspending disbelief. As far as he was concerned, he was in real combat, and felt chastened by the way Selby continually managed to keep out of gun and missile parameters, while still being able to nail him so efficiently. Good thing this was a simulation. He'd have been dead long since otherwise.

He turned his head this way and that, hunting the speck that could grow in frightening milliseconds into the adversary aircraft. The radar told him where it should be, but by the time he'd manoeuvred, it was somewhere else. Selby was bloody ferocious, and was making no allowances for his lack of experience.

Despite being at the receiving end, he accepted the conditions. Better to learn this way, than in the terminal manner of a real conflict.

Christ, he thought grimly as he hauled the

stick towards him and his G-suit inflated, squeezing at him. Where is he?

Everything was realistic; even the sounds of the engines came through on the phones in his helmet. There were clouds up here also, and low-lying ones below. Every weather condition, and all times of day could be simulated. At the moment, he was in the cockpit alone, and conditions were a bright, still day, while aircraft configuration was half internal fuel, but a full weapon load. God knew what it would be like with a full war load, his back-seater in the office, and night conditions. And all that before he flew the aircraft for real.

Sod it! Where are you?

He banked sharply right. The cockpit had a limited six-axis motion capability, but with this to provide the brain with an initial motion cue and the visual images reproducing whatever change of direction was demanded at any given time, it was easy to feel you were hurtling swiftly through the air; that you were standing your aircraft on its wing tip, trying to get a missile lock on the maddeningly difficult-to-acquire blip that danced about you, itself trying to get into the vulnerable cone behind your tail, your six. Despite having all-aspect missiles that made head shots possible, a pilot still preferred attacking the six. Your opponent couldn't shoot back. A head-to-head could be suicidal if you got things wrong.

In the first instance, a head-to-head shot was your best bet, provided you could keep the engagement at long distance. But the difference between healthy long distance and a distinctly risky close-in knife fight could sometimes be measured in seconds. He who sees first wins . . .

So where was Selby?

Palmer pulled the stick, slammed the throttles open and went into a steep climb. He brought the throttles back, kept pulling on the stick. Inverted now, the nose began curving tightly towards the scenery below. The Gs mounted and the barest of tremors went through the stick, indicating that the stall was approaching, though the systems would not actually allow it to happen. Assuming they were all on-line the Super Tornado's own control systems would in real life prevent mishandling.

A slight graying at the edges of the computer visuals warned Palmer that the same maneuver in a real situation would have brought him to the edge of a potential G-induced blackout. A severe condition would be G-loc, or G-induced loss of consciousness; a total, prolonged blackout that could sometimes prevent a pilot from regaining control of his aircraft before hitting something hard; or give a potential adversary the opportunity to nail an easy, non-maneuvering target.

Palmer eased up on the stick. The graying disappeared. He pulled on the stick again. There was Selby!

"I've got him!" Palmer heard himself shout.

The missile seeker had begun to give him the

tone. The seeker diamond was blinking, hunting round for the acquisition box; then both box and seeker disappeared.

"Oh shit!" Palmer said in frustration.

Almost immediately, he heard the ominous sound of Selby's own tone in his helmet.

He slammed the stick to the left while kicking right rudder. He centralised, slammed the stick the other way until he was again inverted, then pulled hard, reversing his direction. The tone died, but almost immediately came back.

"Jesus!" Palmer muttered, breaking hard to the right and pulling tightly into the turn. He broke lock again. Thank Christ for that, he thought feverishly. He realized he was sweating.

Now where was Selby this time?

Then the tone was back, insistent and deadly. There was a thump and a muted explosion, and the cockpit rocked.

"Fox two," he heard Selby say.

That was the fourth time he'd been nailed.

"Very impressive," Thurson said. He had watched the combat on one of the monitors and was now standing to one side with Jason, keeping out of the way of the students and instructors.

"Selby and Palmer?" Jason asked. "Or the equipment."

"All of it. Selby, Palmer, and the equipment."

"Poor old Palmer will be feeling a bit miffed. He was rather comprehensively bested."

"Yes, but as has recently been said, he'll improve. Besides, he did fight back rather aggressively. A good thing, don't you think?"

The doors to the domes had opened, and out of the red one came Selby. He waited for Palmer who came somewhat sheepishly out of the blue dome. They were both wearing full kit.

Selby gave Palmer a friendly pat on the shoulder and said something to him. Palmer returned a rueful grin.

Thurson said to the instructor: "Have Selby and Hohendorf been at it yet?"

"Oh yes, sir," the instructor answered. "They're our best customers. They've had four combats so far."

"And the outcome?"

The instructor grinned. "Inconclusive. Is there something I don't know? Are those two having a grudge match?"

"Good competitive spirit," Jason said, after a sideways glance at the Air Vice-Marshal.

"I see, sir," the instructor said warily. He wasn't going to argue with the Wing Commander.

"How do you rate them?"

"There's not much I can teach them about the basics of air fighting. Between us we're now working out tactics to counter those of all possible threat aircraft, mixing them with all sorts of weather and light conditions. Those two are very keen."

"As they should be," Thurson commented drily.

Selby and Palmer, who had gone into another room to remove their gear, now entered wearing their flying overalls. They saw the Air Vice-Marshal and Jason, and paused uncertainly.

Thurson went up to them. Jason followed.

"Good work," Thurson said, including them both.

Palmer said: "I'm afraid I was soundly thrashed, sir."

"He does have a certain advantage. He's been doing this job rather longer than you have. I thought you handled yourself well."

Palmer looked pleased. "Thank you, sir."

"Just bear in mind that a potential enemy will be in there, hoping to make dead meat of you before you can blink. The only answer . . . get him first. I've no doubt you can do it."

"Thank you, sir," Palmer said again.

The instructor had been waiting for a break in the conversation. Now he said to Palmer: "You can watch the reply. We'll freeze the action at certain manoeuvres to analyze it and see where there's room for improvement. When we've done that, we'll study the print-outs to check the launch parameters on your missile releases."

Palmer nodded. "If you'll excuse me, sir?" he
said to Thurson.

Thurson gave his permission. "Carry on, Richard."

"Sir." Palmer joined the instructor at the console.

Thurson turned to Selby. "Impressive work.
How do you find the new aircraft?"

"Everything I could wish for, sir. She's crisp, responsive, agile, unbelieveably powerful . . . Need I
go on?"

Thurson smiled. "I think you've convinced
me." He glanced at his watch. "Now I'd better leave
you to get on. Nice work, Flight Lieutenant."

He caught Jason's eye and together the two
men left the computer room. This was literally a flying visit—he had to be back in Whitehall by four.

Selby went over to the console to join the others. Palmer was examining his print-outs in disgust.
"Look at that." He began to read off the concertinaed
sheets that had come off the printer. "Conditions at
acquisition: 117.7 seconds, range 3000.3 meters, azi-
muth minus 0.2, elevation minus 0.2, angle off 72.1,
throttle 100 percent, missile status . . . my God . . .
mach number less than allowed minimum. I
launched three more—bad angle off, poor range,
track-while-scan a fat zero, missile crashed, missile
infrared signal lost and finally, this one: max flight
time exceeded." He flung the sheets down. "Hell—I
might as well give up."

"You're being hard on yourself, Richard," Selby said. "I've been told you've taken two other guys on and won each engagement. One was a fighter jock with operational experience. Can't sniff at that."

"Who said?"

"Tom Wells."

"My old instructor on Hawks?"

"That's right. One word of advice, though-- watch the Gs. Learn your body's limits. A zonked-out pilot's no good to man nor beast."

Palmer turned to the instructor, who nodded. "You came dangerously close, I'd say, on at least one occasion. Show's you're keen, but there is such a thing as being too keen . . . A good show, though, apart from that."

He fingered Selby's print-outs which the machine was now producing, and dismissed them. "No need to check you out, Flight Lieutenant."

"You say such nice things, Mike. Book me in for a session tomorrow."

"Anyone in particular you'd like to be matched against? Hohendorf, for instance?"

Selby thought about it. "Is he booked in?"

"Not yet, but I expect it can be arranged. Unless you'd like to try one with me."

"I'll take you on yet, Mike, but I'd like a two-crew session tomorrow if that can be arranged. Elmer Lee and me, versus any crew you fancy."

"All right. I'll see what I can do. What time?"

"First thing after breakfast."

The instructor grinned. "No trouble getting the slot. Let's hope there's a crew just as keen to take the early shift."

"I wouldn't let the Wingco hear you say that. This is a 24-hour unit."

"Really? I wish someone had told me. Now get out of here so I can teach these neophytes how to stay alive."

Selby gave an exaggerated bow. "To hear is to obey."

The Air Vice-Marshal had picked up his navigator from the Mess and together they were heading for their aircraft, accompanied by Jason and Group Captain Inglis, the Station Commander. Thurson had done an informal tour of the unit, met with and spoken to the crew—both air and ground—checked out the aircraft, visited the full mission simulator and finally, pronounced himself well satisfied.

The three of them stopped short of the waiting Tornado while the navigator went on ahead and climbed in.

Thurson said: "It all seems to be going very nicely. You've both done an excellent job. The financial wolves of Whitehall will be kept at bay. If they howl too loudly, I shall merely say . . . 1992 and all that." He rubbed his hands in a characteristic gesture. "There were a few noises when you asked for the outer perimeter fence, but I managed to convince them that paying for the double fence system was infinitely cheaper than the loss of an aircraft through sabotage. Of course," he went on, "if any of your jocks puts one into the drink or the mountains, that remark may well return to haunt me." His eyes fastened upon them. "I dislike being haunted."

Neither Jason, nor Inglis, said anything.

"Good," Thurson said. "I see that's gone home." He shook hands with each in turn.

They saluted as he turned to walk to his aircraft; then he paused.

"Do you recall the buzzing of our fighter aircraft last year by the Soviets during the Baltic and Norwegian Sea exercises?"

Jason and Inglis nodded. They remembered the incidents clearly; Jason in particular. He had been piloting one of the standard Tornado F.3s, and had been leading a pair on a long-distance combat air patrol, a dry run for future CAPs by the November squadron. A pair of Flankers had popped in for a look above the icy waters of the Norwegian sea. The Su-27s had come barrelling in on either side to split right and left into tight turns before coming back again.

The Tornadoes had held station, Jason watching the antics of the Flankers keenly, noting how they manoeuvred. It all went into his mental file. Finally, bored with the game, the Flankers had turned for home. Jason's detailed observations had since been programmed into the air combat simulator, giving the simulated threat aircraft the observed agility of the real thing. The pilot learning how to fight with his aircraft could then adjust his tactics accordingly. It all helped.

"Ah, yes," Thurson was now saying. "I forgot—you saw the buggers yourself, Chris. Well, there's a new item on the agenda. Word has it that an F-16 lookalike, the MiG-35, may be nearing production. As with these things, much of it is conjecture. No one has yet produced a photograph or if they have, they're not showing. MiG-35 may not even be its proper designation. But no matter. Do keep an eye out, won't you? Which reminds me—let's have the first November squadron declared operational soon."

"If progress is maintained at our present rate," Jason said, "I see no reason why Zero One Squadron should not be operational by the summer's end."

"Excellent. And now, Christopher, you won't forget that invitation, will you?" There was the suspicion of a twinkle in Thurson's eye.

"Er . . . no, sir. I won't."

"Jolly good. . . . Operational by the summer's end, eh? But a week or two before that if you're pushed, I expect. Wouldn't you agree?"

Not waiting for a reply Thurson went quickly to the Tornado, put his helmet down by the ladder and began his walk-round of the aircraft. Inglis said to Jason: "Did I miss something?"

"Such as?"

"The AVM seemed to be advising us to get a move on. I wonder why."

"The usual thing," Jason shrugged. "Something to tell some parliamentary sub-committee."

"No. Seemed a bit more important than that, I thought."

"Well, we're doing our damndest. I don't see—"

Jason stopped. The Air Vice-Marshal, walk-round complete, had paused by the ladder, helmet now trailing in his left hand. On the shoulder of the aircraft, an airman who had helped the navigator with his straps now waited. About the Tornado, other members of the ground crew waited expectantly.

Thurson gave a brief nod, climbed the ladder and eased himself into the aircraft. The airman helped with the straps, then climbed down, moving the ladder away.

Jason and Inglis took a few steps farther back as the engines were started. They waited as Thurson went through further checks, then saluted as the aircraft began to roll. Thurson brought a hand to his helmet briefly in acknowledgment. The canopy closed, and the Tornado began taxiing to its take-off point.

"I wonder if he's bringing his daughter to the Ball." Inglis's offhand remark was almost overwhelmed by the engine noise. "Exceptionally pretty girl. I've seen her."

"Lucky you," Jason said, eyes firmly on the departing aircraft.

Chapter

11

Neil Ferris had made a friend since coming to
November One: Caroline Hamilton-Jones from
Fighter Control. A woman who was extremely wary
of attachments to fellow members of the RAF and
aircrew in particular, she had surprised herself by
finding she liked the company of the unassuming
Ferris. He was not as she had at first expected, be-
lieving all the myths associated with male Austral-
ians.

Though they'd been out together a few times,
usually to visit isolated highland villages, never once
had he made an obvious pass at her. But he was
clearly fond of her, and now, as they stood together
in the sun outside the squadron buildings, idly
watching Thurson's Tornado take-off with its full
burner climb, she decided she had grown to like him
very much.

"The old man comes here so often," Ferris said,

"I think he'd love to be back on an operational squadron."

"Can't be much fun down in Whitehall, I suppose," she said, "trying to keep the accountants and God knows who else happy. Apparently a lot of people want to close us down. Russia's put everyone in a tizzy with its new moves, and he knows he has to face a groundswell of opinion, not just in Whitehall, but in the NATO countries too."

Ferris nodded. "You like the old boy, don't you?"

"He's not bad."

"Not bad." Ferris repeated the words drily. "I guess I'll have to take that as an example of English understatement."

The Tornado had now disappeared into the bright sky. A pair of ASVs swept low over the main runway to break snappily into the landing pattern.

"Looks like Hohendorf and Bagni are back," Ferris said, following the aircraft with thoughtful eyes. "Hohendorf's incredible. There's a little wager going, on who's best of the lot: him or Selby."

"So who's your favorite?"

Ferris grinned. "When it's so close, I don't gamble."

Caroline closed her eyes, and turned her face up to the sun. "Mm. This weather's wonderful. I came here for a while during the winter, and there were days when we had some pretty wild storms. Come winter, don't go into the drink, will you?"

"I have no intention of going into the drink at any time."

"Oh good." She had turned away from the sun and was again looking at him. "So what are they really like up there?"

"Selby and Hohendorf? Like twins, sometimes. Then at other times they can be so different. Selby seems to have more passion. I can watch them carrying out combat manoeuvres and tell you who's who, just from their style. It's not that Hohendorf has no passion. He's just better at controlling it. He flies with the precision of a surgeon; beautiful, fluid moves. Lightning reflexes. A real professional."

They strolled away across the grass. Caroline decided to change the subject.

"Looking forward to the Ball?"

"Too right," he said. "With luck, the first squadron will be fully operational by then so we'll have something really worth celebrating. That McCann's planning a little spectacular—so he says. He won't let me in on it, but I think he's told Richard . . ."

"Who, of course, is not telling."

"Exactly. McCann's a bad influence on that boy . . . especially now that young Richard is supposed to be sweet on that nice little WAAF who looks after the Wingco."

Caroline looked amused. "The US Air Force couldn't handle McCann. What chance have we got in Fighter Control?"

They walked on. Suddenly, Ferris was serious. "And what about you?"

"He's tried." She gave him a sideways glance.

"The little drongo. I'll break his neck. No, honestly—he can play with any other woman on the station, except you."

"You don't own me, you know," she told him.

"I don't want to."

"And I'm not saying that, just because we've been out a few times, there's anything more in it at the moment. I've got a career that means a lot to me."

"Do you hear me making demands?"

She smiled gently. "No. You're not." She glanced at her watch. "Time for me to go down the Hole." The "Hole" was the name given by all November One personnel to the underground Fighter Control Center, which was linked to the entire Alliance air defense net. "If you're not on tonight's flying roster, perhaps we can have a drink in the Mess."

"You're on. Well, I guess I'd better get up the tower. The boss seems to think it's a good idea for the crews to spend some time with the poor souls, so that we can appreciate the hard time we give them."

"Good thing too, and second only to your coming to see us down in Control." She reached out and held his hand briefly. "See you later."

"You will," he said.

He watched as she went to her car, a little yellow Volkswagen Beetle. The air-cooled engine stuttered into life, and she waved at him as she drove off.

He stood looking at the little car until it was curving along the perimeter track, at the far end of the airfield.

Hohendorf and Flacht had completed their debrief and had left for the kitting room to remove their flying gear. Bagni and Stockmann were still finishing their reports.

Down to their flying overalls, the two Germans headed for the squadron coffee bar. As yet, only three crews were on strength: Hohendorf and Flacht, Selby and McCann, and Bagni and Stockmann. The remainder, who would make up the eventual complement of twenty, were still in training with the conversion unit. Palmer and Ferris, however, were the next crew due to come on strength. Palmer's progress had been rapid and it would only be a matter of days before he became a properly accredited member of Zero One Squadron.

In the bar, Flacht dropped into a chair and stretched his arms. "I've been thinking about the Ball, Axel."

"What about it?"

"You need a woman." Flacht, as with all married personnel, was now housed in family accommodation. Though the November One Mess was more cheerful than the Schleswig Mess, he still felt Hohendorf needed the friendly atmosphere of a home and had invited him over twice since their arrival.

Hohendorf went behind the counter to pour coffee from the filter machine into two mugs. He brought the coffee over, sat down, handed a mug to Flacht. "Don't worry about my love life, Wolfie. I've got enough on my mind with the new ship. And what's more, you don't need me too often at your house. You need time with Ilse and the baby."

"She likes having you around. You know that. Besides, it's good having another face from home. She gets on with the other wives, of course; but you're part of the old squadron. It's important to her."

"I'll visit with you, as long as that's the real reason and not because you think you ought to hold my hand. There are many things for me to do here, and many people in the Mess to talk to. There is so much to learn about our new airplane, the day is not long enough. I have to force myself to make time to go to the gym."

Flacht was reluctant to leave it. "We all have the same work-load, Axel. We all have to keep fit. It doesn't mean we can't relax as well."

"Stop it," Hohendorf said, almost sharply. "My social life is fine. I promise to let you know when I see a woman to excite me."

Flacht shook his head slowly, giving up. "You're hopeless."

Hohendorf remained silent for some moments.

"I appreciate your concern, Wolfie," he said in a quiet voice. "But there isn't a problem. You've got enough to do in the back seat, and looking after your family. You don't have to look after me down here as well."

Flacht drank his coffee. "Anne-Marie could at least have answered your letters."

"They weren't exactly love letters; just general news. Anyway, how do you know?"

"Erika wrote to Ilse. She had called Anne-Marie to ask if she had heard from you. Anne-Marie said yes. You know your cousin. She wanted to know if Anne-Marie had replied. Anne-Marie said she hadn't found the time yet. I'm sorry, Axel."

"What for? What goes on between Anne-Marie and myself is not your fault. And as for that cousin of mine, Erika keeps hoping this sick marriage will get better."

"And you?"

Hohendorf's eyes seemed to lose emotion. "It's dead, Wolfie. I know that, and Anne-Marie knows that. I'd be relieved if she divorced me tomorrow. But she won't. She wants a fall-back position."

He reached for a newspaper lying on a nearby table: it was a *Frankfurter Zeitung* left by one of the other German-speaking aircrew. The conversation was closed.

In the Mess, Selby was on the phone to Kim Mannon.

"Thanks for calling, Mark." There was more

than a touch of sarcasm in her voice. They hadn't seen much of each other during the last couple of months. "I was beginning to wonder whether you were a mirage, or something."

"I did warn you it would be a busy time," he said.

"Yes, love, but I need to see you. Well? When are you coming down? Look . . . why don't I come up instead?" she went on, not waiting for a reply. "We could meet in Edinburgh. Daddy has got that house I've told you about . . ."

"Which is used by your father and his executives during business trips."

"And for family social events, which this will be. It is a family home, you know . . . not a company building. No one will be in residence for the next two weeks. There's a couple who look after it, the Boyds, but they don't live in. We'll be quite by ourselves. How about it?"

"If you had given me a chance to speak, I'd have told you that I've got four days' leave . . ."

She gave a little squeal of delight. "Oh Mark, that's super! When?"

"Next Tuesday. I've got the weekend too, so that gives us six days . . ."

"Hooray! I'll call the Boyds as soon as we've finished, to warn them."

"There's more."

"I am being spoilt."

Selby grinned at the phone. Look at me, he

thought, like a silly kid with his first girlfriend.
Knowing he would be seeing her soon excited him
and he wished he could be with her at that moment.

"We're having a Summer Ball." He gave her
the date. "I'd like you to come."

"Is this open to negotiation?"

"No."

"Then I'll come."

"You could just have said yes."

"I like putting up a fight. It keeps you on your
toes."

"You're impossible."

"That's why you love me. And you know I love
you," she added softly, then hung up before he could
react.

He had been about to leave the booth when he
paused, and called his sister in Aberdeen. The university had begun its summer break, but she had remained to carry out some research.

"Mark," she said. "This is a nice surprise.
You're lucky to have caught me."

"Oh?"

"I'm off on a short coastal trip for a week. Field
work. I've got a passage on a small fishing boat."

"Just you?"

"No. There'll be three of us. Anyway, to what
do I owe this call?"

"I'm repaying a debt."

"What debt?"

"A Summer Ball for a Winter Ball."

"If I remember correctly, you didn't particularly like that little event."

"Something good came out of it."

"Oh you poor, smitten man."

"Wait till it happens to you," Selby told her. "Which reminds me—I've got you a nice escort."

"Safe, you mean."

"His name's Richard Palmer. A good bloke. He'll look after you."

"As I said . . . safe."

"Do you want to come, or not?" He gave her the details.

"Of course I'll come. But don't expect me to fall in love with this Richard Palmer, just because you chose him. Does he know, by the way?"

"Not yet. I had to find out whether you'd come. And no one's asking you to *do* anything. He's just the escort. If you like him, fine. If you don't, fine. Anyway, the poor devil needs a break. I keep shooting him down in mortal air combat."

"I see. I'm the consolation prize."

"Don't be ridiculous, Mo. You'll enjoy the Ball. Besides, I'd really like you to come. It's a rather special event."

"Why don't you do what we've always done? Escort me yourself. Ah," she went on. "Daylight dawns. You're escorting Kim Mannon."

"Yes." He sounded almost sheepish.

"Why didn't you tell me that in the first place?"

"Well . . ."

"Oh Mark. You are in a bad way." She laughed. "All right, I'll come to your special occasion, but don't expect me to stick to your downtrodden friend all evening."

"He's not downtrodden."

"In that case, of course I'll come."

"Good. I'm sure you'll have a good time."

"I'd better," she warned.

Whitehall, London, a day later.

Charles Buntline entered the minister's office.

"No need to ask whether matters are proceeding according to plan, Charles," the minister greeted him drily. "You look like a cat who's been at the cream."

"Good morning, Minister. Kind of you to spare me some time."

"Cut the flannel, Charles. I'm as keen as you are to see this thing work in our favor. We've got a few minutes before the Air Vice-Marshal arrives. I take it you've heard from your man, Stolybin?"

Buntline nodded. "No problems there. All that remains is for us to have an escort crew ready in time."

"And the tanker?"

"The tanker's the least of our problems, Minister. The modifications to the starboard drogue have already been carried out. No one has been told why, naturally."

"You are quite certain this aircraft . . . this

Krivak . . . will be able to make contact with its probe for the refuelling?"

"Stolybin had precise information. The drogue was modified accordingly."

"I see." The minister looked uncertain. "Double agents always give me the shivers . . ."

"I've kept a close eye on him. As far as I am concerned, he's only as good as his last piece of information."

"A wise precaution. Does he trust you as much?"

Buntline said, "We both know we'd dump the other if the going got rough."

"And they say chivalry's dead." Muted voices came to them. "That must be the Air Vice-Marshal. He'll be able to give us an up-date on the escort."

Thurson was shown in.

"Air Vice-Marshal. . . ." The minister shook hands warmly. "You know Charles Buntline, of course. Good of you to come."

Thurson nodded curtly at Buntline, who contrived to be looking out of the window, down at Horse Guards Parade.

"Please take a seat, Robert," the minister said, the first name putting Thurson immediately on his guard. "No need to beat about the bush. We all know why we're here. How are the crews shaping?"

"They're doing very well, Minister. The selection process clearly works. Those already posted to the squadron are excellent crew material, and those on the operational conversion unit are beginning to show the same promise. We shall have a highly-skilled team on that first unit, just as Wing Commander Jason expected."

"That's very cheering news, Robert. We'll be needing two of those crews soon, I expect. And it couldn't be coming at a better time. Rumor has it the Opposition's girding its loins for an all-out attack on defense expenditure; and we're not without the waverers in our own ranks. So this mission of yours could be just what we all need."

Thurson noticed that the mission had suddenly become *his* mission. He didn't bother to protest. Certainly it was his head that would be first on the block if anything went wrong.

Richard Palmer was having a hard time. He was in the middle of the sort of situation any pilot would dread; but to a fast jet pilot, flying the Super Tornado with as much time on type as a gnat, this was the worst kind of emergency possible.

The weather was as nasty as only North European weather could be, a pitch black night, and the cloud base almost down to the deck. But that was only the least of his problems. A short while before, he had been settling nicely into the sortie when a caption on the far right column of the central warning panel lit up. Third down from the top, it said R REV: right engine revolutions.

Almost immediately, the rpm indicator for that

engine wound its way rapidly round the dial before whipping back to the stop. On the heels of that bad news, the caption to the left of the REV caption and one rank up, came on. R TBT, it said. Turbine bearing over-temperature.

Oh shit.

Palmer reacted swiftly. He shut down the affected engine. The left automatically built power to compensate, but he pushed the throttle to full afterburner. There was little trim change and he took the aircraft gently up from its altitude of 200 feet to one thousand. The caption lights went out.

In the back seat, Ferris had seen the repeat on his own warning panel.

"Are we in serious trouble?" he asked calmly.

"Nothing I can't handle," Palmer replied, surprised by the calmness of his own voice. "She's as smooth as silk. We're heading back. I'll make a gentle turn to two-one-zero."

"Two-one-zero," Ferris confirmed, unconsciously going through the motions of tightening his already tight harness.

"Don't worry, Neil," Palmer's voice said in his ear, "I'll get you down in one piece."

Ferris felt a quick rush of guilt. He knew Palmer had not been aware of his furtive movements. Any pilot would seek to reassure his backseater, even in the guise of a joke; but he still felt as if he'd been caught stealing biscuits.

"I have every confidence in you . . ."

"Uh oh," Palmer said quickly. "I have a wing-sweep malfunction. We're stuck at 45 degrees."

"Oh great." He put out a call to November One, reporting their condition.

Palmer looked about him. Nothing to see out there except the black night, and the glowing HUD. At least, there were no other aircraft in the vicinity, and no mountains to speak of; but there would still be plenty of high ground and the odd ruined castle to catch the unwary on the approach. He thought of the ruin he'd marked in his mind as a reference point. No use to him now, even if he could have seen it.

But the aircraft was handling beautifully. The good engine seemed to have ample power to keep the ship under control. He took it out of burner. There was plenty of fuel, but he wanted to see how she handled. The Tornado ASV remained fully controllable.

Then the warning panel gave him more bad news. Third column from the left, third caption from the bottom. The IN glowed.

"Oh shit," he said. "We've lost the Ins."

Ferris saw it on his own panel. The inertial navigation system was out. Shit indeed—how often would one be hit by such a serious second malfunction? It wasn't their lucky day. Ferris was immediately on to November One again, giving the current aircraft status.

"November Tower to Sparrowhawk," Palmer

heard in his helmet. "We recommend a GCA. Do you accept?"

A ground-controlled approach. Palmer decided he was not going to quarrel with that.

"Accepted," he replied. "Neil," he said to Ferris, "do you concur?"

"From where I'm sitting," Ferris began, "it sounds like a very good idea. Let's get back down. The night is mean."

Palmer thought his breathing was sounding inordinately loud, and tried to calm it.

"What is your current engine state?" November Tower was asking.

"Eighty percent."

"Go to max dry re-heat and climb to 3000 feet. Maintain 310 knots."

Palmer moved the throttle to the stop before the combat position on the quadrant. The Super Tornado, even on its one engine, surged upwards as he obeyed the controller's instructions. He levelled off and throttled back. Speed came down, settled at 310 knots.

He peered through the gloom. Nothing. Not a light to be seen. The FLIR—the infrared system—in which mode, superimposed on the HUD, would have given him an almost day-like view of the world, had been the first casualty of the dead engine, going out almost simultaneously. He could have used it now; but there was little point in his wishing for something he could not have.

"Right, two-seven-five," the tower said.

"Two-seven-five," Palmer acknowledged.

"No one told you to descend. Maintain 3000."

Shit. He was allowing the aircraft to run away with him. He had lost 200 feet in the process. Suppose there had been high ground only a hundred feet below? Exit one aircraft and two crew members.

His body felt clammy and he had the bizarre sensation of wanting to wipe his palms, though he knew they were perfectly dry within his gloves.

"Sparrowhawk," a new voice was saying, "this is Peregrine." Tom Wells, his instructor. "You've flown single engine for months," Wells continued, referring to the single-engined Hawk. "Your aircraft is more agile and more powerful, but I have every confidence in you. You can do it."

"Left, one-eight-one," the tower said. "Descend to 1500 feet, 300 knots."

Palmer obeyed the instruction.

Ferris said: "You OK, Richard?"

"I'm fine. Don't worry."

"Who's worried? I'm enjoying the ride."

Some ride, Palmer thought, marvelling at Ferris's calm.

"Wheels down," the tower said.

Palmer complied. "Three greens," he reported with relief. At least, nothing had gone wrong with the hydraulics.

"You're on the glide path, on the centreline," tower said, as if announcing a cricket score. "Holding good. 250 knots. Remember you're at 45 degrees sweep."

Palmer eased the throttle back. At 45 degrees sweep, neither flaps nor slats should be deployed. It was going to be a nose-high, fast approach.

"Cables prepared for engagement," the tower informed him.

At each end of the runway a series of cables, rather like arrestor wires on an aircraft carrier, were built into its surface. Should the aircraft miss the cable, there was still the arrestor net, after which was the final line, the rough gravelly overshoot. Palmer hoped it would not come to that. If you're into the gravel, you're in real trouble.

"One thousand feet, 210 knots," the tower said. "You're on the glidepath, on the centreline. You should be seeing the runway lights any moment now."

And there they were. Dear God, they were beautiful.

"All yours," the tower said.

"Thank you, November Tower."

Palmer held the nose high at 14 degrees alpha, with 190 knots on the HUD and slowing rapidly. The LERXes were giving good aero-dynamic braking. Airbrakes and wing spoilers were out. He flared to 16 degrees alpha as the wheels thumped down. He brought the throttle to idle, keeping the nose high, letting the wings and LERXes do the braking for as long as possible. There would be no thrust reversers to help him. At last, the nose settled down and he moved the stick forward to keep it there.

He tapped the brakes. They worked, but speed was still high. He lowered the arrestor hook. The warning light came on to confirm. He heard a noise that might have been the hook screeching on the runway surface. He kept braking. Oh for thrust reverse! But it was no go on a single engine. Now, he stopped braking as the cable approached. Braking while the cable jerked the aircraft backwards would result in a tip over.

He felt the hook catch, jerking them to a halt before dragging them sharply backwards. At last, the aircraft came to a safe halt.

There were a few moments of silence as Palmer rapidly shut down all systems.

Ferris said, mildly: "Looks as if we might make a pilot of you yet, Richard."

Palmer did not trust himself to speak. His knees were shaking but, oddly, his hands were rock steady.

"You know a good thing when you see it," Palmer said, at last trusting himself to speak. He was pleased to find that his voice was also steady.

Then he reached for, and pulled the canopy release handle.

Light flooded in as the blanked-out bubble of the canopy came open like a giant clam. Tom Wells was grinning down at him from a platform. They were in the full-mission simulator complex. On one level Palmer knew he must have been aware of this. Why then were his knees still shaking?

Wells came down from the platform and onto the walkway that surrounded the cockpit module as Palmer and Ferris began to unstrap themselves.

"The chances of all these emergencies occurring at once during a single mission," he began, "are remote . . . we hope. But we thought we'd throw them at you to see how you'd handle it. And while they may not occur in peacetime, wartime conditions might easily interfere with proper maintenance." Wells looked at Ferris. "Well, Neil? What do you think?"

"He's not a bad little pilot." Ferris grinned. "I think I could put up with going on squadron strength with him."

Wells said to Palmer: "Well done, lad."

You don't know the half of it, Palmer thought as he eased himself out of the front cockpit, praying his legs would not betray him. It had been so real! The motion, the bumps through the dark and unseen cloud layer; even the Tornado's control system's constant ride adjustment had been faithfully simulated. The passage through the clouds had thus been far smoother than it would have been in any other aircraft.

He found, gratefully, that his legs were quite steady.

Wells clapped him on the shoulder. "You've come a long way, Richard. You can be pleased with yourself. And now for that drink you promised to buy me."

Palmer checked. "What drink was that, sir?"

"What I like about you, Richard, is your unbounded generosity."

Palmer gave in. "I'll buy you a drink, sir."

The Zero One Squadron work-up continued. More crews were sent on by the OCU and it began to look as if Wing Commander Jason would indeed have his first fully operational squadron by the end of the summer.

Selby returned from his Edinburgh vacation with Kim Mannon looking so haggard that McCann loudly recommended a month's high-protein diet. As was his wont, he chose his moment when three of the female office staff were within earshot.

Bagni was given leave and he flew off to Florence to see his Bianca, and to invite her to the ball. She declined, saying she would be in New York on business. Bagni returned, knowing he was now in serious danger of losing her.

Ferris and Caroline Hamilton-Jones continued to grow closer to each other, while still telling themselves it was not happening.

Hohendorf heard nothing from Anne-Marie, but the news from Schleswig gave him no cause for alarm. More and more, his anxieties about Willi Beuren receded as he channelled all his energies into his mastery of the Super Tornado.

For Jason, everything was going smoothly. Thurson had not yet carried out his threat to bring his gaggle of VIPs, and Jason counted every day that he did not get warning of their arrival as a blessing. Meanwhile, everyone was looking forward to the Ball.

The gate policemen watched as the battered VW van came up the road and stopped close to the entrance. They made no move towards it, waiting in their booth to see what would happen next.

First, a young woman climbed out of the driving seat, turned and a small child was handed to her by someone unseen within. The policemen watched, intrigued. Suddenly, other people began to spill out until there were ten of them standing near the vehicle; five men and five women, plus the child. They were shabbily dressed, mainly in jeans that were seriously the worse for wear. Some wore headbands.

They began hauling placards from the van, and what looked suspiciously like bundled-up tents. A man put something on his shoulder: a video camera.

The policemen decided enough was enough. One of them reached for the telephone. The other went out to the group.

"I'm sorry, ladies and gentlemen," he began. "You cannot camp here. And definitely no cameras allowed. Sir, please remove your camera and ask your friends to return to your minibus and leave."

"Why should we?" the woman with the child asked. "We're on a public road."

The child, a little girl of about three, stared at the big service policeman with the unabashed gaze that only one so young could muster.

"Wrong, madam," the policeman said patiently. "This is Ministry of Defense property. The road over there is a public highway. Once you turn off it, you're on MoD land. I'm sorry, but you'll all have to leave and sir, please don't use that camera."

The cameraman was not prepared to back down. "Why not? If you're worried about my taking film of your airplanes, I can do that while they're flying anyway."

"You may do whatever you like, sir . . . but from the public road."

The placards were displayed now. One read: DON'T FRY OUR CHILDREN! Another: NO TO NUCLEAR WEAPONS.

Just then, Wing Commander Jason arrived driving the station commander's car and skidded to a halt behind the booth. The sergeant inside came crisply to attention.

Jason opened the car door. "What the devil's going on out there, Sarn't Williams?"

"They just arrived, sir. Corporal Neve's attending to them." Williams unbent slightly. "He don't seem to be having much luck."

Jason came forward to see for himself. It had taken the protesters a while to find the camp, but it was inevitable that they would eventually find their way here. The problem now was to prevent them becoming a permanent fixture.

He watched the corporal's unsuccessful attempts to reason with the group. As a precaution, Sergeant Williams was on the phone again, calling up men from the guardroom to be ready to go to the corporal's aid if necessary.

Jason stepped past the barrier. Corporal Neve saw him, broke off his argument, saluted.

"Sir, these people—"

Jason stopped him with a brief movement of one hand, and continued past him towards the protest group. An immediate silence fell. The camera focused on him.

Corporal Neve strode forward. "I told you not to use that camera."

"Corporal Neve," Jason said gently. "I'll handle this."

Neve came to a halt. Jason went up to the woman with the child. Before she could react he held out his hands. "May I?" He took off his cap and showed it to the little girl.

The woman eyed him uncertainly.

"I'm certainly not going to . . . er, fry her," he said, referring to one of the placards.

The camera remained fixed upon him.

The child made up her own mind. Fascinated by Jason's uniform, she began to squirm in her mother's arms. Too surprised to do anything else, the woman handed her over. The child immediately took the cap and put it on. It slid to one side, tilting on her tiny head, but it didn't fall off.

"She likes pilots," Jason said.

The woman glared at him. "Your nuclear weapons will destroy her. Or perhaps her children. And her children's children."

"We have no nuclear weapons here," Jason told her. "This is an air superiority station. We're here to prevent nuclear weapons ever being used."

"We expected you to say that," someone behind the woman shouted contemptuously. "It's what your bosses program you to say."

"Nobody's programmed me to say anything. I am not a computer. I've told you the truth. Our job here is to see that this little girl, and indeed the whole world, lives in peace. Our job is to prevent war happening."

"Do you have children?" the woman asked.

"Not yet," he replied. "But if your little girl were mine, I'd be proud to think I'd done something in my life to make it more probable that she'd reach a happy old age. Corny though this may sound to you, I—"

"I don't think it's corny." The woman looked at him for a long moment. The child showed no inclination to leave him. "You really meant that, didn't you?"

"This is too important a matter for lying."

"That's not like a politician."

"I'm not a politician. But it just doesn't make sense to me, people protesting against something that's designed to keep them safe. This is not a nuclear base. You've come to the wrong place. It's as simple as that."

The others had fallen silent during the exchange.

Now the disbelieving one said, "You're not going to swallow that bullshit, are you, Lisa?"

"I believe him," she said.

"Christ almighty," came the voice in disgust. "You're a pushover. He plays around with the child and you turn into jelly. Of course he's a bloody politician. All these servicemen are. And that's the oldest trick in the book."

"I believe him," Lisa repeated.

"I give you my word," Jason said to her. "No nuclear weapons. Ever. We're fighters."

The child lay her head on Jason's shoulder, and stared at her mother.

"Come on, Tiffy," Lisa told her. "Time to go." Reluctantly the child went back to her. "Children see things better than we do." She returned Jason's cap and he put it on. "Tiffy doesn't normally go to people."

"I'm flattered," Jason said. "Goodbye, Tiffy."

" 'Bye."

Jason straightened his cap and raised one hand to Lisa in an informal salute. "Thank you for listening." He turned and went behind the barrier.

Neve followed for a few steps. "I think you should know, sir, that man was filming you all the time you—"

"Leave him, Corporal Neve."

"Sir."

Uncertainly, Corporal Neve turned to face the protesters, planted his feet apart, and clasped his hands behind his back.

"You're not really leaving, are you, Lisa?" one of the men asked.

"Yes, Baz—I am."

"But for fuck's sake—"

"This is Ministry of Defense land and that officer could have turned his bully boys loose on us. Dogs, the whole production. But he didn't. Instead he came out to talk. He didn't have to."

"Don't be so wet. He just wants us out of the way."

"You're being very stupid," Lisa said. "I'm going home. You can please yourselves."

"Pull yourself together, Lisa. He's just another PR man."

Lisa shook her head. "No. I could see his eyes and he was genuine. He knew we had come all this way for nothing. What idiot gave us the information about this being a nuclear base?"

"Well . . ."

"You, Baz. That's who. Tell whoever gave you the information to . . . Oh what's the use. Let's get the gear packed up."

* * *

Neve watched as the van turned round and went back the way it had come. The Wing Commander knew his stuff. Neve was glad he would not have to cope with a bunch of crazy women camping outside the station perimeter. If it meant the Wingco had to mess around with that woman's baby, it was worth it.

He looked at the departing van with contempt. Bloody trouble-makers.

Later that evening, Jason received a call in the Mess. Thurson was at the other end.

"Have you seen this evening's news?" Thurson's voice was brusque.

"No, sir."

"Perhaps you'd better not. An HS 125 CC will be flying up to the station in the morning. It's coming for you. Put on your best uniform and be on it. I'll meet you at Northolt."

"Sir, may I know . . ."

"Wing Commanders do not give unofficial press conferences."

"I gave no . . ."

"Watch the news. Better still, don't. I'll see you in the morning. I've already spoken to Group Captain Inglis." Thurson hung up.

Jason replaced the phone slowly. Group Captain Inglis. Not Jacko Inglis. Trouble . . . and bad enough to get him summoned to London. What press conference was Thurson talking about?

"I didn't give any bloody press conference," Jason said aloud.

Then he remembered the people outside the November One gate, and the man with the camera. He did not regret what he had done.

But he had not expected it to become television news.

The twin-engined military version of the BAe executive jet landed at November One at 0700. Jason, who like a man condemned had risen early and had eaten a good breakfast, was ready to go. By 0730, the 125 was again in the air and heading south.

At 0900, it landed at Northolt on the outskirts of London and a few minutes later Jason was on his way to town in the back of the official car, accompanied by Thurson. Thurson was in a funereally sombre single-breasted suit.

Their meeting had been reasonably cordial, Thurson having the look of a man who had much to say, but was biding his time. Nothing about November One was discussed in the car, but Thurson silently handed Jason a copy of a national newspaper. On the front page was a photograph of Jason with the little girl in his arms. The picture showed her playing with the RAF cap on her head. He thought it was not a bad picture. It caught the intense expression on the little girl's face as she peered out from under the cap's brim.

Thurson noted his reaction. "It's a nice hat. It goes with a nice uniform. I just hope our masters let you keep it."

Which brought the silence down until Whitehall.

In Thurson's simple office in one of the solid buildings along the wide thoroughfare, the Air Vice-Marshal said: "Sit down, Christopher." He glanced at the clock on the wall. "We've got five minutes. Suppose you tell me what the devil you thought you were up to."

"May I speak frankly, sir?"

"You might as well. The nation heard you last night, and probably the world by now. Did you look at the news?"

"No, sir."

"What it is to be wise," Thurson said. It did not sound like a compliment.

"I said what I did to prevent a small problem from becoming a much larger one. I had no idea the man with the camera was a television reporter."

"He wasn't, but with the sell-anything mania that's about these days, he quickly found someone with a chequebook."

"I don't think we've come off too badly," Jason said. "After all, if we'd done nothing, or if the service police had been used to move them, that camera would be recording very different scenes by now.

More cameras and more people would have arrived, and we would probably be faced with a permanent camp on our doorstep."

Thurson digested this, and looked at his subordinate thoughtfully. "For a man who dislikes politicians, you appear to know how to wield their weapons."

"I never said I didn't like politicians."

"Not on TV you didn't. For which we can be profoundly grateful, because you'll certainly be meeting some of them now. Enemies. You and I are about to visit an inquisition chamber. Therein are some of the very people I've invited to visit November One. You do remember, don't you?"

"Yes, sir. I do."

"Good. In addition to the Honorable Members, there'll be a gentleman from the Ministry. He'll no doubt have some pertinent questions to put to you."

"I take it, sir, I'm on my own?"

Thurson stared at him. "What gave you that idea?"

"Judging by the nature of your call last night . . ."

"The ministerial secretary was literally at my elbow as I spoke to you. I had to let him see I was on top of things, if you get my drift."

"And today?"

"I fought for the November project, Christopher, because I believe in it. I'm not about to abandon it because a bunch of the unwashed are looking for another issue to protest about."

Jason would not have called the people at the gate unwashed, but he let Thurson have his say.

"If, however, your words get you into more trouble with your audience today," the Air Vice-Marshal continued, "you're going to have to bail yourself out. I'll help where I can, but I can only do so much." Thurson sighed. "My God, Chris. What possessed you?"

"The need for survival, sir."

"Survival, Wing Commander?" The gentleman from the Ministry turned out to be a lady. She had caught the Air Vice-Marshal on the hop, but Jason was not displeased. "Whose survival?" the lady from the Ministry added.

Jason felt he knew exactly what to say. "The child's, ma'am. And every other child's."

"I see. I suppose you feel this laudable sentiment gives you the right to make dubious pronouncements upon matters affecting the defense of this nation."

"I was not making such a pronouncement, ma'am."

"Let me get this correctly. Are you telling me you did not say . . . and I quote . . . 'I give you my word. No nuclear weapons. Ever.' Unquote. I've seen the video, Wing Commander."

The room, oak-paneled with deeply upholstered

leather furniture, was generous in size; but to Jason, it felt claustrophobic. A long table was at its center, at which were seated several MPs and senior service-men, plus the ministerial lady. Jason sat before them on an upright chair. To one side, out of the line of fire, was the Air Vice-Marshal.

"I spoke the truth," Jason told them. "I said 'We're fighters.' Which is correct—we do not carry nuclear weapons, ma'am. I saw nothing wrong in ad-mitting it. If anything, it helps that any potential enemy knows what he may be up against. It should make him think twice—"

"Wing Commander," an MP interrupted. Jim Beresford was a man who saw himself as a man of the people, and played the part to the hilt, stressing his regional accent. "Are you trying to tell us your words would make a . . . 'potential enemy' afraid of your expensive new toys?"

"With respect, sir, they are not toys. They are indeed expensive, but they are lethal weapons. The crews who fly them are dedicated, highly-trained men who chose to do a potentially dangerous job in defense of what they hold dear. They are not kids playing with toys. If their existence prevents any hostile force from breaching our airspace, then they will have proved their worth. If they can further, by their very presence, prevent the *possibility* of a hos-tile incursion being considered by others, then an even greater success will have been achieved. The fact that my men may enjoy what they do does not detract from their high value. I would have no one in my squadron who was not committed to the task. We are, sir, very aware indeed of the costs involved and we make sure we give good value."

The man of the people sat back: "By God, Wing Commander, you're sure of yourself, aren't you?"

"I'm paid to be, sir."

Thurson closed his eyes briefly, but said nothing.

Unaccountably, Beresford looked less hostile. "I'm a politician, Wing Commander. I'd have expected a man like you to be scared stiff of politicians."

"I respect all of you," Jason said, "but I am not frightened of you. No."

"You should be. We could make recommendations to have you dismissed from the service."

"Then sir, you would destroy my career, but you would not change the situation. The requirement to effectively defend our airspace would remain. Getting rid of me won't make it easier."

"But keeping you on will."

"It just might, sir."

"Modest with it too."

The Air Vice-Marshal, observing the verbal battle from his corner, permitted himself the briefest of smiles.

Beresford said: "This might surprise you, Wing Commander, but, even if I may not always agree with him, I like a man who sticks to his principles.

I don't want this country's enemies dropping bombs on me either. That's why I'm coming up to that base of yours. See how you're spending our money."

"Yes, sir."

"Why did you pick up that child?" This from the ministerial lady.

"A positive image, ma'am. It was the very last thing they expected. My intention was to get rid of a potential trouble spot. I also happen to like children. I get on well with them."

"Yes. The child did seem to take to you. The protective warrior."

"She liked my funny hat, ma'am."

The lady from the Ministry actually smiled. "Do us all a favour, Wing Commander. No more press conferences. Please."

"It is my intention to keep well away from the press."

"Very good. That's all, Wing Commander. Thank you for coming."

Jason stood up. "Thank you, ma'am. Gentlemen."

Three hours east of GMT, in a small room that had been electronically swept for listening devices, two men sat watching their own video recording of the protest incident. One of them was the handsome young KGB major Stolybin had pointed out to Charles Buntline in Washington earlier that year.

The recording ended and the major's companion, a grey, stony-faced civilian in an ill-fitting double-breasted suit, leaned forward and switched off the machine.

"That was good work, Comrade Major. Admittedly groups like that are always vulnerable to misinformation. Still, you fed them the nuclear weapons nonsense very neatly."

Praise, from such a source, was rare. The major looked down modestly. "I'm afraid it hasn't really got us anywhere. That Wing Commander's very shrewd."

The plan had been for a permanent protest camp to be established, even if only for a few days, which would have been a good cover for the group's freelance cameraman, who would then have been able to record the movements of the aircraft from close quarters.

The major pointed at the now-blank screen. "More than shrewd—extremely determined. According to that news item he's been working for the establishment of his fully integrated unit for years. And what with the advent of glasnost and the British people's hope for defense cuts, he's been having a difficult time of it."

The senior man frowned. "It is *we* who are having the difficult time, Comrade Major. I must remind you that defense cuts are no longer a Western monopoly. If the man has his way, we'll soon be defending our homeland with pea-shooters. Apart from anything else, he should realize what this does to service morale. There's slackness everywhere. Thank God for friend Stolybin. If, as seems likely, this Wing Commander's unit provides the welcoming committee for the traitor Kukarev's defection, at least we'll be ready for them."

"Stolybin's no fool." The major lit a cigarette, grimacing at its harshness after the ones he'd been used to in Washington. "All we have to do is down Kukarev . . . That way the Wing Commander will lose what little backing he's got, we get rid of a traitor too decorated and famous to touch in any other way, we prove that the West, while pretending to welcome glasnost, still works to corrupt our people, and we send a message to the 'elected Deputies' that we so-called hardliners have been right all along."

His companion nodded. "And what about our man on the spot? I trust he realizes how vital his job is."

"Zitkin? He keeps the reports coming. An ambitious man. He'll let us know the moment there's any movement. For now, Kukarev's simply biding his time and checking up on future aircraft deployments in his area."

"He wants to know what the opposition will be if he's discovered when he makes his break." The senior man fanned cigarette smoke irritably out of his eyes. "He's in for a nasty surprise . . . Do you imagine," he went on, "that the British pilots will present much of a problem?"

The major shrugged dismissively. "I doubt it. They're very new to their aircraft."

"Even so, I wish we could have got someone in there. I'd feel safer with an on-the-ground opinion."

A failure was implied. "I did my best," the major protested. "The screening was incredible—even the most junior non-flying staff were rigorously vetted. I nearly got a civilian cook through, but they dug up some old photograph of him outside one of our Baltic submarine bases fifteen years ago. Deep files."

"Almost as deep as ours." At last, the older man allowed himself a smile. "Did Kukarev really think we had forgotten the father, just because the son went to Afghanistan and covered himself with glory? Like father, like son, Comrade Major. Just a few words from his old friend Stolybin, and he fell. Not all the medals in the world will help him now."

The major drew uneasily on the last of his cigarette. For himself, like Comrade Zitkin, he was an ambitious man, doing his duty as well as he knew how. But the civilian by his side was fired by something more, a hatred that was painful to see.

Two days later Thurson was summoned again into the minister's presence.

"Word has come from Buntline," the minister told him. "Apparently the closing stages of the operation are fast approaching. You will of course be given ample warning of the exact date of the defection. A combat air patrol exercise will be mounted to include a specific area off Norway's North Cape, well within November Squadron's usual sphere of operations. A dummy patrol or two before the event would not go amiss, I feel. Have you selected the crews yet?"

Thurson shook his head. "That has to be up to Wing Commander Jason, Minister. He knows his men far better than I ever could. In any case, I would not care to make the selection—and when I ask *him* to I shall certainly tell him exactly why he may be ordering four of his best men into a possibly fatal encounter."

"If they're as good as everybody claims, they won't get into trouble. In fact, what better way to demonstrate the usefulness of the November project?"

Demonstrate. . . . Usefulness. . . . Thurston held his peace. It was almost as if the minister wanted the project to fail. Its probationary period seemed to be never-ending.

"Use your discretion," the minister was saying. "Choose your time to tell Jason, and then only as much as is necessary for him to mount a well-planned patrol. Now—about the briefing for the crews themselves . . ." He paused deliberately.

After a while, Thurson said reluctantly, "Perhaps it's better that we don't tell them."

The minister nodded. "Good. Good."

"Nobody wants a Korean airline-type incident," Thurson went on, feeling as if he was committing an act of betrayal of the November crews, "nor even skirmishes like those in the Gulf of Sirte. If it's kept low-pitch, with nobody keyed-up, there's much less chance of someone squeezing off a missile too soon. Also, I—"

"I'm glad you agree with me," the minister interrupted. "I'm absolutely convinced that we're doing the right thing in keeping this to ourselves. We should leave as little to chance as possible. All men are capable of mistakes, no matter how good they may be. As you've already pointed out, there are many instances of errors being made, even by the most professional crews. I seem to remember some Americans shooting down a perfectly innocent—"

Thurson decided on an interruption of his own. "The rights and wrongs of that one were never fully established, sir."

The minister flashed him an irritated glance. "Exactly. That's just what I mean—there's always uncertainty . . . Anyway," he went on in a voice that had acquired a sudden coolness, "this operation will test the November crews' mettle. And if they come through, you'll have been amply vindicated."

"Wing Commander Jason will be," the Air Vice-Marshal said with fierce loyalty. "And if they do not come through?"

The minister did not reply.

Chapter

The Ball.

The last Saturday in August dawned brightly, heralding a clear-skied, hot day. A gentle breeze came off the Firth to keep the promised high temperatures within pleasant levels. Thurson arrived to declare Zero One Squadron operational, and this was marked by a full squadron fly-past of twenty aircraft. Their combined shadows fell heavily across the airfield. It was an impressive moment.

The highlight of the day was a stirring air combat display between Hohendorf and Selby. They kept this within the bounds of the station, showing to the full the astounding agility and power of the Super Tornado, and the consensus of opinion, from the hardened instructors to the youngest of ground personnel, declared the fight an honorable draw. Neither pilot had managed to achieve a single kill solution. When they landed, Selby and Hohendorf shook hands, but there was still that indefinable distance between them. Perhaps it was as Thurson had said. They were the top males of the tribe and would always circle around each other warily.

To Jason, their prowess meant he had a pair of formidable hunters on his squadron, and that was good news.

Though the Air Vice-Marshal had arrived with his family—who were guests of the Station Commander—Jason had not yet seen Antonia Thurson. That pleasure awaited him at the Ball.

As the day drew to a successful close, the excitement built. Any free Mess accommodation had been booked solid to cater for the influx of guests, and many married officers had opened their homes to others. Senior diplomats from the USA, West Germany and Italy, who had also come for the occasion, were housed within special accommodation on the station.

Nico Bagni found to his great and pleasant surprise that Bianca Mazzarini had after all postponed her New York trip to come to the Ball. Wolfgang Flacht offered his spare room, which was accepted.

Kim Mannon booked into a hotel on the cliffs above the nearby fishing village, telling Selby she had plans for him later that evening which would be inhibited if she stayed with any of his squadron colleagues. Morven booked into the same hotel. In due course Palmer and Selby arrived in Selby's car to collect them.

Kim Mannon had chosen to wear a black outfit that clung and was just the right side of decorum. While Selby complimented her, Palmer was admiring Morven, who in her own way rivalled Kim Mannon's maturer beauty. She wore a white, off-the-shoulder gown that showed off her youth and innocent grace to perfection. Palmer was staring at her with something akin to awe.

"Right, gentlemen," Kim Mannon said. "When you two have finished ogling, there's a ball we'd like to go to."

For Jason, the evening had begun with something of a shock. During the period before going into dinner, someone had said at his elbow: "Hullo, Uncle Chris."

His "niece" was indeed no longer a gawky, cropped-haired teenager. Antonia Thurson now had rich abundance of dark hair that had been gathered in a loose bunch that ended in a single, central plait. A sapphire-encrusted bow was pinned to it. Violet eyes smiled at him, and two faint spots of color stained her smooth cheeks. Dressed in silvery-gray raw silk, her slim body, at five foot six, brought the top of her head just beneath his nose. The scent of her was intoxicating.

In the confusion in his mind, Jason found himself irrelevantly thinking that she did not look at all like her father; then he regained control of himself and saw the Air Vice-Marshal and his wife standing not far away. Antonia, Jason now saw, looked like her mother, but had Thurson's directness of gaze.

"Miss Thurson," Jason greeted formally.

"Don't be silly, Uncle Chris. I'm still Antonia." The direct gaze held his.

He cleared his throat. "I'll call you Antonia, if you cut out 'uncle.' It makes me feel as old as . . . well old."

"As of this moment, it's history." She put her arm in his. "I think Daddy wants a word."

They went up to Thurson and his wife.

"Hullo, Christopher," Thurson's wife greeted. "You're looking well. I see Antonia's monopolised you already . . . but then she always did."

"You look a little shell-shocked, actually," Thurson put in. "I told you she'd grown."

"The younger pilots will go slightly crazy, sir."

"Yes. They well might, but I'm certain they'll be kept in check. After all, isn't that what Wing Commanders are for? And," Thurson went on before Jason could say anything. "I think I ought to tell you today's show was most impressive. Feather in your cap. That air combat display did more than anything to underpin the purpose of this project. The aircraft could not have had a better platform upon which to show off their capabilities. I've heard murmurs coming from our NATO partners too. It's all good news."

*   *   *

The dinner, too, went off smoothly, the men resplen-
dent in the multi-national designs of their Mess
Dress, the ladies bright jewels among the throng.

Two areas had been reserved for dancing. One
was for ballroom music, the other for disco. Protocol
insisted that the disco would not commence until
midnight.

Dancing was now in full swing, and Jason
found himself on the sidelines, watching. Antonia
was hard put to accommodate all those who wanted
to dance with her, as were Kim and Morven. There
were a lot of single aircrew about.

Jason had gone round the floor once with the
Air Vice-Marshal's wife, and with Mrs. Jacko Inglis.
That had been his lot. He had not asked Antonia to
dance, but at every possible opportunity she had
glanced at him from across her current dancing partner's shoulder. No sooner had the dance ended, however, than another eager young officer would come
forward.

McCann had managed to steal three dances to
everybody else's one—except with Kim: after two
tries Selby's scowl appeared to have warned him off.

Someone drifted over to stand next to Jason. It
was Axel Hohendorf.

"Not dancing?" Jason asked.

Hohendorf said: "The competition is too good.
What about you, sir?" He studied the crowd with benign interest.

"I'm using the same lame excuse." Jason

cleared his throat. "You and Selby were very good up there today. I'm proud of you both."

"Thank you, sir."

Jason looked about him in satisfaction. "I'm proud of the whole squadron."

On the far side of the dance floor Morven, Kim and Selby were grouped together, having a rest.

Morven said: "Mark, I've been wanting to ask you all evening. Who's that dishy man with your boss?"

Selby looked round. "That's Axel Hohendorf. Axel von, actually—he's a count, or a baron, or something."

"I don't care about titles. He looks wonderful in that Mess kit."

Selby stared at her. "You're never interested in him."

She met his gaze, conscious of the tone of disapproval. "Why not? Has he got three heads?"

"What about young Palmer?"

"What about him?"

"Hey, you two," Kim interrupted in soft warning. "No family rows. Anyway, Mark, why shouldn't she be interested in him? I pride myself on knowing a good thing when I see it." She narrowed her eyes. "Baron Hohendorf looks like a good thing to me. Let Morven cast if she wants to."

"For a start," Selby said, "he's married."

"Then where's his wife?" Kim demanded. "This is one of the biggest events in his career and she's not here? What more could she say? Short of sending him a pissoffgram—"

"Kim! For God's sake!" The worried whisper came from Selby.

"As I was about to say, short of doing that, her message could not be clearer."

"There *is* supposed to be a problem," Selby admitted grudgingly.

"Well then. Off you go, Morven. Ensnare the handsome baron." Kim held on to Selby's arm tightly. "Leave her be, Mark. She's a big girl now. You don't have to hover protectively about her all the time."

The bandleader announced a Ladies' Excuse Me.

"There," she went on, "Morven can justifiably ask him to dance. And if you sulk, I'll go and ask McCann. Where is he, by the way?"

Selby glanced at his watch. "It's nearly midnight. I think he's gone off with some of the guys. He's planned something, but God only knows what. Palmer's gone too. He's involved in it somewhere."

Selby found his eyes drawn to where Morven had gone as the music began.

"May I have this dance?"

Hohendorf looked down at her, bowed stiffly. "Of course. My pleasure." He turned to Jason. "Please excuse me, sir."

"Enjoy yourself," Jason said, and watched good-naturedly as they moved away.

Antonia touched his sleeve.

"Don't think you're escaping, hiding out here."

He was instantly overwhelmed by her flushed cheeks, the brightness of her eyes. He shifted awkwardly. "I'm a terrible dancer . . ."

"Good God," a voice close behind him said loudly. "Look at that, my dear. A bold fighter pilot reduced to a shrivel by a slip of a girl."

Jason turned to see a well-mellowed Air Vice-Marshal eyeing him with obvious amusement.

"Well?" Thurson continued. "Are you going to dance, man? Or has someone nailed your feet to the floor?"

"I'm . . . I'm going to dance, sir."

"Jolly good. Off you go. Don't be too hard on him, Antonia. He may be a bit fragile."

She smiled at Jason as they moved to the dance floor. "Are you fragile, Chris?"

I may well be before this evening's over, Jason thought.

"That depends," he said rashly.

"On what?"

He looked round wildly for an acceptable answer. "On what McCann's planned. He seems to have disappeared."

"McCann. Is that the American who kept asking me to dance?"

"The one and only. Thank God."

"He seemed harmless enough."

"Harmless." Jason welcomed the diversion. "He's an excellent navigator, but harmless he most certainly isn't."

"Anyway," she said, "I don't want to talk about McCann."

After a while, he said: "There are plenty of other pilots wanting to dance with you. You don't need an old man . . ."

"Old man! Don't be so silly." The band was playing a waltz and she moved in closer. "And don't be so stiff. This is a waltz, not a march. I didn't want to dance with them. I wanted to dance with you."

Jason cleared his throat. For God's sake, he told himself, this is ridiculous.

"Antonia . . ." he began.

"What's wrong?"

"Wrong? Er . . . nothing . . ." he said after an agonised silence.

"Well then. That settles it."

"Settles what?"

"I'll dance with you for the rest of the night."

Nico Bagni and Bianca Mazzarini were holding each other close.

"I'm so glad you came," he said to her.

"I'm glad I came, too. I was unkind, Nico, and I'm sorry. I suppose I felt jealous of your airplanes." She glanced about the room. "There are many beautiful women here. I think perhaps I shall visit you more often."

"They cannot take your place," he told her.

She leaned even closer. "Nico," she whispered, "may one kiss in this place?"

"Not in here, but I am certain I can find somewhere."

"Then take me there."

"We must wait until the important guests leave, especially the Air Vice-Marshal. They'll go when the disco starts."

"Oh Nico," she said. "I want to make such love to you tonight."

His silence was eloquent.

The waltz came to a halt and as if on cue, a sudden explosion of electronic sound filled the room.

Disco time. But not quite. Into the room filed twelve figures whose attire brought shrieks of astonished laughter. On each head was a helmet with the visor down, its oxygen tubing fixed to a shoulder. On each lower body was a bright orange G-suit, pressure tube hanging from the left hip and held in the left hand. The lead figure had a big ghetto blaster on its shoulder and Madonna was belting out "Open your heart."

To the insistent beat of the music, the figures circled the room, hips bumping and grinding, pressure tubes twirling.

One two three-four *bump,* one two three-four

grind. One two three-four *twirl,* one two three-four *turn.* And so it went, round the room.

Jason stared at the spectacle, his heart sinking. "Oh my God," he murmured. *"McCann."*

He glanced worriedly to where the Air Vice-Marshal had been in conversation with an American diplomat. Conversation was now impossible. The American seemed bemused, but was smiling. Thurson had disappeared.

Suddenly Jason felt a tap on his shoulder. He turned. The Air Vice-Marshal had come up behind him. Oh God, Jason thought. One unorthodoxy too many. There it all goes, down the tube.

But Thurson was smiling. "Time we were leaving," he bellowed over the music. "The rest of the night now belongs to your young warriors."

"Very well, sir." Jason moved slightly away from Antonia.

"No need to accompany us out. Antonia's staying."

"She is?"

"Of course, man. The night's hardly begun. I expect you to escort my daughter home by . . . shall we say . . . six in the morning?"

"It will be daylight by then, sir . . ."

"Yes. It will, won't it? Sorry I can't keep up with you young chaps. Look after him, won't you, Antonia."

"I will," she said.

"Have fun, Christopher. Do you good."

Thurson left unobtrusively with his wife. Behind him, the ballroom was erupting into uproar as the helmeted figures began dancing with anyone they could grab.

"Come on, Chris," Antonia urged. "You heard what Daddy said."

"Oh no," he demurred.

"Oh yes," she said firmly, grabbing him by the arm and steering him towards the noise.

Jacko Inglis went by with his wife, to accompany the Air Vice-Marshal back to the Station Commander's quarters. Jason gave him a look of helplessness as he was dragged into the gyrating throng.

By three o'clock most of the older guests had fled and the younger crews, inevitably led by McCann, were in control of the proceedings. The twelve spacemen had got rid of their helmets, but had retained their G-suits.

Ferris and Caroline Hamilton-Jones had spent much of the evening together. Feeling quite relaxed with each other, they were sitting out the current spate of disco dancing which had spread into the main ballroom.

Ferris said: "How about that stunt of McCann's? Where could he have got twelve Marineflieger *orange* G-suits from? We use olive green. And as for the boss's face when they first came in! I swear, for one second he really wanted to strangle old Elmer Lee."

"I don't believe he's thinking of Elmer Lee at the moment," Caroline said.

Ferris followed her gaze. Wing Commander Jason and Antonia Thurson were deep in conversation, her head close to his in a shadowy corner of the ballroom.

"The Wing Commander gets the AVM's daughter," Ferris remarked. "Never thought the old bludger had it in him."

"Old? He's only thirty-five."

"Yeah, but she's just a kid."

"Kid my foot. You're looking at a woman who's made up her mind about the man she's going to land."

"She told you that, did she?"

Caroline, with the wisdom of centuries to support her, said: "You men are sometimes so hopeless."

Morven was dancing with Hohendorf and from across the room Selby watched, trying to disguise the disapproval he felt. As Kim had said, she was a big girl now.

Noting his gaze, Hohendorf said: "Your brother is not so happy that we've spent so much of the evening together."

"Oh don't worry about Mark. He always worries about men who come near me."

"I can understand that. I have told you about Johann and Erika."

She nodded. "The navigator who married your cousin."

"So you see, I know how he feels. He is right to worry about you. It is natural that he would want to protect you." Hohendorf paused. "You are also," he went on, "very beautiful."

She gave a little smile of pleasure. "It took you all evening to say that."

"But I have been thinking it. I thought it the moment I first saw you. When I saw you arrive with Palmer, I never imagined we would even have danced together. In the beginning, I almost wished I had not come."

"Why?"

"What you have no knowledge of, you cannot desire." He looked at her, as if again seeing her for the first time. "I think I am saying too much."

"No," she told him softly. "You're not."

At four o'clock, Antonia said to Jason: "It's time I took you home."

"Took *me* home? I thought I was supposed to be the one doing the escorting around here."

"Yes, but I think I'm wearing you out."

"You most certainly are not."

"Oh good."

What am I *doing?* Jason thought as he returned to the dance floor.

*   *   *

By five, those still mobile were eating a buffet break-fast. Nico and Bianca had long since departed with the Flachts, and Selby and Kim Mannon were out in the entrance hall, preparing to leave. Morven came out to them and announced that Hohendorf would be escorting her back to the hotel. Transport had been laid on, to avoid the need for the men to drive their guests back. Few were in a fit state to drive.

Selby said with quiet ferocity: "He's *what?* And what about Palmer? You're supposed to leave with the escort you came with. That's the decent thing."

Morven was not to be deflected. "I've already asked Richard and he's quite agreeable . . ."

"Agreeable? What do you expect the poor sod to say? You present him with a fait accompli . . ."

"Listen! Will you? Richard doesn't mind." She spoke slowly, emphasizing each word. "You don't know what he's told me. It's very sad, really."

"All right. What did he tell you?" Selby's voice had all the tones of someone who was not about to be convinced.

"Richard, whom I happen to think is a pleasant sort of person, would much rather have brought someone else here tonight."

"Then why didn't he tell me?"

"He didn't bother. The ridiculously old-fashioned traditions of the Service wouldn't have let him."

"Nonsense. What are you talking about?"

"She's a sergeant, Mark. And that makes her the wrong sort for your Mess. I think it's silly. . . . Gail Graham, he said her name was."

"Good God. That's the boss's secretary. Sergeants have their own Mess. . . ."

"There you are . . . but it's not fair. But Richard doesn't seem to mind. He says she's applied for a commission and has a good chance of getting it. So don't make a fuss, Mark. Don't jeopardize her chances." She saw her brother's eyes focus on something across the hall. She turned and saw Hohendorf approaching. "Well, Mark?" she went on quickly. "We're going now, OK?"

"I suppose so," he answered reluctantly.

Just before six, Antonia said: "Time for Cinderella to go home. I've had a lovely time." She gave him her most enchanting smile.

In the light of the new day streaming through the windows, he considered her the most beautiful woman he'd ever seen.

But she's only a child, he told himself. "Thank you for being so patient with my dancing," he said.

"Rubbish. You've got some good disco moves."

He smiled. "Is that what you call my efforts? Wing Commanders don't have good disco moves. They make fools of themselves if they try."

"That's not what I think."

Jason knew he wasn't going to win the argument. He didn't want to. "I'd better get you home."

The Station Commander's car, complete with driver, was waiting for them outside the Mess. The driver got out and saluted.

"Group Captain Inglis said I was to wait for Miss Thurson and yourself, sir," he announced.

"Thank you. Have you been waiting long?"

"Since 0400, sir."

"My God, man. Someone should have told me."

The driver waited as a pair of Super Tornadoes hurled themselves into the morning sky. November One did not sleep. Throughout the night, two of the OCU aircraft had been on quick reaction alert.

As the quiet of the morning returned, the driver said: "I was fine, sir. I was told not to disturb you."

"Were you indeed. Have you had anything to eat?"

"Oh yes, sir. Plenty. One of the lads brought me . . ." the driver stopped, not certain whether he should say more.

"Good," Jason said, saving his embarrassment. "Thank you for waiting. The Station Commander's quarters, please."

"Sir."

When they reached their destination Antonia gave Jason a gentle kiss on the corner of his mouth before they climbed out. The driver looked firmly to the front.

Jason held the door open for her, then followed to the porch.

She stopped, turned, and kissed him again, this time lightly on the lips. "It was all very wonderful. I . . . I hope you'll find the time to see me again soon."

Before he could say anything to that she turned again, and went quickly inside.

He went slowly back to the car, then paused in the act of getting in. He shut the door, and went up to the driver. "I'll walk back."

The driver was surprised. "Bit of a walk, sir."

"Don't you think I can handle it?"

"You've had a long night, sir."

Jason stared at the airman's ID tag. "Rigby."

"Yes, sir."

"Think the Wing Commander's drunk, do you?"

"Oh no, sir." Rigby had the expression of one who wished he'd kept his mouth shut.

"Good. Because I'm not. I want to walk, and I want to think."

"Yes, sir."

"Goodbye, Rigby."

"Goodbye, sir."

In the Mess, McCann was still going strong. He peered out of a window. "Goddammit! Who turned on the lights?"

"Been daylight a long time, Elmer Lee," another American voice said. "Go back to sleep."

In his orange G-suit, McCann was swaying to a continuing beat which, while now subdued, still came out of the disco room. He leaned against the window. Then he stopped swaying, body going tense like a pointer's.

"Hey, you guys. It's the boss, out on a morning walk."

People crowded to the window. They watched Jason's distant figure silently.

Then McCann said, with the air of someone who believed he had stumbled onto a big secret, "Hey, guys." He spoke the words slowly. "Maybe the boss is in love. He—"

"That's enough, McCann."

McCann turned to see Ferris. "Aw c'mon, Neil. I was just . . ."

"Can it."

Behind Ferris, stood Caroline. As Mess residents, they had nowhere else to go. Their home was where the noise was.

McCann took another look at the distant figure before nodding, as if to himself.

"Consider it closed." He looked at each of them in turn. "All right?"

"That's just fine."

"OK." McCann staggered away, found an unattended young woman. "Let me tell you what it feels like to be only a poor navigator," he began to her sadly.

Caroline watched him go into the disco room. "You can't help liking him."

"If you like itching powder," Ferris said, but without malice.

Hohendorf was in his room, listening to the faint sounds of music from downstairs. He had come back alone in the small coach that had been laid on as guest transport, but he would be seeing Morven again later in the day. He didn't know where her brother was, but he suspected that Selby had remained at the hotel with Miss Mannon.

He closed his eyes as he lay on his bed. He had been staring at the ceiling, wondering how best to deal with this latest caprice of Fate.

"Why, of all the men in the world," he said into the silence of the room, "did that man have to be your brother?"

He fell asleep, the image of her face in his mind. It was six-thirty, and his last conscious thought was of how much he had wanted to touch her bare shoulders.

At midday, there was a discreet knock on Morven's door. She was awake and already dressed in jeans and a soft blue, open-necked denim shirt.

"Come in," she called, securing her hair in a ponytail with an elastic band. She turned on the dressing table stool. "Oh."

"Expecting someone else?" Selby had entered.

"I thought it might be one of the hotel staff coming to tidy the room. What are you doing up? I didn't expect to hear from either of you till the day was practically over. Is Kim up and about as well?"

"No. She's sleeping like a log. I wanted to have a chat."

Selby was in his dress shirt, opened-necked, with cuffs undone, and which was loosely tucked into his dress trousers. His feet were bare.

"A chat? What about?" Morven asked. "As if I didn't know," she added to herself, turning back to the mirror and reaching for her eye shadow.

"I heard that. And yes, you do know what I mean. Are you meeting him? Is that why you're dressed to go out?"

"Yes, Mark," she replied with heavy patience. "I am seeing him. He'll be here in half an hour. We're going for a walk along to the old fishing harbor, then perhaps for a drive. It's a very flexible arrangement."

"Are you out of your mind, Morven? The man's married, for God's sake."

"Please don't raise your voice. I don't want the entire hotel to get the bulletin. Axel told me . . ."

"Axel told you what?"

"Axel told me," she repeated with calm precision, "all about his marriage, and what really happened."

"He did, did he? And he's as innocent as a lamb, I suppose."

Morven stopped what she was doing, and stared at her brother in the mirror.

"There are times, Mark," she began in a voice that had lost its warmth, "when you can be very mean. I know what happened to Axel's marriage. What his wife did to him is very sad. How he managed to fly properly after that is remarkable in itself. You've always told me how you've got to be aware all the time up there. No time for the luxury of a wandering mind. By rights, Axel should have made all sorts of mistakes. But he didn't. Now, he's got over it. He says his flying was never affected."

"He's a bloody good pilot," Selby admitted grudgingly. "I'll give him that. But that doesn't mean I'm going to stand by and watch him hurt my sister."

"He's not going to hurt me, Mark. My God, we're only going for a walk . . ."

"And a drive," he reminded her. "Then, afterwards?"

She swung round. "What do you mean?"

"I'm not . . ."

"Exactly what do you mean?" She saw him eye the swelling of her shirt front. "Mark," she warned, "don't let me get angry with you. I'll pretend I don't know what you're thinking at this moment."

"For Pete's sake, Mo . . ."

"Mark, if I want to sleep with him . . . I will. I don't interfere with your sex life. Grant me the same courtesy. We've always been straight with each other. Don't let's spoil it now."

"Look, I don't want . . ."

She tried conciliation. "I know you're trying to protect me. You've always done that. You've frightened a few boyfriends away too. But do you really believe that if I'd thought any of them had been worth it, I'd have let that happen? Have I ever given you cause to worry?"

"No. Not really."

She wanted a more positive answer. "No? Or not really?"

"No," he said quietly.

"Well then." She stood up. "I'm not going to give you anything to worry about. I like Axel. He's actually a very gentle man . . ."

"Not in the air, he bloody well isn't. He's an aggressive sod."

"Isn't that what a fighter pilot ought to be?" She leaned forward and closed one of the buttons of his shirt. "You men. So possessive. You should be glad it's Axel. If it had been McCann, he'd probably have made more than one try for my knickers by now."

"And I'd have throttled him, back-seater or no back-seater."

"Oh ho. As I said . . . possessive. You've got more than enough to keep you occupied with Kim on your hands. Don't add more. And you'd better get back before she wakes up."

Selby unconsciously glanced at the door. "Listen . . . the man's married to a woman who's got a whole bloody airline. He's not going to give that up—"

"Mark." Warningly.

"All right, all right. I'll leave it alone for now, but I'm not happy."

"I'll take note of that. And don't *worry*. Axel's so correct, it's bloody frustrating." She stooped to check her face in the mirror. "God. I look awful."

"You look stunning."

"You're a biased brother," she said. But she was pleased.

"Naturally." Selby kissed her on the cheek. "I'd better get back. Just be . . ."

"Don't say it."

He sighed, nodded slowly. "Fine. I won't."

As Selby left, she stood again to the mirror. "I know he's the one," she said to her reflection. "And it's not me you should be worrying about, brother mine."

They walked down the narrow, sloping lane to the harbor. Though the former fishing village now catered mainly for holidaymakers, there were not many people about that Sunday morning. Morven and Hohendorf came to the end of the lane, crossed the street that skirted the seawall, and wandered onto one of the small moles that formed a haven for small craft within. The firth was calm and the tide was partially out. The few boats were lying on their sides where the water had retreated to leave moist, slate-colored sand. They were tethered by long ropes to stubby concrete posts set into the mole, and at the edge of the street.

Morven sat down on the warm, embedded stones of the mole. Tufts of grass sprouted between the spaces.

"Did you have any trouble?" Hohendorf asked her.

He had arrived at the hotel up on the cliffs soon after her talk with Selby. He'd left the Porsche there. On the way down they had not spoken, enjoying the walk and each other's company.

"He came to my room," she now replied, not wishing to elaborate.

Hohendorf, in a lightweight suit and a white T-shirt sporting the head-on view of a Tornado at speed, looked out to sea.

"Your brother does not like me," he said, "and I cannot quite understand why."

"I don't think he dislikes you. He is wary."

"But why? What have I done to him?"

"For a start, you're as good as he is. He's always prided himself on his abilities as a fighter pilot. I suppose he doesn't want someone as good as he is on the same squadron."

"I am not sure that is all it is," Hohendorf said thoughtfully. "Of course we circle about each other like a pair of stags . . . but I think there is something else and I do not understand what it is. Perhaps Mark does not know himself. I wonder, for example, if he would help me if I got into trouble up there."

Morven tossed her head indignantly. "Of course he would. Mark's not the kind of person to leave *anyone* in trouble."

Hohendorf persisted. "Perhaps, my dear, I am not just *anyone*. . . ."

She swung round. "Would you help him?"

"Of course."

"And he would help you. You're both airmen, for God's sake."

A silence fell between them and though they were close to each other, they held their bodies warily apart.

Then Hohendorf, offering the olive branch, said: "It cannot help that he sees me with you, especially as he knows I am married."

"He thinks you will hurt me."

"I understand that. But how could I even consider hurting you? I would rather not see you again."

She hunched her shoulders. "Is that what you want? That we don't see each other anymore?"

"No," he said quietly. "It is not what I want."

She leaned against him, relieved, turning her head out to sea. "That's all right then."

After a moment's hesitation, he put an arm about her. "Last night, I wanted to kiss you."

"Why didn't you?"

"Well . . . I . . ."

She snuggled against him. "It's all right. You don't have to find an answer."

They stayed on the mole for a good hour, saying very little, enjoying the warmth of the sun and the closeness of their bodies. Visitors walked along the mole and came to stand behind them to look out to sea. Morven and Hohendorf took little notice, and the visitors went quietly on their way. The world about the girl and the tall young pilot had temporarily faded out of existence.

At last they stood up and, arms about each other's waists, walked back up the lane towards the hotel.

"I'm coming back next week," she began. "I've got to do some field work in and around the Spey Bay area. If you can manage a day or so off, why don't we meet?"

"I would like that," he said. "I have seen Speymouth from the air, of course. Where shall I meet you?"

"There's a little guest house on the road to Spey Bay. Not luxurious, but very cozy and run by a lovely family. I've stayed there before. We can leave the car and go for a real walk on the Speyside Way. A true nature trail, if you're feeling fit."

He smiled. "I'm feeling fit."

"Do you have a back pack?"

"Yes. I do plenty of walking near my home in the Teutoburger Wald."

"Oh well. This will be just a stroll to you."

"I have a feeling," he said, "that this stroll of yours will test me to the full."

"As if I'd do a thing like that." She pressed him closer. "I'll get lots of food and we can go up into the hills away from everyone. Why don't we drive to Spey Bay now so you can check the route? It's a nice day. We can have tea at the guest house."

"It is OK with me," he said. "Let's do it."

Later in the Mess, Hohendorf heard a knock upon his door.

"Komm."

Selby entered. Hohendorf watched him with expectant wariness. Selby came straight to the point.

"You know how I feel about my sister seeing you," he said.

"Yes. I do."

"I just want you to know you'll answer to me if you hurt her."

"I would feel the same way about my own sister, if I had one."

"Yes. Well." Selby was unsure of how to continue. It was not the reaction he had expected. "You are a married man, Hohendorf. How would you react to your sister going out with one?"

"I would not try to direct her life, although I would advise caution. But I would trust her to make her own decisions. Have you ordered her to stop seeing me?"

"Me? Order Morven? You must be joking."

"Then trust me. I will do nothing to hurt her."

"Your word as an officer and a gentleman?" Selby spoke the words almost as a joke, but the German took them very seriously.

"Yes," he said. "My word as an officer and a gentleman."

Chapter

The operational week began smoothly.

Flacht got his strike in first. He and Hohendorf were in flying overalls in the squadron coffee bar, and had recently landed from a high-level sweep to Iceland and back. They had been paired with Palmer and Ferris. Selby and McCann were up, accompanied by Bagni and Stockmann.

"Don't think I didn't notice what was going on," Flacht told him, "just because we left the Ball early. So when are you going to bring her over to us? Ilse would like to meet her properly."

"Hey, Wolfie. Hold it, hold it! I've been out with her once."

"And already you're looking the better for it. Working better too. There was an extra bite to your flying today."

"Nonsense."

"Nonsense, he says. I'm the one who has to sit

in the back. She's put some electricity into your blood. You were a robot before. Now, you're on fire. You've come alive again for the first time since Anne-Marie left. I wish Johann were here to see it."

"Ah," Hohendorf said, self-consciously dismissive. "I'll be seeing him and Erika soon. I'm taking some leave in two weeks. I'll be flying over to see them."

"You can tell the old reprobate when you see him I can navigate circles round him now."

"I can see he's really going to like hearing that," Hohendorf said drily.

Not wanting to delay any longer, Thurson brought his group of all-party MPs up to November One two days later. Among them was that "man of the people," Beresford, despite subtle efforts in London to keep him off the invitation list.

They were in Fighter Control when Jason joined them on his return from a sortie.

Beresford collared him immediately. "Well, Wing Commander," he announced, "I'm here."

"Yes, sir," Jason said, hoping his dismay did not show. When they had met for the first time down in London, Beresford had been surprisingly friendly. But up here he'd have his reputation as a back-bench firebrand to consider.

"Stop calling me, sir, lad. I'm not one of your superior officers. I'm Jim Beresford. Call me Mr. Beresford if you must, but I'd prefer Jim." He glanced round at the other MPs who were trying to look as if they understood what was being said to them by Flight Lieutenant Caroline Hamilton-Jones at one of the computer terminals. "Look at that lot. When they leave here, they'll have as much idea as a fart in a bucket."

Beresford was a sturdy man, roundish about the middle. He had the solid face of one who had worked manually in a hard profession. His eyes seemed watery and a little vague but, as Jason knew from experience, this impression could not be more wrong.

"I've had a good look round at the station," Beresford was saying. "I'm impressed. I know how much you've worked for it. If this place can do what you claim, it may turn out to have been a good idea."

"You're being cautious, Mr. Beresford."

"Jim, lad. Call me, Jim."

"Very well . . . Jim."

"And I'll call you Chris. Right . . . Now can you show me how that flipping Christmas tree works?"

The "Christmas Tree" was the operations screen.

"Of course." Jason picked up a remote control about the size of those used for switching channels on a television set. "We normally use the computer terminals to place different windows on-screen, as well as different levels of magnification. There are, of course, several other functions. For the purposes of the demonstration, I'll use the remote." He pressed a switch. The screen altered. "Here, you can see the whole NATO area, from Norway to Greece . . ."

"And you can go beyond, I imagine."

"Er . . ." Jason hesitated. ". . . yes. But I'm afraid I'm not authorized to show you."

"Of course," Beresford remarked drily. "I'm only one of them what pays for the stuff . . . Don't worry. I expected as much."

Jason pressed another switch, held it down. The screen changed scale.

"We can select any country within the Alliance, lay a grid over it and focus on any square within to view a particular tactical situation. For example, here we have the UK . . . moving . . . to our own area. There."

"Are those two blobs moving about in there your fighters?"

"Yes. One is piloted by Capitano Bagni from Italy, with Captain Stockmann from the United States as navigator. The other has Flying Officer Palmer as its pilot. He's our youngest, and promises to be a top ranking pilot. He had to be good in the first place, to get here. You'll appreciate this, Jim— he doesn't come from a privileged background. He worked very hard to get where he is."

"Good for him. You sound as if you're proud of him."

"I am. I'm proud of all my crews. His navigator is Flight Lieutenant Ferris, from Australia."

"Truly international." Beresford watched as the images whirled about each other. "What are they up to?"

"Air combat training. We do much of it on the ground in simulators, to cut costs and to allow the crews to get used to taking the aircraft to limits which would be the least of what they could expect in actual warfare. Simulators are becoming so sophisticated these days that transfer to the aircraft itself has become much smoother. But of course they can never totally replace actual experience in the air.

"For the more complex battle scenarios we go to America or Canada, where there's more space. We also go to Sardinia where there's a fully-equipped air combat range. But all these deployments cost time and money, and in addition, slots have got to be booked well in advance because of demand. We're hoping a range will be built in the North Sea area. We could get a lot more training done, with less time wasted waiting for slots to become available." He pointed at the images on the screen. "Would you like to hear how they're doing?"

"Can we?"

"Oh yes. We can put them on the speakers."

Jason pressed another switch and the airmen's voices came through, swelling into the room.

Everyone paused to listen.

*   *   *

Palmer watched Bagni's aircraft disappear from his
HUD. Grunting to fight the G forces, he pulled into
a tight turn after it. Nothing.

Ferris was moving his head about, eyes searching the sky.

Then the radar warning went mad. "Break
right!" he called. *"Now!"*

Palmer obeyed, and lock was broken. But Bagni
had already called Fox on him twice. He had to get
one in. At least.

In Fighter Control, Beresford was listening with rapt
attention, his eyes glued to the screen.

Jason said: "We can change to side view, and
give a 3D image."

The screen altered again, and this time the terrain beneath the aircraft showed peaks and valleys,
with the high ground colored red.

"They seem a bit close to those mountains,"
Beresford remarked.

"Not as close as it looks. When air fighting, absolute minimum height above high ground is 5,000
feet. All manoeuvres must have this as the pull-up
altitude. Most manoeuvres end at 10,000. Anyone
who disobeys this rule knows he will be carpeted and
grounded for a while, or even washed out of this unit,
if he doesn't have a damned good reason. Not excuse,
you'll note. Excuses are not accepted here."

Beresford nodded, still watching the screen. "I
can see you mean business."

"Aircraft and crews are expensive items, and lives are priceless."

"You're talking my kind of language, Chris."

"Where is he, Neil?" Palmer was saying.

"Below us," Ferris replied. "Stay up here. Let him come up."

Palmer listened for a tracking warning. None came.

"All right, Richard," Ferris said. "He's coming. He's not tracking because he doesn't want to warn us. When I call the break, go for it. OK?"

" 'kay."

"Right. Hold it . . . hold it. *Break left!*"

Palmer flung the Tornado into a hard left turn, hauling on the stick, grunting like a walrus. The aircraft pulled itself tightly round. Bagni's Tornado began to creep into their HUD, then stabilised.

"You've done it, Richard!" Ferris crowed as the G forces lessened. "Now zap him before the wily bugger gets away. You pulled some heavy Gs back there, matey. We hit 9 for a while."

There was no reply from Palmer. The other aircraft was still within the parameters for a good shot. Ferris felt the Tornado's nose drop slightly. He wasn't worried. Palmer was obviously concentrating on making certain of the shot. Ferris decided not to interfere.

*   *   *

In Fighter Control, Jason was giving Beresford a running commentary.

"Bagni is pulling the sucker trick on Palmer," he began, "or is trying to. The question is whether Palmer will allow himself to be drawn."

"You'll have to explain that, lad."

"As you can see, Bagni is holding a fairly straight course." Jason pressed a switch on the remote. A red line crossed the 3D view from left to right. "That's the base line. Hard Deck we sometimes call it. For the purposes of the exercise, it simulates ground level. Bagni will go as close as possible, then pull up. If Palmer has not been keeping a sharp lookout, he will be suckered into the follow-through and cross the line. If that happens, he's lost the engagement."

"And if that was the real ground," Beresford said, "he'd be dead."

"Exactly. In either case, he loses the engagement."

"This air fighting business is rough."

"The real thing will be a lot rougher. I'd prefer it if the real thing did not occur."

"So would we all."

"Which is why we want the other guy to know it'll never be worth his while."

Ferris was still not worried, but he thought a little warning wouldn't come amiss.

"Watch out for his next trick, Richard. He's trying for the pull-through. He wants to drag you through to Hard Deck, but he himself won't touch it. Don't get target-fixated, old mate."

About forty seconds had passed since the turn. Palmer was still silent. The Tornado hurtled on down after Bagni's aircraft.

"Watch the baseline, Richard," Ferris warned. "We're pretty close. And there he goes. He's pulled up, Richard, and we're going into the baseline. We've lost it. Never mind. Go up after him, Richard. The baseline, for Chrissake. Oh *shit*. We've just gone through. The boss is going to have our guts for garters."

Ferris broke off, suddenly furious. What the hell was Palmer up to?

Jason and Beresford watched as the Tornado crossed the red line and continued earthwards. Everyone had heard Ferris's voice. But a new tenseness had come over Jason's body.

Beresford was watching him.

"You think something's wrong, lad," he remarked quietly.

In the Tornado, Ferris was desperate. "Richard! Come on, you drongo! Pull that bloody stick. Are you looking for a wash-out? *Richard!*"

The Tornado continued to lose height. Then the voice warning system, pre-empting the sound of the low altitude attention-getter, was activated. The computers had decided that if the aircraft continued upon its present course, impact would occur.

"Altitude!" the voice began. "Altitude!" Then: *"Pull up! Pull up!"*

Lights were flashing, and the ground proximity tone sounded.

But Ferris had already decided to take action. He yelled into his mike on the emergency channel. *"Pilot incapacitated! Initiating command eject!"*

Even as he spoke, he had reached for the lever to his right, and moved it forward.

Both seats left the aircraft cleanly, but he had waited much too long. They fired into a mountainside, killing both men instantly. The unoccupied aircraft flew steadily on for some moments, then ploughed into a valley in a ball of fire that scattered wreckage over a wide area. A sole main wheel rose high into the air, seeming to hang motionless as it reached apogee, before falling back to earth and slamming into the ground. It did not bounce, but remained firmly embedded in the spot where it had made its impact.

Wreaths of dark smoke rose towards the bright sky.

A horrified gasp went round the control room. Now there was stunned silence. All eyes were on the screen where the computers in their unemotional way had marked the aircraft with the sign of the coffin.

"Oh Neil! Oh my dear God . . ."

A woman's voice. Jason turned to look. Caroline Hamilton-Jones stood by the computer console, tears in her eyes.

Beresford put a gentle hand on Jason's arm. "I'm sorry, lad. Truly sorry."

Jason sighed. "Thank you . . . I must go. Things to do."

He put down the remote and walked away, stopping by Caroline Hamilton-Jones. "Caroline . . ."

Her mouth was contorted with grief. No words came.

"Look—why don't you take a break?"

She wiped her eyes and shook her head.

He touched her gently on the shoulder, then crossed to where Thurson was standing. "I'm going with the crash crew, sir," he said. "See what can be found."

"Yes. Of course."

One of the MPs found enough voice to say, "I don't believe I just saw two men die. It seemed so. . . ." He ran out of words.

Beresford had caught up. "There'll be some flak after this," he said to Jason. "I want you to know that I'd like to be in your corner. I can see what this is doing to you, and I'm very sorry. But politics are politics, lad. I'd be letting down my party if I didn't speak out."

Jason stared at him blankly. "What exactly are you saying?"

"I'm saying I'll bring you down if I have to. I'm sorry. You're a good man—but there are wider considerations. Money. Airbases or schools. Maybe that's what it comes down to. You've got troubles enough, lad, I know that . . . but I couldn't live with myself if I didn't warn you."

Jason turned away. Jim Beresford was part of a battle that belonged to another day.

Bagni circled the area of the crash, horror chilling his mind. He had killed Palmer. He had dragged the younger pilot too low. Palmer hadn't had the experience to see the danger for himself.

"I killed him," Bagni murmured. He was speaking to himself, but Stockmann had picked up the low whisper.

"You're talking bull there, Nico," the backseater said. "This had nothing to do with you. We hold here till the helo arrives, then we head for home."

"I did kill him," Bagni insisted. "I dragged him down."

"Nico, you're talking shit, I tell you. This was a weird crash. Something was wrong. He didn't even try to pull up after you. His ship went straight in. It was almost as if the guy had gone on holiday. Here's the crash helo. Come on, Nico. Leave them to it. Let's go home."

Bagni turned the Tornado for base, seeing Palmer and Ferris in his mind's eye. Palmer shy, quiet. Ferris dry, easy-going. They would not be in the Mess tonight.

Bagni screwed up his first landing attempt, and had to go round again.

"Nico," Stockmann called. "Quit horsing around and put this goddam bird down. You did not kill Palmer and Ferris. Now put us down."

It was not his best of landings, but he got down in one piece. After the extensive debriefing, he went to his room in the Mess and shut himself in.

He sat on the bed, and watched his hands tremble.

The news, as so often happened on units, went the rounds of November One like wildfire, long before the official announcement. An airman had popped into Jason's staff office where young Sergeant Graham, who was not afraid of Air Vice-Marshals, held the fort.

"Have you heard, Sarge?"

"Heard what?"

"A Tornado's down. Palmer and Ferris."

Her face went gray with shock. Even as the realisation hit home, the phone rang.

Mechanically she picked it up. "Wing Commander Jason's office." Tears were streaming down her cheeks.

The airman stared at her uncomprehendingly.

At the other end, Jason said gently, "Sergeant Graham, Sparrowhawk's down."

"Yes, sir. I know—" Her voice broke.

"Gail? Gail . . . words aren't much good, my dear, but I'm truly sorry."

She hadn't known that he was aware of how things were between her and Richard. How things had been. . . . But a good commanding officer missed very little. She began to sob openly.

"Dear God," Jason muttered. "What an unholy mess. Look. I'm going over to the crash site. Get Corporal Lovell to stand in for you and go off for the rest of the day. I'll talk to you when I return."

She controlled herself. "If it's all right with you, sir, I'd rather stay."

"You're sure?"

"Yes, sir. I'd prefer it."

"Very well." He paused. "I'll see you when I get back."

"Yes, sir."

She rang off. The airman went silently away. She sat on at her desk, fingering the letter that had arrived that morning, addressed to her personally. She had wanted to give Richard the surprise when they met later that day.

Her acceptance for a commission had come through.

Tom Wells, as the instructor who had known Palmer longest, wanted to deliver the news personally to his parents. Inglis gave permission, and Thurson found him a seat on the HS 125 taking the MPs back to

London. A car was made available at Northolt and a few hours after the crash Wells, in civilian clothes, was standing outside the modest semi-detached house on the outskirts of Reading.

Palmer's mother opened the door to his ring. "Yes? Can I help you?"

"Mrs. Palmer, I'm Tom Wells . . ." She stared blankly. "Perhaps your son has mentioned—"

She brightened. "Mr. Wells. Oh yes—Richard's often spoken about . . ." She tailed off. Her hand went to her mouth as she made the connection. "Oh no," she whispered. "Not Richard. Not Richard. Just now, I heard the news on the radio that an airplane had crashed in Scotland. You've come to tell me it's my Richard. You have, haven't you?"

Wells felt his eyes grow hot. "Mrs. Palmer, may I come in?"

She stood back dazedly to allow him through. She closed the door and went ahead of him with slow, emphatic steps. They went into a small, neatly furnished lounge and sat down awkwardly.

"Tell you what," she said brightly. "Make some tea, shall I?"

Not knowing what else to say, he said: "Yes, please."

She immediately stood up and went to the kitchen. He heard her moving around. He stayed in his seat, rooted to the spot by his inability to reach her. Surprisingly quickly she returned, bringing a well-laid tray. There were biscuits. He stood up to help with the tray.

"Thank you," she told him politely, and began to pour. "My husband's out. Milk and sugar?"

"Yes, please. One sugar."

Carefully, she carried out his request. "There you are," she said, handing him the cup. Then she sat back, and smiled at him.

She could not have switched on the kettle. The tea was cold.

Wells drank it.

"Biscuit?" she asked.

"Yes, please."

She handed him the plate. He took one.

"Thank you."

Unnervingly, she continued to watch him with that fixed smile. Then the unnatural resolve gave, and her face crumpled. Still sitting bolt upright, she began to weep in a soft high-pitched wail that sounded like a small animal in pain.

Wells put down his cold tea and went to her; but she waved him away.

"Why didn't you look after him!" she suddenly said accusingly. "He said you always looked after him. Squadron Leader Wells this, Squadron Leader Wells that. Why didn't you look after him?"

Wells didn't know what to say. He was grateful to hear a key in the door.

"Hello, love," a male voice greeted. "Got company, have we?" It was a sturdy, cheerful voice and a moment later its owner, a sturdy, cheerful man in corduroy trousers, tweed jacket, a checked shirt and knitted tie entered the room. He first looked at Wells. "I know you. You're Tom Wells, Richard's instructor."

"That's correct, sir. You visited Richard during advanced training. Your wife was ill at the time."

"Yes. I remember." Even as he spoke, the older man had been taking in the scene, putting two and two together. It didn't need genius to work out why Wells was there. "Let me see to my wife," he said to him. "I'll be right back."

She struggled to her feet. "I'll see to myself, Harry. You . . . you talk to Mr. Wells. He's come a long way. I'm going upstairs. You can tell me what he says later."

She allowed her husband to help her to the door. Wells stood up as she left the room. She didn't look back at him. Mr. Palmer stood in the doorway, watching her go up the stairs.

"Won't be long, love," he called after her. Then he returned to Wells. "Life has to go on, Mr. Wells." He sighed deeply. "That's what they always say, isn't it?"

Wells nodded silently.

"Thank you for coming," Palmer said. "I know it can't have been easy."

"I wanted to do this, Mr. Palmer. A phone call's not right, or some total stranger at the door. I cared for Richard. He was one of the best young pilots I've ever had the privilege of training."

"Thank you for saying that. I know it's not the usual stuff—dear sir or madam, your son was brave and did his duty . . . You know the crap I mean."

"Yes. I do."

Palmer's voice was husky. "He always wanted to be a pilot, you know. Ever since a boy. His room's full of stuff about airplanes. We've kept all his models." Palmer hesitated, staring at his hands. "I could show you if you like. Would you like to see?"

"I'd be honored."

"It's just upstairs."

Richard Palmer's room had been kept tidy by a loving mother. Everything was spotlessly clean. Models of aircraft were arranged neatly on shelves fixed about the room. Others hung on lengths of string from the ceiling. Bookcases were full of aeronautical works, from boys' stories to the most advanced aerospace technology. There were photographs of Richard at all stages of flying training; photographs from university days; photographs from schooldays; photographs of him as a small child and finally, as a baby. It was a shrine.

I've got to get out of here, Wells was thinking.

Palmer picked up a model. It was of a Hawk. "I made this one. He stopped making them when he went to university, so I took over." He sat down on the unused bed. "I'd been hoping to play with these with a grandchild one day. Do you know he met a girl recently?"

Wells was surprised. "No. I had no idea."

"He was going to bring her down to meet us. Well . . . it's all gone now." Palmer put the model of the Hawk gently down and stood up. "Thanks again for coming, Mr. Wells . . ."

Wells gritted his teeth. There was one last formality. "Arrangements are being made to have Richard flown down, Mr. Palmer. If you need anything . . ."

"No. We're fine, thank you. Would you think it rude of me if I said we'd prefer a quiet service? Just family."

"I understand."

"But ask the girl, if you can find out who she is. Gail, he said her name was. We'd like to see her, if only this once."

"I'll make enquiries."

Palmer held out his hand. "Thank you. Would you mind showing yourself out? Richard's mother—you do understand?"

"Of course," Wells said, and made his way downstairs and out of the sad house.

The next morning, Bagni knocked on the door to Jason's office.

"Come in," the Wing Commander called.

Bagni entered and saluted with unusual formality. Jason frowned. "At ease. You wanted a word with me?"

Bagni came instantly to the point. "It was all my fault, sir."

"What was your fault? You're not going to take the blame for that crash, are you? I saw it all on the screen, Nico. Yours was a legitimate manoeuvre. You were not to know Palmer had suffered G-loc. He blacked out."

"I dragged him down . . ."

"Let me ask you a question . . . If this had been a real combat would you have carried on with the manoeuvre?"

"Yes sir, but . . ."

"There isn't a 'but' in there, Capitano Bagni. You're a fighter pilot. So was Palmer. What happened to him was not your fault."

"Sir, there is something else."

Jason's eyes watched him steadily. "Go on."

Bagni took long seconds, wrestling mentally with what he had to say. "Sir, I request to be grounded."

Jason's eyes held Bagni fast. "Do you have a good reason?"

"Yes, sir. I am afraid of landings. I always have been. One day I will kill myself and my back-seater. It's only a matter of time."

"I see."

Jason got slowly up from behind his desk and went over to a window. A pair of Tornadoes were hurtling down the runway. He waited until their roar had faded before speaking.

He turned to face Bagni. "I studied your file very carefully, before selecting you. No reference anywhere to bad landings. You are either very good at hiding such an apparent handicap from your assessing officers, or you're just one of those pilots who *believe* they're afraid of landings. It's a fantasy fear, Bagni. And now you've added it to this foolish guilt about Palmer's death."

"I have lived with this for a long time, sir."

Jason said: "Look, Nico, you're one of the finest pilots on the squadron. In fact, you're one of the top three. I have no intention of losing you. If I thought you were below the standards I expect, you would not find it necessary to ask. I would ground you myself. Tell you what. Show me just how afraid you are. We're going to work the circuit. I'll be in the back seat. As your aircraft is not a trainer, there are no dual controls. I shall be completely in your hands."

Bagni's eyes widened in shock. "Sir! But . . ."

"No more buts, Captain. Be ready for take-off in an hour."

Jason made Bagni carry out ten consecutive take-offs and landings. Each was perfection. Bagni put the aircraft down with barely a jolt.

"You didn't need ten of those," Jason said after the last one. "The first convinced me. How do you feel?"

Bagni was chastened. "You trusted me. I was not afraid."

"You never really were. Any more than you were responsible for young Palmer's death."

In the back seat, Jason shut his eyes briefly in silent thanks. His shock tactics had worked. Perhaps Palmer's death had.

He mentally uncrossed his fingers. If things had gone wrong, Bagni would have splattered them both across the runway. But Bagni had got everything right. He might have been able to get away with faking the first landing, but not the following nine. There had been no hesitation in his execution of them. Every one had been precise, with the indefinable touch of an artist. Bagni knew his job.

Jason left the aircraft with relief. He would not have liked losing such a pilot, but if Bagni had even fumbled any one of the ten landings, Jason would have grounded him.

Away to the east, at the base on the Kola Peninsula, Kukarev lay on the bed in his room, staring at the ceiling, a tightening knot in his stomach. An hour before, he had returned from a low-level sortie over the Barents Sea. The knot in his stomach was due to the fact that he now knew the date of his final departure. He had been given the date of the end of his detachment. He gazed at the ceiling and thought of the enormity of what he was about to undertake, and what had driven him to it.

It was Sergei Stolybin who had made it possible. They had once been flight cadets together, but Stolybin had washed out and had gone on to join the KGB. Once, on a survival course deep within the Arctic wilderness, Kukarev had risked his life to save Stolybin from freezing to death. Stolybin had never forgotten, and they had remained firm friends throughout the passing years.

At first Kukarev had kept to himself his hatred of the men who had brought his father to disgrace and death, and his mother to a weary grave soon after. But he had never married, to avoid both emotional vulnerability and possible official blackmail afterwards. And once he had mentioned to Stolybin a hypothetical scenario of a pilot wanting to go West.

His friend had avoided committing himself, and a full year had passed after that, with Kukarev wondering whether friendship could withstand the KGB ethos. On every posting, he had expected arrest. But nothing had occurred and he had continued to rise in his career.

Then one day, in Kabul of all places, Stolybin had met up with him and in a bar that night had mentioned to him casually that if a hypothetical pilot wanted to make the hypothetical trip West, there might be a hypothetical way. They had gone on from there. And now the trip was no longer hypothetical.

Kukarev continued to stare at the ceiling. He hoped Sergei Stolybin had not compromised his own safety by helping him. They had kept their meetings to a minimum, but that did not mean Stolybin was himself not under possible surveillance.

Kukarev had brought up the subject on one occasion.

"Surveillance is something I know rather a lot about, Pyotr Ivanovich," Stolybin had said. "And flying is your game. Let's each concentrate on his part. Don't worry about me. Worry about how you're going to evade anyone they may send after you to turn you back, or to shoot you down. I'll handle the surveillance."

In Aberdeen, Morven's first knowledge of the crash was through the news media that night. Because the names of the victims had not yet been released, she was hit by a sudden blind panic and wondered about the safety of the two men most important to her.

Her hand hovered over the phone, and she felt anguish over whom to call first. She decided on Axel and felt blessed relief when he came on the line. Inevitably she was shocked to hear it was Palmer and Ferris who had died. Ferris she'd met only briefly, but Palmer she'd felt she knew well from their time together at the Ball. He'd seemed such a good, gentle person.

She called a second time, and got her brother.

"Poor Richard," she said. "What happened? I asked Axel . . ."

"Called him, did you?"

"I called you first," she lied, feeling guilty, "but you weren't around . . . so I asked for Axel." Hohendorf would not betray her, she knew.

Seemingly mollified, Selby said: "There's an inquiry on . . . you know . . . usual stuff. To determine cause, to apportion blame if any, to take remedial action, and so on. We've got some educated guesses, of course, but I can't tell you about that."

"Will you be all right?"

"I'm fine. We're all cut up, naturally; but nothing stops."

"I know. Have you heard from Kim?"

"Yes. She called just now. That'll be why you couldn't get me."

"What about Richard's girl? The one he couldn't take to the Ball . . ."

"Very sad case there. As you know, she's the boss's sec. She didn't want to, but he's made her take some leave. I gather she's got family to go to . . . Morven? Are you there?"

"Yes, Mark," Morven replied. "Still here. I was just thinking of how things can change so quickly . . ."

"Best not to dwell upon it."

"Of all people, I should know that."

"Yes," he said.

The question of Selby's mortality had never arisen in Morven's mind. Having a brother as a jet fighter pilot had been good for her image at school, and his possible death had simply never occurred to her. Now, it was different. An item on TV had come painfully close to home.

"I've got to go now," Selby was saying. "Look kid, don't worry."

"I won't."

They both knew it wasn't true.

"Mark . . ."

"Yes?"

"Tell Axel to be careful, will you?"

Silence.

"Mark . . . ?"

A sigh. "I'll tell him."

"Promise."

"I promise."

" 'bye."

" 'bye, Mo."

Three days later, sixty miles from land, Hohendorf and Selby were returning from a paired high-level patrol and were practising an ultra-low approach to base, as had been directed for the sortie. Height over the sea was thirty feet. They flew a 500-meter lateral separation pattern and were due for a pull-up to 5000 feet within one minute. At 450 knots, that would leave them with a remaining six minutes transit time.

Just before the pull up, a huge flock of birds rose from the sea and slammed into Hohendorf's aircraft. The force was so great that the Tornado appeared to stop in mid-air and only Hohendorf's swift reactions in pushing the throttles hard against the stops into full combat afterburner and an instinctive pull up prevented the aircraft from plunging into the sea.

Inevitably, November One aircraft had hit birds before, but damage had been minimal. The engines had been deliberately designed for high-speed low-level transits, and to facilitate bird ingestion they did not have fixed inlet vanes. The birds would go straight through, be turned into mincemeat, cause some damage, but not sufficient to stop the affected engine from running. No aircraft had been seriously affected and, as far as Hohendorf knew, no type of Tornado had been lost under such conditions.

But there could always be the exception that proved the rule.

In this case the birds were large gulls—Hohendorf could see the smeared head of one on his windscreen—and a great number of them had been drawn into the engines. Even more had spread themselves over the windscreen and canopy, their entrails forming a red-streaked cloak, causing the sun's rays to send a baleful glow into the cockpits and streaming astern in a crimson mist. Mercifully, the canopy had remained intact.

Hohendorf and Flacht had their visors down, as was the hard rule for low-level flight: whatever came through a shattered canopy could make a nasty mess of a visorless face, and although birds, particularly geese, could sometimes be found at ridiculous heights, low-level without visors was asking for trouble.

The Tornado staggered up towards 10,000 feet, its engines fighting to regain power over the mangled carcases clogging its vanes.

"Christ," came a voice in their headphones. An anxious Selby. "You look as if you're shitting blood, and your canopy's painted red." He had moved his own aircraft closer immediately he'd seen the birdstrike. It had all happened so quickly. Nothing had come near his own Tornado. "What's your status? Have advised November One of birdstrike."

"Better answer him, Wolfie," Hohendorf told Flacht. "Check out the systems while I get us to height."

From the rear cockpit, Flacht had already pressed one of the display tabs to bring a full systems state on-screen. Both the front and rear cockpit central warning panels were showing more lights than either crew member wanted to see, and the multifunction display Flacht had selected seemed to be giving nothing but bad news, much of which had already been confirmed by the warning panel. The list was ominous.

"You don't want to hear this," Flacht said.

AICS, the list began, N RPNS. No response.

The air intake control system was shot. Surprise, surprise.

EOS	N RPNS
ERS	N RPNS

EFCS	N RPNS
ESS	N RPNS
EIS	N RPNS

Engine oil, engine reheat, engine fuel control, the list seemed to go on and on as the display went swiftly through its pages of unwelcome information. The engine systems were taking a hammering: oil, fuel control, ignition, starting . . . That meant no re-light facility, should they suffer a double flame-out. The ram air turbine would pop out automatically to generate limited power for the controls, but its effectiveness would depend on many other things not having gone wrong.

Flacht passed the information to McCann, who patched it through to November One.

"Merlin two-four," Hohendorf began to his companion plane, using the sortie call-sign, "when we get to height, look me over, will you?"

"That's a roger, two-one." It was McCann who answered. "How's your visibility? You guys look covered."

"Visibility practically nil. If we lose nav systems you may have to guide us in, with GCA help."

"Will do, Axel," came Selby's voice.

Hohendorf switched channels long enough to say to Flacht, drily: "When he thinks I'm going to die, he calls me Axel."

"But we're not going to die," Flacht said. "I'd never forgive you."

"Don't worry, Wolfie. I'd never forgive myself."

"Hey you two!" came McCann's voice. "Quit whispering. Let us in on the secret."

Hohendorf reverted to the original channel. "What's the matter, Elmer Lee? Getting lonely?"

"Thought you'd lost radio," McCann retorted.

Hohendorf felt his face twitch in a grim smile. Elmer Lee was worried. He knew what was going on in all their minds. After Palmer and Ferris, no one wanted another crew and aircraft loss. He could imagine the state of things back at November One.

At last, they reached 10,000 feet and he levelled off slowly. The engines were still struggling for power, but at least they had taken the aircraft to a safe height. If they both died on him now, he might just be able to glide to base. It would be a one-shot landing, but even if all the fly-by-wire channels went to sleep, the mechanical back-up would still give enough control to get him home. Admittedly the usually smooth, crisply-maneuvering Tornado would try to turn itself into a flying pig, but these things were all relative.

I can do it, he said in his mind.

The engines were coughing, losing the struggle.

Flacht was saying: "We're still in D809, but November One's cleared its southern section of all activity for the duration."

D809 was one of several designated danger areas where intense military flying was conducted.

"Good," Hohendorf said. "One less problem to

worry about. If we lose CSAS, I'm still going to put her down rather than eject. Do you concur?"

"I hate swimming," Flacht said, "so I think I prefer to stay in here where it's nice and warm."

"As long as it doesn't get warmer."

"You guys are ghouls," came McCann's voice. "You know that?"

Hohendorf smiled again, and concentrated on nursing the wounded aircraft.

Selby had carried out a careful inspection of the Tornado, moving his own aircraft about it. A bird had impaled itself on one of the missiles and was shearing away bit by bit in the slipstream. Other strips of carcase were smeared about the airframe, but no serious damage appeared to have been done to the outside. The canopy remained covered in blood.

Hohendorf had come out of afterburner, but kept the throttles at MAX DRY. Engine power was well down, but he was able to hold at 280 knots. The wings were spread fully forward and the aircraft seemed to have settled down. CSAS, the command stability and augmentation system, was still on line. If it held till touchdown, he'd be very pleased indeed.

Even as he thought that, the engines both went out simultaneously. One moment they were on; the next, they were not. The sudden dying of their comforting background noise was more unnerving than the birdstrike itself had been.

"That's it, Wolfie," Hohendorf said. "We're gliding home."

The ram air turbine had popped out, giving them sufficient hydraulic power to operate the tailerons. But there would be no relight. To make sure, Hohendorf went through the procedure; but the engines did not respond. Given the thumping and grinding noises that had come from them, this was not altogether surprising.

He informed Selby, while Flacht warned November One. GCA was ready to talk them down, while Selby played watchdog. The aircraft had become as basic as it could get without actually falling out of the sky.

Gingerly, Hohendorf put the Tornado into a glide that he hoped would lose height at a rate that would take him to the runway threshold by the time flying integrity was finally lost.

The wings, flaps and slats, extended before the loss of main power, developed sufficient lift to enable him to come close to the correct angle. In a silence broken only by the rush of air over its airframe, the Tornado ASV glided steeply earthwards, maintaining flying speed, the wings and LERXes working together.

Selby's aircraft followed at a safe separation, but close enough to warn of any new danger.

"You're holding well, Axel," he told him. "Attitude looking good."

Hohendorf did not acknowledge. It was unnecessary to do so. Peering through his reddened screen, he could catch only the most fleeting of glimpses of the outside world. He was totally dependent upon Ground Control and Selby's aircraft for guidance.

At ten miles out, Ground Control gave him a new heading. He turned the aircraft, watching the standby attitude direction indicator carefully.

"Maintain," came from the ground. "Shallower if you can."

He couldn't. The glide continued. ADI starting to waltz. Stabilise.

"Wheels down," came another directive. "Runway at 2.5 miles."

He reached for the lever with the wheeled shape at its end. Nothing happened. Calmly, he reached farther left to the emergency landing gear lever, tucked away near the stores jettison panel.

It worked. With relief, he heard the wheels come down. The resultant drag caused some reduction in airspeed and he steepened the glide to compensate. Watch that pitch angle!

"All wheels down," came from Selby. "Do you have confirmation?"

"Three greens," Hohendorf acknowledged.

He was trying to keep stick movements as minimal as possible. This was not the time to slip into pilot-induced oscillations, and lose control through over-correction.

"You're doing nicely, Axel," Selby said. "Perfectly in line with the runway."

"If only I could see it."

Oh God. In his mind he was seeing Morven's face. Did that mean he was going to die? Seconds ticking.

No! He was not going to be taken away from her.

"Fifty seconds to touchdown," advised Ground Control.

"All right, Axel, start bringing the nose up. You're almost there. *Don't* change direction. Your nose is perfectly lined up."

In the back. Flacht maintained his silence. It was going to be a narrow thing but there was nothing he could do now, and Hohendorf did not need further distraction. He was completely confident in Hohendorf's piloting skills. They would get down. He was sure of it.

GCA was keeping out of it too. Having guided him safely home, it was now up to the chase aircraft and Hohendorf. Strategically positioned about the airfield, the crash services waited.

Jason had gone to the tower to watch and to monitor the situation. Inglis had gone too. They could see the growing specks that were the two Tornadoes, coming in over the Firth. One was slightly higher and behind the other, which seemed at a suicidally steep angle. The entire control room was holding its breath.

"He's got guts," Inglis muttered to Jason in a

voice so low, it was as if he thought Hohendorf could hear him.

Jason nodded, eyes fastened upon the aircraft. "It's a flatter angle he needs really, just at the moment."

"Threshold coming up, Axel," Selby warned. "Let's have the nose up, past the horizon. That's it. Get ready for the flare. Make it good."

Hohendorf complied, feeling for the change in the aircraft, checking flying speed, judging the flare so that as the nose came up and speed began to decay, the aircraft would sink reasonably gently onto the blessed surface. One chance only. One chance, one chance . . .

"Threshold!" Selby called. "Height's good. All yours."

Hohendorf brought the nose up further. Oh God. Where was the runway? If they touched too soon they'd dig in and cartwheel. An age seemed to pass as the aircraft sank, reaching with its wheels for the hard ground. 150 knots and 15 alpha.

Bump, squirt. They were down! Down, down, down. They were staying down. The gear was locked. No collapse. Hold the nose up. Hold it as long as possible. Let the aircraft decide.

The nose came down as lift decayed, met the runway in an almost leisurely manner. Hohendorf began braking immediately. There was sufficient hydraulic pressure to operate the system. The aircraft came to a halt. The readied cables and erected barrier were not needed.

Hohendorf gave a long sigh as he turned off everything left to be switched off, leaned back in his seat and shut his eyes briefly.

Flacht said: "I don't want to hurry you, Axel, but much as I like it here, I think we should leave . . ."

"Wolfie," Hohendorf said, "we made it. We're alive."

"I'll kiss you later. Shall we go? What if there's no power left to raise the canopy? What if an engine catches fire? Besides, all the blood up there is giving me the creeps." There was a raising lever in Flacht's cockpit, but he hardly dared touch it. "What's more, the crash crews will want to clear the runway for Selby and McCann."

"Right as usual, Wolfie." Hohendorf pulled at the jack handle. The canopy hissed softly upwards, tearing at entrail residue that had glued itself to it.

"Ugh!" Flacht peered at the smear marks on the aircraft as normal daylight again flooded in. He began to swiftly release himself from the airplane.

The first of the crash crews had arrived and were staring at the Tornado.

"What were you trying to do, sir?" someone called up to Hohendorf. "Wipe out the entire bird population up here?"

"I missed a few. Better luck next time, I suppose."

They were all grinning their relief as he and Flacht climbed out. It would not have been much fun trying to salvage what would have been left of them, had his landing failed. Welcoming hands patted them on their shoulders as they walked towards the vehicle waiting to take them off the runway.

Hohendorf paused once to look back at the Tornado. It already had people swarming all over it, preparing for a tow to a repair hangar. It seemed disdainful of the humans, as if it knew it had done well.

In the control tower, Jason and Inglis had picked up binoculars to view the final stages of the landing. Inglis lowered his, but Jason was still focused on the aircraft as it was towed away.

"Astonishing airmanship," Inglis began. "Hohendorf deserves a medal. He saved us an aircraft, not to mention two lives. Something for Selby too. He called those final shots perfectly. Hohendorf trusted him implicitly and had he misjudged it, we would have been scraping an unholy mess off the runway."

Jason took the binoculars away from his eyes and nodded. He felt the same way.

"I had earmarked them as Flight Commanders," he said, giving the binoculars to an air traffic control assistant to put away. "Tom Wells and two more instructors from the OCU have been standing in, but Helm and da Vinci are going to need them more than ever soon, to work on the new intake for the second squadron. I'd thought of giving one flight each to Hohendorf, Selby, and Bagni."

"When?"

"Sometime in the autumn."

"A good time as any," Inglis said. He drew Jason to one side. "Whatever it is you feel goes on between those two," he continued, "it is clear they work very well together. So it can't be as serious as you think."

Jason said nothing.

Hohendorf and Flacht met up with Selby and McCann in the squadron coffee bar.

"Well hi, my main man," McCann greeted Hohendorf exuberantly. "Was that some flying, or was it? You guys had my guts in jelly, I can tell you."

Hohendorf smiled, held out a hand to Selby. "Mark . . . thank you. I needed you, and you were there."

Selby shook the hand, his own smile coming slowly. "Part of the service. Glad you made it, Axel." He paused. "Are you going to tell Morven?"

"Not unless you think I should."

"It would worry her, especially after what happened to Richard and Neil."

"Exactly what I was thinking," Hohendorf said.

Selby nodded slowly. "Then it's settled. She'll not hear about it from me."

"Nor from me."

But Morven did hear of it.

She met with Hohendorf for his leave as had been planned. After he'd parked the car, they set off with their backpacks for the Speyside Way, the day pleasantly warm for the long but easy walk along the river. She had brought food as promised, and he'd complemented that with a bottle of fine wine.

They walked for an hour on the wide path, through lush hedgerows and woodland, towards Fochabers. From time to time, dark pods among the gorse bushes that bordered the path would explode with sudden sharp reports, scattering their seeds in all directions.

Hohendorf ducked mockingly. "We're under rifle fire." He smiled at Morven. "I'm not tired yet. How about you?"

"I can go on as long as you can," she said. "Perhaps longer."

But she did not return his smile. She had been subdued ever since they'd met, and this disturbed him.

"Is something wrong?" he asked.

She shook her head. "Nothing's wrong."

They walked on in silence. He shrugged. For his part, Hohendorf was enjoying the magnificent Speymouth scenery. Now and then, he paused to look down upon the river. The path had climbed to nearly two hundred feet above the valley. Each time he lingered, she continued walking, and he had to lengthen his stride to catch up. They went through Fochabers without stopping and eventually, their path took them to a sign that recommended the view. He turned to gaze out across the valley. Below them, a lushly green island seemed to swim in the waters of the Spey.

"Let us stop here, Morven," he said. "We can eat, and I want to talk to you." He leaned against a wooden railing to watch her.

She came to a halt, reluctantly it seemed. He looked about him, found a likely spot at the base of one of the numerous Scots pines, away from the path.

"We'll have our picnic here," he told her and, taking off his pack, sat down.

She joined him, and rested her own pack next to his.

His eyes were upon her, but she looked away.

"Please tell me what is wrong," he urged. "We have walked a long way, most of it in silence. I thought this was to be a happy time for us."

It seemed ages before she answered. Then her tone was bitter. "Why didn't you tell me you nearly died last week? And don't try to deny it."

He was utterly surprised that she knew. How had she found out? Surely, Selby would not have gone back on his word?

"Who told you?" he countered.

"Not Mark." She said it coldly. "He doesn't think I'm worth the truth either . . . I found out by sheer chance. I was in a pub up here and I heard two airmen talking. They were drivers, and one of them was going on about someone carrying out a landing without engines, after a birdstrike. He described the state of the airplane in graphic detail."

"That doesn't say I was the one."

"He said, and I quote . . . 'It was the German bloke, wasn't it? The one with the Porsche.' And his friend said: "Yeah. That's the one." They had their wives with them."

"They should not talk so much."

"There was more. They said how you and your navigator would have been scraped off the runway, if you had made a mistake."

"But I didn't." He spread his hands. "And Mark was very helpful too."

"I suppose you both made a pact not to tell me."

"There was no need to cause worry . . ."

"What do you mean 'no need'?" she said furiously. She hit him suddenly on the chest. "Don't you dare do that to me again! Don't you dare treat me like some helpless little silly. . . ." She kept hitting him until he put his arms about her. She laid her head against his shoulder. "Oh Axel . . . you could have died."

"But I didn't . . . Look—I'm very much alive."

Her head came up. Her eyes moistened as she stared at him. "How can you joke about it?"

"I am not joking. You must believe me. We had a little luck. It could have been very different; but that is the reality . . . the difference between living and dying. It is the razor's edge. For everyone, actually, but mostly they don't notice. The car misses them, the stone falls a moment after they pass. On one side . . . life, and on the other . . . death. The razor cut well for us that day."

Her eyes searched his. "I must be crazy. I have a brother who's a fighter pilot. You'd think I'd have known what to expect by now, wouldn't you?"

"And to make life even more difficult, I am married—although I would hardly call it that—and your brother does not like me. We are both crazy." Hohendorf smiled at her. "This means we are well suited."

"You're talking too much," she said, and kissed him.

After a while, he said: "Your brother's not so bad. He stayed with me all the way. I think Wolfie and I would have had a very difficult time without his help."

"There. You see? He must like you a little bit."

"I would not go so far," Hohendorf said cautiously.

"Kiss me," she said. "You're still talking too much."

They kissed again, this time with passion. Hohendorf's diffidence began to fade, and soon they were grappling at each other. Neither was fully conscious of clothes being feverishly undone; of flesh meeting eager flesh; of . . .

Entry.

Morven had managed somehow to unlace one of her hiking shoes. Now she kicked it off and pulled her leg free of the restricting jeans to make it easier to pull him deep into her. She gave a loud sigh that was at once of pleasure and of long-awaited satisfaction. Her body worked sinuously beneath him and she kissed him as he moved within her, making whimpering noises all the while.

Hohendorf knew now that he had wanted her from the very moment he had set eyes upon her. He had wanted to feel her body next to his. He had wanted to feel himself going into her. He had wanted . . .

An unbelievably powerful force took hold of him. He seemed to swoop upon her, lifting her off the ground and squeezing her to him as he felt his whole being flowing into her. She hung on to him tightly, body trembling, answering his urgency with her own. She shuddered against him for what seemed an eternity.

At last, bodies clasped tightly to each other, each gave a long, drawn-out sigh before they relaxed slowly against the grassy earth. While in the bushes about them, the dark seed pods exploded.

"Morven, Morven," he said gently, and kissed her softly upon suffused, enraptured lips.

*   *   *

"We'd better make ourselves presentable," she said at long last.

Their bodies were still locked against each other. "This is a popular walk. We might shock some poor soul who's come up here for the view."

"We're far away from the path."

"Not that far. Come on, you."

He moved reluctantly. Then his diffidence made a return. "Are you sorry?"

"Do I look it?" She began dressing.

"No."

"Then I'm not. QED." She paused to look at him. "Are you?"

He stared at her still radiant from their love-making.

"No," he said softly. "I am not."

She smiled. "Good."

After they were fully dressed again, she began laying out the food. It was now his turn to smile. He enjoyed watching her. Her every movement, her voice, brought pleasure.

"What are you smiling at?"

"I'm smiling at you."

"Then stop it. You're making me blush."

"You're beautiful when you blush. You're beautiful when you don't blush."

She stopped, then leaned over to kiss him. "Get the wine."

He did so, opened it with a flourish, then poured

some into two glasses he had taken out of a small, well-padded cardboard box.

"I'd expected plastic cups," she said, taking the glass he handed her.

"Fighter pilots are trained to be ready for every eventuality. Or so they tell me." He raised his glass. "To us."

She raised hers, looked at him over the rim. "And were you ready for this? Did you expect it?"

"What do you . . . ? Oh no. I did not expect anything. I brought the wine because—"

She was laughing at him. "Oh Axel! If you could see your face. So shocked." She leaned forward again, nearly spilling her wine. "I think," she continued seriously, "I'm falling in love with you." She gave him a quick peck on the lips then leaned back again, against the bole of the tree. "Now let's eat."

"I think I am too."

"In love with you?"

"No," he said, equally serious. "With you."

She stared into her wine for a long moment. "Let's eat."

When they had finished the wine and the food, they leaned together in contentment, shoulder to shoulder against the tree.

"What actually happened to Richard Palmer and Neil Ferris?" Morven asked. "Mark never told me. He said there were educated guesses, but he never explained."

Hohendorf rested his head against the tree.

"What happened," he repeated. "G-loc. That's what happened. The crash recorders confirmed what nearly all of us had already suspected. The inquiry will go on for a long time to check every detail and to make quite sure, of course, but that is what we believe."

"What is . . . what did you call it . . . ?"

"G-loc. It means G-induced loss of consciousness. Some modern jet fighters can turn so quickly and tightly, if you are not G-prepared, you lose consciousness during a very high-G turn. It can take perhaps as long as four minutes before you are again properly awake."

"My God," Morven said quietly. "How dangerous your job is."

"Nonsense. Considering what we fast jet pilots do, I think we are some of the safest people in the world. You would not get me to fly an airliner, for example."

"Why not?"

"I like the fast reactions of my ship. It is almost as if I am thinking with it. The airplane is just another part of myself. I think it, and I am there. With an airliner . . . it is different. I am not suited."

"You sound almost as if someone is trying to persuade you."

"My wife. My father-in-law. They have tried. It is old history."

"What about your cousin? How does she feel about you, and about Johann?"

Hohendorf thought about it for a while. "Erika," he began. "Erika understands. Of course like everybody else, she worries; but she would worry if we drove trucks. She knows it is what we love to do. She would never try to stop it. But Anne-Marie—"

Morven put a finger upon his lips. "Sshh. Let's not talk about her any more."

He gave her a gentle look. "No. Let us not. I am very happy with you, Morven. I have written to my mother about you. I know she will like you also. I never dreamed . . ."

"There you go. Talking again."

She silenced him with a long kiss.

The Baltic.

Beuren and Johann Ecker were heading back to base after a long patrol, keeping low. For months now Beuren had taken the Tornado down to thirty feet, with barely a qualm. His control down on the deck, while lacking Hohendorf's style, was good. Beuren seemed to be a man transformed. Perhaps the poor showing during Red Flag had been the turning point. Whatever it was, it had worked.

Ecker did not expect Hohendorf's kind of artistry from anyone except Hohendorf himself. But Beuren was doing very well. The previous months had shown it. It was possible that he had felt intimidated by the other's brilliance. With Hohendorf gone

to the new special unit, Beuren had had room to
flower.

Ecker glanced out at the rushing gray of sea,
seemingly mere inches beneath his feet. A uniform
drabness had wiped out the horizon, and sea and sky
were one and the same. Over on two-nine-zero, a ship
that had been on the radar for some time appeared
suddenly, apparently floating in the air. It was a
common illusion under such conditions and your instruments were the only things you believed.

Ecker checked the altitude read-out. The Tornado had gone lower. They were now at 20 feet and
doing 500 knots.

"A little more height, Willi," he advised
calmly. Nothing to worry about: the aircraft flew
steadily. But a little prudence . . .

There was no response from Beuren.

"Willi," Ecker murmured in the same calm
voice. "Take us back up to 30 feet." He glanced out
of the cockpit. The greyness seemed to have become
denser.

Still no response.

"Willi, are you OK?" Ecker glanced at his instruments. The Tornado was definitely creeping
lower. "Willi! Pull-up!"

There was a sudden cry of anguish from the
front seat and the Tornado jerked skywards. It began
to roll.

"Willi, we are upside down! Roll 180." At least
they were now a few hundred feet up, but that would

not last for long if Willi didn't come to his senses . . .
"Willi, roll 180 and pull up. We're diving."

After what seemed an age, the Tornado shakily
rolled the right way up and climbed unsteadily. It
levelled out at 5000 feet. Whimpering noises were
coming from the front office.

Oh God, Ecker thought in horror. Willi's gone.

"Willi," he said as calmly as he could, "give her
to me. We'll let her take us home, but you'll have to
put us down. Willi? Do you understand?"

The aircraft was now in a gentle dive.

"Willi!"

The Tornado slowly came out of its dive.

"Take her," Beuren was saying. "For God's
sake—you take her."

Ecker swiftly activated the aircraft's auto-
control systems. "You'll still have to put us down,
Willi. Do you understand?"

"Yes. No. I don't know what happened."

Scheiss, Ecker thought. Just when I believed he
was doing fine.

The Tornado found its own way home. More by
luck than good judgment Beuren got them down. It
was the heaviest landing Ecker had experienced in
his entire career. He fully expected the landing gear
to buckle, but somehow it survived.

As soon as he could, Beuren reported to
Wusterhausen.

"I request to be grounded, Chief," he said.

Wusterhausen looked at him balefully. "After that landing, I'm not surprised."

"I mean permanently. I don't want to fly any more."

Wusterhausen's eyes narrowed. "Do you realize what you're saying, Willi? This will ruin your career. You're a good officer—"

"I'm a lousy pilot. You nearly lost an aircraft and crew out there today, and the only reason I'm standing here talking to you, is because Johann Ecker was on the ball. I'm quitting before I kill someone."

"You won't change your mind?"

"No, Chief."

"Very well. Send Ecker in to me. Put everything in your report."

"Yes, sir." Beuren saluted, and left.

Ecker entered a few minutes later, and Wusterhausen could see by his face just how serious it was.

"Well, Johann?"

Ecker described all that had occurred. Wusterhausen listened grim-faced. Then: "Is this what was worrying you and Hohendorf all those months ago? The fact that Willi Beuren was losing his nerve?"

"Axel had a hunch, Chief. It was I who convinced him he should not destroy a man's career on a mere hunch . . ."

"Instead, you chose to put two lives and an air-

craft at risk. Suppose it had been someone else in the
back seat, who did not have the luxury of being fore-
warned? At least you were on your guard. I expect
my officers to come to me with such problems, Johann, and leave it to me to decide who is fit to fly,
and who isn't."

"We—"

"Don't interrupt. You'll say you were thinking
of Willi. Do you believe what has just happened to
him was a favour? Don't interrupt! You should both
have trusted me. Now you may speak."

"You're absolutely right, Chief. But it was a
very difficult thing to do."

"And do you think I *like* grounding my pilots?
Willi is a good officer. His career will change, but it
needn't be over. Neither of you had any right to keep
something like this to yourselves. Hohendorf has the
makings of a squadron commander, I would have expected him to understand. I know how hard it must
have been, but sometimes, an apparently harsh decision proves to be the best for all concerned."
Wusterhausen paused, then went on in kinder tones:
"Don't fall into the same trap twice."

"No, Chief."

"Fine. That's all, Johann. I'll need your report,
of course. At least, Willi's wife still has a husband,
and his children a father. Which is a lot better than
sitting here trying to think of the right things to say
in letters to his family. Thank you. It was good
work."

Ecker began to leave.

"Johann . . ."

Ecker paused by the door, looked back.

"You were both nearly killed out there today, Johann, yet when that man came in here to ask me to ground him, I could see it was breaking his heart. Knowing the reality, why do we do it?"

Ecker turned to face his commander. "I asked Axel the same question once. Because we love it, he said, and because we're needed. Luckily for us, both reasons coincide."

Wusterhausen stared at him. "Philosophers on my squadron. What next?"

"Axel's not on your squadron anymore, Chief."

"No," Wusterhausen agreed soberly. "He's not. More's the pity."

Summer Into Autumn

Chapter

In the aftermath of the tragic November One fly-ing accident, while awaiting the results of the official inquiry, most newspaper editors were anxious for a follow-up. One tabloid daily ran a story alleging drunken parties at the base, and scandalous behavior, taking the recent Ball as a pretext. Another had somehow got word of the flying rivalry between Selby and Hohendorf, and even the latter's romance with the former's sister, and blew both up into a lurid tale of sexual jealousy and near-lethal airborne feuding at the taxpayer's expense. No names were mentioned, of course, but Selby had no difficulty re-cognising himself and Morven.

Discussing the piece with Kim on the tele-phone, he discovered that clearly Reggie Barham-Deane's hand must have been at work. The newspa-per had to have got its story from somewhere, and

Kim admitted that she'd talked with Reggie: she might well have mentioned something.

"We were having drinks, for God's sake, Mark. Daddy arranges these little get-togethers. Reggie's always there and I can't exactly refuse to speak to him."

"But why *Morven*? Why did you have to tell him about Morven?"

"Did I? I suppose I must have. I'm sorry, Mark. I didn't know it was supposed to be a secret."

"A secret? It's not even true. She danced with him at the Ball, and they went down to the harbor together the following morning. That's all there is to it."

She made skeptical noises but she didn't argue. "Anyway, I do blame myself. I should have known better than to tell Reggie *anything*. After all, he's just the sort of man to try to make trouble for you. In fact he even warned me once that he'd do just that."

Selby frowned. It wasn't himself he was worried for. None of these stories did anything to help November One. A campaign for its closure was developing. The media were so rabid that even Hohendorf's birdstrike had finally made headlines: his survival being presented as no more than a lucky chance. Selby didn't know how serious all this was, but he saw every day that Jason was worried. And when autumn came and Parliament was in session again, God alone knew what the November One opponents would get up to.

The perfect summer weather continued. On the 6th of September Thurson again found himself in the minister's office. Buntline was not in attendance.

"We've got the date," the minister said, "and the flight plan. You may now tell Jason."

"And the selected crews?"

"No change. They are to be told nothing."

"With respect, Minister, I think they deserve some warning of what may be in store. If this defector is detected, he is bound to be pursued. In which case, our crews may become involved in a shooting match. At least, allow us to warn them just before take-off. That way security will be maintained, if that aspect worries you . . . though I must say none of our crews are security risks. They would not be at November One if they were."

The minister was shaking his head. "I cannot agree to your telling the crews. They are simply to know they will be carrying out an extended combat air patrol in the specified area. And before you object, Air Vice-Marshal, let me remind you that the Palmer and Ferris crash is very much in people's minds. You need some points to keep the wolves at bay. The entire November project is in serious danger. This mission may just be what we all need. It would not do to look a gift horse in the mouth."

Thurson, well aware of the political situation,

forced himself to stifle any further protest. "Very well, Minister," he agreed. "I just hope this particular gift horse doesn't bite us."

Kukarev sat in his room, studying weather reports for the general region of the Kola Peninsula. Such work was part of his established pattern and anyone choosing to look in on him would have found nothing to cause suspicion. He was well-known for his attention to detail, and an interest in the weather conditions came into that category. It helped to promote the image of a dedicated operational test pilot.

The weather for the next four days, he was pleased to discover, was as favorable as it was likely to be in early September. He hoped it would hold. His departure was fixed for the 10th. There was no way now that he could change it. He had given the details to Sergei Stolybin the previous weekend in Moscow, using a legitimate two-day break for the purpose. Stolybin had promised to arrange the rendezvous with a British tanker. If not . . .

Kukarev shrugged imperceptibly as he considered the implications. He would be making the first part of his flight at low level and therefore highly expensive in fuel. If the tanker did not make the rendezvous, it would be the Norwegian Sea for him . . . provided no pursuers got him first. Even in summer, the Norwegian Sea was not the place to go swimming in. An immersion suit would have helped a little, but he would not be wearing one. It would not be expected of him, since his officially-cleared flight would not be over water.

He thought of the sailors who had perished after the submarine accident in April, in that very area. He hoped he would not be joining them.

There was a knock on his door. He made no attempt to conceal what he was doing.

"Come," he said.

Captain Zitkin put his head hesitantly into the room. "I hope I'm not disturbing you, Comrade Major."

"No, no you're not," Kukarev lied pleasantly. "I'm just going over the weather reports."

Zitkin entered and closed the door softly behind him. "Thank you, Comrade Major." His smile was ingratiating. "I know how conscientious you are . . . everybody does, but I wondered . . . as you're about to leave us, did you have a chance to speak with your friend in Moscow?"

Nothing escaped Zitkin, Kukarev thought with distaste.

"I did, as a matter of fact," he answered. They had spoken, certainly, but of far more interesting matters than an incompetent *Zampolit* captain. "He will be in touch. He knows who you are now and I spoke very highly of your abilities."

"The Comrade Major is very generous."

"It was nothing. Very simple to do."

Zitkin eyed the print-outs on Kukarev's desk. "So you'll be leaving us on the 10th?"

"Those are my orders."

"To another base in the area?"

"You know I cannot reveal such information, Captain." Kukarev put military firmness into his voice. In fact a *Zampolit* had access to the highest-grade material, but his eyes held Zitkin's until the other backed down.

"My . . . my mistake, Comrade Major."

"Yes indeed, Captain. No more questions about my movements. That could be a very serious offense."

"Of course, of course," Zitkin said hastily. "My apologies."

"I shall forget this lapse, and we shall say no more about it."

Kukarev nodded at him and he went out, again shutting the door softly behind him.

Kukarev stared at the closed door for some moments, a slight frown on his brow; then he returned to the weather reports. Zitkin, he decided, was corrupt enough to go far, despite the so-called spirit of reform. Zitkin's kind would be fighting back, and the resultant discontent could well give the hardliners an excuse to start all manner of unpleasant adventures. When there's trouble at home, find a war; any war. History was littered with precedents. The current unrest in the republics served to confirm that lesson.

From where he sat, Kukarev could see the tree-line at the far end of the main runway. Beyond that, just under 200 kilometers to the north, was the Barents Sea; the gateway out, after his planned feint to the south.

A war to cover up unrest at home could well destroy the Motherland. He knew there were people around mad enough to do it. The same kind who had destroyed his father.

He stared at the distant treeline. He had no regrets.

At the Schloss Hohendorf, Anne-Marie looked out of her mother-in-law's window, down the long, tree-lined drive. She had turned up unexpectedly the day before, and had been given a less than warm welcome. It should not have surprised her, but being the person she was, it did.

What do they want of me? she now thought. I am not a good military hausfrau. I never will be. All in all, Anne-Marie decided, coming to the Schloss had not been a good idea.

If she had not been feeling so ill at ease, she would not have wandered listlessly into the countess's private apartment. Anne-Marie turned from the window and in doing so, her eyes fell casually upon a loose pile of letters on the dressing table. Idle curiosity took her to the table where one of the letters held her attention. She recognised her husband's writing. She stared at it and perhaps, if she had been feeling less resentful, she would have turned away: but she chose to read it instead, and the damage was done. They were not the kind of words she wanted to read.

"I must tell you about someone wonderful I've met" the letter began. "I know you'll like her."

Anne-Marie felt the heat of anger building behind her eyes. She read on, turned the page. Finally she replaced the letter with a steely calm. The anger behind her eyes was building into an all-consuming rage. If Axel wanted to dally with a trollop, that was fine; but to tell his mother all about her—that was something else altogether. How dare he humiliate her so?

She left the bedroom and went straight to her own. She was Axel's wife. No woman was going to usurp her. She picked up the telephone and dialed a Munich number.

"This is the Baroness von Wietze-Hohendorf," she said into it when the call was answered. "I want the company Citation at Greven within the next two hours." Greven was the Munster/Osnabruck airport, less than 30 kilometers away. "Call me here at the Schloss Hohendorf when it's airborne. I want Herr Linden to fly it. No. No one else. What? No. I expect him to be available." She hung up and began to pack.

Corporal Neve watched as the hired BMW coupe approached his barrier. Ever since the trouble with the people in the van early in the summer, he had viewed all unfamiliar vehicles with the suspicions of a guard dog. The car stopped.

His interest perked up as the tall, elegant blonde got out. He knew she was trouble as soon as he saw the expression on her face. Why did he always get them? After the business with the van, a young woman journalist had tried to pass herself off as a fiancée of one of the pilots. He wondered what the blonde's story would be.

Anne-Marie looked him up and down. "I am the Baroness von Wietze-Hohendorf," she announced in English. "The wife of one of your pilots. I wish to see him."

Neve restrained himself. What next, he thought.

"You must first register at the guardroom, madam."

She stared at the chevrons on his sleeve. "You are a corporal?"

"Yes, madam."

"Very well, Corporal. I have come a long way to see my husband. He is a Kapitän Leutnant. I want to see him. You will either let me in, or get someone who can."

Bullying Corporal Neve was the very worst way to get his co-operation. He could be stubborn enough to make a mule seem a model of helpfulness.

"If madam would please check in, I shall call to see if Mr. Hohendorf does in fact have a wife."

Anne-Marie glared insolently at him. "Are you calling me a liar?"

"No, madam," Neve answered patiently. "This is a military establishment. It is my duty to ensure all visitors are properly registered."

As he spoke, another civilian car drew up. Neve peered in at the driver who showed an ID. He raised the barrier. The car had to maneuver its way round the BMW. Neve lowered the barrier once more.

"Please move your car over to the side of the road, madam. Large vehicles come through here all the time. It could suffer some damage."

Anne-Marie hated losing to anyone, particularly to those she saw as functionaries. She tried again.

"Suppose I ignore you and walk through?"

"There are armed personnel in the guardroom, madam. You would not get very far."

Hohendorf was in the simulator section, having just completed another inconclusive air combat session with Selby, when the call came through. He listened disbelievingly, then put the phone down.

Selby saw the expression on his face. "Bad news?"

"From where I am standing . . . yes. Come with me," Hohendorf continued. "There is someone I would like you to meet. It might help me and it will certainly help you to understand. First, we must go to the Mess to change."

Intrigued, Selby followed.

"Whom are we going to meet?" he later asked as they drove towards the main gate.

"My wife. She claims the service police are trying to shoot her. Knowing Anne-Marie, they are probably acting in self defense."

Anne-Marie watched as Hohendorf climbed out of the Porsche. She was standing by the guardroom window. There was not a single armed person in sight.

How handsome he looked, she thought.

She ran up to him and hugged him. "Oh, Axel!" she exclaimed softly. She kissed him on the lips. "It's so good to see you! These . . . these people would not believe me when I told them you are my husband." She had spoken to him in rapid German. She had seen Selby get out of the car, but only now chose to acknowledge his presence. "And who is this? Introduce me."

Hohendorf said coldly, and in English: "What are you doing here, Anne-Marie? Why did you not warn me?"

She drew her head back, but still held on to him, pale eyes seeming to dilate. "Axel? This is a strange welcome," she stubbornly continued in German. "Are you trying to humiliate me before all these people?"

"The humiliation is of your own making," Hohendorf replied. "You arrive out of the blue after months of silence; you ignore every letter I have ever sent you and now *this?* What possible reason could you have for coming here?"

"Axel . . ." Anne-Marie interrupted in a strained whisper. "Stop. What are you doing? Let us not discuss our private business here. Let us go to your room. All these people are watching."

"We're going off the base. You can talk to me, then you can go back to Germany. I see the car is an English one. No doubt it is hired. That means you came by the Citation."

She nodded. "Yes."

"And I suppose Linden flew it over here, like the good lap dog he is. You gave an order, and he jumped."

Her eyes widened slightly. "How dare you . . ."

"Oh Anne-Marie. You are so predictable." There was weariness in Hohendorf's voice. He turned to an increasingly embarrassed Selby. "This is Mark Selby," he said in English.

Anne-Marie stiffened and suddenly released him. "Selby," she said in a low, hard voice. *"Selby . . ."*

Both Hohendorf and Selby stared in surprise at her.

"You know his name?" Hohendorf demanded.

"It's her name. Her *damned* name!" she shouted.

Corporal Neve stared at her from his post at the

barrier, and heads poked out of the guardroom windows to look.

She rounded on Selby. "And what is the little harlot to you?"

A shocked Selby heard himself reply stiffly: "My sister."

"Your sister." She again turned to her husband. "And you dare introduce this man, this pimp, to *me*?"

"Control yourself!" Hohendorf gripped her arm. "Remember who you are, and where you are. You could only have known that name from reading my mother's letters. Anne-Marie, you have gone beyond the bounds of—"

She wrenched herself free. "Don't you dare tell me . . ."

"Get into the car."

"No!"

"If you cause a disturbance here, Anne-Marie, I can have you forcibly removed. And I promise you I will."

That seemed to stop her in her tracks. She eyed Corporal Neve, then went to the Porsche, climbed in, and slammed the door shut.

Hohendorf said to Neve: "Thank you for sending for me."

"My pleasure, sir," Neve said. There was the barest hint of a smile on his face as he turned away.

"I want to talk to you later," Selby said to Hohendorf, then swung on his heel and walked back in the direction of the Mess.

Hohendorf stared at his retreating form for some moments before getting into the Porsche to drive off the base.

Inside the car each of them silently nursed their anger. Hohendorf drove slowly, not allowing his feelings to be vented on the Porsche. Fifteen minutes later he pulled to the side of a narrow road, near a small stream. He climbed out, and walked to the bank. The water flowed peacefully.

Anne-Marie waited. Finally he heard her open the door. She shut it, and came towards him.

"You made a spectacle of yourself," he said to her in German. "You embarrassed both Selby and the corporal. These people are not your servants, but personnel of a military unit. I want you to return to your Citation, and get your lover to fly you home."

"And your little whore . . ."

Hohendorf's eyes were blazing as they turned on her. "Don't you call her a whore," he said with a calm that was more potent than any shout. "You are in no position to call even the most common tart a whore. Morven may not be a baroness, but she is more noble than you could ever be."

"So . . ." Anne-Marie tilted her head speculatively, "you really are in love with . . ." She stopped just short of repeating the insult, and smiled unpleasantly. "Forget it, Axel. You'll never get a divorce from me. I won't have everyone knowing I was pushed over for some . . . some . . ." Again, she paused, not knowing how far she dare goad him. "It's no use presenting her to your family."

"I shall. And when I tell my mother you've read her letters, I doubt if she'll think kindly of you . . ."

"I shouldn't have needed to," Anne-Marie snapped, unrepentant. "She had a duty to keep me informed of what you were doing . . . Now take me back, please." She turned, and re-entered the Porsche.

Hohendorf followed, got in silently. The drive back to November One was done in a mutual silence which continued when she got out and climbed into the BMW, and drove off.

She did not look back.

In his room in the Mess, Hohendorf said to Selby: "Now you know everything. I do not normally explain my private affairs but because of Morven, I felt I should tell you."

Selby looked at him steadily. "I appreciate it. I realise it could not have been easy and I'm sorry I had to witness what happened by the gate."

"And . . . ?" Hohendorf let the question hang.

"Morven is a grown woman. She makes her own mind up."

"What are you trying to tell me?"

Selby tightened his lips briefly. "I don't want my sister involved in a squalid triangle . . ."

"A *triangle*?"

"You know what I mean. Your wife doesn't look like the kind of woman to give up easily. Morven could get hurt. I'm not going to allow that."

"Is that some kind of ultimatum?"

Selby gave what might have been a sigh. "No, Baron von Wietze-Hohendorf. This is not to be pistols at dawn. I'm merely saying I care for my sister very much, and I don't want her dragged into anything that might cause her pain."

"You are saying that *I* will cause . . ."

"You . . . perhaps not . . . But you're not alone in this, as we've both just seen. My sister is important to me . . . And even if you could marry her tomorrow, which you cannot, I would try to stop you. Pilots like us have no right to marry. And you know why. You understand that perfectly."

"No! I do *not* understand! And you do not. I am in love with your sister. She means everything to me . . ."

"Fighter pilots are in love with their airplanes. I ought to know. I cannot prevent you from seeing her, any more than I can stop her from seeing you." Selby paused. "But I don't have to like it, do I?"

He went out leaving Hohendorf staring after him.

Later that same day, Wing Commander Jason wandered into the Mess with a tall, black USAF Captain in tow. McCann, Selby, and Bagni were in the lounge.

"Gentlemen," he began, "meet Ralph Cottingham. He'll be coming to Zero One when he's finished at the OCU. I've been hunting Ralph for months. Some time ago, before you bright sparks got here, we had a tussle with a bunch of F-15s and F-16s, whom we nailed . . . all except one: an F-15 that would not stay in one position long enough to get clobbered. He got away. I decided then that pilot was the kind of man we could use at November One. As I've said, it's taken a while to find and obtain his secondment to us. There was a price to pay, of course." Jason gave a sly smile. "I had to promise the USAF I would not send McCann back."

"I know they love me really," McCann said, as they all grinned at him. Then, being McCann, he went up to Cottingham palms held upwards. "Gimme some skin, bro'."

Captain Cottingham looked down at his pushy fellow-American for long moments, unsmilingly. McCann's gesture of welcome began to turn into a strained fixture as Cottingham continued to stare him out. When McCann had realized just how stupid he could be made to look before his peers, the tall black man relented.

Cottingham slapped his own palms down.

"Awriiight!" McCann grinned his relief.

The introductions were continued and when a suitable opportunity had presented itself, Cottingham hauled McCann into a corner.

"Don't you ever give me what you think passes for cool again, Lieutenant. Got it?"

"Yes, sir. Yes sir, Captain."

"Just you remember it."

"I will. I will."

Cottingham released him and began to walk away.

"Captain?"

Cottingham paused.

"What's it like flying a bird like the '15?"

"I've heard about you, McCann," Cottingham said. "The man who wanted to be a hotshot fighter jock, but kept breaking the birds. What's the F-15 like? Only those who fly it can ever know."

Cottingham went on his way.

"The ASV's better," McCann shouted after him. "And no one can replace Richard and Neil," he added quietly to himself.

The Air Vice-Marshal chose the next day to drop his bombshell. He summoned Jason to London, with Inglis, the station commander.

"Three days?" Jason exclaimed when Thurson had finished. They were in closed session in a small and secure Whitehall office. "Sir, that gives us very little time."

Thurson was unmoved. "It gives you plenty. The mission is scheduled for the tenth. You have till then. It's a Sunday, so things should be quiet over there . . . always assuming they still respect the Sabbath out on the Kola Peninsula." Thurson gave a tight smile at his own joke.

Jason was unamused. "This defector, sir—how do we know it's not a trap? The Soviets cry provocation, and there we are with egg on our faces. Besides, I thought defectors went out of fashion."

Thurson sighed. "We do not have any choice in this. I hardly have to remind you that some people would be delighted to see you make a mess of it."

Jason saw November One being set up as a prime scapegoat. "You're telling me it's an order."

"Very much so. You are to plan a detailed training mission, with *live* weaponry. It will not, of course, be a combat air patrol as such—rather a mission with specific objectives."

"And the crews?"

"They are to be told no more than is necessary to get them in the right place, in the right condition, and at the right time."

"And if they do run into trouble?"

"We both know how good they are. I'm certain they'll know how to handle themselves. Depending on the situation, we may be able to advise them by secure datalink. What will be your choice of crews?"

"My best." Jason looked at Inglis for support. The group captain nodded slightly. "Hohendorf and Flacht," Jason went on, "and Selby and McCann."

"I agree," Thurson said. "I was highly impressed by their air combat display when Zero One squadron was declared operational. I'm confident they are right for the job."

"And the diplomatic repercussions, sir?" Calmly from Inglis. "After all, it's a shooting war we're talking about."

"That's an aspect we leave to government, thank God." He turned to Jason. "Do you think I want to give this order? We have no choice, and that's all there is to it. I'm relying on you, Christopher."

The 10th of September dawned brightly on the Kola Peninsula. As the weather reports had predicted, it was going to be a fine day. A slightly chill wind, presaging the long winter to come, fanned down from the northern icy wastes near the Pole; but it was a light wind, with no teeth in it.

Fully kitted up, Kukarev did a careful walk-round of the Krivak. He checked its compound delta wing, slightly reminiscent of the F-16XL; the deep twin slatted air inlets behind the curve of the cockpit for the single big engine; the two moveable canards either side of the cockpit, the long nose with its powerful radar, the tall landing gear. It was a cleanly-designed aircraft that looked even cleaner today, since it carried no weapons.

No external fuel had been cleared. But at least the internal tanks were full. He was not expected to need more on his flight to the Krivak manufacturer's inland testing ground.

He had just peered into the vast tail pipe when a voice said: "Goodbye, Comrade Major."

He turned. "Comrade Zitkin. How nice of you to come and see me off. Someone must like you. It is difficult to get past the guards. Ah . . . but of course . . . a political officer can go anywhere on this unit. You are very zealous. That is good."

"I hope you will mention this to your friend."

"Oh I will. I will."

"Well, I must leave you to get on, Comrade Major." Zitkin stepped back and saluted smartly.

Kukarev returned the salute casually, and watched as Zitkin strutted away. The crew chief came up when the walk-round was complete, and Kukarev signed for the aircraft. Then the two men saluted and shook hands, as was the custom.

Kukarev climbed up into the cockpit. He secured his straps then calmly went through his checks before starting the powerful engine.

Zitkin was already on the phone in his office as the Krivak roared down the runway, climbed steeply and banked hard, turning south.

"Are you certain he has turned south?" the voice on the phone said. "Not towards the west?"

"No, Comrade General. Definitely south. I've just watched him take-off."

"Very well." The other sounded bored. "It is a feint, obviously."

The line went dead and Zitkin replaced the receiver. A feint? Briefly he wondered what the comrade general had meant. The KGB had never told him why they wanted Kukarev watched, only that he was a traitor planning to do great harm to the Motherland.

Zitkin sat back, reminding himself that it was not his place to question the KGB's motives. It was a sufficient honor to have been asked to carry out a surveillance of such importance.

In fact, a half-wit could have done the job. A half-wit had.

The general put down the phone. "That little worm. Why do we have to use such people?" He looked unenthusiastically out of a window. It was raining in Moscow.

"Because they are worms."

"Well, Sergei, your little scheme is off and running. I hope it works."

Sergei Stolybin answered calmly: "It will work. Everything is ready. We have him. We also have a great propaganda victory."

"If he makes it to the other side, *they* will."

"He won't make it. He'll run out of fuel, or he'll be shot down—with or without his NATO escort."

"No fuel? But I thought they'd set a tanker up?"

Stolybin hummed a few bars of a Western song. September in the Rain.

"And what about the Krivak itself?"

Stolybin sat forward. "If we're stupid enough to let someone steal it from us, we deserve to lose it. What do I care if a few Air Force generals get chopped? The right ones will remain. The hard ones—the ones who know what self-preservation's all about. And they're the ones Russia needs."

The general eyed him thoughtfully. "You still hate the Air Force, don't you? Why? Me—I do my job. But you, Sergei, you bring emotion to it. So much emotion."

Stolybin's mouth drew into a tight line. "I could have been a pilot myself. It's a long time ago, and you probably won't understand me, but I wanted that. I wanted to fly. I wanted it so much I could taste it. And they *failed* me. They claimed I wasn't good enough. General Kukarev was on the board. That traitor . . . that lackey of the West . . . that crypto-capitalist . . ."

The general calmed him. "Whom you later denounced, Sergei. That was excellent work. It set you off on a career that has impressed us all."

A savage rancour still burned in Stolybin's eyes. "Do you know, Comrade General, what really turns my stomach? I'll tell you—even today, even as young Kukarev's up in the air with a stolen aircraft, a traitor, determined to betray his country, what turns my stomach is that in spite of all that he believes himself to be honorable. And if he were to discover that I had betrayed him, he would not be surprised. I am KGB and he would expect it of KGB.

I am not Sergei, the friend whose life he once saved. I am KGB, and therefore not really human at all."

The general looked at him sideways. "You do not like being KGB?"

"That's the funny thing, Comrade General. I do."

Chapter

"Gimme my speed jeans, baby," McCann sang as he zipped the left leg of his G-suit, *"let me show you how. Yeah, gimme my speed jeans, baby, Let me love, let me love, Let me love you now . . ."*

"Elmer Lee," interrupted a long-suffering Selby.

"Yo."

"What do you call that noise?"

"Singing, my man. Singing."

"Well kindly stop it. You're giving us all a headache." They were in the kitting room, suiting up for the flight.

"No soul. You've got no soul, Flight Lieutenant Selby, sir, pilot and coffee bar. Dunno why I fly with you."

A short distance away between the racks, Hohendorf and Flacht listened to the banter as they too got their gear on. It had been a long briefing; over an hour. No explanation had been given, but the mission for that day was an unusually long combat air patrol that would take them all the way to Norway's North Cape. Air-to-air refueling areas had been designated, references for intercept practice with target drones had been given, weather conditions annotated, sortie profile planned, combat weapons and fuel loads selected, and so on.

The notices to airmen—NOTAMS—for the day had looked like a telephone directory, with over a hundred entries covering the areas likely to be crossed and bordered by their flight-path.

Hohendorf read off some of the areas to look out for in his mind.

> Item 21—Practice firing 2NM around grid 9J
> PSN (position) . . . with height given
> as 625 feet.
>
> Item 30—PJE (para-jumping exercise) VMC
> 2NM around VG22
> PSN . . . 0800—SS FL95

That meant the para jumps in that area would be carried out from 9,500 feet in good visibility, from 0800 to sunset. Definitely an area to avoid. Ingesting parachutists was not a good idea.

> Item 40—Testing of rockets and sea distress
> signals INM around PSN . . . 1500
> FT
>
> Item 42—Glider aerobatics at Venlo PSN
> 5122NO163E SR–SS 3937 FT

Nothing to worry about there. They weren't going anywhere near Venlo. The gliders could aerobat from sunrise to sunset to their hearts' content.

Item 60—Overflight by all MIL aircraft prohibited due to air-sea rescue in progress 5NM radius around PSN . . . 5000 FT

The list of warnings and avoidances seemed endless, but all had to be noted and acted upon. Ignorance of the notices was not a defence, should any incident occur. Flacht would have a copy with him, as would McCann.

"Right, gentlemen," Selby called. "Are we all ready? Let's go and hear what final words the boss has to say."

Trussed up in their over-water gear plus all the accoutrements necessary for survival in their high-speed, high-flying machines, they waddled towards the small briefing room where Jason was waiting.

"I won't go over points of the briefing already covered," he began when they had taken their seats. "Today, as you'll have been told, you are carrying a full war load . . ."

"Loaded for Bear," McCann remarked, referring to the NATO name for the big four-engined Soviet long-range aircraft that persistently tested the NATO air defences.

"Yes, McCann," Jason said patiently. "But don't go shooting down any, will you, please? There's a good chap. The Russians wouldn't like it; I most certainly would not, neither would the Air Vice-

Marshal and through him going ever upwards, all
sorts of highly placed people. Our combined ire
would shrivel you into a little puddle of grease. Have
you got that?"

"Strength five, Boss."

"Glad to hear it. To continue . . . you have live
firings in areas Hotel-96, Hotel-38, and Sierra-59.
Target drones will be operating in these designated
areas. Altitudes, times and headings are not given.
Hostiles would not forewarn you. Your intercepts
are therefore to take place as and when you are able
to detect the target drones. On correct detection,
your radars will give you a visual image of the target
on your tactical displays. Do *not* fire before correct
identification. If you do, it will count against your
proficiency ratings.

"As you already know, the first refuelling exercise will take place after your first intercept in
AARA 2, at 30,000 feet. The tanker will contact you
on completion of the intercept. Second refuelling,
however, will occur in a specially designated area for
this mission. This will be AARA Delta 8, in grid
square Victor 3 at 35,000 feet. This will place you off
the North Cape. Remembering my warning to
McCann about prowling Bears, keep a sharp eye out
for their more agile comrades. I think we all know
what I'm referring to.

"They sometimes like to play. Let's not give
them any frights. In these days of glasnost we should
be even more on guard. We want neither to be

caught out, nor do we wish to initiate anything that might give us our own nightmares."

"In other words, don't shoot unless we're shot at." McCann again, wondering why the Wingco was bothering to say all this.

"I would go much further, McCann," Jason told him. "Do not *put* yourselves in a position where you will be shot at. This," he went on, "will be a totally autonomous sortie. There will be no communication whatsoever with base, and no voice communication with the tankers. Secure data link will be used. This is to be as realistic as we can possibly make it, without actually going to war. Voice comms between your two aircraft are to be kept to an absolute minimu. In fact, only an emergency should necessitate such contact.

"Callsign for the mission is Goshawk. Hohendorf and Flacht are Two-One; Selby and McCann, Three-One. Two-One leads. Finally, it remains for me to say this to you: *qui desiderat pacem, praeparet bellum.* Vegetius in the 4th century. *He who wants peace must prepare himself for war* . . . Milton, however, had other ideas: *for what can war but endless war still breed?* But I give you Jason, 1989: *watch your step, and don't bring me any nightmares.* Any questions? No? Very well. Off you go, gentlemen."

As they later approached the aircraft, McCann said to Selby: "That was quite a speech from the boss. Did he look worried to you?"

"No more than usual, Elmer Lee, for a man who's got you in his squadron."

McCann chose to ignore the genial insult. "I dunno," he said thoughtfully. "This Kansas kid's corns are itchy."

"Leave your corns alone, and get up into your cage."

Kukarev decided he had gone far enough south. He didn't want to waste fuel. He made a gentle sideways movement with the stick and the Krivak flipped onto a wing. Kukarev pulled slightly towards him and the aircraft whipped round in a tight turn, to head north. Kukarev kept low, to avoid giving his country's SAM batteries time to acquire him. All his active search systems were off and only the passive warning units were operating. They gave off no signals for anyone to lock on to, but would register any search radar or infrared source seeking him out.

He had planned this route over the months and had flown sections of it at intervals. It was relatively clear of electronic or other prying eyes, and he hoped he would make it to the Barents Sea before the flight plan deviation worried a controller enough to send someone looking.

The Krivak streaked northwards.

The general put down the phone. "He's off the radar."

"He's made his move," Stolybin said tensely. "We've got him!"

"But we don't know where he is. According to the radar people, he's gone very low. Perhaps he's not heading north at all. The Krivak has a very low signature. It can hide very successfully by masking itself with the terrain."

"There is no need to hunt for him, Comrade General. An ambush has been set. We know where he'll be."

Stolybin spoke confidently. But his face now had a thin film of sweat upon it.

A squadron of the Su-27s that had been at Kukarev's detachment base in the south, had found themselves suddenly rotated back north. Just before Kukarev made his turn, two of them had taken off and roared skywards. Shortly after, a pair of MiG-29s from a squadron sharing the base had also taken off, keeping low. An IL-76 tanker was waiting for all four aircraft, near Bear Island.

Unaware of all this activity, Kukarev flew on, maintaining his bearing. He kept a constant lookout, restless eyes monitoring his alarm systems, scanning the sky about him for unwelcome company, watching for a telltale puff of white that might mean a SAM launch. But nothing alarming happened. His luck was holding.

He glanced anxiously at his fuel state. Still

plenty, but he'd be glad when he could head for the upper reaches of the sky where he would burn fuel more efficiently.

Suppose he was flying to nowhere? What if no NATO tanker was waiting? What if no NATO escort? It would be a cold and lonely death in the Arctic waters.

He pushed such thoughts out of his mind and kept the Krivak going north. Soon he must ease off to the West. His estimated time of arrival over the coast was now only five minutes.

Within the cockpits of Goshawk Three-One, subdued sounds of high-tech machinery at work was a lullaby that sent no one to sleep. In the back seat, McCann monitored the steady pace of his own breathing while in the front, the HUD told Selby he was cruising at 30,000 feet on a heading of 350. Speed was a relatively gentle 400 knots. The wings were at 45 degrees sweep. A speck over to the right and a little ahead, leading them, was Goshawk Two-One.

The aircraft, on a seemingly unending sea of white cloud-tufts, sped towards their first intercept in the designated grid area.

Selby routinely checked his systems. Nothing onscreen betrayed the presence of the target drones. Perhaps they would not put in an appearance in this area. He hoped they would not get past him. As yet, however, McCann had given no indication of possible trade.

Then on his headphones, Selby heard a new sound: music. This was accompanied by singing from McCann. "Elmer Lee?"

The singing stopped, but the music continued. "Yo, buddy."

"What the hell's that?"

"Me being happy."

"I'm glad you're happy, Elmer Lee. I really am. But do you have to be happy on the phones?"

"I've got a cassette in one of the slots, using a spare channel, cockpit circuit only. No one else can hear. Dave Brubeck. 'Take Five.' Don't you like it?"

"Give it a rest, Elmer Lee, and keep your eyes open."

The music stopped. "What say I sing instead?"

"God, no."

"There you go."

Selby shook his head. How many people, he wondered, could say they had flown a fast jet at 30,000 feet, listening to Dave Brubeck?

The sea of white tufts stretched before him.

In Goshawk Two-One, Flacht said to Hohendorf: "Two minutes to Hotel-96."

"Anything yet?"

"Screen's clean." Flacht had the tactical display on one of the MFDs.

"After sixty seconds in-area, I'm going low. Call it."

"All right." After a short pause, Flacht continued: "Ten seconds. Nine . . . eight . . . seven . . . six . . . five . . . four . . . three . . . two . . . one. _Go._"

Hohendorf, grunting against the mounting Gs, flung the Tornado onto its back and pulled the stick towards him. The aircraft dived steeply into the cloud bank.

McCann said: "Two-One's just gone low."

"Then it's the high road for us," Selby said, lit the burners and went vertical.

At 40,000 feet, he came out of burner and went into a gentle climb to 50,000, where he levelled off. He throttled further back. The wings spread out to their 25-degree maximum, and Selby took the aircraft into a wide, loitering circle.

"If there's anything up here," he said, "we'll find it."

"You bet your ass we will," McCann said.

Hohendorf had levelled out at 500 feet.

A bare minute later, Flacht announced sharply: "I've got trade. Two targets. One at fifty feet, bearing 270 and coming at us . . . 350 knots at 90 miles, the other at 30,000, bearing 050 at 70 miles. 500 knots. Three-One should have him, so I'm giving priority to the sea skimmer." Flacht watched as the targets' images were displayed.

DRONE J/13A, the readout said. DRONE C/M2-R.

Well, they wouldn't be shooting at the wrong

targets, Flacht thought. No stray aircraft seemed to be wandering in the area to attract the missile.

The computers advised him that Drone J/13A should take priority.

"Target bearing now 201," he told Hohendorf.

Hohendorf turned for the intercept.

"Speed now 400 knots," Flacht said. "They're going to make us work. Select Skyray One. Let's get him before they start getting. Ah. That's it. We've got lock-on. He's turned, range increasing . . . but we've still got lock-on. Range now 95 miles and increasing . . ."

Hohendorf got the tone in his helmet. "I'm taking launch," he said. "Launching." The first of the four Skyrays hurled itself explosively out of the semi-recessed bays of the aircraft's underbelly.

The drone had begun to alter course.

Then Flacht said: "We're getting countermeasures, but Skyray is ignoring it. We're still locking on."

On his helmet symbology, Hohendorf saw the targeting box firmly squared, though the target was itself still invisible.

Flacht watched the missile's trace on-screen. "We're holding . . . and *hit*. We've got a hit!" he said with satisfaction. A bright flaring had briefly surrounded target A on the tactical display. Then another bright flare lived momentarily on the screen. "And I think Three-One has just scored too."

Hohendorf took the ASV into a steep climb. "That wasn't too difficult."

"If we ever have to do it for real," Flacht began as the two aircraft confirmed each other's kill by secure data link, "I hope all engagements turn out so well."

"One thing we can be sure of, Wolfie. They won't."

"I was afraid you'd say that."

"If you wanted an easy life . . ."

"You shouldn't have joined," they finished together.

McCann watched as Goshawk Two-One came into view above the cloud layer. He had turned the music back on as soon as Hohendorf had finished his attacking dive. This time "It's a Raggy Waltz" was playing.

"Elmer Lee."

"I'm here. Haven't gone away."

"I thought cowboys liked country music."

"I keep telling you guys I'm no cowboy. I'm a city dude. And I hate country music." Just then, a set of coordinates pulsed on his nav display. He cut the music. "Tanker's in place. Left, two-two-zero." He watched as the symbol of Hohendorf's ASV began its heading change. "Goshawk Two-One's already getting into the groove."

Selby checked the contents of his wing tanks. The 500-gallon streamlined containers—capacity rounded off from the 495 gallons of the standard F.3 ADVs—were nearly empty, but the airframe tanks were still awash. If anything should occur to cause them to miss the rendezvous with the tanker, they would still make it home without getting to bingo.

They made the rendezvous, their tanker being a Victor K2 with bright lines on either side of each of the outer wing refueling pods. The markings were there to help with lining up for the feed. As experienced feeders, neither Selby nor Hohendorf needed them, but they were godsends to rookies.

After their top-up, both aircraft swung away from the tanker and headed towards North Cape for the next engagement.

McCann went back to Brubeck.

It was McCann who saw it first. He immediately stopped the tape and stared at a trace on his tac display. "What the hell's this?" He transferred the display to Goshawk Two-One.

Selby said: "What have you found?"

"Something that shouldn't be there. We're not in Hotel-38, or Sierra-56 . . . and Hotel-96 is way back south. No target drones are scheduled for this area and this, whatever it is, is moving at one hell of a lick. I've got 600 knots on him, at 20,000. This guy's no drone. I'm checking him out."

He tapped keys and the screen glowed a bright red at him. NO DATA.

"Shit!" McCann exclaimed. "Mark, this guy's

an unknown. I mean we've got the 'NO DATA' caption. One of theirs?" His voice now had an edge to it. "He's over a hundred miles off, but he's coming our way. And . . . hell, he's accelerating. 800 knots now."

"Pass it on to Two-One . . ."

"They've got it . . ."

"Then give me a patch."

"You got it."

Selby got part of the tac display. He would only need it for a quick head-down reference. If this turned out to be a hot engagement, life would be conducted through the HUD and the helmet display, while McCann set up the fight.

"Two-One's just confirmed there should be no drones within a radius of at least 250 miles," McCann was saying, "and . . . oh shit . . . I've got two more inbound, chasing the other guy. What the hell? I'm checking these guys." He soon had the answer. On the screen, familiar images had appeared. "Mark, buddy . . . I think we may have trouble. I've got *Flankers,* for Chrissakes."

"What? You're joking . . ."

"Unless the chips in this baby have gone on furlough, what I've got are big juicy Su-27 Flankers, and they're looking mean. Hold. I've got something coming in from Two-One. We don't get involved, the man says, unless these guys turn for us. But we watch them, clear the decks for action, and go defensive. We also prepare for voice contact if this thing turns really bad." McCann tightened his harness and lowered his visor.

Selby acknowledged with a grunt, and prepared himself for an engagement against targets that for once would be firing back. He felt a cold, almost pleasurable tenseness. A picture of Kim Mannon came into his mind. He banished it. She had no place up here. His universe was now enclosed within this one patch of sky. There was some cloud, but far below. Mainly, there was emptiness, with the dark of the high sky above.

He preferred it that way. Even the subdued paintwork of the ASV would be a liability against cloud. But clouds could be helpful too: they hid you from sight, if not from radar. They also screwed up infrared missiles. Even so, he preferred to be in the open with the high bright sun above. It was a better decoy for an IR missile with your name on it, and with nothing but sea beneath you, visual acquisition of your aircraft would not be easy.

He checked all his weapons, and primed himself for possible combat. His head turned this way and that, eyes searching the sky.

In Goshawk Two-One, Flacht said to Hohendorf: "What do you think they're up to?"

"We'll soon find out, Wolfie. They must know we're here. What's the range?"

"Still over a hundred miles. They don't seem to be coming nearer, but they're still heading west.

Perhaps they can't see us yet. The UK net must have them, but nothing's come through from there. Do we send what we've got down the line?"

"The briefing said no communication whatsoever. Let's play it that way. We'll just watch them, and keep out of the way."

"Missile!" Flacht shouted suddenly. "They've launched at the first target. Another missile! My God, Axel. He's *evaded!* He's made it. And . . . we're now in Victor 3. AARA Delta 8 is 110 miles. . . . Axel," Flacht went on in a suddenly tight voice, "our second tanker—it's somewhere in that area . . ."

"Find him and warn him!"

"We've got no coordinates, no call sign . . ."

"Find him, Wolfie. As for a call sign, you'll just have to warn him as Victor K2 on voice contact. So *find him!"*

"Searching."

Hohendorf glanced at his fuel levels. All internal storage full and plenty still in the wing tanks. But the way things seemed to be developing, he might have to jettison those on the wings to maximise speed and manoeuvrability.

In the back, Flacht had been quartering the air-to-air refuelling area and putting the range of the radar to its full stretch. He was getting a better response than he'd hoped. Just under 150 miles had come up. If the tanker was indeed there, he'd find it. It should have arrived on station by now.

While the search was going on, the attack computer had stored the last positions of the Flankers and placed radials at ten-mile intervals about them and was continuously updating. The Flankers would not know they were being tracked.

"I've got him!" Flacht said. An image had come on-screen. VICTOR K2, the caption said. "The tanker's at 145 miles, bearing 270." He checked his tac display. "Axel . . . that's the new heading of the Flankers. They're going after the tanker!"

"Warn him!"

"Victor K2, Victor K2," Flacht began urgently. "You have inbound hostiles. I repeat. Inbound hostiles at flight level two zero zero and climbing. Bearing zero niner zero. Hostiles are two, repeat, two Flankers. Victor K2, Victor K2 . . . this is Goshawk Two-One. You have inbound hostiles . . ." Flacht repeated the entire message.

Answer! Answer! he begged in his mind.

Every second counted. Weren't they awake out there?

There was a silence that seemed to stretch for centuries. In Flacht's anxious mind, that silence seemed to fill the entire sky.

Then at last: "Goshawk Two-One . . . we read inbound . . . *hostiles?*" The voice, disbelieving, was a woman's; with an American accent.

Flacht was astonished. With unconsciously greater urgency, he spoke to the tanker: "Victor K2, Victor K2. Yes, hostiles! *Get the hell out of there!* My God," he added to Hohendorf. "A woman."

Hohendorf had himself been surprised by the female voice, but women were getting into some areas of military flying now. There were all-female transport crews in the US, but he had never heard of any on the K2s that served the November One aircraft. She was perhaps the navigator, or even the co-pilot. As far as he knew, there were no female K2 captains.

He felt sickened. If the Flankers decided to take out the tanker there would be nothing he could do to prevent it. His orders forbade him to fire on them, and the Goshawk pair were still too far away to be able to place themselves between the Flankers and the tanker.

The Su-27s had as yet made no overt hostile move towards either the tanker or the Tornadoes. The only attack had been upon the aircraft for which there was still no identification data. Certainly nothing identified it as belonging to the NATO alliance. And if it belonged to the Eastern Bloc, then it was none of their business. But the aircraft had been fired upon, and was still racing towards the tanker. Why?

"Watch your step . . ."

Jason's words echoed in his head. The Flankers had attacked one of their own aircraft. He could hardly take retaliatory action for that. But what if they attacked the tanker?

"Wolfie," he began to Flacht, "give November One a data link view of the situation."

"We're not supposed to get in touch . . ."

"I don't think this was the kind of scenario the boss meant. Do it, Wolfie."

Flacht made the link between both aircraft, and November One.

"They do not acknowledge," he announced after a brief pause.

"What?"

"And the Flankers are formatting on the tanker," he added.

As if to confirm, the female voice was back. "We . . . we have a hostile on each wing. They seem to be just looking us over."

She sounded worried, and she had every right to be, Hohendorf thought grimly. The K2 was virtually a flying petrol station. One hit and it would go up like a small volcano. He tried not to think of the four crew in there.

"Are you still linked to November One, Wolfie?"

"They're getting everything. They must be. There is no indication of a loss of contact. The Flankers are pulling back," Flacht went on sharply. "Perhaps they'll be going home now." He sounded relieved. Then he was shouting, horror in his voice. "Oh my God . . . *they've launched. They've launched at the tanker!"*

"Goshawk!" the woman screamed, then contact ended. A brilliant glow flared in the cold blue distance.

*   *   *

"Bastards!" McCann yelled from the back seat of Goshawk Three-One. In his mask, his voice sounded unearthly. "C'mon, Mark! Let's get the murdering sons of bitches. Mark! *C'mon, goddammit!"*

"We don't have the lead, Elmer Lee. Calm yourself."

"Goddammit. What is Hohendorf waiting for?"

"Do you want to go to war over a tanker?"

"There were four people in there, one of them a woman."

"There were a lot more people in the Korean airliner. The world did not go to war then."

"Are you telling me . . ."

"I'm telling you," Selby interrupted firmly, "to wait for the pair leader's instructions. I'm as shocked and angry as you are. Let's just keep ourselves calm, shall we?"

Then Hohendorf's voice, cold from a seemingly total lack of emotion, said in the phones: "Goshawk Three-One . . . if attacked, jettison tanks and engage."

"Now you're talking!" McCann crowed.

"Shut up, McCann!" Selby said, then went on to Hohendorf: "Roger, Two-One. If attacked, jettison and engage."

Hohendorf had used an open channel, and Selby knew why. If the Flankers were monitoring, they would know what was in store. There was still time to avoid a fight. He was enraged by the unprovoked attack upon the tanker and all his gut reactions cried out for revenge. But he knew Hohendorf was correct in holding fire.

A new tenseness had come over him. *Christ,* he thought. *If it happens, this will be for real. There are men out there I've got to beat, if I want to continue living.*

Kukarev had known despair when he discovered the Su-27s waiting for him. They had come from the direction of Bear Island, and he had known then that he'd been set up. His sense of bitterness and betrayal was complete. Only one person could have set him up. Sergei Stolybin. His friend.

The Su-27s had attacked immediately, but—although unarmed—the Krivak had been able to escape so far. Its countermeasures were intact, and its agility had made it able to evade the missiles, four of which had been expended uselessly by the Su-27s.

When Kukarev picked up both the NATO fighters and the tanker, he was confused. Were they also part of Sergei's game? Briefly their presence gave him hope—until the destruction of the tanker. Sergei had closed all doors. Kukarev knew he was lost. Even if the NATO fighters avenged the tanker, he was himself finished. His evasive manoeuvres had eaten into his already small reserves of fuel. Without the tanker, he might as well eject and let the cold waters far below swallow him.

Sergei had won. But why? To what purpose? A

secret hatred? Some political expediency Kukarev couldn't even guess at? Certainly Sergei was KGB, but he was a human being first. They were friends. They had known each other all their lives, even before the arrest of Kukarev's father.

He beat at the controls in bewilderment. Sergei was his friend.

Beep-beep-beep-beep-beep . . .

"They're tracking us!" Flacht said tightly to Hohendorf. "They're going to engage!" Even as he spoke, he had begun jamming the tracking signals from the Su-27s. "They must be crazy!"

In the same instant, Hohendorf jettisoned the tanks and the Tornado, made even lighter, reefed into a hard left hand turn as he shoved the stick over and pulled it towards him. The warning beeps died and he reversed the turn, losing height swiftly.

When he had levelled out at 10,000 feet, the fifty mile distance from the Flanker that had chosen him as meat had increased to seventy. He did not worry about Three-One. The head-down display told him that Selby had made his break to the right and had gone high, also increasing his own distance. McCann would be setting up a Skyray launch even as Flacht now was.

The computers had said that the new ASV could turn close in with both the Su-27 and the MiG-29, but there was nothing like the real thing to prove or disprove computer predictions. With the stake

being your own life there was no need to push it if
you could zap him at arm's length.

"What have you got for me, Wolfie?"

"I've got him plotted, but we're not transmit-
ting. No point warning him."

"He might be doing the same to us. I don't believe those stories about their weak radar."

"I don't believe them either. Decoy him a little.
Let's fly straight for a few seconds. I'll give him a
quick flash, then we'll be ready for launch."

"All right . . ."

Beep-beep-beep-beep . . .

"Scheiss! He's fast, Wolfie!"

Bmmmmmmmmmmmmmmm . . . !

"He's launched!" Flacht yelled. "I'm jamming,
but break him, Axel! *Break him!"*

Hohendorf slammed the throttles against the
stops. The burners came on in a double explosion,
and the ASV swept its wings and flung itself into a
vertical climb.

"It's following!" Flacht called, staring at his
display. "I'm still jamming, but it's ignoring it. No . . .
it's altered course slightly . . . now it's back on . . .
ughh!"

Flacht grunted as Hohendorf cut the throttles,
and pulled on the stick. The ASV began spreading
its wings even as it came tightly over onto its back
and began plunging seawards. When it was vertical,
Hohendorf quarter-rolled to the right and pulled at
the stick again. As the G symbol on the HUD

counted upwards, he eased on the stick, and again slammed the throttles into combat burner. The wings began sweeping back and the Tornado continued to hurtle towards the sea at 90 degrees to its original heading.

"It's wondering what's happened," Flacht was calling. "Sorting itself out . . . it's coming! We've got seconds, Axel. *Do* something!"

Hohendorf said nothing. He was busy. The sea was getting closer.

"It's nearly here!" Flacht shouted, and hit the chaff dispenser.

As the cloud of metal strips billowed behind and to one side of the aircraft, Hohendorf cut the throttles and pulled hard on the stick. The Tornado began to spread its wings, brought its nose up and leaped skywards. Again the throttles went forward and again the wings moved themselves to full sweep as the speed built. The Tornado screamed towards the heavens. They had cleared the sea by fifty feet.

The missile wasn't so lucky. Confused by the sudden cloud of chaff, it wandered off target. As if realizing it had been fooled, it began to reject the chaff and was starting to correct its course. But its great speed worked against it, giving it a poor turning circle. It plunged into the sea, sending a great spout of water upwards as it detonated.

"Oh very stylish, Axel," Flacht told him.

"No time to congratulate ourselves. Let's get that bastard. I'm switching to helmet sight. That was a very smart missile, Wolfie. All right. Where have you got him?"

"Go right, one one niner. We have him at eighty miles. You should have him when I put some light on."

The radar was still sleeping, but continuously updating. Flacht would track only long enough to achieve lock-on. At eighty miles, it seemed that the Flankers' radars were not acquiring the low-signature ASV's.

Flacht switched on. Immediately, the tac display showed the Flankers' current positions. It also meant the SU-27s' radars had picked up the brief emissions. They were already altering course when Flacht switched off.

"They're running in," Flacht said. "I have our target nicely framed. Skyray Two's on. Ready?"

"Yes."

"You're on."

Immediately, the helmet's target indicator box framed the area of sky where the selected target was, and the direction arrow pointed. Hohendorf turned his head, watching as the arrow shortened upon itself until he was looking exactly at the apparently empty section of sky where the target was. The box began to pulse, and the Skyray began its own distinctive group of short growls that went in an upward sound curve. The growls turned into a continuous yelping as the box pulsed more quickly, then into a single tone as the box glowed a solid red.

Hohendorf squeezed the release. "Skyray launched," he said and immediately altered course violently. The Skyray was autonomous now and would be making independent adjustments on its way to the target. "Let's see how he handles *this.*"

A brief radar illumination of the Flanker by Flacht showed it to be taking avoiding action.

"I think he knows we're interested in him now," Flacht commented drily.

"I'm tempted to give him another just to keep him happy," Hohendorf said, "but I'd better not. He has a friend around, remember."

"I've done a quick sweep. Nothing within even extreme range."

"It doesn't mean he's not there. Three-Two's probably sorting him. Keep a sharp lookout."

Flacht was watching his display. He raised his head to do a swift scan of the sky about them, then turned to the display again. He turned on the radar. The missile tone was still on their phones, signifying continuing lock.

"I think our friend's in trouble," Flacht said, voice rising in excitement. "I don't think he expected this. Not so soon. Oh he's really turning, trying to break lock. You've got ten seconds, my friend," he said to the unseen pilot maneuvering frantically out there for his life. "Nine . . . eight . . . seven . . . six . . . five . . . four . . . three . . . two . . . ONE! *And there he goes!*" The pulse flared briefly. "We've got him, Axel!"

Hohendorf said nothing. It was some compensation for the tanker and the four who had died; but he did not feel elated. He hoped he had not just started a war.

"Goddam!" McCann said to Selby. "Hohendorf just creamed his guy. I tell you buddy, I never thought he'd get away from that Russki missile. That thing seemed to have his name carved on it."

Separation between the two Tornadoes was now 20 miles and Selby, keeping an eye on the tactical situation, had maintained a secure distance of 80 miles away from the second Flanker. The Su-27 had carried out a series of manoeuvres in the hope of closing the range, but McCann had decoyed him and Selby had danced the ASV invisibly with his opponent, always maintaining the separation and remaining out of missile lock. He had wanted to see how Hohendorf coped. Now, he was free to sort out his own target.

"I don't think he's going to be too enthusiastic now," McCann was saying. "His buddy's gone. He must be feeling very lonely with us two sharks around."

"Do a frequency check. See if he's asking for help."

McCann did a frequency scan to see which was being used in the target sector. The computers spoke silently among themselves, and one of the displays gave a graphic read-out of the search. Then a series of numbers came pulsing on-screen.

"Found it! Now let's have a listen . . . Jammed. He's talking all right. I've got a voice pattern, but nothing's coming through."

"Leave that channel open," Selby said. "You never know what might turn up."

"Goshawk Three-One," came Hohendorf's voice, again on the previous open channel. "He's all yours. Nail him."

"Roger, Two-One. He's my meat."

"Hah!" exclaimed McCann.

"What's up?"

"He heard us. He must be monitoring. As soon as Two-One got in contact, the voice pattern stopped. Now it's going like all hell's broken loose. I'll bet you my shirt he's calling up buddies."

"I don't need your shirt, Elmer Lee. I agree with you. Let's sort him out and say goodbye to this place."

"Amen," McCann said as Selby wheeled the Tornado round and prepared for the attack. "I've got him nicely for you. He's running, the bastard! Get him!"

"Don't worry, Elmer Lee. He's not going anywhere. I have lock-on."

The Skyray had begun the first of its sequence of using tones. It went through them quickly and on the continuous note Selby unleashed it.

"She's off the rail!" he called.

McCann kept the target illuminated now. "Look at him. Boy! Is he twisting on the hook. Oh no you don't, buddy," McCann went on in a teasing voice. "Little Elmer Lee's got you good."

"And little Mark. You know . . . the one up front."

"Uh . . . oh yeah, Mark. I guess you've done something, being just the pilot an' all." McCann gave a sudden yell. "And we've got a Fox on the guy! Let's go home, Mark baby. Let's get the hell away. We've got the word from Two-One. It came from base."

This time, the recall had come from Two-One via data link.

"About bloody time too," Selby said. "I was beginning to think November One didn't exist any more."

"Hey . . . wait a minute . . ." McCann said the words slowly, and with some astonishment. "You are not going to believe what's coming on. You are not going to believe it!"

"Come on, Elmer Lee. Cut the suspense. Switch it over." Selby began to read the decoded message from November One as it appeared on his display. "Holy shit."

"Hey," McCann said, aggrieved. "That's what I say."

"Quiet, Elmer Lee. I'm reading." Selby stared at the brief message.

GOSHAWK AIRCRAFT WILL ESCORT AND

DEFEND DEFECTING SOVIET AIRCRAFT. ENDS.

"Christ," Selby said. "They were trying to shoot him down, Elmer Lee. Where is he now?"

"Coming up fast from behind. He must be pretty good. He dodged those missiles with some nice moves. I've just had a thought."

"This should be good."

McCann ignored the sarcasm. "He was heading for the tanker. Right?"

"Right."

"But not to shoot it down."

"Obviously. He wanted . . . Oh my God."

"Yeah. You got it in one. He must be pretty low on juice, and I don't see a gas station within a few hundred miles."

"Shit. The poor sod."

"So what do we do? How do we escort and defend something that's going to head for the cold blue long before we get back?"

"Shit," Selby said again. "Why didn't November One tell us?"

"Why didn't the boss tell us in the first place is what I'd like to know. He must have known something like this was going down, but he let us come out here like sucker bait. 'Don't bring me any nightmares,' " he mimicked.

"Put a sock in it, McCann," Selby told him firmly. "Let's not run off at the mouth about something we know nothing about. Wait till we get back . . ."

"*If* we get back. That guy out there sure as hell isn't going to make it."

Selby found he could not argue with that.

Kukarev had followed the fight on his attack radar and had been very impressed by the skill of the NATO pilots. Clearly, they had not needed his help.

He glanced at his fuel read-out. It gave him bad news. Unless those fighters up ahead were somehow rigged for fuel transfer, he would be going swimming.

Flacht watched as the range decreased. "We'll have a visual soon," he said to Hohendorf. "Although I don't know what good that will do. The only help he really needs is fuel." They had reached the same conclusion as Selby and McCann. "Ah! There he is."

They watched as the Krivak performed a stylish barrel roll before eventually taking up position between the two Tornadoes.

"That," Flacht said, "is a beautiful ship. And new, I'd say. There's nothing in the book that's anything like it. A very beautiful ship."

"And a very brave man," Hohendorf remarked soberly. "He knows the only way for him is down, but at least he enters with style."

The Krivak had formatted on Goshawk Two-One and its pilot could be clearly seen, looking across at them. Hohendorf raised his visor and gave an American-style salute. The Krivak's pilot raised his own visor, and returned the salute.

"Now what?" Hohendorf said. "That's a dead man, Wolfie."

There was a pause, before Flacht came back excitedly: "Perhaps not. I sent November One our reading of the situation. Take a look at what's coming on your display."

Hohendorf read the data link message:

SURFACE SHIP IN SIERRA-09. AREA CLEAR OF TRAFFIC. ESCORT AIRCRAFT TO DESIGNATED AREA. PILOT TO EJECT.

DO NOT REPEAT DO NOT COMMUNICATE WITH AIRCRAFT EXCEPT BY SIGN LANGUAGE ENDS.

Hohendorf gave a low whistle. "Looks as if he may have a chance after all. If we don't make radio noises to alert his friends. Pass it on to Goshawk Three-Two."

"I'm doing that now," Flacht confirmed.

"Tell them I'll take him down. They're to stay up here and watch out for any more company."

"That is some sweet aircraft," McCann was saying as he looked the Krivak over. "Think our guys could take it on?"

"Only time and the politicians will tell."

"Something's coming in from Goshawk Two-One," McCann said sharply. "Well, what d'you know . . . Seems our boy's not going for a swim after all. I'm patching it on to you."

Selby read the message. "Perhaps it was just a lucky coincidence—a ship being in the area, I mean."

"If you believe that, Mark, you believe in Santa Claus. I tell you, the boss knew something. That's why he gave us that little speech. Goddam," McCann added, aggrieved. "Goddam."

"We can't be certain."

"Sure we can." He paused, reading his screens. "Here's the rest. Two-One's taking him down and we're to be sentry at the gate. Coincidence? You got to be joking."

Kukarev was himself looking the ASVs over, admiring them with a pilot's eyes. They'd certainly given the -27s a rough time. No doubt their crews would now be wondering how they would rate against the Krivak. She looked good. She *was* good. But the Krivak had problems only a very small group knew about. While her agility wasn't in question, her radar was another story altogether. During his recent test flights it had consistently failed to maintain acquisition. He'd be set up for a good kill, then suddenly the radar would go to sleep and acquisition would be lost. The earlier Krivaks had suffered even worse problems. It was one of the best kept secrets.

Kukarev's attention was caught by the aircraft

on his left waggling its wings. The pilot seemed to be indicating he wanted him to descend.

Why? Kukarev wondered. Was there another tanker?

He nodded vigorously to show he understood, and followed the NATO fighter down.

"There he goes," McCann said admiringly. "Shame we've got to lose that baby. I'd have loved to give it the once-over."

"You and a lot of other people, I suspect. Still, they'll have the pilot. He must have some pretty interesting information."

"Yeah. If he gets out OK."

Flacht called out, "He's coming." He twisted round in his seat to watch the Soviet aircraft as it took up station behind and a little to the right. "I feel nervous, seeing him back there."

"Don't worry, Wolfie. He's got no weapons."

"No missiles, obviously. But what about a gun?"

"He's a friend, Wolfie. He needs us more than we need him."

For fifteen minutes the Krivak kept perfect station behind them. Eventually a Royal Navy frigate came into sight below and the two aircraft flew over it.

Hohendorf formatted on the Krivak and

pointed to the ship, then mimed the ejection sequence.

The pilot again nodded to show he understood.

"Better him than me," Flacht said, watching as the Krivak gained a little height before levelling off. "It's cold down there. I hope they get to him in time."

As soon as he saw the ship, Kukarev knew what was coming next. He would still be going for a swim but at least, the fishes would not be having him today. Stolybin had not had complete success. That, at least, was something.

Kukarev had a final look round the cockpit of the Krivak then, patting it as he would a horse, he pulled the ejection handle.

"He's gone!" Flacht exclaimed, watching as the canopy explosively parted from the Krivak and a tiny shape hurtled upwards. Then the shape became two. The seat itself tumbled swiftly. The man dangled beneath a mottled canopy. "Good chute!" he went on. "He's OK!"

Over to the northwest, there were small puffs of white as the Krivak hit the water, and broke into several pieces which tumbled beneath the surface. Eventually, they would reach the seabed, more than 12,000 feet down.

Hohendorf banked round the frigate, which had already lowered a boat. There was a streaming whiteness climbing the bows of the small craft.

"They're making good speed," he said. "He won't have long in the water. Let's go home, Wolfie. Tell Three-One we're coming up."

The frigate's boat had measured the distance well and within less than a minute Kukarev saw four tough young faces staring down at him; but they were friendly faces. Then strong hands were hauling him in.

"Come on, mate," one of them said. "Let's be having you out of there."

Kukarev's English was sketchy, but he understood the sentiment. He was very happy to be out of the water. Without his immersion suit, he already felt as if he were freezing. His helmet, with its display technology, he had deliberately left in the water. No point making things too easy for the West's scientists. The sailors appeared not to notice as they put warm blankets about him and the boat sped back to the ship. He looked over the stern. The helmet was nowhere to be seen.

Once on the frigate and after a change into dry clothing, Kukarev was taken to the captain's cabin. It was not a naval officer who awaited him but, unexpectedly, a civilian. The man came forward to shake his hand.

"Welcome, Comrade," he greeted in perfect Russian with a satisfied smile. "My name is Charles Buntline. Some gin, perhaps?"

* * *

The two Tornadoes were close in, rushing home with wings swept, at low level. Though they used more fuel in this configuration, there was a tanker rendezvous at Hotel-96, close enough to home to avoid unwelcome attention. But you never knew. So they kept low, hiding from any high-flying bogeys that might have come out for revenge. The closer the ASVs got to home, the further the hostiles would have to fly, their own fuel state becoming ever more critical.

It was McCann who gave the alarm. He had carried out a brief upward sweep of the radar, long enough to pick up traces, but not enough to betray their own position. "I don't like this," he muttered. "I don't like this at all."

"What don't you like, Elmer Lee? And try not to give me bad news."

"I'll get out and walk, if that would make you happy."

"No such bloody luck," Selby said with resignation. "Let's have the bad news."

"We got company."

"Judging by your voice, not people we'd like to meet."

"Nope."

"Tell me."

"Two bad boys. MiG-29s."

"Oh shit," Selby swore. "All the way out here? They haven't got the range. They couldn't have flown Norway, so they must have come right down the coast, via North Cape."

"And at low level, because I got them at 500 feet. Mighty expensive on fuel."

"A tanker or two, then."

"Yup."

"They're being bloody keen. What in God's name is going on?"

"Don't ask me, kiddo. I'm only along for the ride. I figure their buddies told them they were being creamed and called out the cavalry. 'So near but so far,' " McCann began to sing. " 'So . . .' "

"You're singing again." Selby was scandalised. "I don't know what the hell you think you've got to sing about."

"Maybe because this back-up team will be working round to close the door up ahead. Of course, they could always have *their* back-up team too, I guess."

"You're a barrel of laughs, Elmer Lee."

"That's me. Ol' Elmer Lee, the laughing barrel."

Flacht said: "From Three-One. Two MiG-29s up ahead at 500 feet, moving on an intercept course from left to right. 130 miles."

Hohendorf remained silent.

"Axel . . . ?"

"I heard you." Hohendorf fell silent again.

They were 320 miles from Norway's long and

rugged western coastline, and were soon to cross the Arctic Circle on their way south.

"Bodø's out there on our left," Hohendorf went on after his pause. "They've got F-16s on the airfield. Why haven't they come out? Our friends out there are well within intercept range."

"The MiGs would have done a low level well out to sea. They have probably not been detected."

"The satellites might have seen something."

"They don't always see everything."

Hohendorf knew that was true. Because he trusted his own aircraft, did not necessarily mean he had complete faith in all forms of technology. Blind faith was not sufficient to keep a man alive.

"I think," Hohendorf said, "there may be other reasons."

"Such as?"

"Perhaps we shall find out when we get back."

"If we get back."

In Fighter Control at November One, Caroline Hamilton-Jones watched the tactical screen with mixed feelings. She felt anger and bitter sorrow for the tanker crew, elation and relief for the Goshawk pair, and confusion about the whole incident. What had really happened out there? What was the aircraft Goshawk had been escorting? Why wasn't November One sending re-inforcements to help the Goshawk patrol?

She knew the answer immediately she'd asked

herself the question. To begin with, reinforcements from November One would have arrived too late to have been of any use, and secondly, no one wanted a major escalation. World War III was something nobody wanted to happen. That was why no planes had come from Norway. Now, the data link said Goshawk had detected Mig-29s. They would have to fight again, and do so on their own.

She glanced up at the gallery where Jason and the Air Vice-Marshal were in the company of the senior controller. The AVM had arrived quite unexpectedly. She had not given this much significance: Thurson was by now well known for his unannounced visits. But now something within her was saying that perhaps his presence was connected with the havoc far out there over the Norwegian Sea.

After all, Jason had already been up on the gallery when Thurson had arrived and had seemed to greet the AVM without surprise.

She turned again to the screen. A computer-generated window near the right hand border displayed the tactical situation as seen by the Goshawk crews. In the tenseness of the room, she knew everyone there was willing them to survive.

Flacht said: "I've got them nicely plotted. 100 miles and closing. Another Skyray? Or are you going for a Krait?"

"We've got the same old problem, Wolfie. We can't fire until they actually act like hostiles. We may have the tactical advantage, but they have the political. For now. What I cannot understand . . . is why they are here. I have to assume they don't know their boy in the Krivak has ejected, and are still on the job of stopping him."

"And us. They're here for revenge too. They'll certainly know what happened to their friends. They want our blood."

Hohendorf sighed. "So we'll keep our weapons ready. They did not come all the way out here for a Sunday stroll . . . but we must still challenge. We must let them know we have seen them."

"Then this could be a knife fight." That would mean the short-range Kraits, perhaps even going to guns.

"It could, Wolfie. But perhaps they'll decide to go home instead."

Flacht would not bet his life on it, but he illuminated the distant targets with no attempt at deception, sending out an open but neutral challenge. He had to take the risk and force the Soviets to make the first aggressive move.

Immediately, the MiGs changed course for a head-on pass. No warning tones of either infrared or radar tracking sounded on his and Hohendorf's phones. Both Goshawk aircraft remained close to each other, separated by less than 500 meters.

The MiGs still came on in tight formation, making no move to go into an attack phase.

"Perhaps you are right," Flacht muttered, as

the range closed. "Perhaps they have decided to go home." He sounded hopeful.

"Perhaps . . ."

The hope was short-lived. Thirty miles out, the warning tones erupted with unnerving suddenness. Infrared. They were being scanned for a short-range missile attack.

"Break!" Hohendorf shouted to Selby.

Each already knew what he had to do. They went for a cross-over. Selby, on the right, broke left and stayed low. Hohendorf broke right and went high. The tones died immediately, but Hohendorf knew the Fulcrums' combined radar and infrared scanning systems could work independently or in concert. The pilots also had their own version of a helmet sight. The close-in fight was going to have to be conducted ferociously and swiftly. Time was life.

McCann's head swiveled this way and that, scanning the world outside the cockpit. This was his job now. This close, the fight had to be conducted more visually. There was still head-down instrument work, but in the main it was an eyeball job.

He glanced at the attack display, seeing what was up on the HUD in front of Selby. The tracking box was dancing to the left as Selby's 7G turn put them on the tail of their MiG. As long as Selby kept it that way, it would only be a matter of time before he got a Fox or gun solution. The MiGs' first pass had been baulked by the rapid break and the division of height. The trick was to deny them another chance.

Seconds. That's all it would take.

The MiG pilot was no beginner. While in the turn, he quarter-rolled onto his back, pulled into a steep dive then pulled his nose up as he completed the split-S to head off to the right.

Selby had been quick to recognize the maneuver and reversed his own turn quickly, banging out the boards to help tighten the turn so that, as the Fulcrum began its own tight pull up, he was still there hanging on to its tail pipes. He kept the air brakes out and wings spread, but full power on too.

The MiG pilot had a counter to that. He suddenly seemed to rocket skywards. Selby brought in the air brakes. Like a hound unleashed, the ASV hurled itself upwards, sweeping its wings as it did so. It began to catch up, but the Krait's twin seekers were still not happy with the kill parameters.

Hohendorf had found himself a long way from where Selby was fighting for his life. His own Fulcrum was no easy meat either. It was clear that the MiG-29 pilots did not want a long-range engagement, having seen what had already happened to their comrades. They had deliberately decided on a close-in tangle, where they had hoped that their high agility would win the day. But it was not working out exactly as planned, for they had not reckoned on the ASV's improved agility and massive reserves of power.

Even so, as Hohendorf was finding out, in the hands of a master practitioner the Fulcrum could make things very difficult.

Flacht's head was being banged about from side to side by the violence of the maneuvering and his own attempts to keep an eye on their wily opponent. Every time the Krait got a pulse, it would break off as the MiG-29 danced out the missile's kill envelope. He hoped Hohendorf would not let the Fulcrum get within gun range. The MiG's gun was supposed to be phenomenally accurate. Four rounds on target and that was it, he'd once heard someone say. As far as he was concerned, four rounds were four too many.

He craned his neck, looking up and behind at the vulnerable spot behind the tail. No MiG. No tracking alarm either. Where was he? Check the display.

There he was, low down on the deck; but he wouldn't be able to stay there for long. The MiG was no match for the ASV low down. The ASV's swing wing gave it the edge. No other aircraft had the same handling.

Flacht knew Hohendorf had seen their opponent, for the nose of the Super Tornado went down like a bird of prey homing in on its kill. But the MiG was rising again from the depths.

At last the Krait had lock-on and had begun its electronic, modulated hissing. Hohendorf always

thought the sound chilling. It was as if the twin seekers were slavering.

The MiG was pulling over the top, clearly hoping to come down behind, either to try for a tail shot,
or to get the ASV in the helmet sights.

Bmmmmmmmmmmmmmm . . . !

"Scheiss!" Hohendorf heard himself say for the
second time that day as he again found himself on
the receiving end of an incoming missile. He pulled
into the vertical, heading for the sun.

Flacht had been looking upwards and had seen
the flash of the launch come from the inverted MiG.
It was a helmet launch, the fire control system
linked to the angle of the pilot's head rather than
to the aircraft's attitude. The MiG's pilot must have
been looking through the top of his canopy too.

Flacht immediately began a sequenced launch
of six decoy flares and hit the IR pulse jammer.

Hohendorf waited as long as he dared, then
chopped the throttles. Anything the Fulcrum could
do, the ASV could do better, and with variations.

He didn't wait for the speed to decay completely but ruddered the aircraft over on a wing in
an apparently untidy stall. He knew he had no fear
of spinning out of control because the aircraft's spin
prevention system would ensure it did not. He could
do what he wanted. The MiG couldn't.

As the Tornado fell seawards, its tail pipes relatively cool when compared to the high blazing sun
or the flares, the Soviet missile fed itself upon the

hotter options after having first been seduced by the unreachable, glowing ball in the heavens.

"That's your last shot," Hohendorf muttered, feeling the sweat dampening his skull.

He slammed the throttles into combat burner and again the Tornado leaped away on swept wings, opening the fight distance. He wheeled the aircraft round tightly for the run-in. The MiG had turned too and was coming head-on.

The Krait seekers were going mad with joy. Hohendorf launched just as the MiG sent another missile at him.

Simultaneously, both aircraft broke hard to deceive the respective incoming missiles. But the MiG pilot had left his launch a fraction too late and had been forced to take avoiding action before he had properly achieved lock-on. Also the Krait was faster than the Soviet missile, and more accurate.

The Fulcrum exploded in a ball of orange fire as Flacht again dispensed more decoy flares and Hohendorf put the Tornado into a series of G-intense 90 degree turns, all the while increasing his distance from the missile. In the end, its imperfect lock caused it to take the flares instead.

Flacht heaved a sigh of relief.

"I heard that sigh, Wolfie," Hohendorf said. "Were you worried?"

"Worried? Of course not."

Hohendorf smiled, and searched the sky for Selby. He felt good.

*   *   *

"Looks like we're the only ones at the party again," McCann said. "Two-One have got their meat. C'mon, Mark! Let's get this joker."

"What . . . do you . . . think . . . I'm doing, you . . . colonial ape? Picking at . . . my sodding . . . navel?" Selby's grunts punctuated his words as he strained against the crushing G-forces.

He'd hauled the ASV into a turn that was approaching 9G. The MiG-29 was determined to keep the fight as close as possible. God alone knew how far from Two-One the fight had taken them. McCann had seen the end of the fight from his display, but had told Selby nothing about distance. No time to worry about that now. If this MiG scored, distance would cease to be relevant.

The Fulcrum's pilot was going for a gun shot. That could only be the reason for this furious turning fight. He would know now that his comrade had been taken out. He was alone and facing certain death unless he could fight and win. A run out was not an option, as that would only leave him vulnerable to a missile shot. It had to be decided in the close arena.

McCann was swivelling round in his cockpit, constantly on the move, tracking the MiG with his eyes.

"He's gone low!" McCann called.

Selby pulled into a steep climb, pulled back on the throttles, and as the wings spread, kicked firmly on the rudder. The ASV pivoted on a wing tip. He corrected and was now in a steep dive, his vertical reverse having conserved space, placing him on the tail of the Fulcrum. But the MiG was already countering, turning hard towards him.

As Selby flashed through without getting lock for his gun, the MiG shifted upwards slightly before turning again in an attacking curve.

McCann had his head craned round, watching the mongoose-like nose tightening its turn inexorably.

"Goddammit, Mark! The guy's gonna have a solution anytime now . . . Aaah *shiiit!*"

Selby had flung the Tornado onto its back and had pulled hard. The aircraft seemed to double back upon itself. McCann thought he heard a rasping sound as the MiG flashed past going the other way.

But Selby was turning again, heading back on full burner now, cutting into the MiG's turning circle. He had tightened his turn by putting the boards out again when they were tail to tail, so that the MiG pilot would not see the air brakes and know what was happening. As a result, the MiG pilot was surprised to see the ASV's nose pointing at him while he was still in the turn.

He immediately began to tighten his own turn, hoping to spoil the shot he knew was coming. It was too late.

Selby got the tone and the box, and squeezed the trigger. For a fraction of a second, the gun

burped at the MiG, then the target was out of the
box. It flew steadily on.

Damn it, Selby thought. I've missed.

Then the Fulcrum's turn widened, and its nose
dropped towards the sea far below. But no smoke
came out of it. It seemed in perfectly good shape.

"Hey!" McCann began excitedly. "You've
scared him off, my man! Perhaps he's reached bingo
fuel. It's a long swim home."

But the MiG made no attempt to raise its nose.
Horrified, they heard the human sound of harsh
coughing.

"He's on the emergency channel!" McCann
said in astonishment.

"Give him an open one," Selby ordered. "Clear
this one. Others might need it."

121.5 was the international emergency channel
and he did not want it cluttered. Also, you never
knew who was listening.

"Fulcrum, Fulcrum," McCann called, and gave
the MiG pilot an open channel frequency that would
link him with both Tornadoes.

The Russian had clearly followed the English-
language instructions, for they heard his coughing
on the new channel.

"The guy's hurt," McCann said soberly, realisation dawning. "Good shooting, Mark. You must have
taken him in the cockpit."

Selby felt subdued. Blowing the aircraft away
was one thing. Hearing the man suffer on was—

"Can you eject?" he asked, wishing he could speak Russian.

The reply seemed a long time in coming. When it did, the voice was weak. "No. I cannot." The English was surprisingly good. "I . . . have lost an arm, and . . . the other . . . I can only move . . . fingers."

Selby looked in the direction of the stricken plane. The helmet sight, still activated, framed the spot where the MiG was, within its targeting box. Selby turned it off, shocked by its unthinking ruthlessness. His mind was reeling. He was *talking* with a man he had killed.

"Are you sure you can't reach the release handle?"

What a question! Even if he could eject, how long would he last? He was already dead.

The coughing came again, as the aircraft continued its unstoppable plunge, dwindling until it disappeared from sight.

"I am . . . very . . . sure."

There were no further transmissions from the MiG.

Then Hohendorf's voice came on: "Goshawk Three-One. He has gone in. Let us go home."

It was only as they formulated on Goshawk Two-One that they realized that they had been hit. Flacht had been looking them over. "There are holes in your taileron," he said. "How are your controls?"

Surprised, Selby replied: "No anomalies. All systems are on line. Look me over, will you?"

Hohendorf manoeuvred Two-One in order to do a visual inspection.

"There is nothing else," Hohendorf assured him. "He scored some hits. Unfortunately for him, you were the better shot."

"Yes," Selby said. He did not feel triumphant.

In tight formation, they made the rendezvous with the tanker, then continued their way home. They carried out a paired landing at November One where everything seemed normal, as if they had not just come from a battle in which people had died. But then, instead of returning to its HAS, Selby's aircraft was placed within a high-security hangar, with the crew still aboard, and later, with Hohendorf and Flacht, they were given an intense debrief by the unit's Intelligence officers. The Air Vice-Marshal and Jason were there, but took no part in the proceedings, content just to listen. Later Jason, accompanied by the AVM, ushered them into the small briefing room.

"I have been authorized," Jason began, "to tell you something about what occurred on today's mission."

Thurson sat to one side, watching each of them carefully.

"An intelligence group," Jason continued, "whose identity is of little interest to you, was responsible for an operation which it was hoped would result in the defection of a Soviet pilot and his aircraft, an as yet unidentified single-seat, single-engined fighter, supposedly highly agile. You've seen it. Unfortunately, because of what happened to the tanker, we've lost the chance to examine it closely on the ground. We'll require your detailed impressions, of course, and we'll also be studying the radar and infrared signature videos. The pilot at least, seems to have survived."

"We were meant to keep him safe," Hohendorf said quietly.

Jason looked uneasily at the Air Vice-Marshal before replying. "Not exactly. You were meant to be a deterrent. Your options were in fact very limited, but if something went wrong and the operation was discovered, your presence was meant to make any pursuing fighters think twice about interfering—especially so far from their own bases."

"It didn't work, sir, did it?" Selby asked, his voice flat and lifeless.

"No. It didn't." Jason paused, frowning. "Obviously, his comrades got to hear of the operation—God knows how. They must have seen it as a perfect opportunity to catch us out. We can only guess at their exact motives; but presumably they let the defection run, then set up an ambush with the intention of taking out both the defector and every NATO aircraft involved, knowing that they could rely on us to hush up the whole ugly business. Which we certainly would have, for the sake of morale, if nothing else."

He shifted to make himself more comfortable

on the hard briefing room chair. "But you, gentlemen, by your outstanding performance, prevented that. When I was asked to supply two of my best crew for the mission, you four were my first choice. And I was right. You reacted superbly."

"We were suckers," McCann said flatly. "Just plain suckers. With a navy ship waiting to pick up the pieces."

Jason stiffened. Beside him, Air Vice-Marshal Thurson decided to take a hand.

"McCann?"

"Sir?"

"You are an officer in the NATO air forces, are you not?"

"Yessir."

"Then I take it you are aware of the proper way to address a superior officer."

"I am, sir," McCann stood his ground. "But in return I expect to be told when my superior officer decides to shove my ass into the meat grinder."

Jason turned to the Air Vice-Marshal. "With your permission, sir."

Thurson nodded, his eyes on McCann.

Jason said: "You all, I believe, support the idea of the November squadrons. You would not be here otherwise. There are still a good many people who do not, and would like to see us fail. It was one of these people who thought of using this incident to test our mettle. To make us or, preferably, break us. I had no choice but to agree, knowing that any failure to supply crews would be looked upon as a sign of my lack of faith in the entire project, with all the consequences that would bring.

"I am not apologising for sending you out. As fighter crews, you are well aware of the bottom line. All your expensive training ultimately has only one end purpose, to defend the integrity of the NATO Alliance and its forces. But I do agree, in some measure, with McCann. Men should know when they are being thrown into the meat grinder. What you were faced with today will shock complacency on both sides of the political divide. It is to be hoped that the lessons learned will sink home.

"We cannot bring back the tanker or its crew, and the Soviets cannot bring back their four aircraft and men either. No mention of the incident will be made on an international scale, however. It never took place . . . and none of you will talk of it." Jason pushed his chair back. "It remains for me to tell you that I am proud of you all, and delighted that you made it back to us safely. All your drinks are on my Mess tab tonight." Jason smiled.

McCann said: "No limits?"

"You're driving a hard bargain, McCann. I shall probably live to regret this."

"You'd better believe it," McCann told him. "Sir."

Later that evening in the Mess, Selby and Hohendorf were sitting quietly beside a low table at the far end of the lounge. McCann had taken the Wing Commander at his word and was in the bar, picking out four of the most expensive bottles of wine on the Mess list.

"Going to say anything to Morven?" Selby asked.

Hohendorf considered. "As much as I'm allowed to. And you?"

"I don't know. That would be involving our women. A pilot shouldn't do that. No right to. I've always believed a pilot has no right to get too deeply involved, or marry."

"Pilots *do* marry," Hohendorf said. "Look at me. I married."

"And see what happened to that."

"There was no love, Mark. Just a business agreement."

"Love . . ." Selby shook his head. "Now there's a word."

"Only if you're afraid of it. I think you *are* afraid of it. It means responsibility."

Selby shifted uncomfortably, changed the subject. "We worked well out there together, you and I. Everything seemed to fall into place."

"I never doubted it would." Hohendorf shrugged. "We grew up."

They saw McCann approaching with a tray of bottles, Flacht close behind with the glasses.

"As soon as I can get some leave," Hohendorf

said quickly, "I'm taking Morven to Germany to meet my mother."

Selby seemed about to protest. He changed his mind, helped to clear the table for the wine. As he watched the bottles being opened he was clearly thinking of something else.

"Responsibility," he murmured softly to himself. If any of his three companions heard him, they made no comment.

The general looked across his KGB-issue desk at Sergei Stolybin, a cold gleam in his eye.

"I do not think, Comrade," he said, lowering his gaze to the dossier before him, "that you will be receiving any medals for that particular day's work. In fact, there are those among us who would be delighted to see your future activities curtailed. For a very long time . . . in a very cold place. And we do have such places. Even now."

In London, across a wider, more elegant desk, the minister held audience with Thurson and Buntline. Fine sherry was being served in crystal, tulip-shaped glasses.

"Come, come, Air Vice-Marshal," the minister was saying, "don't look so down in the mouth. This was a successful operation. Everybody's very pleased. You should be too—the future of your November project is secure now."

"A successful operation, Minister? Eight people were killed."

"Four of them from . . . er, the other side. Hardly our fault. Superb work by your crews. My word—you and the Wing Commander must be proud of them."

"We are, Minister. And the tanker crew?"

Piously the minister laid aside his glass. "Ah . . . dreadful tragedy, of course." He brightened. "But we all know that air forces lose aircraft and crews almost every day. Accidents, so forth. Not at all by hostile action." The tanker crew dealt with, the minister rested his elbows on his desk and steepled his fingers. "I'm sure you'll now agree that we were correct in not allowing your crews to know what to expect. Proof of the pudding, and all that. In the event, they were fired upon first, and subsequently acted well within international laws. Both sides are of course prepared to bury the whole incident. *Quid pro quo* . . . if you get my drift."

"Four of ours, for four of theirs." There was a bitter edge to Thurson's voice.

"Quite." The minister refused to be shamed. "Most unfortunate about that aircraft . . . the . . . er . . . Krivak. But we do have the pilot, of course. So we're actually one up."

Thurson hid the distaste he felt and watched

as Buntline emptied his glass and held it out for a refill.

"Debriefing's already well under way," Buntline said, looking at Thurson, "as you know. Early days yet, but things are looking very good indeed. Lots of technical and political info. A positive gold mine, that man. A lot of hardliners back in the Motherland are going to be very upset . . . and someone I used to know is bound to cop it. Serves him right." This was said with venom.

The minister dealt with Buntline's glass, and then his own. "The operation was worth it, Robert," the minister said to Thurson. "Advanced the cause of peace. Both Jason and yourself have come out of this very well. Guilt won't bring back the dead. The whole thing's a credit to November One . . . to all those involved up there in Scotland."

Thurson drank his sherry, not really enjoying it. The minister was right, in a narrow sort of way. The operation *was* a success. The cause of peace advanced? Perhaps. And feeling guilty most certainly did not bring back the dead. Pity he did not like the minister. Pity he could not stop himself for thinking that the minister's career was being advanced through the skill and courage of men like Selby and Hohendorf.

"What's all the mystery?"

Selby entered Holyrood Park via Duke's Walk, then turned the 4x4 left into Queen's Drive. The road began to climb. He did not reply to Kim Mannon's question. He had picked her up at Edinburgh airport and after greeting her with a very long kiss, had virtually bundled her into the car.

The road encircled the great escarpment of Arthur's Seat, with its accompanying hills and crags. Selby stopped where it curved by the side of a small lake. He got out, went round to her door, and opened it.

"Come on," he said, taking her hand.

She gave him a bemused look as she climbed out. "Mark . . . what's got into you?"

"Don't ask questions. Come on," he repeated. "We're going up there." He pointed at the craggy hill next to the lake. A high, dark wall dropped perpendicularly to the water.

"What!" She looked at it in horror. *"Up* there? My shoes!"

"It slopes over to the right. Take a look. See? It's quite easy, and not as bad as you think. Come on."

When they had finally made it to the top, she looked about her; at the city, and the Firth of Forth spread below. A slight breeze came up the hill at them, teasing her hair.

"It's lovely up here," she said, peering down at the lake. "I've been coming to Edinburgh for years, but this is the first time I've come to this place. I probably never would have if you hadn't brought me. But I still don't understand . . ."

"Marry me, and have my children."

Her mouth hung open, eyes staring at him in confusion.

"Your father won't like it, of course," he continued into her shocked silence, "but as he's not the one I'm marrying, it hardly matters. If he disowns you, you'll have to make do on a Flight Lieutenant's pay."

She blinked at him, her mouth now opening and closing slowly. At last, she said: "Mark . . . I . . . I'm . . ."

He had moved to the edge of the bluff. He looked across the lake, at the high cone of Arthur's Seat with the criss-crossed lines of the many paths that marked its slopes.

"If you don't say yes, I'm going to jump into this lake."

She giggled nervously. "Don't be ridiculous. I thought pilots never jumped if they could help it."

"That's out of airplanes. We hate that." He tried not to think of the MiG pilot, who hadn't been able to.

Behind him, a slow smile had come upon her face. "So you'd jump for me, would you?"

He looked down at the lake. "One way of getting your attention."

"I suppose I'll have to prevent you from jumping."

"Looks like it."

"Why did you decide to ask me now?"

"Why not? Why not just say yes?"

She came up, placed herself between him and the edge of the bluff, put her arms about his neck, and kissed him tenderly on the lips.

High above them, unseen and unheard, a pair of November One Tornado ASVs streaked across the deep blue.

Born in Dominica, Julian Jay Savarin was educated in Britain and took a degree in History before serving in the Royal Air Force. Mr. Savarin lives in England and is the author of LYNX, HAMMERHEAD, WARHAWK *and* TARGET DOWN!

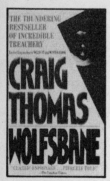

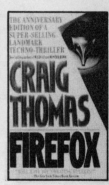

🕮 HarperPaperbacks *By Mail*

Craig Thomas, internationally celebrated author, has written these four best selling thrillers you're sure to enjoy. Each has all the intricacy and suspense that are the hallmark of a great thriller. Don't miss any of these exciting novels.

Buy All 4 and $ave.

When you buy all four the postage and handling is *FREE*. You'll get these novels delivered right to door with absolutely no charge for postage, shipping and handling.